NIGHTMARE'S LORD—

I brought the cup to my lips to rinse the ill taste from my mouth. I didn't want to drink. But I had forgotten. The cup was empty. I peered down the long funnel of its walls and watched.

Inside, there was no bottom, no goblet, no Great Hall in my father's castle. Only the night sky, stars and black Kuoshana, endlessly growing, changing, swirling one into the other, and in the center, a face forming. Brow ridges, eyes, cheeks, nostrils, lips, teeth. A man's face. The man in my dreams. Edishu's face looming at me. Watching with that hideous smile. Laughing!

I smashed the goblet to the floor, shattering the clay into a hundred pieces, and I screamed. I screamed long and loud and hard. "Go away. Leave me alone. Make it go away!"

SUNDER, ECLIPSE & SEED

ELYSE GUTTENBERG

A ROC BOOK

ROC
Published by the Penguin Group
Penguin Books USA Inc., 375 Hudson Street,
New York, New York 10014, U.S.A.
Penguin Books Ltd, 27 Wrights Lane,
London W8 5TZ, England
Penguin Books Australia Ltd, Ringwood,
Victoria, Australia
Penguin Books Canada Ltd, 2801 John Street,
Markham, Ontario, Canada L3R 1B4
Penguin Books (N.Z.) Ltd, 182–190 Wairau Road,
Auckland 10, New Zealand

Penguin Books Ltd, Registered Offices:
Harmondsworth, Middlesex, England

First published by Roc, an imprint of New American Library, a division of
Penguin Books USA Inc.

First Printing, December, 1990
10 9 8 7 6 5 4 3 2 1

 ROC is a trademark of New American Library, a division of
Penguin Books USA Inc.

To the memory of my mother, Esther Guttenberg, who gave me the gifts of voice and history. And to my father, who told stories at night.

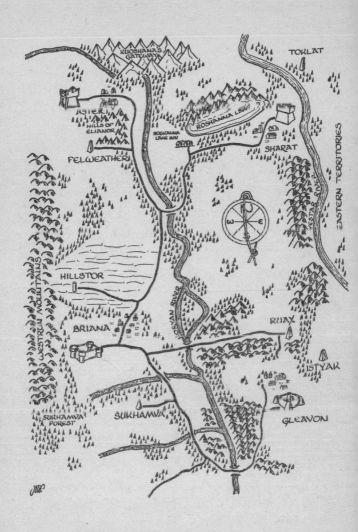

I arise from dreams of thee
  In the first sweet sleep of night,
When the winds are breathing low,
  And the stars are shining bright.
              —Shelley

Prologue

I am inside my mother's dream. I feel her pulse beating, loud and even, as if it were my own. The dream is vivid and unmarred, perhaps because she has thought about it so many times over the years and it has become as much memory as dream. I see the world clearly, as she remembers it before I was born.

She is in Lakotah, the Sumedaro temple. All about, cold drifts like a cloud through the empty hallways. The dream priests are gone. Those who came to seek their council or have their dreams watched have long since returned to their homes. Only my mother, Ivane, Lady of Briana Keep, is there. She is kneeling, straight backed, her forehead bent low to the polished wood railing, holding her own private vigil.

When at last she looks up, her neck is stiff with the long hours of prayer and I feel the ache crawl through her shoulders. She has been crying. Where the lines of salt tears dried on her cheeks, the skin feels mask-like and tight, as though she had become one of the statues guarding the entrance to the fire altar.

Much of what I see through her eyes is familiar, though this dream was first conceived a lifetime ago in the rippling past. On the center wall high above the candles, the carved panorama of the gods stares down at her. The wood is waxed and shining, kept better than it would be today. In the large center panel, Jokjoa, the father god, emerges. Thick, wild curls fall about his shoulders while his arms are lost in a knotted embrace with the mother goddess, Oreill. Below them, the sister goddesses Sunder, Eclipse, and Seed are shown as children, tumbling and playing within the protective arch of their parents' bodies. They are tossing stars overhead like playthings, and around their waists are belted leather pouches holding the tokens of Kuoshana, the skyworld.

11

My mother had not been raised in the north, and I have heard that when she first came to Briana, my father, Morell, had sent her to his priests to learn their Sumedaro ways. But she was an opinionated woman, and no matter how often they tried to explain to her that dreams must be shared in the full light of day, still, it was only in these solitary moments that she sought out the gods.

"A dream," Ivane cries out to the carving, and her voice, thin and sounding very young, takes me by surprise. "Just to be away from here, anywhere. It doesn't matter. But a jarak dream as strong as any I've ever known. Of something new. More than my husband's indifference. More than these walls where I know every rock and stair and tower. Anything. Before I've lost the will."

She bites down hard on her lower lip till the blood pulses like an echo, yet she seems not to care or notice. Nor does she pay any attention to the temple itself, and if I am to recall any details, it must be my eyes peering out through hers that do the watching.

I am certain she must have come to Lakotah before, this way, at night, in secret, longing for a dream. She would have lowered herself to her knees and begged Jokjoa to grant her a true jarak dream such as the Sumedaro priests are able to conjure and follow through the night. She must have wished she'd been trained like them, taught to summon whatever moment they desired from the night as simply as painting a starflower in the goddesses' hair.

I had seen a painting Ivane did of the skyworld like that, with Oreill asleep, her hair a black wash of night and the stars as pearls adorning her braids. Each pearl was meant as a dream waiting to be called. In the lower corner of the painting, Ivane had placed the figure of a Sumedaro priest. The bearded man was shown asleep in his own bed in the temple house. Then, higher on the canvas, she had painted a second, lighter, more ethereal body floating through Oreill's hair and plucking one of the pearls.

Apparently she thought highly of the painting when it was done because she kept it for herself and hung it in her own room. But she had once told me she was not satisfied with her work. Images were only replications of real landscapes. She had known times, she said, when painting seemed more than merely reproduction, closer to a true dream than a copy, but only rarely, at the height of concentration, when with her brush she too became as a Sumedaro and captured the jarak dream with her power.

Tonight, this dream of mine is the clear, true image of her dream. But hers is not jarak. And now I begin to see that her dream is distorted by memory and by time, and I'm not sure I have the ability yet to separate the truth in it from the yearning.

The hall is hushed, the light dim. Ivane has no answer.

The cold begins to touch her and I feel her discomfort grow. She reaches to the floor where her cape has fallen and pulls the heavy wool close about her neck, then turns to leave. At the door she takes a sip of the wine left behind for visitors and glances back toward the statues. She repeats the litany of the Sisters' names: Sunder, of death, Seed, of life, and Eclipse, of deceit. Above them the image of Jokjoa seems to have taken on a kinder, less harsh aspect than earlier, and the half-open eyes leave Ivane unsure whether the statue really did sleep as deeply as the priests claimed, or if, by some magic of the wood, it could truly waken and hear her cry.

"A dream," she dares the wooden figure as she opens the door to slip out. "Only give me a dream and I'll pay any tribute you ask." But she is already gone, thinking ahead to the morning and the more prudent wish that she could paint faces as cunning as the expression that statue held in its grain.

Outside, snow has fallen across the courtyard and Ivane runs quietly across the shadowed ground. She had sent her servant, Allard, away when she entered the temple, but she knew he would be waiting in her room. By now he should have a warm fire crackling in the hearth and the shutters drawn tightly against the cold. Most important, he would have eased her return with a story for Morell should her husband think to come looking and find her bed untouched.

But the hallways are oddly deserted and Allard is not at the door. Ivane's tension stiffens to a knot. True, it was too late in the night for most people to be about on this side of the keep. But Allard should have been there! She hadn't given him leave to make the ride into town. Possibly he'd gone down to the kitchens in search of a late-night meal or conversation. Still, that wasn't like him to leave before she'd returned safely for the night. Or had Morell arrived first and dismissed him?

As quietly as Ivane is able, but not too slow lest she appear suspicious, she pushes open the latch and lets the heavy door swing inward. The room is empty; her desk, table with brush and colors to be mixed, easel, her bed, all seem untouched. Ivane steps inside. At once a wave of warm, scented air soothes her fear. Morell is not there after all, and although there is no sign of Allard, the room offers familiarity and safety. Tonight, she sighs, sleep will come easily.

Ivane piles her cape onto an empty chair, unties the fastenings of her dress, and slips it from her shoulders. The fire's sweet warmth eases the ache in her muscles and leaves her feeling careless and more relaxed. She drinks down the wine Allard left on her table, then slips between the covers of her bed.

Suddenly everything darkens. I should withdraw from the dream, return to my own body, lying asleep so far from here, and quit this prying into my mother's memories. But before I can decide, I realize Ivane is not finished. None of the tight, receding sensations I usually feel toward the end of a jarak dream are present. Would that I had the skill to follow more surefootedly here. But to follow a dream within a dream, this is a difficult thing. I wait. Then again the room begins to clear.

Now the window of my mother's room stands open. A crisp wind comes blowing over the sill, circling the floor, and sweeping across the bedcovers. The tie that had bound her braid has come loose, and her brown hair lies in light waves about her pillow. I would like to lift my hand and caress her hair as I might have done when I was a child, but I cannot. I am only a watcher here, powerless to touch or speak.

The red embers in the fireplace have kept the room warm, and Ivane's shoulder lies naked, the bedclothes kicked down about her waist. Her skin gives off a rich scent of oils and wildflowers.

A slight noise disturbs her. "Allard?" she calls from her half sleep. "Are you back? Would you bring water?"

"Your servant is not here this night, lady," a man's voice answers.

"Morell? Is that you?"

"No. Open your eyes. Do you recognize me?" The voice sounds in a tone both deep and sweet at the same time.

From the darkness a hand reaches, then lingers on the soft hollow of my mother's throat, surprising me. I wasn't ready to find the touch so real. So warm. I feel like a trespasser and almost pull myself away. How can it be right to watch this way, stealing uninvited into my mother's dream? Peering into her bedroom? Yet I cannot turn away.

Ivane rouses herself, opens her eyes more fully, and searches the dark corners of her room. No torch was lit to soften the blackness. No moonlight crept in through the window. "Who's there?" she calls out and pulls her blankets up about her neck, as uncertain as I am whether she sleeps or wakes or walks some other land.

The man leans closer. I . . . we . . . feel the warmth of his body, the trace of his scent: musky and alive. In the darkness his hand brushes her forehead, traces the line of her jaw, then slowly, moves away again.

Ivane does not cry out nor—and this I don't understand—is she afraid. Instead she closes her eyes, turns toward the warmth of the stranger's unseen face. Her heart races, but it's my blood that seems to rush, dizzy with waiting.

"Sit up, there against the pillows," the stranger asks. "So I may look at you."

She hesitates, but when at last she discerns the calm light of the man's dark eyes, she nods and does as he asks.

Suddenly he moves closer to her, his hand on her shoulder, urging.

"Who are you?" she asks.

He says, "I will not answer, for if I speak too loudly, then my name will be heard and known. And my name is a thing that you especially must never repeat."

"But how can you expect me to—"

"Quiet! No. There is danger in knowing, lest my name be used against you and against the child. Now, enough talk. Morning is not far off and what we must do here can wait no longer. I have sent your servant home to lie with his own wife. Tonight, ours will be a deed of double stealth."

Several long moments pass while Ivane searches for meaning inside the man's words, but I am not so sure that it isn't just a riddle of her own wishes. Still, her dream is strong. It is almost too difficult to hold myself apart. With one slender finger my mother traces the outline of his lips. "What are you, then?"

"Do you not know already?" the man answers. "Open

your eyes. Look, this once. For never again will I allow you to see the face of Kuoshana, save perhaps in the few simple dreams you may invent in the morning light."

My mother's thoughts are clear in my mind. Is this so very different? she asks herself. She is Lady of all Briana. And who—no, whatever this man is, she will not show fear or betrayal. She has never before felt passion or desire for a man other than her husband. And passion she understands. Morell's passion. Her own, buried, though it may be. Hadn't she already borne him two healthy children, strong babes who came into the world with hearty cries? Surely, no one will be the wiser if this third child is to be hers alone and belong to no mortal man. In her own country this would have been a woman's right. Here, in a week, maybe two, she could find a way to invite Morell back to her bed. He would come. For that, at least, he would come.

Hurriedly Ivane's arms reach out; she winds her fingers into his wild hair, draws him toward her, closer, till they are touching. She turns, and like her, my breath catches.

One last thing I feel . . . this stranger's hands . . . warm and searching . . . and then she closed her eyes and the darkness edged in around me.

There was more: talk of forgetting and something about tokens which must be found on earth. Or in a dream? Was that it? I couldn't say. A second dream had begun tugging at me, calling, a dream more certain than that dim, aching memory. Whatever remained belonged to my mother, not to me. For myself, I'd followed as far as I was able.

1

The morning I first dreamt of Theron, I woke to find the narrow, close walls of my room layered with a damp, earthen smell. The air was alive with the first hint of spring thaw after a lifeless winter. I opened my eyes, reached out to touch the slate tiles and wooden sill. Warming but cold.

Still, it spoke of good tidings for the coming Springsnight festival, as though Jokjoa and Oreill were content and only Seed, the goddess of birth, was awake and watching.

I shivered and then remembered. I'd been dreaming again, a true jarak dream. But there'd been another dream first, hadn't there . . . ? It was hazy, though, and difficult. It was my mother's dream, filled with longing. I must have been following it. But this one, this was so clear. A jarak dream. It had to be.

There'd been a man in the dream, tall, thin, and young. I almost reached out, thinking I could stroke his hair. But no. The man was no closer to me than I was to Kuoshana, skyworld of the gods. Had I my mother's talent with a brush, I would have sketched it out on canvas, so clearly could I recall his face, the way the hair at the center of one eyebrow split and panned out, like the open wingtips of a falcon, spread wide to catch the wind.

I shut my eyes again, hoping to bring back the dream. Behind closed lids the darkness cleared and the man's figure returned, this time with his face muffled beneath the furred hood of a heavy jacket. He was outside on a roadway, walking his horse past a large group of men. On the far side of the road, horses and wagons were staked out for the night, and several priests nearby chanted their warding prayers against the ancient havens from which, it was said, no dreamer ever returned.

The young man's horse wore a great beribboned blanket, and silver bells dangled from its gaudy halter. I could just hear their slight jingling as he led the horse toward several large, multicolored tents erected on a small rise. And then I recognized the markings on the flags—gray and purple, the colors of Queen Lethia's standard.

Now I was certain. This had been no ordinary dream, winding freely of its own accord, but a jarak dream, filled with sight and sound and smell. The man in the dream must have been Queen Lethia's son, Theron, my sister's future husband. And if I was any judge of distance, the dream showed Lethia and Theron were already less than two days' journey from Briana. A messenger on horseback could have made the trip in less time, but a group that size would have been traveling for weeks before that as well, up from their southeastern territories at Gleavon, over the washed-out bridges with their crowds of travelers and merchants, all making their way toward Briana's Springsnight festival.

Wouldn't Mirjam be furious to know I'd seen her Theron first? And in a jarak dream? When neither Mirjam nor anyone else in the family, for all the laurels they hung at Lakotah temple or the Sumedaro priests they consulted, ever had had the first hint of a true dream.

Except for me. How long had it been? Two years, three at the most since I'd first guessed my dreams were jarak, that the places I traveled at night were as real as the room I slept in? And I'd told no one, not my sister, Mirjam, who would have herded me away to the priests to be mauled and wondered at, or to Hayden, our brother, who would have run to Morell with the story. I'd decided from the start, I'd keep them secret, hoard them.

Besides, I listened to the priests, heard their sermons explaining how our jarak dreams are gifts from the gods. But their answers never seemed to venture far enough, never satisfied me. How much more vital would it be if— perhaps—while the truth of our jarak powers flowed from the gods, the details belonged to the dreamer, something born of our own imaginations, as surely as my mother created pictures with her hands, objects to be saved and wondered at.

No. I'd keep this one hidden, not let the dream priests at Lakotah trick me into telling. Not that it made any difference, not really. Just that I'd been so hungry for something to call my own—and what else did I have? Mirjam was as beautiful as the day. And Hayden would soon have the crown. What was there for me except a face so plain that everyone laughed, and a shouted curse from our father whenever he found me underfoot?

From the room next to mine, Mirjam interrupted my thoughts, calling out to our guardswoman. Ceena wouldn't answer, not when my sister spoke in that voice, as though she called some common servant.

"Did you start a fire?" Mirjam called again. "I don't care if it is spring. It's cold as the mountains in here."

No answer.

Ceena would be standing by the far wall, finishing the last round of her Silkiyam ritual exercise. Step, pull back, breathe, and turn. I pictured her naked feet moving across the hard floor. Morning and night, never a day forgotten, always the same moves.

I remember the first week Ceena came to live with us, wrapping her quiet spells around me. Mirjam kept her distance, mumbling something about how it was just as well the rest of the Silkiyam had disappeared; how they refused to believe, as Father said we must, that only the Sumedaro may enter another person's dreams. But I pushed my way forward to the main hall, where Morell was boasting of the strength of his new Silkiyam guard, of how he'd seduced her away from her secretive life with promises of weapons and horses—and the freedom to use them.

Mirjam had her mind made up from the start. Ceena, with her large eyes rimmed under heavy brows, was too tall and thin for my sister's house-bred manners. And it was my hand Ceena took first, before Mirjam's, with a firm clasp like no woman I'd ever known, and all I could see were her eyes, the same color as the river-blue veins that snaked across her long, muscular arms. It had gone that way ever since, Ceena filling us with stories of her lost Silkiyam clan, while I listened wide-eyed and Mirjam ran to her priests for fear there might be a grain of truth still living in those blaspheming tales.

Satisfied with my dream, I pulled on some clothing and started toward my sister's side of our room. Ceena was standing at the window, her long neck showing beneath her hair as she watched the courtyard below. The light snow that had fallen during the night was melting already. I could hear the workers calling out to throw more straw about the paths and sweep the piles of horse manure over toward the stables. From the kennels came the high yelp of dogs crying for the morning scraps to be tossed their way. And farther away, toward the outside gates, a carpenter's hammer pounded out another walkway to protect Queen Lethia's too gentle feet from Briana's mud.

Mirjam hadn't noticed me. She was standing at her mirror, brushing out her braid from the night before. The mirror had been a gift from our father and the carvers had taken great care, shaping the rare red wood into a delicate oval. Mirjam would be taking the mirror with her when she left as Theron's bride, and for the first time it occurred to me that I might miss my sister, the way I had watched her brush her light hair on a thousand mornings and smelled her perfumed oils.

Different as we were, it was difficult to imagine life without her nearby. Mirjam was smiling. She looked radiant, and I knew well enough that beside her I was plain to the point of being ugly. The wild curly hair that capped my head and shoulders was thick and untamed. My face was narrow, with too wide eyes. How aptly my mother had named me, Calyx, which is not the heart of the flower but the protective leaves that bind the petals, keeping them safe until ready to open. Which is better than being named after a flower, since I have always thought strength a more useful trait than the beauty I'd never have.

I had been sitting for a sketch my mother labored over the first time I realized how different I looked from Mirjam and our brother as well, with his coal black eyes. Hayden took after our father. Lord Morell had the face of the soldier he was: dark and hard as the man's own fire. Our mother's face was fairer, and somehow I'd always assumed I leaned more toward her people than Morell's. But that day, sneaking a look whenever I could toward her easel, I saw my face as she must have. My mother's hands do not lie. Watching her charcoal move across the paper, I learned that I was none of those.

"He'll think you're very beautiful," I said, remembering Theron and his rich furs.

Mirjam turned, surprised. "You startled me," she said. "Who were you talking about?"

"Theron. When he sees you. He'll love you, of course. You'll be his prize. His beautiful princess."

Mirjam looked at herself in the mirror, then with a slight laugh said, "Well, I certainly hope so. That is the idea, of course."

Mirjam's trim, oval face seemed older, as though the mirror was a doorway into some imagined future and it was to the girl in the mirror she spoke, not to me. "At the beginning, when the only things he knows about me are what he sees, then my face will be my weapon to win his trust."

"But you'll be his wife, and a princess in Gleavon," I said, not understanding.

"Yes, of course." Mirjam's voice took on her usual tone of practiced impatience. "A wedding here and a crowning later, in Gleavon. But that isn't enough. Think of our own mother."

"She isn't a princess."

"No. And it wouldn't have made any difference if she was. She's never been anything but a foreigner here. Even after twenty years. Maybe it was different when they were younger, before we were born. I wouldn't know. But if I was Father, I still wouldn't allow her any power."

"Allow? She's isn't Morell's servant to allow or not—"

"You sound very certain of yourself." Mirjam waved her hand to quiet me. "But that's what I'm saying. I don't want to be in her position, a wife, when any stranger has more access to Morell than she has. I want to be there at Theron's side when decisions are made, problems, wars even. If you'd keep your eyes open to what goes on around here, dear sister, you'd understand it's not any title I'm talking about. It's the power to command. Our father has no title, yet he has absolute power. And Hayden, who has no power, except what he can wrangle out of Father, is soon to become a prince."

Mirjam went back to brushing her hair, and I wondered for a while about the different kinds of solace we'd find. When the silence became too noticeable, I said, "Hayden will have the crown then?"

"It's only a small circlet of gold. Our elder brother wouldn't even have a gem set in it. Did you hear what Father said?" Mirjam lowered her voice till it resembled Morell's. " '. . . A crown will remind them what I've done for this land, strengthened their homes and fields against these damnable winters. No more of wandering like those Kareil nomads, searching for meat . . .' And that's true enough. But this crown, do you think people will say Hayden is poor because it isn't more finely made? I wonder, do you think Theron wears a crown?"

"Theron?" I looked away, guarding my dream. "No, but I wouldn't know, of course."

"I hope if he does that it's finely made. Foppish men never appeal to me. But then, I wouldn't want a great oaf of a man either."

"They say Lethia is a grand queen. That she dresses in gold-embroidered silks rather than wool."

"And that even her slippers are sewn with pearls. Yes, I heard the same talk. Her man who came last spring, the one who discussed my betrothal with Father, remember the white fur at his collar? Do you know anyone at Briana who dresses so richly? And did you hear that Queen Lethia had a jarak dream? She's bringing it to one of Father's Sumedaro priests, Jared most likely, to have it told."

Lethia? Bringing a dream? I stopped. Was it possible? I thought I'd heard every straw of gossip about the lady, but this was new, and coming from Mirjam, who held any jarak dream as holy writ, it very well might be true. Now I wished my dream had gone on long enough to follow Theron inside that tent. Perhaps Lethia had been inside. I would have liked to see her face, to know what sort of woman breathed beneath the curtain of tales I'd been hearing.

And now it appeared Lethia was a dreamer as well. So be it, then. But why should that make me feel so uneasy? Morell never dreamt. And Mother says she hasn't had a jarak dream since she was a young girl. So unless Hayden or Mirjam keep secrets as well as I, there were no other jarak dreamers in our family. Why should it matter to me if both Lethia and Theron had the power? But what would a queen such as Lethia need with yet another priest? The Sumedaro are able to follow the sleepers into their dreams, to go where they're sent but no further. When the dream is finished, the priests tell what they saw. Why wouldn't one priest do as well as another?

And what of Theron? If he was a jarak dreamer—and of course, he had to be—wouldn't he have seen me as well? The Sumedaros say jarak dreamers are drawn to each other. Theron was older than I, probably trained by his priests. Certainly, he would be the stronger dreamer, the one to pull me toward him? And then, of course, he would know about me, that I was a jarak dreamer. Which meant that if I didn't talk to him quickly, he might give away my secret.

Mirjam had not seen me stumble. She had a piece of cake in her hand and was brushing the crumbs loose while she spoke: "They say she didn't understand the dream. That's why she's bringing it here, to have one of our priests speak it for her. But why would she do that? What's wrong with Gleavon's Sumedaro? And if she didn't want them, couldn't she just send for another priest, what with all her wealth?"

"Which will be yours someday," I said, hoping to turn the conversation away from dreams. But it was a mistake.

Mirjam turned on me, her eyes calculating, so much

Morell's daughter, as I would never be. With all her talk of bridal finery and how many ladies she'd command in Gleavon, she had not missed the audiences last winter when the marriage had been arranged. Lethia's lands were wealthy and fertile. Snows there melted earlier in the spring and came later in autumn. But Lethia lacked the numbers necessary to defend her borders, armies that Morell had in abundance, and suddenly I realized that Mirjam probably knew the exact count of every horse, soldier, and acre of wheat waiting at Gleavon.

"And what of you, little sister?" she asked. "What shall we leave for you? Hayden is to be king of Briana someday, and I doubt but there'll be wars and more lands that he'll add to his name before he'll sit and be a farmer. And I shall be a queen as well, when Lethia is gone and my Theron grown to his own crown. It's what I've always wanted. To be queen. For my children to grow up strong, with lands of their own. Oh, and rich, of course," she laughed. "With gold bracelets on my arms and all the silk gowns I wish.

"But you?" she surprised me suddenly, stepping closer and taking my chin in her hand. I didn't trust the sharpness of her touch, elegant but demanding. "What is it you want, Calyx. Pearls? Gold jewelry? Don't try to tell me you wouldn't like a few new dresses of your own, something to help you a bit around the edges? You're Morell's daughter too, and there'll be a fair enough dowry waiting, no matter your looks. Or do you already have a lover somewhere? One of the guards maybe? Someone not too young, but ambitious, someone who'll close his eyes so he doesn't have to see your face while he's dreaming of the captainship Morell might give a son-in-law?"

I tried to pull away, but for all Mirjam's fine ways, she was older, stronger. She held me, pinching my chin in her hand. I tried to answer. "I am content . . ."

Ceena rose from her chair, watching, but Mirjam, daring her to interfere, refused to let me go. Though I would have loved to take a bite out of Mirjam's little finger, I stood motionlessly, waiting. Our guardswoman stepped closer; she'd seen our spats before. But before anything could happen, there was a light rapping on the door. Mirjam's eyes narrowed, and she threw a look of pure loathing at me, then pushed me away. Ceena went to open the door, while Mirjam smoothed her gown.

"You're so young," she sneered. "A child only, in children's clothes. But don't worry. There'll come a time for you. Our father will find something for you, though I, for one, am not sure where it will be."

A serving girl entered the room and waited for permission to speak. "Excuse me, ma'am." The girl made an awkward bow. "I've come from the lady's quarters. Your mother, Lady Ivane, asks for you to come attend her this morning, ma'am."

Mirjam walked to the window and spoke without looking at me: "It must be you she wants, Calyx."

"She asked you both come, ma'am. This morning. Before breakfast."

2

Morell and Hayden were there in my mother's rooms when we arrived. I hadn't expected that. My parents saw little of each other anymore, and for years I'd felt that Ivane's quarters were a sanctuary. Everything about the place was hers. It breathed her touch and smell, the sharp odor of paint thinner and lacquer, oils and dyes. The entire well-lit room was littered with easels and the half-filled canvases that consumed her days.

Morell and Ivane were lost in another of their arguments and paid us no attention. Jared, Lakotah's elder Sumedaro, stood looking out a window, his own guards near at hand. Jared had been gone that winter, away at Aster Sumedaro temple. He still wore the heavy, rugged clothing more common in the northlands. He seemed older than I remembered. His thin hair had grown long and more unkempt, and his beard, which had been a rich brown, was grayed now. In the far corner two of my mother's ladies worked intently on their embroidery, too polite to raise their eyes. Near them my mother's musician strummed his viol so softly the sound could hardly be heard above my parents' voices.

Morell stood before my mother's chair, glaring down at her. "You will not slight me this way," he said.

"And why should it suddenly matter so much to you whether I sit at your table or not?"

"You know very well why it matters. And you will be there. I will not have Queen Lethia thinking there is anything but strength and unity in Briana Keep."

"She'll see your soldiers, your stables and weaponry. Who wouldn't see where your strength lies, Morell?"

"Then she'll see my wife as well. At my side. And smiling. Do I make myself clear?"

"You certainly make yourself loud." Ivane rose and looked behind Morell to where Hayden stood, trying to cover his smile. "But I'll make you a bargain," she said. "I will be there, if only for Mirjam's sake. But you can't continue to underestimate the importance of this dream Lethia's bringing. She mustn't be allowed to speak it openly, before the townspeople. At least not till Jared's priests have it first. Alone."

"She's right, I think." Hayden stepped forward. "No matter how many of our own Sumedaro you keep hidden in Gleavon, we still have no idea what her dream really is. Or what she'll claim it is. It's too much of a risk to have her speak freely."

"Risk?" Morell shouted. "Of course it's a risk. It's the one we're going to take. Lethia's no simple woman. If she wants this dream heard, there's no way I can deny her. She'll have thought out every possible trick we can throw at her, and have a second and a third, all equally hazardous, in its place. And Hayden, don't tell me you're another one thinks there could be trouble in the towns over one dream?"

"It can't hurt to be a little careful," Hayden said. I was awed at my brother's bravery in contradicting Morell.

"Let me explain one thing to you, Hayden. And if you want that crown I'm giving you to mean anything, you'll learn you're the one who has to rule the priests, not the other way around. And one dream, no matter that it comes from Jokjoa himself, one dream cannot matter. Do you know why? It's because our gods are vanished, Hayden. Gone! Asleep! Call it what you like. It's for us to act. You and me. And you too, Ivane, though you've never understood the first thing about ruling.

"If the gods give us dreams—as you're so fond of saying—

it's because they're sleeping. And if they're sleeping, which they must be because surely we don't see them, then they don't matter. And all of your mincing talk about sleep and dreams and old ways or new ways doesn't change a thing. It's my father and grandfather—your grandfathers, Hayden—who built these towns when all around us was nothing but a fool's clan of nomads. Nomads, all of them, playing with their magic and without the sense to come in out of the cold. If you think I'll see it all torn down for one spoken dream, you know a good deal less about me than Lethia does."

"All right, Morell," Ivane said. "There's truth in what you say. But don't forget those Kareil clans you call nomads, and the Silkiyam you don't even mention, survived more generations than your family can chart. And if they used magic, it's because that was as the world was meant to be—and they used it well enough to stay alive. What Lethia understands that you do not is the power her dreams can have over the townspeople. They're hungry. Everybody's hungry, what with these bitter, unyielding winters. They need something to hope for. Why can't you see that Lethia's the one will have her way if it's her dream they find instead of yours?"

"Lethia is coming here because of me." My father's voice was set. "Not Lakotah temple."

"Morell," Jared, coming down from his window seat, tried to speak softly. "The temples are not a thing to be used and traded—"

"Besides, it's not true," Mirjam broke in, her chin raised to face Morell. "Lethia is coming here because of my marriage."

Father stopped for a moment, then put his arm around Mirjam. "You see, Ivane. One of our children, at least, understands what this is all about. We use the temples to control the people. It's that simple. As to Lethia . . . we have the army, she has the gold. It's through a marriage of those two that our strength lies. And besides, what could happen? If two years from now she decides to turn on us, do you think that men born here in Briana, these soldiers we'll be sending back with her, men whose families and lifetime friends are here, would fight for her against their own people? No, Ivane. I don't think that will happen.

"Come, Hayden. It's time to go. Mirjam, my sweet, dress

yourself as prettily as if you were the goddess Oreill. We want to show you off to the queen. And"—this he said after a pointed glance at my well-worn dress that made even Hayden shift uncomfortably to the side—"keep your sister out of trouble, won't you? And Ivane, when you come down to this dinner, try to remember, for Mirjam if for no one else, that you and I also once forged a political alliance."

"There was a time," Ivane said stonily, "when you would have said it was far more than politics we forged."

My father's face reddened. "What you still don't understand is that these are not the same times as when we were young. Then it was all very well to bring scores of priests with you up from the south. But that's all they were. Priests. Dreamers. And for some reason I cannot grasp, you fail to see that for all their fine talk of faith and gods—it's not enough. Not anymore. Not when we've an army to house and crops that do nothing but wither before they can ripen . . . And so you will remember, you're not to speak a word, Ivane. Not if I have to keep Norvin standing watch over you the entire evening." My father turned, nodded to Hayden to follow. My brother lingered only long enough to offer Ivane and me a nod and a silent smile before following him out the room.

For a moment no one moved, then finally Mirjam spoke up, her voice light and I thought too gay for this company. "But here you are, Jared, back in time for the Springsnight festival and everyone is being unpleasant. Come, give me a kiss. Aren't you going to congratulate me on the wedding? And here I am talking so much and I don't even know when you returned from the north. Have you had time for breakfast? Mother, shall we call for spiced wine? Am I the only one who feels so chilly this morning?"

"Mirjam," Ivane said, and I could feel the awkwardness opening between them.

Mirjam managed a half smile. "You're looking well, Mother."

"Thank you. Though these long winters take their toll and whatever else your father says, it does seem they weren't nearly so difficult when I was your age. But we hardly see each other anymore, do we? And you"—Ivane's eyes danced across Mirjam's face—"you are lovely, as usual. No, more than that. You are beautiful, daughter. And this spring marriage looks to become you well."

Ivane returned to her chair while a serving girl came around with mulled wine, bread, and cheese. The warm drink seemed to renew her strength and she sat straighter in her chair. She had taken off the painter's frock she usually wore over her dress, and without its fullness I think she might have passed for a man. Yet for all the tired lines of her face, Ivane still looked very much the Lady of Briana Keep. Her fine, light hair was twined skillfully about her head, and the heart shape of her face and high cheekbones were as perfect as those of the chiseled statues in Lakotah's hallway.

Self-consciously I pulled at a ringlet of my own disobedient hair. Ivane had not called us to her room to listen to Father's ranting. And Jared, tapping his finger continuously on Ivane's chair, seemed to be waiting for something.

If, as an elder Sumedaro, Jared were called to enter Lethia's dream, he would be able to bring full memory of that dream back to the light of day. He could watch the dream, or speak it, but he could not change it. Neither he nor any other priest, no matter what Lethia might be hoping for. Down in Briana town, the people paid handsome prices to sit in the rathadaro couch and have a dream spoken. But even they knew a priest's powers were limited: good enough to help a lonely woman recall the feeling of a man's kiss, but not enough to bring her lover to the door.

Only one man, the Elan Sumedaro, could shape his own dreams and he was nothing more than a legend. Sometimes Ceena would speak of things my tutors claimed were lost to the ages: how the three Sisters had divided the world into clans, the better to maintain the balance Jokjoa and Oreill had begun when they set the world in motion. Oldest of the clans were the Kareil, the nomads who were the keepers of the Sisters' laws and history. The Sumedaro town dwellers were the far-sight jarak dreamers, gifted with Jokjoa's vision. And then there were Ceena's people, the Silkiyam of the forest, who named themselves by which of the Sisters they followed: the Kanashan, who followed Sunder's warrior path; the Estair, who studied Eclipse's magic of change; and the Heya people, who lived the way of birth and growth that Seed ordained. And above these three clans walked the Elan Sumedaro, the only one with the power to change the truth of his own dreams.

"Mother . . ." Mirjam said, "what was it Father didn't want you to say?"

Ivane sat back in her chair. "Your father is afraid I'll say something to shame him. I have never been good at holding my tongue. It's just that Morell would not want your dinner spoiled by my bad manners."

"But what could you possibly say?" Mirjam risked a glance to see how much of this I understood.

"Nothing, of course. There isn't a thing I know about his plans, the border wars, the size of Lethia's army. It's not treason he fears from me. I only meant to warn him. But he doesn't listen. It's a difficult thing for him to accept advice from me . . . we're so different. But if Lethia speaks her dream in front of the open temple, as I have heard she may, then . . ." Ivane turned to Jared to finish.

"Mirjam," Jared said, ceasing his finger tapping, "the town is filled with people during Springsnight. They come from every territory, riding, walking, even sailing downriver, hoping to hear the priests speak their dreams, say something hopeful and longed for. In all honesty, it shouldn't be so strange for Lethia to bring a dream she doesn't understand to Briana. She could say it was more convenient, that with all the preparations for this trip, she had no time in Gleavon.

"But it also happens that a caravan of the Kareil clan will be passing this way, as they sometimes do. Lethia's people would have known they'd be here, and she also knows how much the townsfolk look to the Kareil, especially in these times when the world itself seems to have turned against us and we're so helpless against it. For Morell, the timing is difficult. Volatile. He'd prefer no one called attention to the old legends."

"I don't understand." I said, confused by my own layered dreams of the night before. There had been my dream and Theron's and a dream my mother must have had where she'd wanted to give me something. But I couldn't shift the fragments back to remember it. "Is it Lethia's dream that Father is afraid of, then, or the Kareil?"

"It's more the Kareil folk, I imagine. No one knows what Lethia's dream is. But Morell seems to feel he understands Lethia, and that her dream won't change anything between them that matters. On the other hand, he doesn't want any Kareil tales influencing the meeting. Were Ivane to somehow" —Jared sent a questioning glance toward Ivane, but she returned it with nothing more than a look of calm, unreadable silence—". . . get involved with the Kareil," he continued, "Morell would be furious. He knows the power of a fist or of a mounted soldier. It's the townspeople's faith and the possibility that they can be pushed to action through their faith—actions which can't be reduced to a military formula—that's what he fears."

"The Kareil bring hope with them," Ivane said gently. "But not Morell's kind. He has no use for their ways, and he'd much prefer the people looked to him as they've done in the past, not to gods he can't control. But enough now, both of you children. I am content. There's been enough of anger here." Ivane rose and crossed the room to where one of her painting easels stood below a window. Some small piece of work waited there, covered over with a cloth so it couldn't be seen. She returned quickly, walking up to Mirjam and taking her hand. She pressed a ring into Mirjam's hand, something small, a flash of light.

"I have a present for you," she said. "And I want you to wear it, to remember that I am glad, truly glad for this marriage."

"Mother?" Mirjam began, her voice uncertain for the first time that day.

"The ring is an old one," Ivane said. "You'll have other presents, of course. Finer ones. But this one is special also. My mother gave it to me when I married Morell. It was hers before that. And before that . . . I don't really know, except that it's belonged to my family, belonged in the south at least, for as long as any of us could remember. And it seemed the right thing to do to give it to you. My daughter. My first to be married."

Mirjam took the ring as though she wasn't certain what to do with it, looked at it a moment, then slipped it on her finger. The light shone again, golden and rich, but only for a moment, like sunlight shining through a hole in the clouds before it's covered over again. Then it disappeared so quickly I couldn't be certain what I'd seen.

Mirjam hesitated, then said, "It's pretty. Thank you. What's this part? It looks something like a hand . . ."

"It's the hand of Jokjoa, same as the one on the fire altar," Ivane smiled. "You like it, then?"

"Of course I like it," Mirjam said loudly. "It does look old. Do you know? I always wondered if there wasn't power in the statues . . . Don't you laugh at me for saying that, Jared. I don't mean the gods themselves, of course. But what if the three sisters saw the candles on the fire altar and thought they were stars, maybe they would come down to visit earth themselves."

Smiling as sweetly as if we'd never argued, Mirjam turned to show me the ring. I was surprised at how old it did look, tarnished, rough, and plainer than I'd expected. The smooth band was wide enough to fit an image of two arms coming together to clasp hands in the center. When it was new, the hands must have been highly detailed, for though it was polished from wear, the impression was just visible: fingernails, knuckles, even veins must have once been prominent. I reached toward it, wondering at the light I'd seen, and quickly traced the curving front. A rush of warmth rose up to meet my touch, a sudden heat that seemed to jump from the stones across and into my hand, but there was nothing frightening about it. It was lovely, bewitching almost. Mirjam must have felt something of it also. She snatched her hand away and closed it into a fist, but she said nothing and her face remained smooth. But the light and warmth had been there, I was sure of it.

Jared too must have seen it. He turned suddenly, searching. But the moment had passed and he shook his head as though deciding he'd been mistaken.

"It's very nice," I said to Mirjam, and she turned a half smile at Ivane.

Jared stepped around from Ivane's chair. "Take good care of it, Mirjam," he said. "You'll not find another like it. Ivane showed it to me, and I'll admit I nearly tried convincing her to donate it to Lakotah. But she'd none of my suggestions. Said it seemed to her it was meant to adorn her daughter's hand. And I can see already she was right. It shines brighter on your finger than it would have shut away in a case."

"I like to think it was a premonition," Ivane said. "A feeling that my daughter ought to have the ring I was given when I married. But I have another present, Calyx. For you." She walked back to the easel, picked up the piece that had been standing upright, then stood for a long moment, her back to me, till she turned around again. "It's a book I made. Look. The pages are empty. It's for you to write in."

I must have looked puzzled. Certainly I'd never expected

a present, and certainly not something odd as a book. I flipped through the white band of pages, blank, all of them. They gave off a crisp, finished smell, pleasing and enticing in its own way.

"I painted the cover myself," Ivane said. "I hope you like it."

Jared laughed. "Don't be afraid of the thing, Calyx. It's only a book. Look here, it was my idea. At least partly. I was telling your mother how we give one to each of the new Sumedaros when they first come to the temples for training, though of course none of the others have your mother's handiwork on the cover. They're required to copy their jarak dreams into it each morning, at night also during their early training. But it wasn't meant only for dreams. I thought, and your mother agreed, you might like it to record your thoughts in."

"I'm sorry it isn't more," Ivane said.

"No. It's beautiful, really," I said, afraid I'd offended her somehow. "I was surprised, that's all. You never gave me one of your paintings before. I'll take good care of it. Thank you."

"The idea for the cover came from a dream. No, not a dream, not really. I never seem to remember my dreams—"

"Ivane," Jared interrupted. "We talked about that. It's all right . . ."

"Well, a daydream then. Or an idea." Ivane spoke without looking up at any of us, carried away by some memory of her own. "The kind I hold in my mind when I'm completely involved with my work, and it seems I envision the entire scene I mean to paint all at once. Details, colors, light. Everything. Then Jared mentioned the idea of the journal, and I thought of the painting. I'd done it years earlier, but I knew just where it was stored. The two seemed to go together, Kuoshana's gateway—that's what the house is supposed to be—the door that opens on both skyworld and earth, and a journal which is a door between your thoughts and the real world. So I thought you'd like it, you see."

Mirjam coughed into her hand.

"Jared," I said quickly, "I'm sorry. All this business with Lethia and I haven't even asked after your travels. I am glad you're back again. How was your stay in Aster?"

"It's kind of you to ask, Calyx. But to tell the truth, I

don't enjoy it as much as I used to. Roshanna town is smaller than Briana, not as rich, of course. But at least it used to be quiet."

"And Aster? What is it like now?"

"Dark. Cold. These haven't been easy times anywhere. Actually, there was trouble. The town itself had a very hard year. Frost ruined most everything but the earliest crops. Game hunting hasn't been what it once was. The herds have moved along different routes, perhaps because of the deep snows. About the only good thing anyone says is that there's plenty of firewood for the taking."

"They've heard all that, Jared," Ivane interrupted. "Tell them about the dreams. Which, if Morell would listen, he'd see what I mean about Lethia and the power a dream could hold right now."

"Well, it is true. There were complaints. All the time. People demanding that my priests enter their dreams. Not just speak them, mind you, that would be one thing, but actually change them. Try to change the weather or something, I don't know. Shape the world somehow. Make it more to their liking. As if we wouldn't if we could!"

I nodded, but my thoughts were racing. With all this talk of dreams, I still had Theron to think of. More than ever I didn't want Morell to know about my jarak dreams. It wasn't that the dreams granted me any power, but my father had a way of twisting things so, of using what people said against them. I couldn't trust him any more than I could trust Mirjam. And Ivane had given me an idea. If the townspeople believed the Kareil clan could help with their dreams, then I also could find the Kareil in Briana and have them read the dream of Theron for me. Then, when I went to Lakotah with my family, I could give the priests another dream, a lesser one. My thoughts would be clear of the jarak dream and safe from their meddling.

Mirjam must have decided she'd spent all the time she could afford in talking to our mother. She kissed Ivane, bid her as sincere a thanks as she could manage, and made her excuses to Jared. And while it may have been true that she had enough work to keep us both busy for days with Lethia's and Theron's arrival, I had other plans besides running kitchen errands for my sister. Once outside the door, Mirjam started on her list of new demands, but I mumbled some excuse about changing my clothes and ran off, leaving her alone in the corridor.

In our room again, I sat down on the bed in my alcove, hungry for a moment's privacy. A journal? What was I supposed to do with a journal? I wasn't used to writing in books, committing my secrets to paper. But Jared had said the Sumedaro priests did just that. But surely my dreams were different from theirs. They learned with teachers, elders who taught them each step on a path, while I had, of necessity, to keep my dreams private. Still the idea was compelling in some ways. Later perhaps, I would consider it again.

If nothing else, the cover was beautiful. A miniature canvas on which Ivane had worked her magic. It bore the mark of her style—rich blues and purples in the foreground, browns and lighter shades as the scene faded into the distance in the background. The picture was of a country farmhouse: dairy, bins, stables, everything just right. But on a whole the composition was simple: realistic yet childish as though, for all the completeness of detail, half-open windows, lights within—there were no people but I could see the place was meant to appear lived in—still, something was missing.

In Lakotah hall we were taught of such a place—the valley where earth and skyworld joined and the gods themselves had once stepped out of their dreams. Of course, Ivane wasn't claiming that her painting was an accurate portrayal of Kuoshana, only an idea that had come to her in a daydream. It would be fitting in a way to commit my dreams to this book that was covered by Mother's dream. The ring was an heirloom; lovely or not, it held real value. And while the book was no equal to the worth of Mirjam's ring, there was a value to the painting, coming as it had from my mother's own hand. I had never owned one of her works before. She rarely gave a painting away. Most were stored in one of her back rooms and seldom looked at once they'd been completed. On impulse I dug through the chest at my bedside till I found a blue velvet scarf I'd worn when I was younger. Carefully I wrapped the book in it, folding it over and over into a neat square, then placed it at the bottom of my chest, where it would be safe. Later, I would decide about the journal.

When I looked up from the chest, Ceena was watching me from across the room. "What do you think?" I asked, wondering where the Kareil would be camped. "Can Mirjam oversee the kitchen and get married without me?"

"She has enough girls down there to chatter with about her ring without needing you to hang on her arm as well. But you'll have to tell me what you're planning."

"Don't worry," I smiled. "Only a small trip to Briana. And it wasn't you I was trying to get away from. Besides, there's nothing to keep us here, is there, not on Springsday?"

3

Before the morning sun had risen to its height, Ceena and I slipped away together, taking a seldom used stairway that skirted both the kitchens and the chaotic Great Hall. From the moment we set foot on the wide, stone-paved road leading down from the keep, I felt as if I could move more freely. High overhead, great whips of cloth, blues and reds, caught the wind and fluttered like the wings of a great bird, mocking and rebellious. The crowd was louder and much denser than it had seemed from my windows, and we were picked up and carried along in its pulse, down the sloped road out to the open heart of Briana.

Even without hearing the odd cadence in their accents, you could tell the travelers from the clothes they wore: gaudy cottons and patched wool, all speckled in mud. And with it the poverty showed through: sharp-boned horses walking with tired gait, wagons in need of repair, and loads that seemed less full than in past years.

For almost as long as I could remember, hard frosts had come more often than our farmers looked for them, killing off new shoots in spring and freezing crops before they were harvested. Then, just as everyone looked for a thaw, great waves of snow and rain would come, saturating the ground until the fields were a deep grave of black muck that would not dry.

Through it all Briana, the city that was the heart of Morell's territories, sprawled haphazardly across the dished-out val-

ley below Lakotah Hill. Closest to the protective walls of
the keep, lines of chimney tops coughed up gray ropes of
smoke. Farther out, on the flat bottomland, fields had been
cut out and the forests pushed still farther away to the south
and east. In the center of it all, the marketplace had taken
root and grown into a system of covered walkways, tents, and
stalls that would have rivaled my mother's palette for color.

"Look, those are Lethia's colors," I said, pointing to the
gray and purple flags already stretched like a bridge between two tall houses.

"Your father has an eye for detail," Ceena said without
turning to look. Usually my guardswoman kept her emotions hidden under a mask of self-control, and it was difficult to read her voice. But I knew Ceena spoke more freely
with me than she did with other people. Perhaps with Hayden spending most of his time with Morell and Mirjam as
mistrusting as an ignorant serving girl, there was no one
else for her to confide in. Ceena was alone—more than an
exile, for an outcast had hope of someday finding the familiar eyes of a countryman—her people were gone, and she
was never able to forget it.

"He means to show Lethia they're equals."

"Until Lethia turns her back and rides away," she said.
"When Mirjam is gone, Morell will not sit at home writing
letters to his married children. He'll be counting the gold
she's brought him and playing at those war maps he's so
fond of."

"And Lethia?" I said, working to keep pace with her.
"Two days' safe journey away from here and she'll have
counted her new foot soldiers so many times, she'll know
their faces better than Mirjam's. But what difference does it
make? Aren't they both getting what they want?"

"I think it will make a good deal of difference, though not
in the ways they think."

Off to our left in front of an open tavern, wild strains of a
musician's pipe tumbled through the air. I stopped in front
of the doorway to watch a crew of jugglers practicing their
trade. Children fought to get closer to the center, to catch
one of the balls. One of them, a scruffy little boy, tripped
over my feet, balled up his fists, and started to curse. But
where he thought to find an average-sized girl, he met
Ceena instead, my Silkiyam guardswoman standing taller
than anyone else in the crowd. The boy must have recog-

nized her as one of Morell's and he backed away, the bluff gone out of his face.

I shook my head and laughed, but I knew well enough to be glad Ceena was with me. "I want to find the Kareil," I said suddenly. "My mother said they'd come in to Briana."

"Kareil?" Ceena's step slowed. "What would you want with them?"

Someone in the crowd pushed past me just then, but I shouted as if it were more, stalling while I decided how to answer.

Ceena looked at me, then said, "I don't know what you think. Here I was believing you'd no other wish than to hide from your sister's jabbing finger, when I should have remembered . . . You don't often do things without a reason, Calyx. But whatever truth you're hoping to gain from the Kareil, you'll only be disappointed."

"Disappointed? Why? Have you already come here?"

"Not this time. But there were others. Years went by between the time I left my home and when Morell first brought me here. I've told you that before." Ceena's eyes were dark with her memories. "Some of that time I spent with Kareil, hoping they'd have news of my people. But if they did, they never spoke of it. No matter how I asked, how I waited. They're a secretive clan. Protective. One season they allowed me to travel with them. No longer than that. Perhaps it was for the best . . . They've survived, after all. And who am I to speak without the eyes of time, to say which things are wise, which wasted?"

Suddenly feeling the cold, I shivered and pulled my collar closer around my neck. Ceena watched the streets closely, more alert than she'd been before. "This death hold Sister Sunder has on the land goes deeper than what we see here. Though why, I don't know. When another hard winter has come and gone and not a farm anywhere in the north brings in its full yield, do you think people will care whose bed Mirjam sleeps in?"

"But at least Briana and Gleavon won't be at war. Isn't that worth something?"

"Yes. But it won't stop the fighting that's still to come. There's more here than either of those two understand."

I waited, hoping Ceena would say more, but we were in the thick of the market already, surrounded by noise and clutter, and Ceena, at least, was wisely reluctant to shout.

She led the way forward, searching the tents and banners. Her height was small advantage there in the confusion of banners and scaffolding, but whether people recognized her or not, they had a way of stepping quickly to one side when they noticed her, and paths tended to open more quickly than they otherwise might have.

We turned a corner onto the market's pottery section and I slowed, giving Ceena's arm a tug in that direction. My mother's servant, Allard, and his wife, Serell, kept a stall there, not too far from their home and workshop. Their eldest son, Micah, was a friend of mine, and as soon as we neared their tables, I recognized the air that always layered his clothing, the smell of the wet mountain clay he worked with his hands.

Micah and I had been born the same day, the same hour of the same day. The birth date itself had been uneventful, no stars reached their ascendance, no change of seasons or time of great dreams were announced. But for the two of us, sharing our birth dates had been like having a great secret which, when we were younger, we thought no one else would ever know, and it had drawn us together, made friends of us.

Two women stood beneath Serell's banner. They were dressed much as many other visitors, in bright outer clothes with layers of long skirts and close woolen caps. The one on the right haggled over the price of a small brown glazed bowl while the other woman dawdled with her purse. They seemed serious, intent on their bargaining and they flashed knowing looks when they thought Serell wasn't watching.

I looked for Micah, found him beside one of his gangly younger brothers, a look of bored impatience on his turned-up mouth. His eyes lit up when he saw me, but he signaled to keep quiet, glanced quickly to make certain his mother wasn't watching, then ducked down, and crawled under the table. That was as far as he managed. Serell's round face focused sharply and she called after him:

"Micah!"

Trapped, Micah looked from his mother's gray eyes back to mine. "Where are you going?" she asked, then: "Never mind. I can see well enough. By the Sisters, Calyx, what are you doing down here today, of all days?"

"It's all right, ma'am. I won't be missed. They're too busy at the keep to trouble with me." At mention of the keep, the two women looked over to see who had spoken. They looked me over with a cursory glance, then, apparently deciding I wasn't worth their trouble, turned their interest back to the pots.

"Is Allard coming down tonight, then? But you wouldn't know, would you?" Serell said. She started to say something to Micah, but fortunately for us, the woman with the purse began counting out enough coins to make Serell forget her arguing, and Micah took the opportunity to hastily pull us along.

Like three conspirators Ceena, Micah, and I bustled off and quickly were lost in the maze of turns and alleys. With a coin from my purse, I bought steaming meat pies at one of the less crowded stalls, and watched as Micah ate his down in two huge bites. I couldn't help but notice how much taller he'd grown over the winter, much more than the year before when we'd joked about the way his eyes had gained a clear range over the top of my head. Micah seemed to enjoy the freedom we'd brought him, and his blue eyes danced constantly across the tabletops. Yard goods and leather bags, shirts, jackets, copper pots, there was little that had not come in from some foreign city, and he looked as though he wanted to touch it all.

"Have you seen the horses?" he asked, pointing toward the stables on the opposite end of the market. "They were brought in by the herdful last night."

"No," I said, trying to care, but somewhere, back in the streets with Ceena, I had lost the appetite for all this. I wanted to find the Kareil, tell my dream, and be left alone. Even Micah's cheeriness wasn't enough to shake me from my goal. "We were looking for the Kareil clanfolk. Have you seen them?" I asked.

Micah shrugged and when I looked at his face, the disappointment was clear. I should have known it would be a mistake to talk about dreams with Micah. Though he lived a hundred miles closer to me than Theron did, Micah seldom remembered me in his dreams, scarcely remembered his dreams at all. It used to annoy me that the only friend I truly cared for could not find me in his dreams no matter how often I recalled him in mine. Down in the streets of Briana there is a name for someone who cannot remember their dreams: sensume. It's not a pretty name. It never used to bother Micah that he couldn't remember his dreams, but he'd grown touchy lately, more withdrawn, and I worried a little at the way he turned his eyes away when we spoke.

"What do you want to know for?" he asked.

"Nothing. Except maybe, Queen Lethia's dream," I said quickly. "Have you heard about her dream?"

"Yes. But Calyx, if that's all you're going to ask about, I don't know. People talk about how she looks, how old she is, why she hasn't remarried. No one knows what the dream is. All right? Can we talk about something else? Here. Come over here. These horses were brought in from an outlying farmstead. The best in years, they were saying."

Micah elbowed his way forward, clearing our way toward a series of long, hastily built stables. We were on a far corner of the market grounds now; the gathering here was thicker, louder. There was a street brawl going on not far away; a circle had gathered. Ceena, seeing the dust rise at the center, took me by the arm and kept me close. Several of the men must have been drunk, and their swearing and threats came out in a slur of thick voices I could only half understand.

Ceena bent close to whisper something and I thought she meant to order me back to the keep, which at that moment I might not have minded. I didn't like the look of the crowd here, pressing in and so loud as they were. But instead Ceena pointed to a clearing over on our left. The crowd had shifted away from the fighting, and was gathering now in front of a domed black, hide tent. A platform had been set up. Horse auction, I thought at first, but was mistaken. Two people, both nearly as tall as Ceena, had moved from the tent to the center of the platform and, as silence slowly took hold of the audience, began singing.

"Kareil clan." Ceena's voice was low, respectful. "Listen to them, Calyx. It isn't every year they come this way."

Ceena led me along the outer fringe for a better view. The two figures were both dressed in long, plain robes cut in a style I didn't recognize. One of them, a woman—to judge by her narrower shoulders—had a high, sweet voice and I strained forward to listen.

I must have seen Kareils sometime before, but if I had, it had been years ago and I'd forgotten the beauty of their singing. When I heard it now, I was swept up into the twining harmony. The man was playing along on a small

reed pipe, but he lowered it after a while, and on a note,
joined in the singing:

In the darkness, nothing knew
Only the gods, in dark Kuoshana
slept.

In the blackness, nothing sang
Only the gods, in black Kuoshana
dreamt.

On the earth, the god's dreaming
grew the waters,
grew the wildlands.

There on earth, the god's dreaming
brought the people
taught the havensong.

Of Oreill, the mother, suckling
Sunder, Eclipse, and Seed,
her children.

Of Jokjoa, father, laughing
dreamer, liar, man,
all three.

And on earth Elan Sumedaro
walked in dreaming
and in waking

Fought Edishu, dark Edishu
he who was the god's
own nightmare.

As soon as they finished, the two singers lowered their
hoods to their shoulders and surveyed the audience they had
drawn. Two other Kareil men stepped up behind them. For
the first time I noticed a second black, ribbed tent standing
off to one side of the clearing. Its low-cut door was propped
open and another Kareil, an older woman, stood by the
entrance.

In a thin voice that sounded almost as sweet as the reed
pipe, the woman called out, "We watch dreams for those
who wish it. Who'll speak their dreams for the Kareil?"

The two Kareil singers disappeared into the tent and

returned a moment later. One of them dragged out a bright rug and unrolled it on the ground. The second followed behind with an armful of pillows, laid them out, then jumped down to an opening in the closely packed crowd.

"Come," he said, "speak your dream for the Kareil. We take no money. We only follow the Sister's instructions."

Ceena stood close behind me, her curiosity as sharp as mine.

The two Kareil who'd been singing were seated now, cross-legged on the pillows, hands resting in their laps, nothing in their demeanor resembling temple priests in the rathadaro couch. There, they stand with hands outstretched while the dreamer sits before them, head bowed. These people were smiling, their faces open, with none of the austere trappings that marked the Sumedaro.

On my right a thick-bellied, half-drunken man pushed his way to the platform. "What kind of a priest are you doesn't charge for a dream?"

"It was Jokjoa's commandment that our clan remain nomads, friend. Not beggars or merchants."

"I'll take it if it's free, then." He smiled as his friends pushed him onto the platform. The man acted like a buffoon as he sat down and held out his hands to the Kareil, but the tall, gray-robed man joined hands solemnly, closing his eyes. Now I could hear his murmuring Kareil tune begin as the man started rocking gently from side to side, more as if he were away in the forests than here amid this raucous mob.

Ceena took a step back and looked carefully around the crowd. She was right to be cautious, of course. The guards my father had stationed about the market were noticeably absent down here. We'd lost track of Micah, and when I thought about it, I didn't like the sideways glances these people shot toward me, a little too concerned with the size of the purse at my side. But I'd made my plans, and whatever the rabble, it was the Kareil I needed.

Impulsively I ducked from Ceena's reach and jumped to the platform in front of the Kareil girl. She was younger than she'd seemed from a distance, closer to my own age, and I couldn't help but wonder if she really would know how to read a jarak dream.

"Sit down," she smiled. "Here, next to me."

I looked back at the faces that were now staring up at me,

Ceena's among them, and I turned away quickly before my guardswoman had a chance to call me back.

I shook my head. "No, inside. Only if you'll let me go inside."

The girl looked at me, shrugged as if to say it was no matter to her where she sat, then rose, and motioned for me to follow. The tent was dark inside and larger than I had thought with its black roof rising overhead. The smell of spices sweetened the air, and it was quiet, the sounds outside muffled. No one would be able to hear, which was good because I'd as soon have returned to the keep than have my jarak dream spoken out there, with so many listening.

The girl waited till she saw I was ready. "Here, give me your hands," she said. She had a beautiful voice, easy and trusting, and I sat down on a wide, bright pillow in front of her and held out my hands.

"No, not like that," she said. "Make a loose fist. Put them in my lap." She covered my hands with hers. The girl had a long, narrow face with olive skin and brown eyes. Her hair was wavy and thick, held back from her face with a wooden pin. She was very pretty, but in a different, wilder way than anyone I knew, and I had to force myself to stop staring at her.

"Do you always watch the most recent dream?" I asked.

"Not only. I can trace any dream you carry in your memory. Does it matter?"

"There was one . . ." I said, hesitating, but before I found the words to explain, she had closed her eyes, drawn a deep breath. There was a warmth rising from her, stretching out to include me, comforting and safe. For a while the warmth seemed to pulse, grow stronger, and I forgot my dream of Theron, forgot Mirjam and Lethia, forgot everything but the lightness of this touch. Then, across the arch of her hands, a blue light began to show, gently at first, then stronger, vibrant, like nothing I had ever seen before.

"Close your eyes," she urged. "Your dream will be there."

I did as she said, expecting the blue light to disappear, but it was there again inside the darkness. The warmth grew, flowed through our hands, light and warmth rushing together till it seemed we were joined together. The girl began humming a slight melody, wordless and sweet. Time seemed to slow on all sides. I have no memory of where I went, what I thought or did.

Then, suddenly, I was alone. Light cracked through the darkness. I blinked once, twice, opened my eyes. I was awake. The Kareil girl was watching me intently.

At first she said nothing, but the smile that had welcomed me to her pillow was replaced by a look I could not read. "You have jarak dreams," she said, her eyes searching my face, unwilling to let go. She wanted something from me, but I didn't know what. Not money. I had distinctly heard the Kareil say they were not beggars.

"What did you see?" I leaned forward, expectant.

"Kuoshana. You dreamt that you passed through the gates of Kuoshana and visited Jokjoa. There were stars braided through his hair. One of your Sumedaro priests was visiting and—"

"What? That's all?" I interrupted. "Are you sure there wasn't something about a young man? He had a horse. There were guards."

"I'm sorry." The girl shook her head. She seemed surprised. "I only followed where you led. Your dream . . . it was very beautiful. Jokjoa was there—"

"But that wasn't a dream," I snapped. "I know what you saw. That's a painting my mother did. She has it hanging on her wall."

"It may have been a painting for your mother, but for you it was a jarak dream. It was real."

I didn't like the way she was looking at me now, her eyes boring into me as though she would not be satisfied until she had seen every facet of my being and would not settle for only the one dream.

"No! I remember it too well. That was no dream. How can it be real if I didn't dream it? It was only a painting." Annoyed, I stood up. My legs felt stiff and cold. Now I thought the girl looked ridiculously young to have been watching a dream. How could I have ever expected an untrained child to follow my jarak dream, and what did I know about these Kareil people, anyway? That they smiled? Sang? The Sumedaro at least were trained in the temples, they were watched and tutored and only allowed the privilege of following a dream after years of waiting. "You're sure you found nothing else?"

"Nothing else. But understand, friend, that if you dreamt it, it was real. You were in Kuoshana."

"Yes. You said that. But a lot of good it does me." I

wheeled about. For a moment I thought the girl would follow me, but she stayed there, staring after me as I left.

Outside, the sky glared bright but cool. I squinted, trying to find Ceena, but the mass of people seemed even thicker, louder than before. Confused, I jumped down, called her name, but my voice was drowned out in the commotion. I started walking, farther and farther away from the Kareil tents, thinking that if only I could get away from there, I'd find Ceena and we could go home.

I turned a corner, found myself in a section of the market I'd never seen. Then, just as I turned to leave, a man came up behind me, his arm heavy around my shoulders. "What'd ya do inside that tent, honey?" he asked, his voice gruff, his face shadowed.

I tried to push away, but before I could move, another man pulled me to him, his breath rank with wine. "Did you like it? Did you have to pay them?" He loomed over me, his grip tight, digging into my skin.

"Leave me alone!" I cried, but my voice had no strength.

"Bet she had to pay," the man laughed, pulling me in against his chest, his hands pawing me, hard and rough, searching through my clothes. "She's got no face, so she ought to have some money."

"What a' you got, honey? A little something for Jacko? A little something in that purse?"

"Stop it!" I tried to jump away, to free myself, but the man's grasp was like iron, and all my weight was nothing against him. His hands twisted tighter round my arms.

Then somehow, thankfully, Micah appeared. "Leave her alone," he cried, and he grabbed the man who'd gone for my purse, spun him around, and tried to hit him. But the man stood rooted, taller and heavier than Micah. He shrugged off the attack, then crossed his arms over his chest, laughing. A circle had gathered, watching, hungry. From one side a third man jumped in, rubbing his huge forearms and sneering. Someone else swung for the first man's jaw, and with a cracking sound, sent him sprawling to the mud. Everywhere men began piling in against each other, kicking and punching. Before Micah knew what happened, a man's fist shot out, slammed into his stomach. Helpless, Micah doubled over, his face ashen, groaning.

"Micah!" I shouted, then wished I hadn't. He tried to look up to see if I was all right, and missed seeing another blow because of me. He flew backward into the crowd, only to be tossed back again.

I started in kicking again, raging against my helplessness. I tried to bite the man holding me, to twist away, but it was useless, all of it. At last my legs weakened under me, and all I could think of was how the youngest of Morell's soldiers went about with dagger and sword, and I had nothing, nothing to fight with.

And then suddenly Ceena flashed into the center, her eyes steady, head held higher than anyone else's, judging the conflict.

None of them knew what happened, so lost were they, so drunk. For one long moment Ceena stood motionless, and I thought they would attack her, realized I'd never seen her in a real brawl, that she was outnumbered and weaponless. What good would her Silkiyam pride be now when all the moves I'd ever seen her do in Morell's yard were nothing but shadow dancing?

Ceena's hands came together in what looked like prayer, and she held that stance for one moment . . . two . . . until slowly, as though the prayer had become a dance, her head moved to one side first, then the other. I'm not certain what happened next, only that I'd never seen her like that before. Her eyes flared, that much I followed, they changed, focused inward. Her head snapped forward suddenly, and her eyes, mortal again, stared out at the crowd. Then she struck.

One by one she fought them till they crawled away from the circle, groaning, beaten. She kicked to the side, sent one man flying while she took another around his neck, pressing in till he couldn't breathe, couldn't move. She moved with a lightness that confused them, arms and legs whirling too fast for their drunken eyes to follow. She used no weapons, only her body, but she whipped through them all, legs kicking high, motion a blur.

The two men who had first grabbed me watched her, opened-mouthed in disbelief, till at last it must have entered their heads just who Ceena was and why she meant to protect me. They pushed me away then, as quickly as if they'd touched a fire. "Damn it! That's Morell's woman. The one's supposed to be Silkiyam," one of them hissed at the other.

"Then who the . . . ?"

"Damn, if she's not the lady's bastard daughter, that's

who she is. Though how the hell we were supposed to know?"

The fighting was almost over now. Those who weren't laying facedown in the mud were running for the alleys. In two strides Ceena came up on the men standing over me. She stood glaring down at them, but she didn't move to strike. They dropped my purse to the ground as they backed away a step, then took another step, and another, till finally they turned and dove into the crowd.

I lay there on the ground, mud-splattered and too stunned to remember how to move.

Micah appeared beside me, his face swollen, one eye nearly closed. Blood ran down from his nose and lips, and he wiped it. "Are you all right?" He put his arm around me to help me stand, but my legs felt weak and I stumbled. "Are you hurt?" he asked.

I shook my head, refusing to speak. I was filthy and ashamed. All I could think about was the way Ceena had moved, how no one else in all Morell's command knew how to do what she'd done. Sunder's Kanashan.

Ceena pushed Micah aside to reach me. She was unhurt, her breath as even as if nothing had happened. Her arms were strong but quiet now. She lifted me up like a child and I buried my head against her chest, unwilling to think of all the things that had gone wrong.

4

My room was empty and dark when Ceena finally brought me home. I wasn't willing to speak about anything, not even to thank her. All I wanted was to be left alone. And I'd been so relieved to find Mirjam gone, not to have to explain myself, the way I looked. It wasn't enough the Kareil had left me with that dream of Theron still untold, or that Micah had been hurt on my account. Now there would be my father to answer to. There was no hiding such things from him. He'd hear about the street brawl, of course, and that I'd been with the Kareil. He'd hear about Ceena. And when he did, it wouldn't matter what excuse I gave: Theron, a jarak dream. He'd probably believe it was my mother's doing somehow, that she'd put me up to it. But it wasn't. It was my fault, all of it. My father might beat me. He'd done that before. Not to Mirjam, of course, or Hayden. Not them. But me he would. And yet, if I thought about it, there were worse punishments than a beating. But he needn't know that.

I shivered, chilled by my own helplessness. Desperately I wished I could hide, leave Briana Keep far behind. I waited, unwilling to move until certain I'd heard the door brushing against the sill in the outer room, heard Ceena's footsteps fading beyond the hall. I could never protect myself against my father, not if he took it into his mind to move against me. But I'd as soon keep my jarak dreams to myself as let him know about them. The Kareil girl had failed me with her ridiculous story. But maybe there was still another way to hide the dream?

As soon as I heard Ceena leave, I dropped my clothes in a careless pile, then, naked and lonely as a little girl again, climbed into bed, pulled the blankets high over my head, and lay there, half in, half out of sleep, too frightened of everything to move. I vaguely must have heard the gates rattling open and the heavy clanging of horse hooves on the stones that marked Lethia's arrival. But I never went to the window or cared enough to see the bustling commotion below. It was sometime much later when Ceena finally returned to my room. I heard her scraping about, moving kindling and logs in the open hearth, and later again when Mirjam came in. They talked a little. I heard their muffled voices, but I didn't want to listen.

There was the matter of my jarak dream to plan, the one pearl I would not let my father take from me. If I could have another dream, not a jarak dream but something real enough to throw to the priests, they wouldn't think to look further. No one in our family was a dreamer; there'd be no cause for suspicion. And without suspicion there'd be no action. They'd take the newer dream, the false one, and that would be the end of it.

I could dream of Micah! He was so easy for me to find in my dreams, we'd done it before, planned it. And it never mattered before that Micah didn't remember his dreams. I

could still send mine. To the cliff tree, where we'd met
before. The memories were strong enough, surely I could
find my way in a dream.

My heart quickened.

Fall asleep, I urged my body. Sleep. Dream of Micah as
he'd once stood there beside me in the full light of day. By
the cliff tree, the broken trunk, the one place in all Briana
that belonged completely to the two of us alone. The place
where I had once dared reach across the emptiness between
our bodies and filled the space with a kiss on his lips.
Scratchy, and wet, the kiss felt with the first whisper of a
man's mustache tickling my cheek. And the softness of
Micah's searching mouth had been so sweet. We were surprised, almost shy with each other when it was finished. I
remember Micah looking at his feet, his hands, anywhere
but at me. Almost the same look he'd given me in Briana
this morning: shy, distant. Could one kiss change our friendship? But I couldn't take the kiss back. Micah could have
said something about it today, if he had wanted to. But he
hadn't, and I could still dream about it.

And there was time. Morell would not have my farsight
dream. Nor any of his Sumedaro priests either. I would
never consent to speaking it. I would have this dream instead. By the cliff tree, up the path, and over the rock.
Surely I could find it.

Ceena was shaking me.

"Wake up, Calyx," she said, her voice coming muffled
through the layers of blankets that had twisted about my
face. "Wake up. Lethia arrived during the night."

I rubbed my eyes. I'd been sleeping in a tightly curled
knot, hands clenched into fists, jaw snapped tensely in place.

"Come. Can you wake? Mirjam's already about. She's
gone on ahead to Lakotah for the Morning Watch. They'll
all be there, Lethia and Theron. Morell. You'll be looked
for."

When I didn't answer, Ceena pulled the coverlet down to
my shoulders. "Are you all right?" she asked, but all I
wanted was to burrow back into the safety of sleep. The
world seemed so bright, I thought the sun would blind me
after the long night.

"Here, roll over," she said gently. "Let me look at your
face." Ceena turned me toward her as easily as if I were a

poppet and pushed the hair out of my eyes. She felt my forehead first, then my cheeks. She was so close I could smell her familiar musky scent. With it came the memory of the way she had fought in the marketplace. And her eyes, not beautiful by Mirjam's standards, but something else. Stronger. Silkiyam.

"No bruises," she said. "You don't seem ill."

"No. I'm ill. No. No, I'm not. I'm fine. Just tired." I tried to answer her. I wanted to, but I was confused. My body ached, muscles felt as though I'd been buried under an avalanche. But there was something else . . . not just the market brawl . . . something in the past night that I couldn't yet face, that prevented me from looking back.

Ceena wasn't satisfied with my answer. She ran her fingers through her cropped hair, leaving it standing nearly straight, a dark halo around her face as she watched the fire lick the gray, soot-covered stones. I wondered if my father already knew about yesterday, or if Ceena thought I was feigning illness so as not to face him. And then she spoke, her voice so low and frank, it surprised me even before I understood what she said. "Calyx," she said, "you've been dreaming."

"No!" I shook my head. "It's not true." Naked as I was, I sprang upright, wanting to deny her words, thinking that now I would have to protect both this new dream of Micah as well as the one I'd had of Theron.

"It was only about Micah . . ." I said, then stopped, frozen, as the dream I'd been struggling to deny came thundering into daylight. There had been a new jarak dream, one so vivid I could almost feel it lingering in the room. Not Micah, certainly. Not Theron. But someone. Who?

And then, hideously, the memory flooded over me in drowning waves. There was a man's face, pocked and demanding. He was looking at me. Staring. His mouth gaping and hungry, lips cracked with yellow blisters, malformed.

Ceena found a robe to cover my shoulders, then sat beside me on the bed. "You cried in your sleep," she said. "I didn't understand the words, but your voice sounded frightened. You kicked about."

"I dreamt of a man—"

"Wait." Ceena brought over a water pitcher from the center table and handed me a mug to drink. "Don't speak yet. Just listen. You're a dreamer, Calyx. No, don't try to argue. You've probably known it for a long time, though by the Sisters, I don't understand how I missed it—"

"No more than I understand how I'd never seen you fight that way before."

"All right, then," she nodded. "Your father thinks he keeps one of the Sisters' Kanashan warriors tied to his household. But he's never asked me to prove myself. There's more that I never learned than that I did. And no matter what you saw, the truth is I'm slow . . ." Ceena looked away from me, as if grappling with her own unanswered questions. "I was only a child, you see. Too young. Much too young. I do one of the forms and Morell's captains think they've never seen anything to match me for strength or agility. And it's suited me that way to have them think what they will. Which, I see now, is exactly what you've done, allowing others to make their own assumptions. But you, you're young and untrained. Though that in itself may be good. But jarak dreams are different. They must be watched. Known. By the dreamer, if no one else. This dream of yours, is it your wish to have a temple priest speak it?"

I shook my head.

Ceena opened her hands. "I thought not. Give me your hands," she said. She was staring directly at me, her face set firmly, hands open, waiting not as a temple priest would but simply and trusting, just as the Kareil girl had opened her hands to me. For a moment I was afraid Ceena would hate me when she knew my dream, or look at me the way that Kareil girl had.

"How could you know I had a dream? You're not a priest." I backed away from her. "You told me once that no Silkiyam would ever be a dream priest. You said—"

"I said no Silkiyam would steal a dream as the priests do. Your temple priests watch dreams, but that's all they know. They cannot shape them as the Elan Sumedaro once taught the Silkiyam to do."

"Is that what you want to do to my dream? Shape it? Change it?"

"No. I'm sorry. Don't think I mean to take your dream upon myself and change it. I couldn't do that even if I wanted to, which I never would. Among the Silkiyam, I belong to the Kanashan clan—trained in the ways of death, of endings, a warrior. Dreams belong to the goddess Eclipse, she who lives as a trickster, with illusion and potentiality, not Sunder, who taught the Silkiyam the Kanashan ways of strength. And if I never find another Silkiyam, the loss of their knowledge will not change the truth of the world. A true jarak dream does not belong to the dreamer alone, any more than it belongs to the temple priest who takes your money. It belongs to you first, then the earth, and then Kuoshana, where it must return to rest."

I listened, but I had no strength to argue. There were so many facets. Ceena said one thing, Mirjam and the priests another. Micah saw only the strength of my faith, but the truth was, I was as filled with doubt as he. Did my jarak dreams really descend from the gods? But how? And why? And that Kareil girl, who was only a child herself, she'd confused me all over again. And what good were dreams if Sunder, Eclipse, and Seed had the power to undo them?

I let out a breath, then lay my folded hands in Ceena's cupped palms, completing the circle of the dream just as my family and their guests would be doing in Lakotah's faltering candlelight. Did it make a difference, after all, if here there were no lapping flames to sanctify the dream, no image of father Jokjoa or mother Oreill to bring the dream home from skyworld?

My hands were warm inside Ceena's large grip, tight and safe. I closed my eyes, forcing the memory forward. "There was a man. He must have been looking for me, but I'm not sure. He was turned away first, watching in another direction. But then he looked right at me. He . . . he laughed when he saw me. I couldn't hide. I wanted to. But there was nowhere to run that he couldn't find me. That was all, a message he wanted to tell me. That he had found me. But not just found, hunted me down as though I were an animal. And he was ugly. Terrible. Skin all gray, pocked. Thin, long lips. Old, I think. But not his eyes. They were alive enough, with a power that tried to force me to look at him, and it took all my strength just to turn away from him. That's all. Nothing else happened. Are you done? Or do you Silkiyam have another way of ending the dreamwatch?" I pulled my hands out of hers, shuddered, and walked away, arms crossed over my stomach to curb the sick feeling inside.

"No, that's all," Ceena said. "Except . . . did he touch you?"

"What? Touch me? No! He didn't have to. Wasn't it enough that he saw me? Nothing else happened. Just the man. What more would you have?"

"Edishu," Ceena whispered, but I hardly heard her. I was standing over the small enameled washbasin. Around its edge a crust of frost had formed overnight. I pushed a sleeve of my robe up high and used an elbow to break through. Again and again I splashed the icy water on my face, ignoring the burning cold that ran from my face down my neck.

"What? Did you say Elan Sumedaro? Jared and my mother were talking about that also."

"No. Edishu. Jokjoa's dream. When I was a child, when I still lived in the havens, we were taught that long ago, in the earliest days, Edishu was god-spawn, a dream too real to be held in the shadow of night."

I raised an arm, questioning. "We hear the same stories. But they're old. None of the Sumedaro take them seriously."

"Which they'll regret someday. Edishu escaped the prison of Jokjoa's dream, only to be snared again by the Elan Sumedaro and imprisoned in Kuoshana. Again and again throughout the ages it's happened. Edishu returns, the Elan Sumedaro rises against him, weakening his hand and forcing him back to Kuoshana. But too much is at stake—the world itself—and Edishu does not lightly give up his attempts."

"Nightmare stories," I said as offhanded as I could manage. "Something the sensume tell when they don't have dreams of their own. Surely you don't believe that? Even Morell and Jared agree that the gods will not waken, that they seldom look to earth anymore. Besides, if it were true, wouldn't our jarak priests warn us? Wouldn't they double their warding chants? Their prayers?"

"No," Ceena shook her head. "That would mean admitting there was something they couldn't understand, something beyond their control."

"Jared admits there are things he doesn't understand. I've asked him. But his answers never . . ."

"What? A Sumedaro priest risk his furred collar against Morell's word? Not likely. Not while he enjoys the fit of his robes. Yet it is true. The gods still dream. How do you think they continue giving us the gift of our jarak dreams, if they've forgotten the path themselves? And Jokjoa's dreams are the strongest of all, as Edishu's very existence proves. He's hungry for life since he's been denied any true life of his own. But Calyx, your life's more sheltered than you realize. Don't you see how bad it would appear if someone in Morell's own family believed in these northland tales?"

"The Kareil folk we saw in town yesterday, they'll be singing of the Elan's battle against Edishu. Only he has the power to enter both Kuoshana and earth at will and brought his dreams with him, whole into the day. The Waking Dreamer, they called him. World Walker. Bridge Builder. Listen for it. Their clan is said to have descended from the Elan Sumedaro's offspring, the Jevniah, and those people hold much store in the old ways of the earth."

"Why would I dream of this Edishu?"

"That I don't know. But your dream's been told. It should be safe now, woven into the tapestry of the Sisters' magic."

I watched out the window while Ceena talked. There were fires blazing in the distance now, in the empty fields past the outskirts of Briana, and it seemed as if the entire land was ablaze. Yellow, white, and blue flames shot up in a hundred spires. Even across this great distance I could hear the early morning revelry, pipes and flutes and drums raised to greet the Springsday. But all the while my thoughts reeled around and around. Edishu, searching out the life he longs for and has been denied. And those eyes, blazing fires in a dead pit of a face. Fire born out of the dreams of gods. Was it possible? If we dream, is it because the gods allow us a small fragment of their own vision? Edishu. Edishu. I did not like the sound of the name. And I did not like to think that he had seen me.

"And if he does?" I asked, a cold draft on my back as I turned around to face her.

"If he does what?"

"Escape. You said, look to my own dreams."

"That, yes. And wait."

"But what if the Elan Sumedaro couldn't get into our dreams because this Edishu god was already there, blocking the path?"

Ceena watched my face as she answered: "I don't know the answer to that. These are legends, and old stories can't always answer new questions. You can ask new questions, but the asking will change the answers. I don't know if the Elan Sumedaro has the power to block Edishu. But your dream's been safely spoken, and it should not return."

For a long moment we were quiet, each of us thinking our separate thoughts, and then Ceena said, "When I first learned of the histories, I was a child sitting under the light of a thousand stars. They were sung through, over and over again, a circle without beginning or end. But the circle was closed. Complete of itself . . . There was fighting—raiders in the heavens—during the years before I came to Briana." Ceena stared across the room into the fireplace. "And I doubt any of the people I knew are left in the northlands. If they are, I doubt even more strongly they'd recognize me or allow me to live with them."

"What kind of fighting?" I asked gently, curious but all too aware how easily Ceena turned inward sometimes, refusing to speak. This time, though, she held my gaze steadily, as if this she wanted me to know.

"War has as many faces as the goddess Sunder," she said. "The people of the forests, my people, the Silkiyam, we have always lived in the havens. You know the word?"

"It's a northern word. It means home, doesn't it?"

"Home. Yes. And sanctuary. Asylum. Cloister. The Silkiyam do not live in open villages like Briana. Nor are we nomads, like the Kareil. It's the havens we live in—either its forest or barren highlands places of power, marked by the Sisters' hands.

"My family had five children. Five. It seemed a good number when I was young, all of us strong. The Silkiyam divide themselves into three clans, one for each of the Sisters. My family belonged to Sunder's warrior clan, the Kanashan. When I was seven, I was taken to the hill caves to live with the teaching masters. Kanashan requires devotion if one is to take the vows, and I did not see my family again for several years. After that, the Sister's hand was on the mountains, and one winter, half my village did not live to see the spring thaw. The cold, and thieves from down-country breaking through the haven's warding magic, took care of what was left. I'm here because I gave no vows to my people. There was no one left in my family to accept them, releasing me to fight. Kanashan incomplete is useless."

"Is that why you came to live with us? Because your home was destroyed?"

"I had no home. And there was no one left who I could find to serve." Ceena's voice was hushed, distant. "But that war is not over and I think now it never will be. The havens were the heart of the Silkiyam, the heart of the land, and the last few places of power on earth. Take the Silkiyam away from their homes, and all the Sister's magic will do them no help."

"But you're Silkiyam. Couldn't you go home if you wanted to?"

"I was trained to serve my people through Sunder's way. I would have been Kanashan-sworn, but I was too young to take my vows. Now I wonder if the remaining Silkiyam haven't armed themselves with Eclipse's magic and hidden the doors. Had I been older, I might have known how to find them. That day, I'd been out hunting for food and missed the fighting. I never found out exactly what happened, but when I returned, our homes had been ransacked and everyone was gone. Some dead, but most simply disappeared. I was a child. What could I have done? Had I been there, I probably would not have survived."

"Who would have done this?"

Ceena searched my face. "In truth, I don't know. But I believe it was Morell's father—his men, that is, though it almost doesn't matter."

"Not matter?" I whispered, the voice gone out of my throat.

"Calyx, listen. I have no love for your father, but neither do I hate him for that deed, ugly as it is. Morell's father, Nealon, may have had his hand in it, but what's closer to the truth is that if he hadn't done it, someone else would have. Outlanders. Easterners. All of them fear the old ways, fear to have the power placed in things invisible to the eye. Today they choose instead to believe in only what can be known. A person's word, the knife's edge. The world is changing, and if I carry the burden of hate in my heart, then I'm the one must live in hate. Hate eats away at its keeper, diminishing her life. Hate is Eclipse's weapon, not the Kanashan way of Sister Sunder, lover of death though she be. She teaches us to separate the two. But that's the way of things now. To live, the Silkiyam go deeper into the forest. Sometimes I think they may have allied themselves with the Kareil folk and taken to the open roads. There could be safety in such a thing."

"Is that why you agreed to take me to the Kareil? You wanted to see them yourself?"

Ceena shook her head. "You may look to your own dreams, child. Or wait. As I do. As my people do."

"Wait for what?"

"For the Elan Sumedaro, the Waking Dreamer, to bring the power back to the havens. Among the Silkiyam it's said the Elan Sumedaro will return to us out of our need and grow to be a common dream shared by all."

"Do you dream?"

Ceena raised her eyebrows and laughed. "I'm no Sumedaro. And I've never been granted a jarak dream. When I do dream, it's of the feeling of a Kanashan motion, the world cupped like an upturned hand, filled with honeyed water to strengthen me. Or I dream of the forest where I lived when I was young."

"Kanashan. That's what you did in the market, the way you moved?"

"Yes, that's what I did."

"But you're not . . . ?"

"Sensume? No. I don't believe there is such thing as sensume. Not if you mean a person who has no dreams. No, we are human. We dream. It's that simple."

It was much later in the day when I was finally summoned to join the family for dinner. In the dim evening light I rummaged through the bottom of my chest, noticed the scarf in which I'd wrapped my mother's book, and pushed it aside to find a dress I hoped would prove passable. The dress was old, though it had once been very fine. There was a hint of braiding tucked around its oval collar, and I imagined that its pale blue color suited my dark skin. When I slipped it on over my head, the dress was as tight as a child's outgrown gown, but I tolerated it, thinking that the best clothing was always uncomfortable.

I had only to wait a little longer and I would meet the man who was to be Mirjam's husband. I still wasn't sure which one of us had called the other in the jarak dream. But I would know when I saw Theron's face. I would sense it in the way he looked at me. And if he was a jarak dreamer, maybe, after everything else, he would befriend his wife's younger sister, recognize me as a true-born friend, and allow me to come live with them in Gleavon Keep? Surely he wouldn't turn me away?

The plan sprung to life as I walked down the stairway to the Great Hall. I would be free of Morell and the towering walls of Briana. Ceena would come with me. I would hide away on a wagon. Or learn to ride and disguise myself as one of Briana's soldiers accompanying Queen Lethia on her return trip. I could be off having adventures and living in freedom. It would all be so easy. I would speak to Theron, I promised myself. As soon as I had a chance to meet him alone.

5

The keep's central hall was filled with people, walking, standing about, laughing, drinking, all clamoring for a look at the queen and her son. As soon as I saw him, there was no doubting Theron was the man in my dream. Tall and very comely, he had the same pale complexion and split eyebrow I had marked earlier. He stood in a small, closed circle of guests, Mirjam to one side and on the other an older, tall, and very commanding-looking woman who could only be Lethia.

They were a regal pair, my sister and her prince. Theron was as trussed and ruffled as any man could be; Mirjam floated in a gown more fit for her wedding bed than that crowded hall. And me, with my wrinkled dress, I probably would have been sent around to the kitchens for my supper had I tried to come in the front door. Why, just this once, hadn't I taken more care? I pushed impatiently at my hair, twisted my skirt, then gave it all up. Mirjam and Hayden were family, and no matter how I looked, I had more right to be seated at that table than any invited guest—queen, prince, or beggar.

I walked straight up behind my sister, ignoring the pointed stares and broken conversations that accompanied me. Mirjam was speaking, her voice as honey sweet as I'd ever heard it.

"Oh, Calyx," she said, her voice dropping slightly when she saw me. "You're here."

I had fixed a smile on my face, but Lethia was watching me intently, and I stumbled, confused by her interest. "They only just called me to dinner," I said too loudly.

I couldn't help but stare back and forth, from Lethia to Theron to Lethia again. She and Theron were of one face, but where their shared features were overdrawn on him, on her they were fascinating. Her narrow jaw was proud and elegant, her eyes deep, and for a woman the same age as my mother, she could have rivaled Mirjam for beauty had she wanted.

"Mirjam, daughter, you haven't introduced us," Lethia said, releasing me from her locked stare. "This must be . . . ?"

"My younger sister Calyx, you've met everyone, of course. Why, no! How forgetful I am. But you haven't been downstairs at all yet, have you?"

Warmly Lethia said, "Calyx, I am so pleased to meet you at last. I worried you were ill when you didn't join us earlier."

"You're gracious to be so concerned. I was not ill, only . . . occupied. I hoped it wasn't rude."

"No, child, not at all. But when you weren't at your impressive Lakotah this morning, I couldn't help but be concerned. You had no ill dreams, then?"

"Dreams?"

"You must forgive my sister's lack of attendance on temple duties," Mirjam offered in my defense, but the comment was misplaced. Lethia meant something more than my temple dreams, I was certain, by something in the way she turned her head to watch me.

"Of course. I didn't mean to chastize our cousin. Only that in Gleavon, when we dream, we always go first to be shriven. Isn't it the same in Lakotah?"

"The custom is the same in all the northern lands, my lady," Mirjam stepped between us to answer. "How could it be otherwise, with the Sumedaro priesthood to lead us in Kuoshana's path? Calyx follows me in this as in all things. But this is to be a feast. Shouldn't we, just this once, not speak of temple matters? Calyx, tell me, what do you think of your new brother?"

Relieved, I turned to Theron. "I am honored, sir, of course. And I hope we will have time to become friends?" Then, afraid there might never be a better chance to speak with him about our shared dream, I added quickly, "But you look familiar somehow. As if we've already met."

"Met?" he answered. "No, I don't think so. I don't see

how that would be possible. I've never been this far north before. Unless you travel much?"

"No. Briana's borders and that's all."

"Then a portrait perhaps?"

"No, I'm certain, there's been no painting. But with all this talk of dreams, I couldn't help but wonder . . . Do you remember having ever dreamt of me?"

"A dream? No, not a dream. There isn't a dream I have that isn't temple-spoken. I have so few dreams." Theron smiled while his eyes never left Mirjam's face. "I'm sure I would remember—"

"But you could have had the dream and then forgotten. That happens sometimes, before you have a chance to speak it in the temple?"

"Calyx, that's enough," Mirjam said. "If Theron says there was no dream, leave it at that."

"Yes, of course. Excuse me, sir. I didn't mean to offend you."

"Well, Theron," Mirjam said, taking his arm in hers, "I told you she was outspoken. And what do you think of her?"

Theron looked as if he were noticing me for the first time, then snickered suddenly, and moved to cover his mouth with his hand. "Compared to you, my darling, what is there to think? Or compared to . . ." and he gave a callow laugh at his clever, unfinished joke.

Lethia remained as she was, her face lovely but unreachable. Mirjam, however, did not mind the jest. "Calyx favors a cousin's cross in the family, don't you think, though she has Mother's eyes. We never understood where her hair came from."

Theron nodded absently, and I was stung as painfully as though she'd thrown dirt in my eye. He had no interest in me. That much was clear. But when he looked back at Mirjam, he pulled himself up taller. I think he even wet his mustached lip with his tongue as though he were waiting for us all to be gone so he could reach over and kiss her. And how could he not want her? Mirjam was so perfectly beautiful. Her hair was braided with tiny pearls and hung down like a waterfall below her shoulders. She was dressed in orange and yellow, a gown so tightly cut that anyone could have drawn a perfect outline of her body.

Whatever I may have hoped for from Theron, I felt certain now I would never get it. And though I still couldn't be sure if he'd shared the jarak dream with me or not, he probably thought no more of me than he did of one of Mirjam's hired serving girls standing in a corner waiting to be called. Yet perhaps that was just as well, for even as young as I was, I knew myself well enough to understand that I would not want a man looking at me the way this Theron stared so transparently at Mirjam. It wasn't the desire on his face that bothered me. That I understood well enough. But that with Mirjam staring, first demurely to the floor under the heat of his gaze, then meeting his eye as strongly, playing with him, he seemed to be saying he owned and possessed her fine body and no one else in the world could challenge his right.

I stood up taller, forcing myself to take hold of my plain, aproned skirt as though it were as fitting a gown as either Mirjam's or Lethia's. "Excuse me, my sister is too kind," I said, stepping in front of Mirjam to face Lethia again. "Mirjam thinks she has the best of this marriage for herself, but it appears to me that all of Briana gains an ally in this newfound union you've given our two lands, Lethia."

"Indeed?" she said, and under her smile I forgot the strength of her demanding gaze. "I had not sought to find such grand words from a child so young. You are younger than Mirjam, yes? And I wonder, you have more of a politic bent, don't you? Here, take my hand and walk with me. Over there by the window, where the air is fresher. We were so many days on the road, it seems I've become more a creature of the wind than of rooms and halls and temples."

We walked over to the window and stood there, looking out through the thick, warped glass that was Morell's pride. Lethia laid her slender hand on the stone sill, producing a dark shadow that moved as she moved, each finger so perfectly articulated that I thought the shadow would remain forever, a bas relief sculpture etched into the stone. She was telling me about her journey out of Gleavon, and lulled by the rich timbre of her voice, I felt, more than heard, the steady gait of horse hooves marching across the still frozen dirt road and the constant whirl of wind in my ears.

But the next moment the spell was broken. She pointed across the open courtyard, out beyond the rows of horses and tents her soldiers had pitched, over to Lakotah's open doorway. Her finger seemed to slice the air like a knife drawing a straight line of blood in its wake. "Lakotah is a fine temple, beautiful, really," she said. "But now tell me, in truth. No one else is listening, so it will be our secret. Why weren't you at Lakotah this morning?"

I caught my breath. This had been deliberate, then. But why? What could she possibly want to know? I started toward the others, thinking to pretend I'd misheard her, but the entire room had emptied out as if it too had been under Lethia's spell. Mirjam, Theron, Norvin, Lethia's people, they'd all gone ahead to the Great Hall for the feast. Protect your dream, I warned myself, from her as well as Morell. I turned back, shrugged my shoulders as offhandedly as possible. "Because my father ordered me to stay in my room until he called me down."

Lightly now, Lethia said, "I'm so sorry. Certainly you would have enjoyed it. Your father's Sumedaro . . . what was his name?"

"Who? Jared?" I answered, hoping this might be the end of it. "Tall man with thin hair, he would have been wearing northern robes? He'd be most likely to lead the dreamwatch."

"Yes, that's him. He's an excellent Sumedaro dream speaker. He spoke Mirjam's dream, a sweet dream for a girl about to be a bride. And Theron's as well."

"Theron's dream? Theron spoke his dream?"

"Yes," Lethia seemed to enjoy my discomfort. "Theron's. But why should that sound so important to you? That's the second time now you've asked after Theron's dreams. And you young enough to be sent to your room like a whipped puppy. Or is it that you're so anxious to be wedded yourself that you must ask after the dreams of a man waiting for his bride to come to bed?"

"No, no, it wasn't that. I . . . yes. He dreamt of Mirjam, then? That's all?"

"Of course that's all, and quite enough for my son to remember any dream," Lethia added. "But didn't you have a dream to be spoken yourself, Calyx?"

"No. I slept late. Mirjam didn't want to trouble me."

Outside, the sky had darkened and the outlines of Briana's high stone walls were lost to the night. "Pity," she said as she started away from the window. "I had thought . . . but no. Never mind. Come." She took me by the elbow. "They'll be looking for us."

"Yes, I'm very hungry," I said, relieved. Then, thinking I could afford to be polite now I was nearly free of this oddly demanding woman, I asked, "And did you speak your own dream this morning?"

"But don't you remember, child?" she asked, her face twisted. "I just told you my dream. It was on the road out of Gleavon. We were camped for the night and I had already set up my tent."

I stopped walking. "Your dream? That was your dream? But it couldn't be. There'd been another dream earlier. I can't remember most of it. But that dream . . . it was Theron's. You weren't there. He—Theron, that is—I knew he was the same man as soon as I saw him. He stopped outside the tent, handed the reins to that old man. Then he—oh!" I stopped, as suddenly the rest of my jarak dream flooded back at me. There had been more, much more, but Mirjam and Ceena had been up and moving about early that morning, and I'd turned away from the dream to listen to them.

Slowly, because I saw now that there were no secrets left to hide, I said, "But I remember now. You were standing inside the door of your tent, watching for Theron. It was your eyes I saw him through. Then you went back inside. It's so strange, though. You were sitting down. A girl was brushing out your hair. You were holding something? What was it? A statue? But you weren't looking at it. You were holding it up in front of you, as if showing it to me. What was it?"

Lethia moistened her lips, but she would not answer me. There was power in that statue, ancient magic. I could feel it now. The entire tent was alive with that power and Lethia did not want me to know what it was. Yet she had led me to it. Surely she would know I had seen it. Why was she showing it to me? To frighten me? Warn me?

"Very good, you save me having to remind you of each detail," she said. "Pity you didn't speak that dream this morning. I would have enjoyed seeing their faces. To hear a jarak dream shared! Your father would not have liked it, to know there was jarak blood hidden so deep in his clan. No, not liked it at all." Lethia turned and walked away, leaving me to run after her, the last one into the feasting hall.

An empty seat had been saved for me beside Mirjam, and I made for it, weaving in and out of serving girls loaded down with their platters, hoping no one would take notice. At the center table, my father's swarthy face was even redder than usual. My mother, seated beside him, looked delicate and pale while Lethia, on his left, only served to make my mother appear more fragile. But Ivane leaned forward and exchanged pleasantries with Lethia, and took such sweet care to fill my father's wine cup that it was difficult not to notice the smile Morell gave Ivane in return.

For most of the dinner, while servants laid out trenchers full of venison, game hens, lamb roasts, and bread, I was safely ignored. Once or twice my brother smiled at me from his place at the table and raised his wineglass in greeting, but we were too far apart to speak. Mirjam and Theron, their chairs pushed together, spent most of the time laughing and whispering together. I tried once to talk to Lethia's man seated beside me, but he kept his eyes down and his mouth full. He had no more use for me than his prince had.

Theron put his arm around the back of Mirjam's chair, so close I could see the rubies set into his rings. But his hand didn't stay long on the chair. In plain sight of every man and woman in the hall, he leaned even closer and kissed her neck. And his hand that came so close to brushing me moved around her shoulder and very low to where her breasts showed above her dress and rested there, his fingers brushing back and forth on her pale skin. Mirjam beamed at him, and it was as if with that unblushed nod, a knot was cut free and the hall grew louder and more boisterous than before.

I studied my hands, my plate, the dark, swirling grain of the tabletop, anything rather than look at my sister. A large flagon of wine sat before us on the table, and I filled my goblet to the top. The wine was thick and sweeter than I expected, and on an empty stomach the drink flooded through me with a forgiving warmth. I refilled my goblet and drank again.

Most of all, I tried not to look at Queen Lethia. She had known about my—our—dream all along! While I had forgotten. And I had been completely wrong. Theron was as near to being a sensume fool as Mirjam, with not a simple fragment of a jarak dream between the two of them. But Lethia had known, for as long as she'd been coming to Briana she had known. She had led me on, her words bleeding with honey, only to show me in the end what I ought to have known for myself. And now, having met Theron, it was impossible to ask him to take me with him to Gleavon. I'd be a servant there, not a sister.

As soon as I set my goblet back on the table, a girl stepped up from behind and refilled the cup. Jarak dreamer, Ceena had called me. Kareil and Silkiyam. Edishu. Elan Sumedaro. What had any of it to do with me? I lifted the goblet to my lips again and peered cautiously down the table toward Lethia.

She was watching me!

I quickly drank the wine, picked at my food. She had Theron's eyes, that much I could say with certainty, or rather he had hers. Riveting midnight blue eyes with a shape almost like a crescent moon that tapered off into the darker night. Mirjam could have them both, I swore silently. I did not like having those eyes turned on me.

Awkwardly I reached for my goblet again. I felt very sleepy suddenly, and too hot. My coarse russet dress itched and pulled in all the wrong places. I saw Ceena standing with several of the other guards near the blazing hearth. Why wasn't she sitting beside me? If only I could go to sleep. I could close my eyes while I sat up. It wouldn't matter. Maybe put my head down on the table. Just for a moment. Hayden might tease me for acting like a child, but no one else would notice. Then I would feel better and the spinning would stop . . .

The next thing I knew, the hall had grown quiet. I bolted up straight in my chair. My mouth tasted terrible. My lips felt dry and pasted. But my goblet was full again and at least I could have a drink. I gulped down the wine and wiped my mouth.

My mother was standing. She must have been speaking and somehow I'd missed it, caught only her last words: "Thank you. My apologies for leaving so abruptly, but I tire too easily." A girl held a cape up to her shoulders, then followed Ivane out the hall.

At the same time I heard the slight, drifting melody of finger pipes trailing in from the opposite hallway. The sound grew closer and louder. Finally three white-robed people walked in, two of them playing their instruments, the third walking silently in the center. I recognized them at once, the Kareil dream speakers from the marketplace, the young girl who had taken my hands and the older woman.

Ivane's singers!

One of them, the tall man in the center, was new to me, and like no one I had ever seen before. His face, eyebrows, everything was white. Colorless. Translucent, like the swirling texture of a marble statue. And his hair too: long, fragile curls of white lying like clouds upon his shoulders.

When the music had gone through its first melody, the tall man, the pale one, started singing. He went through one wild refrain, his voice resonating with trills, then another, and with the third round the two Kareil women put down their pipes and added their voices to his:

Touch us, teach us, Waking Dreamer
Graced with dreams of skyworld's making
Teach us in the ways of shaping,
Day from night and truth from vision.

Armed with bow and dream and dagger,
Rid us of Edishu's waking
With your winter son Jevniah
In the havens grant us hope.

Trees have died and mountains hidden
On the earth the laws forbidden
We who seek the token's treasure
With our need we roam forever . . .

White-knuckled, Morell gripped the table, but he let them go on till the last note hung in the air. Then he rose from his seat, glaring angrily. Norvin, Morell's chief captain, waved his hands, and instantly guards everywhere snapped to attention, hands reaching toward weapons. In a loud, cold voice Morell shouted to the Kareil singers: "Enough. You go. Now!" I think he half expected some treachery to erupt, the way he stood there staring at each face in the hall, watching for some sign of violence, a hand moving inside a shirt, eyes hoping to hide beneath his scrutiny. His long arms were braced against the table as though he would pick it up, platters and food and all, and heave it against the wall if anyone dared cross him as Ivane had done.

Without showing any hint of surprise or fear, the Kareil tucked their pipes away and walked slowly down the length of the hall. At the door all three turned and bowed toward Morell.

"S'matter?" I asked Mirjam, my voice a slur. "Din' he like the song?"

Mirjam looked at me in disgust. "Hush," she said, and slid her chair farther away from mine.

"Ashhk Theron. He'll know." I tapped Mirjam's arm. "Go on. Ask him."

"Be quiet, Calyx, or I'll have you sent away," Mirjam hissed under her breath.

"You can't do that to me. You're not a queen yet," I said, twisting around so she was forced to look at me. "And you won't find me anyway 'cause I know where to hide and Theron can't dream and neither can you." I was going to say more, I meant to. I'd had as much of Mirjam as I could bear, but the wine made my head both light and heavy at the same time and my voice rang in my ears when I spoke.

"What are you talking about, Calyx?" Mirjam snapped, and she looked around to see if there was a servant she could call, but everyone's gaze was fixed on my father.

He stood there at the center of the table, the sweat glistening on his dark chest. Even with all the wine I'd drunk, I knew enough to understand that regardless of what Ivane hoped to set in motion, everything was going exactly as he had planned. I could almost see him counting his new allies on his fingers as he gripped the table: Lethia, and with her, Isiad of Ruax, with his three blond-haired sons and their wives, not without wealth and soldiers of their own; Warren of Sukhamva, an unmarried man who was said to wait constantly on Lethia's pleasure. Then the northerners: Shimoan, from the territories east of Aster; Korinna, who as the single heir had recently become queen in her own right in the western valley of Hillstor. And there wasn't a one of them would have missed Hayden's crowning and the chance to do a little spying on their neighbors. Which was exactly what Morell had wanted—to prove to them that none but he could boast of a town the size of Briana, or soldiers as well trained and numerous as his. He wanted to be absolutely certain they all saw and remembered, and understood what a marriage of Morell's numbers with Lethia's wealth could mean in the northlands.

At last he raised his copper goblet high in the air, and his voice, when he cleared his throat to speak, was as strong as his fighting arm: "To Lethia, and to all of you, my lords and ladies. Welcome and be merry. This is the high feast of Springsnight, the night of winter's break upon the land. And it has been on my mind to name my first-born son, Hayden, as my heir and chief agent in Briana." Morell waited while the crowd took up a thunderous stamping and cheering. Even Lethia's two stolid men on my left were caught up in the shouting. I drank each toast that was raised until at last Morell lifted his hands to restore order.

He began again: "But there is more, and I know you have heard the talk, and I am not one to make long speeches. Only that what you have heard is true, and I would that my son, Hayden, takes on himself the first crown of Briana . . ." Morell waited, but this time there was not a sound in the entire hall save for the crackling fire at our backs and the heavy breathing of the older men who watched, cautiously appraising this lord and his son who would be prince.

"Hayden?" Morell said, and five seats away from me, Hayden rose, straight backed and tall, and faced the company.

Norvin took up his place behind my father's chair. From inside his shirt he produced the crown, a vine-thin circlet of gold, gleaming and perfect in the hall's careening light. Norvin handed the circlet to Morell, who raised it high for all to see.

With measured gait Morell said, "My father ruled in this land and his father as well, all the years back to a time when the people were homeless wanderers on the earth. Let no one here, or in any of the northlands, say Briana never had need of a crown before. But Hayden, say instead that with this crown you declare a love and unity with this land of ours that no other may claim, that this land is yours, and Jokjoa smiled from Kuoshana and threw down a thousand dreams to the Earth when you took the crown upon your head."

The entire room roared its approval, as if they too were being given the crown, and all of Briana, not Hayden alone, were being made royal and god-hallowed with this one small act.

"In the name of Jokjoa and Oreill, the father and the mother, I place this crown on your head, Hayden."

Liar, I thought. In your own name you do this.

Hayden bowed his head in mute benediction.

"Freely, and with consent of all present, we grant you keep this covenant . . ."

With a sword at your back if you dare say otherwise, I thought.

". . . between Briana and its people. And empower you to honor the temple and keep faith with the gods that they shall strew our path with dreams . . ."

Faith in high Kuoshana? How could he speak like that? My ears rang with the hidden malice in Morell's words, but I forced myself to keep quiet. Blindly I grabbed my goblet, drank the wine. But when I tried to put it down, there were two tables and two goblets, each swaying uncontrollably, and I couldn't see which was real and which shadow.

The next moment the goblet fell from my hands and clattered to its side, a river of red wine pouring across the table toward Hayden.

Morell refused to falter, but the look he threw in my direction was of fiery malice. Somehow I managed to find a rag and put the red-stained tablecloth. I think a serving girl came up behind me to finish the job, but that was not until Morell had placed the crown on Hayden's head and the crowd had taken up the cry.

"Hayden! Hayden! Briana!" they shouted wildly, and when I dared look up again, the plain band of gold was already outlined against the black of his hair, gold on black, like stars in a sea of night. But just then Lethia moved into my line of sight. She was watching me mop the tablecloth, her indulgent smile now shaped in a mocking curl. I don't know what I would have done if Theron had not stood up, blocking her from my view.

Red-faced and smiling, Theron held his cup toward Hayden and waited for the hall to quiet. "May I ask first boon, my lord?" he said.

"As your guest and friend, ask," Hayden said, and although I refused to look at him and chance Lethia's smile again, I could tell from his voice my brother was enjoying this immensely.

"Before all present, I ask consent from you, as I already have it from your sister, to be her husband."

In a deep, proud voice Hayden answered, "Then you shall be my brother." He came around to Theron and clasped him with both hands full around his back. And sitting as close as I was, I saw that Hayden's eyes were red-rimmed and wet, and he was nearly crying. Theron too looked as if he were filled with warmth and good feelings, and for the first time since I'd met him, I thought perhaps, after all, my sister had taken a good man.

"I have never had a brother before," Hayden said, more for Theron's ear than anyone else's, and they locked arms with each other and drank together.

When the approving murmurs in the hall died down, Lethia cleared her throat. She spoke in a quiet voice so that everyone had to strain to hear, but the effect was very commanding, as she must have known it would be.

"A toast," she began, and there was probably not a man in that company but wished she had set her gaze on him. "First to my son, Theron, who is heir to all my lands and wealth, and to his bride, whose beauty will light our home. Second to my host, and soon to be brother, Lord Morell, whose hand is from this time forward clasped in mine . . ." She paused as if to consider the full weight of her words, and to make absolutely sure that everyone noticed that pause. "And for you, Hayden, I too have a favor to ask, if you find it proper for a mother-in-law to ask second boon?"

Hayden jerked his head toward Morell, then back again. What was he afraid of? Lethia had already spoken our shared dream at Lakotah that morning, hadn't she? Surely there wasn't cause for Hayden to fear her boon request, though fear it or not, he was bound to grant her—or anyone—favors asked at his crowning.

"Ask Lethia, and if I can grant it, you shall have whatever you wish of Briana."

"Only a small favor, then. I have a dream to tell. One that has not been spoken before. I would like to tell it, here, in front of everyone."

For the first time that evening, Hayden looked shaken. He had known this would come, surely. He should not have been surprised. But I think this public display went against him. It would be impossible in a crowd this size to influence a dream watch. He'd agreed with Ivane when she tried to tell Morell exactly that. It was too risky. There was no way of knowing what her dream could predict. Nor was there a way to deny her request.

"Would you have a Sumedaro?" he asked.

"Not yet. I would like to simply tell it first, so everyone may hear it and I will be shriven. Then later, if I have time enough before we return to Gleavon, I will find a priest."

"In Briana it is more usual for us to take our dreams to the temple, but you have asked for a boon, and it would be unseemly for me to deny your wish," Hayden said, but already he looked paler and younger than before.

Lethia waited only long enough to make sure she had the full attention of everyone in the Great Hall. Then she said, "I saw Oreill, the mother goddess, visiting me. At one breast she nursed the infant goddess Eclipse. Her second child, Seed, clung to her shimmering skirt while the third daughter, Sunder, played with a ball near her feet. But as I looked, I saw that the ball was not a ball at all, that it had a face, eyes, nose, mouth. It was my face! My head! Severed and dead! And I was a plaything of the death goddess, Sunder. I understood that I was dead and that I was looking at Kuoshana through the eyes of a dying woman. And when I understood that, I also wanted very much to see Sunder's face so I could worship the goddess who had claimed my life and remember her as I journeyed through Kuoshana. But the face she bore was a woman's face, not a goddess's. Dark, heavy eyes and tawny skin and black, coarse hair that was left wild and unbrushed. The face of your third child, my Lord Morell. Calyx! There! With my blood on her hands."

What was the woman saying? Me? Trying to kill her? Or was I dead? Had she said Sunder? Sunder had killed me?

With trembling hands I reached for my goblet and drank down what little wine remained in the bottom. It was too much. My stomach lurched and I covered my mouth with the first cloth I could grab, all the while praying to Sister Eclipse not to let me be sick. Not there. Not on the table, with Theron and Mirjam and Lethia all watching.

"Ceena," I heard Mirjam shout, "get her out of here."

From somewhere else, another voice. Hayden's, I think: "Madam, my apologies. She's a child. She drank too much."

"What she does here matters little, sir," Lethia's voice rang through my despair. "You have heard the dream. And

I have changed my mind, after all. Have you a Sumedaro able to speak it for me?"

My mouth tasted vile. The whole world seemed to stink of vomit and soiled filth. If only I could clean my mouth, I thought, I would be all right. This would all go away. They would let me sleep. I slumped forward to the table. Sleep, that was it. Everything would be all right if I could just . . . no! I pushed myself up. Shouldn't do that. Theron's here. Mirjam wouldn't like it. Mustn't ruin her feast. Can't sleep. Not yet.

I brought the cup to my lips just once more. Only to rinse the taste from my mouth. I didn't want to drink. But I had forgotten. The cup was empty. I peered down the long funnel of its walls and watched.

Inside, there was no bottom, no goblet, no Great Hall in Briana. Only the night sky, stars, and black Kuoshana, endlessly growing, changing, swirling one into the other, and in the center, a face forming. Brow ridges, eyes, cheeks, nostrils, lips, teeth. A man's face. The man in my dream. Edishu's face looming at me. Watching with that same hideous smile. Laughing!

I smashed the goblet to the floor, shattering the clay into a hundred pieces, and I screamed.

I screamed long and loud and hard. "Go away. Leave me alone," I begged. "Ceena! Make it go away!"

Morell's chair slammed to the floor as he rose, red-faced and fuming, his fist hammering empty air.

Beside him, Lethia sat, disciplined and unscathed, her hands folded neatly on the table.

"Get her out of here!" Morell bellowed. "And as for you, Calyx . . ." Morell tried to calm himself, and in that single moment my life was saved.

Farther down the end of our table, Jared rose to his feet, his Sumedaro orange robes a shapeless blur in the corner of my vision. But Morell saw him, as Jared meant him to.

"No." Morell slammed his fist to the table. "Not you, Ceena. You stay where you are. Stay away from her." Two guards pressed in front of Ceena, blocking her, though I called her name, crying.

"You! Jared. Priest," Morell said, each word so precise that no one could mistake his intent. "You take her. I give her to you. A present for your temples. And make sure I do not see her again for a long time. A very long time."

6

Pale leaves were unfurling on the trees when our small company finally rode out of Briana. I had made my few farewells; to my mother, who said she believed some good would come of this but cried just the same; to Hayden, who slapped me on the back as soundly as if I were a soldier out on his first march, then hugged me suddenly, in spite of his attempts at formality. It was Ceena's farewell that proved the most difficult. Distant, reticent, she'd wrapped herself in a protective silence I didn't know how to breach. But I was young and excited as a puppy, and after that, no one could convince me that Morell's exile was anything but a blessing.

At the time, it hardly seemed to matter that Mirjam did not come to see me off. I was too busy with my own preparations to notice her callousness, and just as relieved to be out of Queen Lethia's reach. And though I spent more than a few afternoons with my mother, we seemed able to speak only about little things: the weather, the gossip about one of her girls who'd run off with a guard. Whenever one of us circled close to the subject of my coming journey, the talk foundered painfully, and we both seemed relieved to give it up. Sometime at Lakotah's Fire Altar, Mirjam and Theron had been married and toasted, then bedded. Then later, in a procession I had watched from my window but not been permitted to attend, they had ridden off under a sea of gray clouds, southward toward my sister's new home in Gleavon Keep.

Whereas for me, with my single act of defiance I had changed my modest girl's clothing for the hope of someday wearing a priest's widely gathered robes. I had packed only the oldest clothing I could find in my chest: Hayden's discarded tunics, a favorite linen dress, the heavy woolen riding gear Jared advised me on, and no more. Alone in my room, the stars for my witness, I had sworn every oath I believed in: when I turned my back on Briana's sprawling politics, I meant to leave that world behind.

And I, who had never been allowed beyond the keep's main gates after dark, was soon sleeping in a warm blanket roll not three lengths away from the open road. In that bed, with the cold ground for a mattress and the stars my blanket, I did not dream. I lay down too tired and woke too quickly to think about dreams. And for a while I was content.

Jared rode closest at my side, on a dark horse that was larger by several hands than the gentler mare he had chosen me. With his gray hair hidden beneath a richly furred hat, Jared seemed stronger than he had in Briana and not nearly as old. He held his back straight in his saddle and seemed glad to be riding for Aster again. Even his endless finger tapping eased off until finally it ceased altogether and I found myself speaking more easily with him than I had in years. Still, I decided to wait and keep my dreams a secret, at least until I was a Sumedaro myself and knew better how to handle such matters.

Behind us rode the two guards I had first mistaken for priests: Beklar and Damen. Beklar, a small man but as hard and strong as the wind, welcomed me with an open sense of fairness I would have found unsettling had I not longed for it so deeply. His straight, thin-lipped smile was either one in ready song, or drawn into a tight silence, with little use for small talk in between. The first night out, he showed me how to choose a sunbaked rock to lean against while we ate, and how to level a small clearing for my bed using spruce boughs for a mattress. Evenings, while Damen quietly prepared our meal and Jared rested, Beklar kept up a constant singing as we wandered about, filling our arms with kindling.

Each day's journey brought us farther into the lowlands, and the number of farmsteads tapered off, then disappeared altogether as we approached the forested area near the Koryan River. Here the rain came down in earnest; gray, windswept sheets that hit us like pinpricks and brought a halt to the easy conversation of our first days. Whenever I complained of it, Beklar laughed knowingly, saying I'd wish for rain soon enough when winter set in.

Still, we kept riding through wide skies and unending countryside until the land changed again as we moved northward, into winter. The trees, struggling to survive against the cold, grew shorter and more tangled, and the road was a pocked vein of ruts and trenches. We had climbed out of the lowlands again, into the Hills of Elianor, when the freezing rain turned to a thick fall of snow, covering the land in every direction. Far to the west, Hillstor Valley lay, where the young—and as Mirjam had often pointed out—unmarried Queen Korinna lived. Eastward, Shimoan ruled in Toklat. Aster, our destination, cut the middle road between these two lands and lay farthest north of them all.

It was nearly dark one night when Damen pointed out the first farm we'd seen since leaving Briana's warmer lands. Jared pulled his horse to a halt and scanned the low-lying fields.

The farm lay in a rough valley below us, surrounded by gray and white fields of new-fallen snow. Through the shuttered windows a warm light glowed onto the dusk-muffled ground. But for that, the house seemed poorly kept. A fence flapped open in the wind. Clapboards were missing from the walls. The barn and storage shed showed no signs of the hay that should have been bundled safely in their lofts.

At length Jared spoke, his breath rising like a cloud. "We'll go on ahead," he said. "It doesn't seem the kind of place would welcome four uninvited guests. What do you think?"

Beklar kicked his horse, prodding him closer. "It's what I told you. A farm like that has no love for the Sumedaro. They'd look at us as thieves."

"No storage sheds but the one there," Jared pointed. "No silo. Meat they'd have, and firewood. But they wouldn't want to share. Remember the last time we tried a farmstead? We were lucky to make it out of there with our horses and gear still our own. No, we'd do well to push on to Sharat temple."

"Sharat temple?" I repeated. "I thought we were going to Aster."

"We are, but we have the one stop to make. It doesn't change the route too much." Jared smiled, seeing my concern. "Only that we take an eastern turn first and follow the southern shore road around Roshanna Lake. Sharat lies at its eastern border. I spent my youth there, studying to be a priest. It's a quiet, lonely place, different than Lakotah or Aster, which have towns surrounding them. Actually that's why we're going there. There's a new priest we'll be bringing to Aster. The north temple's larger, a better place to school a young Sumedaro. Carth, he's elder priest at Sharat, asked me to come take him north. There's too many raiders about the roads for anyone to be traveling alone.''

"But I thought priests were safe wherever they went?" I asked.

Jared raised an eyebrow. "Most folks out here have no use for strangers, priests most of all. True, there was a time when they'd welcome a Sumedaro, share a meal, their homes. They'd ask nothing more than to have a dream spoken, medicine for their children. But that seems further back than even I can remember. Now they haven't enough to feed themselves, and they care no more for your robes than for a sack of books.''

Beklar raised his chin sharply. "Except that your robes would keep a baby warm and dry paper will turn a stubborn fire to a blaze.''

"The earth's gone hard," Jared agreed. "That's what the people see. The elders tell how different it once was. That the north had been a blessed place. Green and rich with the gods' blessings. Now, they say, there's a curse on the land. And though Lord Morell would try to shut the stories up before they're spoken, they say it's what the old legends warned. That the gods are at war again. Or Edishu abroad—''

"Edishu?" I said, too loudly, wishing I'd held my peace.

Beklar's dark eyes narrowed. "You've heard the newest songs and stories, then?" he asked. "And here I thought Morell had a clamp so tight over Briana's ears that you in the keep would never hear all the talk.''

"Not so tight as Morell wished it," Jared said, and I stole a quick glance at him, if only to make sure he wasn't keeping an eye on me. "Morell didn't succeed in keeping the Kareil away. And as long as folks see that clan alive, even if it's only once or twice in a lifetime, they'll remember the earth is not only Sumedaro. Though," he laughed, "being Sumedaro, I shouldn't be the one to talk of such things. But come. We'll keep straight along this road, forget the farm. Roshanna Lake's as windy as an old man, and it wouldn't be the first time the path was lost under snowdrifts.''

We rode on till we were well past the farmstead. After that we camped each day before dark settled in. While Jared and I unpacked horses and gear, Damen took his leather sling and went off, following the fresh lines of tracks that danced across the mounding snow. Nights, we kept a fire burning and Beklar took turns with Damen keeping watch. No one mentioned the farmhouse again, and I learned a little of what it was like to be hungry and cold, to ration each mouthful of dried meat and cheese. Till finally on a crisp, clear afternoon, we turned off the main road and followed the southern shoreline around Roshanna Lake. Roshanna was larger than any river or lake I'd ever seen, a flat oval mirror reflecting the earth's beauty back to Kuoshana's vain gods. Crusted ice rimmed the edges along-side our path, freezing the slender brown grass and forgot-ten cattails into place. Far opposite, the northern shore robed itself in haze; huge boulders towered from the surface where, ages ago, they must have broken from the jagged lines of hills rising up straight behind.

All that afternoon we rode single file, breaking trail through unmarked snow that came halfway to our horse's knees. Twice that day Jared dismounted and stared into the thick, snow-covered forest. Solemnly he raised a temple icon over his head, invoking Jokjoa's protection, the same as I'd seen Lethia's priests do, always staying far enough ahead of their queen to insure her safety. East, south, and west he pointed, each time reciting the warding chant against the ancient Silkiyam havens which the priests had taught us to fear.

Head bowed, I listened. But I couldn't help wondering what Ceena would say if she were here. She'd told me it was the havens that were threatened by the priests, not the other way around. If Eclipse's magic had weakened enough to force Ceena's people from the havens, then why did the Sumedaro feel the need to guard against them? A forgotten rivalry that had escalated to fear? Jared had once said the havens spun dreams from which no priest ever woke. But I didn't understand that fear either. If our jarak dreams were gifts from the gods, why not welcome the havens which had also been given to us? Why not search for a way back to them instead?

I wondered, but I didn't think Jared would like my ques-tions, and I didn't ask. Instead, it seemed that the cold reached out toward me with a touch so determined that I started, thinking a hand had brushed my cheek, wraithlike and dark. But as I turned to the others, I saw that they too held their heads down, fighting the frost, and I took com-fort, seeing that I was not alone.

And then, after long weeks of sleeping under the stars, we arrived at the easternmost point of Roshanna Lake. The trail turned away from the lake, and we followed into the thicket, pushing on toward night until we reached Sharat temple. The great outer wall loomed up as we neared, a rigid set of lines against the moonlit backdrop of trees and snow. At the wall's center, a heavy door marked the entry. And though it was halfway on to morning when we rode in, the door was open wide, with neither guard nor lamp to mark our coming.

"Here, you can get down now, child," Jared said slowly. "Damen, unpack the horses and see if there's not a ladder up to the hayloft. There'll be clean bedding and we'll sleep warm for the night. I doubt there's anyone awake to welcome us. Come morning, Carth will never forgive himself for his bad manners. We'll have a hot breakfast and bath out of him instead of excuses for the bad season."

I jumped to the hard ground, clapped my hands together inside my bulky mitts, but already I could feel the difference in the air. We were out of the wind at last. Four walls surrounded us and there was a stone courtyard beneath my feet. More than that, I thought, I would never need. Wordlessly I followed Jared's lead into a long, narrow building that smelled wonderfully of animals and grain, wool blankets moist with use, and old, oiled leather. Down at the end of a long boardwalk, clean stalls seemed to smile openly toward me, and almost before I had found a corner to stretch out in, I was asleep.

Next morning, late, I was awakened by a tapping on the bottom of my foot. "Wake up! Can't you smell the porridge cooking? There's warm bread and milk, eggs too, if you want the truth of it. Or are you practicing up on your dreaming already?"

Beklar smiled down at me. He was dressed in clean trousers and a woolen vest, while his dark hair hung to his shoulders, wild and unkempt as always. "You know what it is the new priests do in there?" he whispered, his dark eyes all seriousness. "Before you're allowed to take your vows? First they test you to see if you can fall asleep. You have to know how to sleep if you want to be a Sumedaro. But you'd pass there, no fear."

"Don't you come teasing here." I kicked out, sending a

rain of hay about his legs. "Not when you've eaten and bathed already."

"No, it's true, it's true! How do you think Jared got his robes? If you want to eat, you must first dream your meal. Then produce it, silver platter and all, real as the ground below your feet. Venison with herbed sauces, spiced wine—"

"Beklar, no Sumedaro can do that."

"And who told you that? The Elan Sumedaro could have brought anything he wanted in Kuoshana back from his dreams! Battle-axes! Jewels! A warm sun! And that's what the Sumedaro have to practice as well if they want to be priests! Now hurry yourself."

I stood up, pulled a few vagabond straws from my hair, and tugged my clothes straighter. "Beklar?" I asked, wondering. "How did you come to be Jared's guard? Did you ever want to be a priest?"

"A priest? No. I knew from the start, a life indoors in a temple'd never fit a man such as I. For me it's the distant hills that matter, the air blowing clean on my face, and songs. The best are from the mountains—"

"But any shepherd could say the same . . ."

"You're a hard one, Calyx. Did I ever tell you that? Always pressing for more. Never settling. You're right, of course." Beklar pulled loose a straw to chew on. "Funny thing is, you'll understand when I tell you. More than most. Your Ceena, she's Silkiyam. Right?"

"Yes . . . ?"

"When I was a kid, not even half the size you are now, my family met a Silkiyam man. Just once. He spent the night at our house. But it was enough."

I stepped closer, intent. "What was he doing traveling through a town?"

"Oh, we didn't live near any town. Not then, at least. Far west of Hillstor my people came from. My father was a solitary man. And my mother also. They'd leave us children to mind ourselves and go off hunting together; spring, fall, and midwinter. They lived for it, the mountain country. One day they came home with a man—tall, taller than Ceena. He spent the entire night awake, talking to them. I didn't understand a touch of what he said, if that. I was such a little one. But when he left the next day, I knew I wanted to grow as strong he'd been. To sing the way he did too— sing about the gods."

"And?"

"Well," Beklar said, walking toward a slit in the wall where he could see beyond, "nothing ever turns out the way we think it will, does it? Here I am—a guard, shorter than most for the occupation, but I'll do. A priest's man—and mind you, I keep Jokjoa's laws, even if it is in my own way. And I strum a bit now and then. Everything I wanted, just in different proportions."

"You never told that to Ceena, did you? That you'd met one of her people?"

"Oh, no. I wanted to. To ask her about herself. But she's not the type you can strike up a conversation with, you see."

"That would have been when she was young herself, wouldn't it?"

"I suppose. If she'd even been born."

I looked at Beklar, trying to judge his age. His beard and hair were black, with little more than a touch of gray. Around his eyes a few lines were etched in, but only a few. Ageless, he seemed to me. Timeless. "And you never saw him again? Or any other Silkiyam?"

"Only your Ceena. But come along. Jared'll be waiting."

Beklar led the way down and across through the outer ward into the temple and on through a series of dimly lit, narrow corridors until at last we reached the kitchens. I leaned toward the open entry, my gaze roving over the walls with their shelves of stacked dishes and scoured pots, kettles, knives, and bowls, and I drank it all in, hungrier than I'd realized for the sight of four walls and a solid floor.

Beklar showed me a small table where a washbasin and warm water waited. "I've got to go," he said. "Maura over there, she's cooking and Serebet, that's her with the butcher's knife in the corner, they'll feed you and show you where to meet Jared."

"What's he doing?" I asked, the warm water already dripping to my elbows.

"Only meeting Carth and then Dev, and Avram. He's another new priest I just heard will be coming north with us. Now let me go about my work. The horseshoes need to be checked. With two more in our company, there'll be more work than before, though more to share the load as well. Damen is busy stocking the panniers. We've still a long road ahead, and that nip of frost we took at our heels won't be anything to what we face tomorrow."

When I looked up again, Beklar was gone and the two women, Maura and Serebet, had stopped their work to wait on me.

"Good morning." I offered a smile. "I heard there were two priests joining our company. That would be Dev and Avram?" I spoke politely, uncertain how to address them. In Briana I would have been courteous but short. Morell didn't like the family to be familiar with servants. But I wanted this to be different, to learn to be a Sumedaro, not a lord's daughter anymore.

"Dev's one of our own priestlings," the one who'd been chopping answered—Serebet, Beklar had called her. She spoke quickly, eagerly, as if she'd been waiting all morning to be asked. "Dev's lived here since he was no taller than my side. Avram will be the other. He's just arrived himself from another temple. South of here, though I'm not sure where. His father was a friend of Carth's, they say. Jared's to bring them north to Aster along with you."

Both women were short and gray-haired, with shoulders that seemed to droop from years of water jugs hauled along well-house pathways. It was Serebet's voice that surprised me more. I would not have expected anything so gentle and melodious from someone whose hands were buried to the wrists in a sinkful of vegetable scrappings. "I'll miss Dev," she said, keeping up a steady stream of talk. "Though no one ever stopped to ask me what I thought."

"And you are . . . ?" The second woman, Maura, picked up a pile of neatly folded clothes and held it out to me.

"Thank you," I said. "My name is Calyx."

Maura walked over to have a closer look at me. I could feel her gaze moving across my face, cataloging the faults of my plain features: too much mouth, wide-set eyes that seemed almost to miss what they were looking at, small, sharp nose. No servant in Briana would have dared look at me the way she did, for all the gossip they whispered behind my back. But Maura's smile remained, and I almost thought it was not my beauty, or the lack of it, she meant to judge, but she simply wanted to see who this Calyx was.

While I changed clothes, Maura's hands flew across the counter, scooping up flour, sprinkling water. "Dev will be glad to see you," she said. "He's been aching for someone his own age to talk to. The other lad, Avram, I have a feeling he won't do. Though of course, they've taken up together. Avram's either playing jokes or he's off talking to someone or other. He's a difficult one for Dev to understand, wouldn't you say so, Bet?"

"True," Serebet said. "Hadn't been here but a day or two himself when there was some mischief. Dev got a scolding for it, but Avram, he found a way to apologize himself right out of trouble."

"And we're no use, I'm afraid," Maura went on. "Dev's been so filled with the pain of waiting. That's his youth speaking, of course, but he won't hear of it. Thought you'd never come. Thought Roshanna Lake was the Great Waste itself, and all his jarak dreams would come to nothing but a nagging doubt. Try to ask him what more he expects in Aster, though, and see what he'd do for an answer. Thinks he'll live a holy life, study his jarak dreams all day, with nothing but his faith to bring him food and clothing. Avram's the one will be a good priest. Seems to know his way around every situation. Almost too settled at times for one so young, though, wouldn't you say so, Serebet?" Maura looked up from the counter to see Serebet waiting to lead me out. "Are you ready, then? Well, go on ahead but come back here when you're needing food, Calyx. Old Maura will take care of you. Your stomach or your dreams, either one, I'll fix," she laughed as she waved us on.

Once out of the kitchens, the halls lost their pleasant sense of warmth and good company. Sharat grew darker, narrow and chilly. The temple seemed older than Lakotah. But I think the difference was more in its situation. Sharat was a forgotten place, so far away from the lords in their cities. Lakotah thrived on the crowds, grew rich on Morell's extravagance and high profile. I followed closely beside Serebet as she led the way through a low-ceilinged common hall lined with benches and rugs more worn than any I'd seen in Briana. We turned down another corridor with doorways shooting off on opposite sides. Most of the rooms were empty or sparsely furnished, but through one of them I thought I saw the outline of a stone fire altar, square and low and glowing with the ever present candlelight.

"You'll be a priest someday," Serebet said when she saw me peering toward the fire altar. "And then it won't seem as if you had to wait so long. If tin-eared Maura can hear dreams, anyone can."

"What? She's Sumedaro?" I must have looked surprised.

"Well, of course," Serebet laughed, wiping her hands on her apron. "What did you think we were, farmers? Out here on the shores of nowhere?"

"I'm sorry. I didn't mean to suggest . . . I only thought . . . our priests in Lakotah don't . . . well, you were working in the kitchen."

"That's all right. It doesn't matter. Only watch out, or you'll be too much like Dev, always rushing off to a day that doesn't come. Better to be like Avram, learn how to live with people, adapt. In Sharat we're all Sumedaro and all Sumedaro work. No one out here to do our weaving or shoe our horses if we don't do it for ourselves. It's true we don't dress in fancy robes, if that's what you want, not like your Jared, there. And we don't get many travelers in here willing to trade gold for a dream. Though we could handle them if we had to. We've as many jarak priests here as any other temple in the northlands. But there's work to be done, endless work. Just you wait and see if it isn't the same in Aster. Look, I'll tell you what you do. Trust Dev. Ride with him. He's a puppy, loyal. He'd give the world to a friend. When you're settled in Aster, he'll be a good one to turn to."

Serebet stopped outside a wide doorway. The wooden lintel was plain, undistinguished from all the others we'd passed except for its latch, heavier and equipped with a lock. "Here now, fix your collar. Isn't that better? Now in with you, and may the Sisters walk you through the night."

"May I ask you something?" I said, hand on the door.

"Ask."

"Did you know I'm Lord Morell's daughter?"

"We'd heard."

"And it didn't matter?"

"Of course it mattered. Or it might have if you'd been the other one. Your sister. I wouldn't have said all I did about Dev if you were, though. I'd have been afraid for him falling in love with some fool princess, dreaming about nothing but her, when it's his jarak dreams he wants to mind."

"Thank you." I nodded, thinking I understood the part about Dev, though I wasn't certain if I'd been insulted or praised. But then Serebet left, and I opened the door.

Inside the room a hearth fire had been built so high the air wavered with the heat. Jared stood with his back to me, his hands stretched out before the blazing fire. Beside him a silver-haired man sat with a thick comforter draped over his legs. Two younger men stood near a long table on the opposite side of the room. I assumed Avram was the darker and Dev the taller, with brown hair loose to his shoulders.

But then, for some reason, the table drew my attention so sharply and suddenly, everything else seemed to dim. Shadows darted up from the fire and arched across the high ceiling, dancing and pointing back down to the table.

It was a heavy table, dark and uneven in the distilled light. I started toward it, then stopped, confused. It wasn't the table at all, but something shimmering on top of it that pulled me, stronger than my will. I took a step closer, staring, aching with the thought that whatever it was created that light and no matter how desperately I already wanted to possess it, it did not belong to me.

In the center of the table, draped in a velvet cloth, a bracelet rested beside a plain earthenware goblet. The bracelet seemed to be made of a gray stone, faceted but simple. Light from the fire was bouncing off its surface, casting rainbows of shimmering light in a circle about the walls. It was the two of them that had pulled me, the goblet as well as the bracelet, and ordinary though they were, I felt myself drawn to them as though I had suddenly been handed my heart's desire on that velvet cloth, and I longed to touch them. Either of them. To know they were real. I dared a step closer, my heart hammering.

"Calyx, didn't you hear me?" Jared's voice cut across worlds, demanded my attention. "Carth wants you to come around where he can see you. Stand here, by the fire."

I forced my eyes away from the table. "Of course, excuse me. I was . . . it's so warm in here. We've been riding so long, sir." I turned from the table, fighting myself.

The dark-haired young man, Avram, watched me curiously, while the other, Dev, offered a smile.

"So," Carth laughed, "Jared thinks you'll make a good soldier."

"Soldier? Oh no, sir," I mumbled. "My brother, Hayden. He's the soldier. I'm to be a Sumedaro . . ." I stopped, hearing my voice as muddled and foolish as a child's.

"Don't take him too seriously." Dev walked over and

stood beside me, his eyes dancing in the fire's reflection. "Carth calls us all soldiers. Soldiers of the Sumedaro. That way he thinks it's all right to work us till we drop in our beds at night, too tired to dream. While he claims all the best jarak dreams for himself."

I looked about the room, still confused. Both Jared and Carth were smiling fondly at Dev. Only Avram, shadowed in the far corner, seemed unaffected by Dev's half-joking humor. I dared a look at the bracelet again, at the lights tossed from its surface and the way they shone, brightly first, then against my eyes. But the feel of it drove deeper than I'd realized and my blood sang in my ears, leaving me faint, the room darkening about me. I blinked, shook my head, trying to see, but my knees went weak on me and one of my legs slipped suddenly sideways.

"Are you all right?" Dev asked, catching me by the arm. "Here, look. Carth, she's too tired for this."

Ears ringing, vision narrow, I felt as silly as a little girl, but I leaned against Dev for support, helpless to do anything else as I tried to find my balance.

"Jared, is she ill?" Carth called out.

"No, no, I'm all right. Just tired. The room . . . it's so hot."

Dev helped me to a bench while Jared watched closely, frowning. "She's all right. Aren't you, Calyx?" Jared said. "Just tired. If your mother knew how I'd pushed you, she'd have my head. But when I saw you could take the pace without complaining, I was so relieved. I thought . . . well, I just forgot. Treated you like a boy, didn't I? You're just tired now, aren't you? We're all tired. Still, it's true, the roads only get worse up ahead. And now I've spoken with Carth, I'm glad we didn't have to slow down. Calyx, Carth says we're to bring these"—he touched a finger carefully, almost reverentially, on the goblet's rim—"relics to Aster."

I took a deep breath, forcing the strength back toward my legs and arms. My vision had cleared again and I crossed back to the table. "They're real, aren't they? Ancient? They must be. But what are they for? How did they get here?"

Jared waited for Carth's nod before speaking: "When Sharat temple was first built," he said, "it was the Silkiyam gave the relics to the priests. That's all we know, really. Lakotah had its relics also, as most temples did years ago. Surely you remember Lakotah's? A hand carved of stone,

curled slightly as if it was resting. It sat above the fire altar?
The truth of the relics is long forgotten except that they
were gifts from the gods to guide our dreams. We know
nothing of their power—if they ever had any. Carth here in
Sharat and Hershann in Aster decided it was time they were
shared with the northern people. That's why I called you
here. They're precious cargo and if anything should happen,
any trouble along the way, we wanted you to know it wasn't
just food bags we're carrying."

Carth straightened himself in his chair. "Aster lost its own
relics long ago," he said. "And it's been generations since
these have been moved or put on display."

"Then why move them now?"

"They're a reminder," Carth said. "That's all. A symbol.
Isn't that it, Jared?"

"Yes. A symbol. That's where their value lies," Jared
said. "Of course, they don't do anything."

"If they ever did." Carth sounded as if he'd heard these
arguments before. "Maybe the Silkiyam would have claimed
there was a power to them. Or the Kareil. But those people
would say anything if it served them. As for us, we have our
jarak dreams, Jokjoa's true gift to the world. We've no need
of stories to muddle up what we see before our eyes."

"Not us, perhaps," Dev said suddenly. "But you're not
answering Calyx's question. The relics are being moved
because Carth thinks the townsfolk around Aster need to be
reminded of the Sumedaro's position. In these outlying lands
it's the elders who maintain law—the elders who speak the
gods' will. Sometimes, though, the people don't like what
they hear. Carth wants to use the relics to remind them that
it's the temples the gods speak to, not the towns. The relics
will calm them down. Control them."

"That's enough." Carth's voice was gravelly but direct.
"We've spoken of this. Your allegiance is to the temple, not
the towns. And once you're pledged to Aster, you'll have to
mind what you say better than you have here. Hershann
hasn't known you since you were a boy, as I have, and he
won't be so interested in your opinion. Curb it, for your
own good! If we've decided that the townspeople would
better honor their faith in the temples if they could actually
see a relic in place on the fire altar, then it's an easy enough
way to remind them of our power. Which is not for you to
squander. You understand?"

Dev stared at the floor, biting back his words, and I thought I saw what Maura had meant when she said Dev was always rushing into trouble.

After that the talk turned again to the journey ahead of us and I paid little attention to what was said. Instead I watched the bracelet shining from its place on the table. What harm could there be if I touched it? Only to feel it. Jared had touched the goblet and nothing happened. Surely, it would be all right. I wouldn't drop it. What if I were the one who ended up riding the horse whose saddlebags contained that bracelet? Wouldn't it be better if I could hold it now, first, just to see . . . ? No one had actually said I couldn't touch it . . .

Slowly I reached out toward the bracelet. I only meant to touch it, to savor its weight, to feel the flush of time and creation caught inside the relic.

I never saw Avram stepping to my side as I opened my hand. I'd forgotten he was there. He'd been so quiet, so dark, almost one of the shadows himself.

I reached out. Opened my hand.

At the same time Avram's hand stabbed past mine and he snatched the bracelet from the table.

I pulled back, jerked my hand away. But the bracelet had brushed my fingertips as he moved, and where it touched, my skin burned.

For just the slightest moment, Avram dug his fingers into my wrist, then quickly released them. The dizziness returned suddenly, clutched at my stomach, as if the memory of some precious dream had been stolen by the morning light. I shook my head, looked from Carth to Jared to Dev. They hadn't noticed a thing, none of them. It had all happened so quickly.

And Avram was smiling at me, gently almost, his head cocked slightly to one side as if it was me he worried over, and he said, "Here, let me show you. Beautiful, isn't it? Rath, it's called. I only meant to give it to you. A present. As Jokjoa once gave it to Oreill." He bowed toward me, teasing with an exaggerated courtliness. And the way he spoke was so calm, self-assured. Was this supposed to be a joke, then? Some awkward, boyish introduction? No wonder Serebet had said Dev didn't understand his humor.

While Avram turned the bracelet over in his hands, Dev came over and plucked it from him, then laid it back on the table. I watched, curious to see if the glow would begin again. But nothing happened. Perhaps Jared and Carth and Dev had already seen its glow so many times, they didn't feel the need to remark on it? And the goblet—hadn't I felt a warmth as real as if it had just been drawn, newly fired from its kiln?

"And some say it's made out of pure starlight." Dev smiled. "And if you believe that, you may as well believe old father Jokjoa throws dreams down to you from a sackful of flowers he's slung over his back. And if you're a good little boy—"

"Don't we know a lot?" Avram's voice rose an octave.

"I'll tell you what I know," Dev said, all seriousness. "I know the strength of my own jarak dreams. That they're true, that they're real, that I live for them—"

"And I don't?" Avram snapped.

"Dev, mind your tongue. Nobody said you aren't going to Aster to be a priest," Carth interrupted. "Jared, will you take that boy—"

"Man!" Dev reeled abruptly. "From the time I leave this sunken boat of a temple, I'm a man. Not a boy. A man and a priest. A jarak dreamer!"

"Out of here!" Carth's face reddened. "And mind what you say to Calyx, there. Though, child, I hope you're too smart to listen to his ravings. Believe what you like, Dev. Or say what you will, for by the Sisters I'll never understand what's behind those laughing eyes of yours. But how a Sumedaro priestling dares talk so about the gods . . . Where else do you think your jarak dreams begin, if not the gods? And another thing. Say what you like in here, but when you're wearing those orange robes in Aster, you'd do well to talk more like a priest than a farmer!"

Early in the morning on the following day we rode out, six in a line now, plus three packhorses. Beklar had been right to worry. Once beyond shelter of the bluffs that protected Sharat's northern shore, the snow swirled like whirlpools around our team and the air burned more deeply into our clothes with each passing hour.

With the harsh weather Beklar and Damen grew distant and could hardly spare a word the remainder of the journey. Jared worried constantly over the relics, his mouth set in a firm line whenever he looked at the packs that carried them.

It made me shiver to see him so, as if for a moment I watched out of his older eyes and felt with him what it was to know that everything you did and lived for mattered not so much for yourself, but for some other burden; that your life was little more than a pair of shoulders to carry its weight.

As we rode, I tried to slough off the loneliness that seemed to have closed around us all, but, like the early winter, it would not flee. The rising cold was real, the ache in my thighs where the saddle chafed the skin to a burnished purple was real, the constant hunger, the slick road, this was the life I'd bought myself by screaming like a child at Morell's table.

I tried, as Serebet had suggested, to ride beside Dev, but that proved more difficult than I would have guessed. Dev's mood seemed to swing wildly. Sometimes he raced his horse as though he were still a boy set free at last from his nurse's side. At other times he grew serious and withdrawn. We'd stop to build a fire, pass a mug of broth about the circle, only to find Dev gone off by himself, silhouetted on a rise where he kept some private vigil, quiet in a world of his own making.

Jared didn't seem to worry. Once, when Beklar started toward Dev, Jared called him back. "He's all right," he said. "Let him be. It's all too well I remember the first days of my priesthood, waiting for the stars to open like a path drawn right to my feet. It'll pass once Hershann sets him to work again."

Avram was the one who sought me from the start, drawing his horse up close on the narrow path. "Is this the first time you've ever seen Roshanna Lake?" he asked.

"Yes," I smiled, glad for the company. "First time I've been outside Briana's territory at all. My brother, Hayden, and Mirjam too were always allowed to do more traveling. Because I was the youngest, I suppose . . ."

"I thought I'd once heard that Lord Morell's youngest child was a boy," he said lightly, but I bristled suddenly, thinking this another of his ill-managed attempts at humor.

"And I thought you were the goddess Eclipse, hiding in a priestling's suit," I snapped back.

"I'm sorry," Avram smiled. "I didn't mean to offend you. But even if I'm not a goddess and you're not a boy, I can show you some of Eclipse's magic."

"Priests dream," I said, kicking my horse to a faster pace. "They don't traffic in useless magic."

"No, wait!" Avram called out, and in a moment he'd matched his horse's gait to my mare's. "Don't be angry. Look, I'll show you."

I turned to watch and, seeing him, I couldn't help but smile again. Avram looked as full of mischief as the countryside, and as ruddy as Roshanna Lake itself. While he dug his legs firmly against his horse's flanks, he let go the reins and held his hands out high in the air.

"What are you doing?"

"You'll see. But first you have to call on the goddess Eclipse to make this work."

"What do I say?"

"Say what you wish. But hurry, or the magic won't work."

"All right, I'll try." I sat up straighter and in a mock-serious voice called out, "Eclipse, appear! We call you from the stars. Appear!"

"Perfect! Now watch . . ."

Suddenly, out of Avram's lap, a tiny song bird emerged, trilled a cautious tune, then shook its wings and flew up, higher and higher until it disappeared, a speck of color against the endless gray sky.

I didn't know what to say. I couldn't laugh. He'd tricked me, of course, hidden the bird ahead of time. What I didn't understand was how, or why. Didn't he realize that out here in the cold, so many miles from the warmer lands such a small, bright bird would only die? Waiting for me to say something, he was smiling broadly, obviously proud of himself.

Abruptly I said, "Have you always had jarak dreams? Is that why you wanted to be a priest?"

"All priests dream." He shrugged, surprised by my question.

"But is it the same for all of them, their dreams?"

"Well, I suppose not. That's why we study, to strengthen our dreams."

"For whose sake? Ours? Or the gods? Or for the people who come to the temple? Carth said our dreams were a gift. Did he mean that the gods actually send us dreams, or that our ability was the gift and the dreams are our own?"

"I'll tell you what I think." Avram glanced over his shoulder to make sure no one was within hearing distance. "I think Carth doesn't have the first idea where our dreams come from. Or how it is some of us have jarak dreams and some are sensume. Why don't you ask Dev? He's forever telling me about his dreams. But," he hesitated, "I'd have thought Morell's daughter would tell me all the answers, not come asking so many questions."

"Maybe it's because I am his daughter that I have to ask," I said. "Maybe with so many priests watching me all my life, I never had the chance to ask the right questions before." I looked at Avram as we rode, trying to understand him. At the very least, I decided that whatever had happened between us in Carth's chamber had been my imagination. I'd been jumpy and unnerved by the darkness and close walls. Perhaps it was my fault, that I'd expected my first stop in a Sumedaro temple to be filled with dreams and omens of the future, and the bracelet had somehow heightened those longings. Avram's only fault was that he'd been caught between me and my daydreams. Surely, the whole thing had been no more than that.

I looked away toward the tall, deep evergreens that lined the road, the snow blown loose from their branches, and I thought of Ceena, realizing for the first time that I missed her, her honesty, her faith in what she believed. I asked Avram the question I'd refused to ask Jared, "Why is it that the Sumedaro ward against the havens? Isn't there an older lore that says the havens granted jarak dreams?"

"From what I've seen, most priests are half afraid of their dreams."

"Then why go to Aster?" I asked, surprised to hear such cynicism from a priest. "Why take your Sumedaro vows when you could stay at home, take another vocation?"

Avram laughed at that. "Now I know you're a lord's daughter. Who ever told you a person has the freedom to choose a vocation? Maybe it was different for you, but most people go where they're sent. Same as Jared. Same as Beklar. It was my father who decided that one of us was to be a priest. I was beginning to have dreams, and so the lot fell to me. It's just one of the ways I can be useful." He shrugged. "Things could have worked out worse, I suppose."

"It was the choice I wanted," I mumbled, and our conversation faded. After that we rode on at a drudging pace, heads bowed as the wind dried our cheeks to a crisp red. It wasn't till the third day after that, five days since leaving

Sharat, that we woke to the sight of Aster's hills. We broke camp quickly and rode at a faster pace, our faces turned constantly into the cold. At last, sometime toward afternoon, Beklar sang out, "Aster Valley. There it is!"

7

I reined my horse in and slowed to a walk beside Beklar and Damen. From farther behind, Dev and Avram cantered up, then halted, their breath thick in the wintry day. Aster temple stood in a valley below us, its long walls rising above a dark line of spruce trees.

"Beklar, Damen. Can you make them out? How many down there?" Jared nodded toward a mass of gray shapes huddled against the distant wall.

"What is it?" I asked Dev. He'd ridden up to my side, his horse stamping impatiently, as if it sensed it would soon be home in a stable again.

"Beggars. Look along the wall. Down there. Do you see?" Dev pointed toward the shadows at the base of the temple walls. At first I'd taken the huddled, black shapes for bushes or wagons. Now, following Dev's hand, I saw the shadows were moving about the wall, pacing slowly.

"Aster's legacy," Avram said flatly. "And ours now as well."

"Beggars," Dev nodded, "but five years ago they were honest farmers and merchants, no different than my own parents on their landholdings except that their farms are useless now. The gods took their wealth for themselves and left them a sheet of ice where their homes had been. Where else could they turn if not to the temples for shelter and hope?"

"Enough talk!" Jared urged his horse a step closer toward the height of the road. "You have no idea what you're saying, neither of you. It would be one thing if those people had any faith. But they don't. They're nothing to you. You are Sumedaro priests! The temple is yours, the landholdings yours, and your faith belongs there, inside those walls, not to some pack of beggars who'd as soon steal your life as your dinner!"

I drew back, surprised to hear Jared so vehement. His face was flushed, and even through the heavy layers of clothing I could see his chest laboring with each breath. He turned back around and I thought he would say something to me, another of those warnings after my safety that had become so numerous since leaving Sharat, but it was the gray packhorse he looked at, the one carrying the relics out of Sharat temple.

Rath and Gamaliel, Jokjoa's bracelet and goblet. Every morning before mounting, Jared had checked and tightened their bindings himself, readying them for the new day's ride. But not once in all those days had he opened their wrappings, though I'd watched and waited, thinking often of the bracelet I'd seen in Carth's chamber. Maybe I'd have been better off, I mused, if my mother had given Mirjam's ring to me and left my sister to be content with a journal. Then perhaps this thirst of mine, this foolish envy, would never have begun.

While Beklar fixed the wrappings around his long-necked viol, Jared added a second layer of padding to the bags, then, satisfied that the knots would hold, turned back to Beklar.

"There's two score at the front gate," Beklar said. "And across at that low-domed hill, there"—he pointed away westward to the outer limits of an old paddock—"another twenty."

"Do you expect trouble?" Dev asked, and I remembered the farmsteads we'd stolen past in the dark. I had thought they were isolated incidents, too infrequent to be concerned with. But now I saw from Jared's face, he was none too surprised to see this camp below.

Dev's horse shied and he drew in the reins. "What do we do?" he asked.

"We go in," Jared said. "It won't be the first time I've had to face them. Or the last."

Beklar scanned the outer wall, watching the distant figures. "I've never known them to be well armed," he said. "But they don't have to be. They're too many to fight off. Still, I don't especially want to feel the touch of their hungry hands on my skin, though I'll lay them down if they try to touch any of you, I swear it."

"Can we ride around back?" Jared asked. "There, to the east?"

Beklar looked as if he was considering the ploy, but Damen shook his head. "No, we'd never get in. The rear gates were battened down after last winter."

"Straight in, then," Jared decided. He raised the orange cowl of his cape high over his head, and with his back as stiff and ready as any of Morell's men, he called out our orders: "Make a double line. We go in two abreast. Beklar, you with Avram first, then Damen leading the gray gelding. Whatever else happens, watch the gray horse. Don't risk the relics. Calyx, you stay beside me, and Dev, you lead the other horses. Now! Ride for Aster!"

Jared kicked his horse forward, but even at a gallop the ride took longer than I would have guessed. Down the steep hill, then out the open road we raced, drawing a straight line to Aster's gate.

They saw our approach, of course. It couldn't have been prevented. The crowd rose up, stragglers and small groups gathering together as I gained my first full look at the temple's towering, rock-formed walls. And they were nothing but a crowd, not soldiers and not raiders. I heard their shouts, despite the crying wind and hoofbeats stamping in my ears. Children were there as well, their faces all alike, dirt smeared, hungry eyed, raucous and running in their own chaos. Still, I'd heard my share of battle tales, and I was frightened enough to dig my knees in harder against my saddle as the crowd took up positions along the road, flanking our approach.

Aster's gates loomed larger and larger in front of us until finally we could ride no closer. The crowd opened up, then closed around us, tight and cloying, sealing us in.

Beklar's horse reared beside me, its front hooves flaying the air. All around us people jumped toward safety, fighting each other to be free of the horse's thrashing. Beklar inched the horse toward an opening, cutting into the line ahead of Avram and forcing two, three, four men to leap, sprawling to the sides. Slowed to a near halt by the press, I edged my horse up close behind them, hoping to all Kuoshana our line would stay closed.

There were hands everywhere, hands grabbing my boots,

tugging my leggings, reaching up toward my face. Everywhere there were women, children, men, their cheeks drawn and tight in the freezing air. They kept pushing in all around us, fighting for a chance to reach one of us.

For an instant I lost sight of Beklar, kicked my horse closer toward Jared's broad back, but before I'd closed the gap, out of their middle one woman leapt wildly toward me, digging her fingers into my leg for a hold. Her face was wrapped in filthy rags—for warmth I tried to tell myself—but underneath her eyes were clear with hatred.

"Jarak dreamer!" her voice rang in my ears. "Speak for us, priest! Let us in." She clung to my clothes, tearing at me for a hold, and I whipped about, searching my sides for someone to help. Avram was there, not two lengths away. "Av!" I shouted, but though he must have seen me, my voice was useless in that clamor and he held his place, without turning.

"Get down!" I tried to kick her away. "I'm not a priest! Leave me alone! Avram!" I called again, but it was no use. His eyes were set on the temple door, his horse moving steadily from my side.

"Jarak dreamer!" the woman screamed again, as if stricken. "Shrive me of my dreams!" she hissed and spat suddenly in my face. I kicked my horse forward, and this time the jolt sent her slipping past my stirrups to the ground. Without looking back, I wiped the freezing spittle with the back of my glove. But in doing that, I missed seeing the next attack.

From somewhere off to my left, a man leapt to my saddle, his heavy arm buckled around my chest, holding fast. I twisted to face him, but instead found a glint of silver, a thin dagger, drawn and pointed below my ear. I screamed as loudly as I was able, terrified that I'd already been stabbed. But Sunder was with me, for the knife had not made its cut. My horse lost her footing and somehow the man was thrown to the ground like an anchor, dragging me half out of the saddle with him.

Out of the fracas Beklar appeared, still safely mounted on his horse. Shouting, he maneuvered his way in close enough, found the right angle, and kicked the man full in the chest, breaking his hold on the horse and freeing me. I watched only long enough to see the blood rush from the man's open jaw before Beklar grabbed my arm and helped me right myself in the saddle again.

In front of us, Jared whipped his horse forward. The gates were swinging open from within now, and the next thing I knew, the ground beneath us had changed and I heard the clapping of hooves on hard stone, then afterward the sound of iron bars grating in a latch.

Aster's gates snapped shut behind us, and I sucked in a long draft of clear air. We were standing in a broad, paved courtyard. I could hear again: protected now, the wind had slowed to a hollow drone. The cobbled floor had been swept free of snow. On either side two small pools lay frozen and gray. Once, the courtyard must have looked regal and commanding, but even tired as I was, I noticed at once the gray poverty of the yard: fallen brickwork and gaps where paving stones needed to be replaced.

"Jared! Welcome, Jared!" A barrel-shaped man in brown robes approached from farther inside, his arms outstretched in greeting. On either side behind him a handful of men and women stood about. They stole cautious glances toward the door, and more than a few were armed, though they seemed uncomfortable with the broadswords they carried so grimly at their sides. But these people weren't soldiers; they were priests dressed as children would dress for a game of war. I found myself searching the upper palisade for a sign of real help. What if the attack had exploded into more violence? Where were the soldiers, guards, and archers that Aster's elder priest should have hired to protect us?

Smiling, Jared climbed down and took the man's arms. "Hershann! Jokjoa's fist, but it's a good thing you saw us. What news? Has it been this bad for long?"

"Since just after winter set in, they've been here, like ants on a wall, ever since you left. They've been moving in steadily all along. We do what we can for them, of course. But tell me the truth now, are you well?"

"Yes, yes, of course I'm fine. With Beklar and Damen with me I'd trust myself through much worse. And I've seen beggars crying for food before. But here, let me catch my breath. Now I'll tell you. I've brought you something from Sharat. Avram! Dev! Come here. Meet your new master."

Beklar and Damen took the horses' reins and started in freeing their loads. Still breathing hard, I jumped down, waiting my turn to be announced. Beggars crying? Is that all Jared called the attack? Hadn't he seen what that man had tried to do? And that woman? And why wasn't Jared mentioning my name as well? Hershann would be my master here at Aster also? Avram stepped forward, but Dev looked back at me as if he too sensed the oversight. His eyes met mine only once then, and from the way he kept his arms crossed tightly across his chest, I saw he meant to keep his own council.

"Come here, then, and let me look at you two," Hershann said. Aster's elder had a smooth, round face and small eyes, the kind of man who looked like someone's uncle, but there was little kindness in his manner. "Avram, we've been waiting for you. Your father was a friend here, but he would have told you that, wouldn't he? Though I'd have never thought he'd send one of his sons so far from home without a reason."

"I asked to come, sir. I wanted to be a Sumedaro."

Hershann put his hands on Avram's shoulders. "You have his look about you, the way I remember him when we were young. And it will be to our gain if we can make a jarak dreamer out of you . . . Though I've a feeling you're already a promising one."

"Thank you, sir. I hope to be, under your tutelage," Avram said, his voice so soft I had to strain to listen.

"Well, we shall make very good use of you. And you will learn much, that I guarantee. So! And you are . . . ?"

"Dev, sir. We met years ago. But I'm sure you wouldn't remember. You spoke a dream for me once. You said it was a jarak dream."

"Did I? Well, good, good. I would offer you a meal, but today is the Sister's fast and we wait till sunset tonight to break our fast. I'm sorry we can't talk longer now, but there'll be time. There'll be time. The Sumedaro will be gathering at the fire altar and I must attend them. Rija!" Hershann called to one of the women who'd been leaning against an inner wall. "Rija, come here and show these two boys to the temple. They'll want to partake in the offices. And find Syth. He'll take over with them afterward. You boys follow Rija. The rest of you, go on about your ways. The trouble's over. There's nothing more here. Sister's invocation follows at sunset."

"Now, Jared. Are they safe?" Hershann turned his back on Avram and Dev, dismissing them without a second look as he took Jared's arm. "Have you brought them?" Together they approached the packhorses. Beklar and Damen had already unhitched most of our bags, and the bundles were growing to a pile on the ground.

Jared let out a satisfied breath. "Yes, they're here. The Rath and Gamaliel of Jokjoa. I'd have spent my life getting them here. You'll be pleased."

"Pleased? Jared, you make light of my feelings. I'm honored. It's been a long time, you know. Sometimes I think you have it the better of us, Jared. You travel, see things. While my days are locked in here . . . You can't know what it means to have the relics. How long I've waited to touch them. To own them. For Aster to own them."

"Aster is Kuoshana's gateway, Hershann. There are many who'd willingly spend a lifetime here. I among them. This north country is holy. It becomes a part of your blood, something longed for, the silence, even the winter. What happens here is greater than at any court in the southern lands."

"Perhaps a long time ago, but now? I'm not so certain. You saw that rabble outside. It seems your southern politics has taken to wandering farther north. You take them! I give them to you. In return for your present." Hershann laughed at his own joke. "And if you won't take them as a gift, I'll give them to you in trade. Now show me the relics before they're buried in a vault inside."

Jared called to Damen to bring out the leather-wrapped box we'd carried from Roshanna. Without ceremony Hershann took it, holding it against his chest with the grin of a schoolboy. I think he would have opened it right then, but I'd grown tired of waiting and coughed deliberately into my fist. Hershann stopped short, acting as if he'd just noticed me for the first time.

"Oh, Calyx. Forgive me, Hershann," Jared said. "This is Calyx. I sent you word to expect her."

"Morell's daughter, of course." Hershann smoothed his robes. "How could it be otherwise? My lady, Aster is pleased to have you for a guest. I hope the journey wasn't too strenuous? It's a long ride for a young lady."

"Thank you, sir, the ride was long, but we are at least unharmed," I said, trying to quell my rising suspicions. The last thing I wanted was to be treated as a lord's daughter and a guest of rank.

"Good, good. Now, if you'll run along, I'll have Rija fix

you up a fine meal in the kitchen when she's done with Avram. She'll be your girl while you're staying with us—"

"Excuse me, sir, if I'm too forward, but if Avram and Dev are to keep the Sister's fast with the other priests, then wouldn't it be proper if I kept it as well? I came here to study. To be a Sumedaro."

"A Sumedaro? You, lady? Jared, you never spoke of this. Morell's daughter a dreamer? And what would your father think of that?" Hershann laughed loudly and Jared smiled, but I saw no joke. Hershann's manners were more what I'd have expected of some pandering lord at Briana Keep than any I'd thought to find in a Sumedaro. I noted his richly furred robes, afraid that for all my hopes I'd only found another Briana.

"No, no," Hershann continued. "I expect a letter from Lord Morell is already on its way. Unless you have something with you, Jared? Perhaps Morell meant to house you here while he prepared a suitable marriage? Surely that wouldn't come as a surprise. A man with your father's concerns must deal with these problems. Tell me, did he actually say you were to be a Sumedaro?"

"Well, no sir. He . . . he left me to Jared's charge. The choice was mine to make. It's what I want, to be a Sumedaro, to study the path of a jarak dreamer."

"Well, there we have it. Your father would have mentioned the subject to Jared if he'd meant for it to be. In the meantime, why don't you attend the fire altar with the others, if that's what you want? After that Rija will help you in your rooms. We shall find a place for you while you're with us, and suitable work. If that will bring you comfort, my lady?" With that Hershann took Jared by the arm and left the courtyard, dismissing me.

Morell's daughter! I shook my head, my thoughts spinning. Did that man really think Morell's daughter would wring her hands and sit whining in the corner? Damn Eclipse and the trickery she wove on earth! And if I was to act the part of Morell's daughter, as Hershann seemed to think I should, did he think I would have tolerated such an attack as just occurred outside his gates?

I sat down on the low-bricked wall surrounding one of the pools, waiting, thinking, until the girl, Rija, appeared and quietly asked that I follow her into the inner hall. She was older than I, though not a good deal, with a mouth as thin as a line, steel-straight nose, and hair so light it had almost no color at all. She kept her hair cut straight at shoulder length, and with all her fragile looks, I thought she could have been a second to Mirjam—had the fortune of birth run differently.

She said not a word and kept her eyes lowered politely toward the floor, which was just as well since it would have been difficult not to begin an argument. Aster temple soon proved to be far larger than Sharat, and by the time we'd wound our way through a confusing series of hallways, the long morning had caught up with me and I'd lost the will for argument.

When at last we reached the fire altar, Rija led me toward a front row, close enough that I could feel the heat of its hundred candles against my cheeks. I felt conspicious in my heavy traveler's clothes, a stranger, not to be included with the others. I was one of the last to arrive and the stiff-backed benches were already filled with orange- and brown-robed men and women. Craning my neck around, I searched the long rows for Dev and Avram, and found them already seated far off to the opposite side. I would have liked a chance to speak with Dev, to ask what he thought of that brief meeting in the courtyard, but it was too late. Already, Avram was talking to a man at his side, pointing and asking questions while Dev, head bowed, seemed comfortable in the quiet of his own devotions.

From a doorway off to one side of the fire altar, Hershann entered, walking with a smooth grace that hid his bulk. He had changed into the formal golden robes and triangular headpiece of a Sumedaro elder and faced the assembled priests with arms outstretched. There, with the lights of a hundred candles flickering behind him, Hershann's features merged with the dark shadows. The reflection on his robes danced across the faces of the Sumedaro below him, hurling them into light, then dark, then light again. On the railing in front of him, Rath, the bracelet and the plain earthen goblet, Gamaliel, rested on a shimmering white cushion.

I slid forward, staring at the bracelet with longing. Though as I thought about it, I realized my wish had changed. It was not that I needed to possess it, hoard it as my own. That was not my wish, but to answer its summons! The bracelet had called to me in Sharat temple, almost as if it recognized me. I was to be a Sumedaro, I was certain. I was a jarak dreamer. And the bracelet had known. That was its message. Hershann had no right to treat me so lightly. Why couldn't he see? I was to be a priest, a Sumedaro. It had to be true.

For a long while I sat without listening to the service. The bracelet was as I remembered, its stone cut somehow to reflect the fire altar's dashing light. Then suddenly, as I watched, memory layered itself over memory, searching, spiraling. As though someone had whispered it in my ear, I remembered clearly the ring Ivane had given Mirjam that day. A ring with two raised hands joined together and marking the narrow of each wrist—a tiny bracelet!

Jokjoa's Rath etched in perfect detail on Mirjam's ring; Kuoshana's bracelet, as certain as the stars that banded our skies. The one thing my mother had told her was that it was old—but how old? With a new curiosity I watched as Hershann raised Rath toward the wall of statues rising behind the altar. In plain sight of everyone present, he slipped the bracelet onto his left wrist, then raised Jokjoa's goblet to his lips and drank. When next he turned and spoke, his eyes sparkled with deep satisfaction and I heard the ritual invocation of the Sumedaro priesthood for the first time.

"Of Jokjoa, Father Dreamer, he who named the Sister's Magic," Hershann sang in a rich, bass timbre.

"Beg the dreamer, Hail the speaker," the gathered voices answered. Then in unison they sang:

In dreams Jokjoa sent us power
Sumedaro, jarak power.
In dreams Oreill does give us vision
Rathadaro, jarak vision.
In birth does Seed grant life anew
On earth Eclipse hides all with fulsehood
In death does Sunder guide us toward her
In day the Elan shifts all skyward,
Watches long, Kuoshana's gateway . . .

On my left, I watched Rija sing the words, her eyes lowered, her breathing slow and full. I searched the hall: Avram, no longer speaking with the priest beside him, had joined Dev in their silent repetitions. I alone seemed to keep quiet, too uncertain to sing. Was I supposed to join in or was the ritual only for the initiated Sumedaro? But then, if Dev and Avram were allowed to sing, why hadn't I been instructed in the proper form? In Lakotah we had sung greetings, but this song was different, simpler in the way of older pieces but stronger as well.

When I looked up again, Jared was watching me from his seat in a corner of the fire altar. I nodded my head in recognition. Lying, to show I would be fine here. Better to have him return to my mother with the message that I was not troubled or afraid, rather than risk losing what small chance I had to become a priest. True, I had questions for my mother that I'd never thought to ask before leaving Briana, but they were not the questions I trusted Jared to carry. If I had hoped for some show of assurance from him, a smile or a nod, it did not come. Instead I saw he was tapping his fingers against his knee again, watching me with that same curious, concerned look I had already seen too much of on the ride past Sharat.

What had I done wrong? Had I missed some lesson while Mirjam had run off to Lakotah each morning, her simple dreams always an open book for the priests to hear, while I had remained behind, hidden behind lessons and games and secrets? What was it Ceena had said about this priesthood? That they are blind . . . that they learn a simple trick . . . to follow a dream and think they have great magic . . . but not one dreamshaper among them. But she also said it was the priesthood she mistrusted, not the dreamers themselves. For years I'd been afraid to tell her of my jarak dreams—as I had also been afraid to tell Jared. Now look where that had brought me! Hershann thought I didn't belong here except by Morell's decree, and Jared didn't know the truth of my dreams to speak out in my behalf.

Hail Jokjoa,
Thus we greet you.
World dream sender,
Swift creator.

Hail the Elan
Edishu slayer
Gateway Builder
Waking Dreamer

The chamber grew silent. No one spoke or moved. Caught

up in the quietude, I stared at the polished wood railing, so like Lakotah's yet different also. The same opaque waxed gloss, the same smell of clover hanging in the air. But a different wood, different curl to the railing. High above Hershann's bowed head, the only statue I'd seen since arriving in Aster peered down—the Elan Sumedaro battling Edishu just at the moment he was exiled back to Kuoshana, back to Jokjoa's dream. The figure, I was relieved to see, looked far too handsome, too mortal to remind me of the one in my dream that Ceena had said was Edishu.

As the service came to a close, Hershann surveyed the faces below him, his eyes gloating, his right hand fondling the stone bracelet. All in rhythm, the Sumedaro stood to leave and I stood with them. For the first time I noticed a door standing open to one side of the hall, and beyond that the shadow of three dugout rathadaro couches where the priests would speak people's dreams. Along the inner wall, a line of Aster's townspeople had gathered to wait. Most were warmly dressed in thick cloaks and furred hats, but some of them looked more like the beggars we'd fought at the gates: tired, ill, hungrier for a decent meal than for a priest's empty handshake. It wouldn't have been difficult to convince me that the same man who'd laid that knife to my neck was standing inside, waiting.

I looked up to find Hershann walking toward me, Avram and Dev close behind with an older priest who would be Syth, the one Hershann had mentioned as their tutor.

"Well," Hershann said, his voice all light and easy again, "what do you think of your new charges?"

Syth was a kindly-looking man with small eyes that peered cautiously from his wrinkled face. He looked older than any man I'd known before, with a receding hairline that followed from ear to ear behind his head, and deeply etched skin that made me wish all the more that I could sit and learn at his side.

"They're likely looking boys, Hershann," he said. "A bit thin, but we'll take care of that. And come just in time, at that."

"Aster does need the extra hands," Hershann murmured.

"Hands, yes. But it's priests we need most. And not just priests but jarak dreamers. Did you see the people waiting at the rathadaro couch today, sir? There's hardly enough jarak dreamers among us to watch all the dreams they've been bringing."

"I know, I know. We'll take care of it. I've been thinking we can take Barat out of the library and put him here. He can take on two watches a day along with Orrin. Orrin's good. They like him. But he tires quickly. Calyx, you might take Barat's place in the library. A scribe's table shouldn't offend your father. If that suits you, of course?"

"Work in the library? As a scribe? That will be fine," I nodded, thinking of my mother. "Assuming of course, it doesn't interrupt my studies?"

"Studies?" Hershann scowled. "No, of course not. We all work here, work as well as pray for our dreams. We cook. Tend flocks. Weave. We've masons and farriers, stable hands and washerwomen. Surely, even living in Briana Keep you couldn't imagine it was otherwise? We're like a city, self-contained. Self-reliant. We have to keep ourselves alive. Jarak priests or not, the gods won't do it for us."

"Of course not, sir. I didn't mean to imply that I thought—"

"Well, then, it's settled. Rija will show you the way tomorrow, after the morning meal. Kath will be glad of a pair of young hands to help her with the stacks. Syth, take the boys to their closet. Put them on their journals as soon as possible. Push them. Work them. Avram's father was a strong dreamer, I remember him well. And this one. Dev, claims he was born under Kuoshana's star. For work send them to Galen. He'll know best where to use them. And test them yourself as soon as it's possible."

"Next Sister's morning, you'll have what you want," Syth smiled. "Whatever paths are open to them, we'll know it. And what they can't see for themselves, I'll teach them to find."

And then, before I could ask any of the hundred questions I had waiting, I was alone with the docile Rija again, her face all smoothness and cooperation as she led me to my rooms. The outer room, which was almost a hall in itself, was larger and far more lavish than anything I'd have chosen, and I took an instant dislike to it. A fire had already been laid in the hearth, but even so, a chill sat in the air. Several chests stood against the walls, and beside a wardrobe was a large table with two chairs tucked neatly underneath. From the way it was all placed so carefully with tapestries and rugs, I half expected to see one of Mirjam's girls sitting at the window, her embroidery in her lap.

"Your bed is through there." Rija seemed so openly pleased to have me looking about the room that for the first time that day, she raised her eyes to meet mine. "I think you'll find everything you need. I had one of your men bring your things, but . . . well, there wasn't much. I didn't think you'd mind if I had one of the girls race around, trying to scare up some suitable clothes. They're not the best, I know. But after that long ride—it must have been terrible for you—I hope they'll fit, the dresses. In the morning I'll come help you try them on. Then I'll take you to meet Kath." Rija stopped to straighten some things on the table, then turned to the door.

"Wait!" I called. "Can you answer a question?"

Rija hesitated. "Well, of course," she smiled. "But ma'am, there's really not much I know besides looking after things—"

"No, of course not," I said softly, wondering how best to gain her confidence. "It's just that I haven't met anyone else who . . . well, you understand . . . who I can talk to."

Rija looked at me with a calculating glance that transformed her face. I could have laughed at myself for not seeing it at once, that Hershann would have handpicked this girl as someone he assumed I'd trust and talk to. She'd been instructed, warned. And probably she was allowed to say only so much and no more.

"Of course I'll answer your questions," she said brightly. "After all, I'm here to make you comfortable, aren't I? What would you like to know?"

I started to change my mind, to send her away, remembering all too well what it had been like in Briana, everyone so willing to talk, so patient with me. But what would be the use of wrapping solitude around myself again? And if this was some game Hershann had started, what hand did I have worth the playing? Hershann already knew what I wanted. And I already knew he wasn't going to give it to me, at least not easily. Which meant I'd have to find another way to take it. Steal it. Demand it. Earn it.

True, there were scruples, paths I would not follow, but for now, didn't it make more sense to play my hand?

"Those journals Syth gave Dev and Avram," I said gently. "What do they do with them?"

"The journals? That's all you want to know?" Rija looked surprised. "They'll write their dreams in them. Several times each night and first thing in the morning. Syth makes it his business to watch over the new priests. Sleep in their room. Wake them so often they can't tell which end of a pen is up and which is down. Then he makes them write whatever they remember. That's the part I dreaded most, being woken up like that. Write it down. Write it down. After a while it becomes a habit."

"And that's all?"

Rija shook her head, and her robes flowed gently about her. "That's all for a long time. Later, he'll teach them to choose something, a place or a person they knew. You have to keep your thoughts trained to the one thing. It isn't easy unless you have a calling for it. And it wasn't ever easy for me."

"Then you've been trained as a jarak dreamer too?"

"A little . . ." Rija said something I couldn't hear. "But Aster is a large temple. And the gods don't send dreams to everyone. In the end, we find our place here, all of us."

"Tell me how you came to be here. Didn't you want to be a jarak dreamer?"

"Oh dear, no." Rija smoothed her robes. "My parents sent me here when I was twelve. They were merchants, and successful, but there were too many of us at home, you see. Still, there was coin enough to set me up comfortably here. I'm not complaining. And certainly, no one needs the worry of being a great dreamer."

"And this testing Hershann mentioned?"

"The same thing really. The elders do it, or Syth. He'll set a goal for them to dream, a place, a house, something small, then enter their dreams and watch how well they're able to navigate their surroundings."

"I think I understand," I said. "But one thing more. Will Dev and Avram have private rooms here also?"

"Private? You mean like these?" Rija laughed. "No, no. I share a space with three other women—you'll meet them. Then there's so many others. Fowler, he's one of our strongest dreamers, though he has a sharp tongue, but he's elderly and not well, so we try to be patient. And Idelle, she takes care of the sheep, handles the shearing and the barns. You'll meet them later. We're less than a hundred all counted, and there's room enough for us all. But private quarters like these? They're only kept for visitors."

"Is that what Hershann told you? That I was a visitor?"

Rija studied the floor. "Hershann didn't say anything.

When he heard Lord Morell—your father—was sending you here, he just thought you would require rooms.''

"Rooms? And nothing about studying to become a Sumedaro? Did no one mention that I would study with the others, learn like Dev and Avram to be a priest?''

"A priest? Oh no! Eclipse's hand! You wouldn't like that! This isn't any way for a lord's daughter to live. It's slow, learning the jarak dreams. It has been for me, anyway, and you won't be staying here that long. You'll be marrying, owning lands of your own. Besides, you must be chosen to be Sumedaro, it isn't only given to you, like your work. You will be a smithy and you a weaver and you a Sumedaro. True, some things can be taught, but to be a true farsight dreamer, that's something else. Avram was just telling me about his dreams, and if half what he says is true, he'll make a strong dreamer. And Dev, well, he's wild, can't control his dreams. At least that's what we heard of him from Sharat, though Syth doesn't believe there's a jarak dreamer born he can't handle. You wouldn't like it here after a while. Nothing ever changes. You wouldn't have much in the way of fine clothes or friends.''

"I see," I nodded, then, "Would you mind doing something for me, for tomorrow? I was thinking that I'd like to write a letter home. It's been such a long journey, and I'm sure they'd like to know how I was doing. I was thinking someone could carry it back for me. But I don't have any paper.''

"Oh, I could get you paper and a pen. That wouldn't be a problem.''

"Could you bring them by the morning? Sometimes I wake early, and I thought it would be a good time . . .''

Rija talked on a little longer, then seeing that I had grown silent, fussed about the table one more time, then left.

Alone again, I walked into the second room. A bed! Canopied and well fitted. Only a few days earlier, I had longed for nothing more than to lie in a bed of my own again. Now that I had one, I wished I was riding again.

It wasn't till a long time later that I bothered to notice anything about the chamber. In spite of my disappointment, it was a beautiful room, with a high ceiling and stone walls hung with brightly colored carpets, and two fair-sized windows looking out to the north. Standing there, hands braced on the cold sill, I looked across a forest of mixed spruce; a colorless world, all grays and black, with dark stands of trees crisscrossing against the white snow. Farther north would lie the great ice sheets and somewhere beyond, Kuoshana's gate, with not a single dwelling all the way north between my window and that distant place. I took a breath. Kuoshana's gateway. Source of the jarak dream! I could stretch out my hand, like so. Just stretch it out and touch the vastness of its power. Ah, Jokjoa, Father Dreamer. Is it true that you sleep there, lost in the vastness of your own dreams, protected by the magic of your daughters, Sunder, Eclipse, and Seed?

I closed my eyes, realized suddenly how tired I was. I didn't need Hershann's permission to write my dreams any more than I needed my mother's book.

And I would write them!

Elan Sumedaro, I swore aloud, all of you, whoever you are, hear me! I will be a dream shaper, priesthood or not. And you will listen. This I swear! You will hear me!

8

I sat up, rubbed the sleep from my eyes. My alcove had grown too warm during the night. Ceena, I thought, must have banked the fire higher than she realized. But no, I shook my head, remembering. This was Aster, not Briana—though after yesterday it didn't appear to be the Aster I'd hoped to find. I'd been dreaming of Micah. But more important, I'd made myself a promise last night and the dream must be written if that vow was to hold meaning.

I quickly jumped up, grabbed the long ends of the robe that had been left for me to wear—ridiculous robes—and ran to the outer room. Yes, there it was, the paper I'd asked Rija to bring and the ink. She must have crept in while I slept. How easy it had been to trick her. I sat down, all too aware that someone had been in the room while I'd slept, straightened, built a fire. Later I would talk to them, tell them that if there was only one boon they'd give me, it was privacy I'd ask for.

But Micah . . . I'd hardly thought of him this entire trip. In some childish way I must have hoped to shut the memory of his long fingers and sweet-tasting lips tightly in my heart, to bless it by keeping it secret—and as far from my thoughts as I could.

In another sense, though, it hardly mattered. Micah was gone, wasn't he, and most of my fears and concerns gone as well? But it had been a good dream, I laughed. Not a jarak dream but more like memory, filled with the freshness of Micah's touch and kisses. I dipped the pen in its ink bottle and sat quietly while the memory of my last meeting with Micah filled the room.

How I ever managed to sneak away from my guards in those last hectic hours, I can't remember. But Micah was waiting for me at the cliff tree when I arrived, so Allard must have delivered the note I'd hurriedly pushed into his hand.

"When are you leaving?" Micah demanded as soon as I crested the hill. I was out of breath from the climb, my face flushed with the effort.

"Tomorrow or the next day. I don't know. Whenever they tell me."

"Ceena didn't come with you?" Micah looked behind me down the path. There was only one way up the hill, and the brush ended well before the bedrock outcropping that shaped the ridge, making it impossible for anyone to see us without also being seen.

"No, I'm alone."

"Calyx, what happened? Father told me, but Calyx, you can't leave. Not now. Couldn't you say something, ask your mother's help?"

"Micah, no! You don't understand. I'm happy to go." I was smiling, but he didn't see. He was staring at the ground, two steps away from me, afraid to see the truth written on my face.

"Happy? Happy? How can you say that? Doesn't it mean anything to you what I feel . . . what you said you felt—"

"Micah, I'm sorry. I shouldn't have said that. We're friends." I took a step closer to him, purposefully—for I knew why I'd come—rested my hands on his shoulders. "We'll always be friends, Micah. And more than that."

"More? What more?" His tone was harsh, his voice tight.

"Micah, I don't mean for us to fight. Not now," I said,

then awkwardly, though I had so wanted to get it right, I leaned forward on my toes, raised my face toward his. Gently, yes. And sweet. But I was determined to do this thing with him.

His face flushed in surprise. We had kissed each other before, but no more than that. How could he have dared hope for more? I stepped back, forced my heart to be still, then reached for a lace on his shirt.

Now, at last, he understood. His arms went out, drew me in, and this time it was his mouth that brushed mine. But he stopped, looked into my face. His eyes were so bright, filled with wonder. Asking. When I smiled he kissed me again, too eagerly this time and I cried out—we both cried out—with the surprise of it.

Neither one of us knew for sure what to do first. He found his way to the hem of my brother's oversized tunic that I'd thrown on, fumbled with the knot till I had to help him loosen the thing.

Then we fell. We tumbled. We rolled. Laughed. Pulled sticks from each other's hair. I don't remember how our clothes fell away, but somehow they must have, for we made a blanket of our things to lie on.

In the whole world, nothing seemed to matter except the two of us. We rolled over each other again and again, like puppies biting and crying, until Micah stopped us.

He was lying over me, a sweet longing in his eyes that seemed almost painful. "Are you sure, my love? This is what you want?" he asked. "You're not afraid they'll find out?" His face, so close, had a sad, almost frightened look.

But the sharp roots of the cliff's single tree were dug in against my back, making me feel wilder and more insistent. In answer I found a way to move, took his hands in mine. *It's all right,* I wanted to tell him. *This is our choice, our doing. No one else can be held accountable for our acts.*

"I love you, Calyx," he whispered. "I've always loved you."

"Shh, I know, Micah. And I love you."

"Do you? Do you really?"

"Micah," I laughed. "Don't be silly. Of course I love you. I'll never love any other man but you. And probably no one else will ever love me either."

"I wouldn't want anyone else to love you. I wish we could belong only to each other. But Calyx, you said you were happy to leave. How? I don't understand."

"Micah, shh. Shh! Not now. Just touch me again. Hold me. Please. They'll be wondering where I've gone."

And then we were done. We slept, I think, our clothes piled back over us for a blanket. And afterward Micah looked more surprised than I to see the drying stains on my skirt. Surely there had been other girls for him before this, I teased him. After all, most of the men in Briana seemed proud to make their exploits known. And while I hadn't thought about it before, I'd always assumed Micah had more freedom than I to use his life as he choose. But I didn't really want to think about that. I had planned this all out after Ceena told me that jarak dreams belong to those who share them, not to the dreamer only. But I had wanted something in my life that was mine, only mine. Not something owned by Morell or the priests, certainly not the kind of things Mirjam owned, baubles and toys to be thrown aside when she tired of them. And if even my dreams could not be mine, then what else was there but my body? Only my body. And there was one way I knew to cheat Morell out of selling that, as he had sold Mirjam's, one way to claim it as my own.

Write the dream down, I ordered myself. No matter what it is, write it down. No one will know. And no regrets! You want freedom, jarak dreamer? You want to ride your dreams like the wind, find faith? Truth? Then it's your own path you'll have to forge and follow no matter where it winds!

Quickly I scribbled it down, the dream only, sparse and clear, with no thoughts of my own added. This was going to be a journal, not a diary.

I finished, then leaned back, thinking. In some ways Dev reminded me of Micah—brown hair, eyes, easy smile. Long, narrow shouldered. But there the similarity ended. Micah and I had known each other from the cradle. And Micah loved me. He always had, though perhaps being friends since childhood made love come easier. I was Calyx to him, the face as much a part of the person as the name, inseparable as the years we'd spent together. With Dev it would be different. He would have to look at my face first, then later learn to judge the woman inside. I wonder if he . . . but no—

The door started to open.

Quickly I shook my head, chasing the thoughts away. Just

as I pushed the papers inside a drawer, Rija stepped in, her eyes following my movements. "Did you sleep well?" she asked in that too innocent voice she had.

"Yes I did, thank you. Shall we be going down to break our fast?"

"Oh, I ate hours ago." Rija walked over to the fire, held her hands toward the red, glowing logs. "In summer we eat at dawn, you know. But in winter, sunrise doesn't come till far too late into the day. I wouldn't get up if I didn't have to, not in the dark. And then it all goes on forever . . ." She rambled on, never noticing how I listened with disbelief. "First there's the service at the fire altar," she said, ticking the hours off on her fingers. "Then we take breakfast in the long hall. And then work, always work. It's almost no different than living in a village, but for Hershann's endless ritual. And there you were, sleeping so soundly. I wouldn't dare wake you—"

"Next time, Rija, wake me."

"Oh, that won't be necessary." She turned, smiling. "The food's kept warm—"

"Wake me," I said sternly, "or—never mind, I'll wake myself. I told Hershann, and I mean this: I came here to be a Sumedaro. I mean to work, to be part of this temple. I want to follow the same path, practice the same rituals, pray for an understanding of the gods' will. Can you understand that?"

"Well, yes," she said, turning her gaze to the floor again.

"Good, then I'll get my clothes, and you can show me the way to the kitchens."

"Here." She ran toward the inner room ahead of me. "I'll help you dress. There's one I saw inside should fit—"

"Rija." I held still. "No, none of that clothing. I'll wear what I have. Or I'll wear the robes of a Sumedaro."

"Oh, you wouldn't want to do that," she said in honest confusion.

"I wouldn't? Well, never mind for now. Tell me something. Why are your robes brown and the others orange?"

She shrugged her shoulders. "The difference is small, ma'am—"

"Calyx."

"Calyx. We change depending on our work. I can wear orange if I want. It's the color we wear officially as Sumedaro. When we're doing other things, working in the yards or some such, we wear brown."

"And your hair?"

"Well, we keep it shorter than the townsfolk. But you're not going to cut your hair, are you? That is, please, don't do that. Hershann would be furious with me. Your father—"

"Rija, I'll make you a promise," I said as I rummaged through my clothes for the least road-worn tunic I could find. "When I do cut my hair—and please, don't bother trying to tell me how beautiful it is, because it's not—when I do cut it, I'll make certain you can't be blamed."

Rija stood tight-lipped, and but for my curiosity about the temple itself, the silence might have grown uncomfortable. I plied her with questions as we walked downstairs, and little by little she turned out to be more helpful with her answers than I would have guessed.

Aster, though older than Briana, was built along the same design as most northern temples. The outer walls were built as strongholds, with towering gatehouses and walkways fencing inner courtyards. There were two separate living complexes, with women's apartments to the east and men's to the west. Inside, the temple seemed more labyrinthine, with new corridors crossing older, empty halls, built ages ago when far more people lived within the gates than today.

Once on the lower level, I could have found the kitchens myself. The air grew hot with the rising odor of cooking fat, and the noisy clatter of pans and dishes reminded my stomach of the day's fast.

Rija sat me down—the only person at a long plank table that ran the length of the kitchen's central alley. A moment later she returned with a plateful of steamed meat pies and mulled cider which one of the cooks had run and fetched as soon as he saw me enter. I ate as well as anyone would after weeks of smoky fires and overcooked food, too hungry to care that I was the one person in the temple who had been permitted to sleep past the morning call. Afterward, Rija led the way up a twisted set of stairs to the temple library, a jigsaw of narrow halls and cluttered lofts that housed Aster's history.

We found Kath in a narrow room formed by the library's highest tower. Kath was elder librarian, a title the narrow-faced old woman had kept faith with for thirty years before I arrived. She was standing behind the shoulder of a seated priest, watching as he worked with brush and ink.

"Excuse me. Mistress?" Rija said. "I've brought you Calyx. Hershann said you might make use of her."

Kath turned to look at me. "I know what Hershann said."

"You'll have to excuse her clothing, ma'am. There wasn't time to find anything more suitable and she—"

I stepped forward, interrupting, "Your pardon, Mistress Kath. Rija means well, I'm sure. But this is my clothing, that I brought out of Briana. And it's not that I mean to be of trouble, but—"

"I'll take her, Rija. You may leave now," Kath spoke loudly, her voice surprisingly strong in that quiet room.

I waited till Rija was past the rows of empty desks, well out of hearing. "That was kind of you," I said.

"Then next time you can hush and wait till I've spoken, Calyx of Briana." Kath turned her eyes on mine. "Hershann may have sent you here, but you'll have to prove yourself if you want to stay. There's plenty of folks who fight to work under me. Easy, they think. Warm. The seats are soft. But your neck will stiffen to a knot and your eyes'll run milky with the fumes of mixing ink in the stale air. And if you can't mark a straight line, you're out of here, no matter what Elder Hershann says. Now, tell me, have you ever held a brush?"

"Yes, ma'am."

"And I suppose you can read and copy?"

"Yes, ma'am."

"Then listen." Kath showed a half smile. "I don't care how you dress. Or what your name is. If you want to pretend you're a priest—and didn't you know Hershann would tell me about that?—that's your business with him, not me. While you're in these towers, you'll work under my good grace. If we understand each other, we'll get along well enough. If not . . ."

"Thank you," I said, trying to picture my mother when a messenger arrived, telling her I would be working with a brush in my hand. "I think we'll be able to get along."

For the rest of that day and all through the following weeks, Kath set me to working on old documents: rebinding worn covers, fetching old volumes the priests requested for their lessons, an endless stream of odd jobs that required no skills yet had to be done. She watched me as only a careful master would, hawklike and suspicious. It wasn't until I finally proved to her that I was trustworthy and not flighty that she allowed me to take up a brush or pen.

At last she set me down with a middle-aged priest, a quiet, heavy-set man named Orrin, who insisted that we push our table nearer the window to catch the slanting light. Orrin kept a respectable distance between us, never allowing his hand to brush against mine. But the lessons he taught were worth the annoyance of being called milady or mistress, and sitting there beside him, I found the first hours of contentment I'd known since coming to Aster. Every day he spoke at length and with reverence about the proper use of color and the curve of a line, here thinning, there wide about the base; about how to twist a vine through a letter's stem and the importance of pleasing the eye at the same time as instructing the mind. And as the weeks flew by and it became apparent that I'd never have the sensibility to create the finest original work, there was still a familiarity and ease when I took up the slender pen and set it to the page. My hand was steady and my eye true, as I'd promised Kath, and the hours slipped away as I outlined coiled letters and filled in leaves and borders.

I didn't see Dev or Avram very often, and when I did, it hurt more than I would have guessed to see them dressed in their wide orange robes. Beklar and Damen had already turned south again with Jared, and that I dealt with more easily. Much as life in Aster was a struggle, it seemed a reasonable alternative to Briana. Beklar had looked tenderly at me when they departed, telling me to call on him if ever I had the need. Jared had hugged me to him, promising to carry the letter I'd written to my mother. We both knew he wouldn't mention the part about the priesthood to her, and for that matter, my letter told nothing of my disappointed expectations.

The days of deep winter took on a heavy silence. Not that people shunned me, though there was enough of that, but in addition, the work I did was so solitary there was little time left for friendship or conversation. Once the novelty of copying letters wore off, I found more time for my roving imagination than I needed, and spent far too much of it picturing Dev and Avram seated in the rathadaro couch. Dev's heartfelt faith would have led his jarak dreams to further heights. Syth would be teaching him, showing paths and ideas I couldn't begin to guess at. Even Avram would be a full dreamer by now, though I imagined him more likely to use his wit to bargain for ascendancy than to earn it. But however they came to it, they'd both know chapters more of the Sumedaro path than I. As did Rija—for all her jarak dreams mattered to her. Or Idelle in the fields. Or Galen working outside. Or Kath. Or any of them. And other than scribbling my dreams every morning in a journal, it was a long time before I found a way to vent my frustration.

I'd taken to returning to the library in the evenings after dinner, when the halls were silent and no one was about to question me. I'd found passages in the books I copied that nagged at me till I found a way to return to them. Chapters, fragments I couldn't forget though I wasn't permitted to turn a page during the long hours of copying. Legends were recorded in those volumes, everywhere about me. On the shelves, stacked on tables, even piled in the corners. History everywhere, written lore—perhaps, I dared hope, some of the very secrets Hershann denied me. And they pulled at me, their names, their secrets.

Most of all, it was Edishu I wanted to learn about, that dark figure who had appeared in my dreams. Ceena had said that my dreams were safely read and I was free of them. And I wanted to believe her, but what if she was wrong? I trusted her, of course, more than anyone else I had known. But even she had admitted there was much she'd never been taught; much of the Silkiam ways that—however much it grieved her to consider—had disappeared with the loss of her people.

I already knew that the Elan Sumedaro had fought Edishu. Once, twice, how many times I couldn't be certain. In the legends it was always the Elan Sumedaro, aided by the strength of Jokjoa's tokens, who triumphed over Edishu, condemning him once more to prison in Kuoshana.

But just as often the legends implied that Edishu returned eons later, only to fight again, only to be banished again. How many times had he returned to earth? How many times had the Elan Sumedaro fought him? And if Edishu was locked safely away, then why had I dreamt of him? What if he had freed himself again? What if he found me? Was the Elan Sumedaro already somewhere on earth, waiting, ready? Perhaps I was meant to be a messenger, to find the Elan Sumedaro and tell him that he needed to be ready?

It was in one of those dusty, leather-bound volumes that I found a reference to Jevniah, Elan Sumedaro's son. It was during a Sister's fast, several months after I had first arrived in Aster, in the evening, when Kath and the other workers usually kept to their rooms below. For me, the day of fasting had become a summons to climb the narrow stairs to the library tower, to see it bathed in a quiet light and spend my leisure alone, a manuscript in my lap.

I found the volume I'd been copying from the day before. Kath had taken her finest boar brush and gold paint from their cabinet and asked me to refinish the border work on a worn page. I'd done a fair job at keeping my hand steady, but while I worked I glanced again and again to the opposite page, where the story of Jevniah's birth was laid out in delicate, curling letters:

On earth the Elan walks
In dim twilight, he walks
Spans the bridge that crosses two worlds,
Keeper of the gate of two worlds.
But by day, calls no man brother,
And at night, no woman wife.
Till once he found a Kareil woman
One who sang his name at evening
And she loved him and they gathered
Seed of his dream and dream of her life.
Yet Edishu, bitter fighter,
Sought the Elan's newest child.
Then to save his wife and child
Turned her long hair white with power
Left her dreaming with its power,
Till at six month time they found her,
Whitened, weakened, near to death,
And she gave the babe unto them,
Half unformed at sixth month time
Ripped the vine they shared in common.
White-haired Jevniah, dreamer's son.
Born to carry on the battle
Kuoshana's bridge, the Elan's right.

I closed the book and slipped back in the chair, watching the play of light and shadow on the tiled floor. Edishu! Whatever else Ceena had said, she was right in that the image of his face had not returned.

Edishu! I whispered aloud, then shivered. With no one working in the tower, the fire had been allowed to die and the cold seemed to rise along my legs and back. The Elan Sumedaro had a son, Jevniah. And Jevniah, with his hair as white as the Kareil clansman I'd seen in Briana, was born to carry on his father's battle against Edishu. But what happened after? I knew no later stories to say that either the Elan Sumedaro or the white-haired Jevniah had fought and slain Edishu. Or died themselves in the effort. Nothing that mentioned a final battle, or victory, or defeat on either side. Only battles and songs of battles, one after the other after the other.

I tucked my feet up in the chair, when a thought struck me, and I jumped, catching the book as it toppled to the floor. I understood!

The battle was not over.

If for every story I read, the battle did not end but was renewed again and again, then it was not over. And Edishu might come back in spite of what Ceena had said.

There was a sound. I thought I heard a scurrying somewhere in the corner. But, no, it was nothing. I was edgy. There were too many memories, too much thinking. I smoothed the crisp pages back into place, laid the book on the table. I needed company. I was alone too much, read too much. It wasn't good for me. Even when there were others in the library working alongside me, at meals, at the fire altar, always it seemed I was alone. I started for the door.

I would find Dev, ask him about it. He would know. It was the kind of thing that would matter more to him than to Avram. Dev would tell me. I hadn't thought of asking him before. The battle had been between Elan Sumedaro and Edishu, and later with Jevniah. Maybe Ceena had been wrong. Hadn't she said herself that she'd been separated too young from the Silkiyam to learn all they had to teach? What if it wasn't Edishu I had dreamed of? Maybe my dream had simply been a nightmare born of too much rich food and too much excitement, and all those names had nothing to do with me.

Heart racing, I ran down the stairs, flight after flight until I reached the main courtyard. A light snow was falling, cleansing the grayed yard with a white dusting. Dev and I had found little time to speak since arriving in Aster. Either he'd been working with Syth, learning to control his dreams, or busy with his chores. Carth had been right about that much: life at a temple was little different than life anywhere else. Crops needed to be grown, masonry repaired, clothes mended. With it, Dev and I had found little time together. Women didn't generally sit with the men at meals, but we did sometimes walk together when we found each other in the corridors. But still it was Dev I thought of first, before anyone else.

I found him out in the stables, brushing down a pretty brown and white horse. It was work I knew he enjoyed, having grown up with horses on his parents' land. He'd told me he went to the stables often on the fast days, when busy hands brought steady companionship for his thoughts.

He smiled when he saw me and laid down his brushes, but one of the other priests, Galen, looked out from another stall and climbed forward to join us.

"Oh, but you shouldn't be here, ma'am," Galen said, pulling self-consciously at his vest.

I turned on him. "And why is that?"

"Well, it is the Sister's day, after all, ma'am."

"And the pious should be at the altar? Silent in our meditations? Have I got it right?"

"That's true, ma'am. And it's dirty business here in the stable. I only thought—"

"To help me on the road to true piety? Here under Jokjoa's skies? But that isn't a skinful of wine on that nail over there, is it, Galen? Oh, pardon me, I'd forgotten that even our elder Hershann takes a proper sip while fasting . . ."

Dev put his hand to my arm. "Galen, will you excuse us? Calyx was just telling me that she'd found a broken bit of chain and wanted to know if it belonged in the stable."

Galen fumbled for an answer, but Dev and I were already gone, silently agreeing that we'd need more privacy than the stable allowed.

"You're looking well, Calyx," Dev smiled, but I couldn't help noticing how much thinner he looked, that his face was drawn tighter and more serious than he used to be.

"Thank you," I said, "though I have a feeling a full meal wouldn't hurt you."

"You aren't trying to say that Galen and I both shared a bite to eat on the Sister's fast."

"No," I laughed. "I know better than to think that of you. I was just annoyed with Galen, the way everyone around here seems to know exactly what's best for me. What I should feel and think. But hadn't I heard there was a fever going around? I wouldn't want to hear you'd caught it."

"It's true." He turned to brush a light dusting of snow that had settled about a column base. "There's been altogether too much of fevers and sickness. More, they say, than most years. And uglier. We were worried about Syth, he's old enough as it is. Frail. But he seems to have been spared any real problems this time around."

"But your lessons? If Syth were ill . . ."

"They go on. Syth is a good instructor. And I miss him. But other priests help. What you said about Hershann just now. It reminds me. Don't you feel as if we were young when we came here? So innocent. But"—he looked up at me, smiled—"that isn't why you came, to talk of my worries."

"I have a question," I said. "I was reading. There's so much I never learned in Briana. And they . . . well, you know as well as anyone, they've refused all my requests to take my vows of study. I was wondering, do you know how the Elan Sumedaro died?"

"Die? He didn't die." Dev shook his head, but I could see he took my question seriously. "Did Rija tell you those things?" he asked pointedly. "Or was Kath trying to scare you? The Elan Sumedaro may have returned to Kuoshana, but that doesn't mean he died. He isn't mortal. He can't die. But none of the legends say he won, either. They fight each other, the Elan and Edishu, but neither ever wins. We live on the balancing point of their battle."

"What about Jevniah?"

Dev studied my face for a moment, then went on, "The stories say Elan Sumedaro left his son, Jevniah, as a guard should Edishu return. It was after his son was born and Edishu banished that the Elan Sumedaro returned to Kuoshana."

"And that's all?"

"Of course that's all. What more do you want? Carth used to carry on about the old legends, saying he wished he could wipe out every song that's survived, that they mislead the people."

"What did Carth say about Edishu?"

"Nothing," Dev laughed. "The truth is, Calyx, most priests I've known don't have much to say about it one way or another. Carth spent more time complaining that he couldn't get any work out of me than answering any questions. Hershann or Syth—they're not much different."

"Then do you think Edishu could ever return?"

Dev stood with his arms folded across his chest, looking down the line of chipped columns and empty walkways. "Now, tell me why you want to know. It's not often you ask a question without a reason."

"I want to know if you believe it."

"Which part?"

"Any of it! That a man could walk in Kuoshana. That he could change the world through his dreams. That Edishu is real. That—"

Dev shook his head slowly. "I wish I could give you all the answers, but the truth is, I don't know. I do believe there was an Elan Sumedaro. I believe that because it doesn't seem possible that my jarak dreams are the pinnacle of all that we are capable. Don't you ask yourself sometimes, Calyx, who are we that we should be capable of reaching the fullness of our potential? On the other hand, maybe our jarak dreams are all that there is. We go looking for more because it's comfortable, easy to be given answers."

"No. That's what my father wanted me to believe, that none of it's any more than children's stories. But that's too easy. Even Jared said there's more to it than that. My guardswoman in Briana, I've told you about her. She was Silkiyam. She read my dreams. She said I . . ." I stopped, started again. "She said the havens were real, that the Silkiyam still live there. That our priests only stole dreams and had forgotten the older, stronger ways. While the Silkiyam knew how to change dreams the way the Elan Sumedaro did. And if Edishu is real—"

"Wait." Dev touched his hand to my arm. "You're still only telling me part of the story. All these questions, they're because Hershann won't let you study. Avram warned me that you'd be jealous. Is that it, that you can't get over your disappointment? Because if that's all, then I can tell you now, there are no secrets. Dreams, yes. Jarak dreams but no secrets."

"How can you say there are no secrets?" I shouted suddenly. "You have it fed to you, spoonfuls at a time. And you lap it up as if you could never be satisfied! But what do you do with your dreams? How do you use what you learn? Journal keeping isn't enough. There must be more to it, or the Elan Sumedaro could never hope to fight Edishu."

"That's what I'm trying to tell you, if you'll only listen. Of course there's more. But we don't know what it is. The Elan Sumedaro fought with Jokjoa's tokens, but all we have is our dreams. We don't use them. We only *have* them."

"How can you be satisfied with that? You're a priest!"

"All right, all right. Do you want people to hear you? You shouldn't talk this way at all. People look at you, don't you know that?"

"Of course I know that. I learned long ago why people look at me and it doesn't interest me at all. But you! Dev, you're a priest. A sworn Sumedaro! Elan Sumedaro. Jarak dreamer. Sumedaro. Do you hear the names? You can't deny the connection. You must use your dreams somehow. You told me once you wanted more than anything to learn to dream better, stronger—"

"Then I am right," Dev stopped me. "You wanted to be a Sumedaro and now that you can't, you think I'm learning secrets. That they have a way to empower our dreams. Like Sunder's death magic, or Eclipse's, or Seed's?"

"And do they?"

"No. But wait . . ." Dev took a breath. His face softened. "I have an idea, a way to satisfy you. Though don't ask me why I'm saying this. I'll make a vow, Calyx. Whatever we learn—me, Avram, the other priests—whatever we're taught, I'll teach you! I'll repeat it, everything. My memory isn't perfect, but I'll do what I can. Will that make you happy?"

"Happy? No." I shook my head, but I was smiling. "It will help, though. Thank you."

For a long time we stood quietly, watching the courtyard, the open night above us, clear with a thousand stars. Then slowly he said, "Let's walk. I want to show you something." Dev seemed almost sad just then, though I hardly paid attention; my thoughts were reeling too quickly to ask what he felt.

Wordlessly Dev led the way to a low door along the base of the northern wall. It was a gray-timbered door, old and narrow, one I'd never given much notice. Dev pushed the heavy latch and let the door swing open, then ducked inside, motioning for me to follow. But for the crescent of light filtering in behind us, the corridor inside was dark and so small that I could feel my hair brushing against the roof, the sides pressing near my shoulders. A torch was mounted on the wall. Dev struck a flint, lit one, then another, waiting till the light flared. "This way," he said softly.

"Where are we going?"

"To the oldest room in the temple, just to sit where it's quiet. Syth took us here once, but he feared the room. He kept on complaining about the dark and the cold and said he preferred the daylight to this burrow. I've come here several times since then. Always alone. No one will find us. Not that it's forbidden. Forgotten would be closer to the truth."

The corridor we traced through had a musty odor, dank, but I followed close behind Dev, our torches opening the dark around us. The walls were made of flat, irregularly shaped stones, with no similarity to anything else in Aster. Chips of quartz crystals and jade caught the torch's reflection and sent it shooting off like the shards of a broken mirror. Dev had to duck often, watching out for low beams, and we went on that way until suddenly the corridor took a sharp turn to the right and ended in another door, its heavy timbers splintered with age.

"Here, this is it." Dev held his smoldering torch aloft, throwing an elliptical shadow against the walls and floor. "Look at the walls. There. Jokjoa and Oreill."

"The father and mother," I whispered. "But how old can this be?"

"I don't know. No one does. But look there, the Sisters. Have you ever seen anything like it? Look at Eclipse, the lines of her arm, as though her magic was inseparable from her body. And there, the Elan Sumedaro. If only I could have lived then, when people must have lived so much closer to their dreams, to the gods."

I had never seen carvings like these before. The Elan Sumedaro was in profile, a strange, flat figure with the body turned full toward us. The arm that should have been behind grew out the side so the entire effect was of a twisted, improbable body, distant and impersonal. Edishu was portrayed in the same unnatural manner, almost as though the artist had never learned to use perspective. There was no dimension, no trick of shadow or raised detail as my mother would have used, only the feeling of a distant, unknowable past flowing into ours. Except for their eyes: there was life! Warmth. Compassion. The Elan Sumedaro's especially, which I would have imagined as fierce and hard, they were gentle here, like a woman's more than a man's.

"What is this place?" I whispered.

"The heart of Aster," Dev said, his voice quiet with awe. "The haven from whose ruin Aster was built. Before this the land belonged to the gods."

"Why did you bring me here?" I asked, suddenly afraid.

There was power in this room, an air stronger than anything I had ever touched or breathed or known before. And it called to me with a yearning as sweet as Rath's had been in Sharat. As if the very floor I walked on knew my name and was beckoning, pulling me down into its heart, down through the layers of stone and planking into the soil, into the haven below the temple . . .

I was standing in a clearing in a quiet forest. Soft grass cushioned my feet. The air smelled of fresh summer fruit—ambrosia and blossoms and warmth. Sweet, sweet warmth. And I knew it was an older earth I touched, one that had never known winter or hunger or impotence.

I walked a bit, no more than a few steps, when my toe hit something hard. I bent to look, thinking it would be a rock, but what I found instead was a fragment of a clay bowl with a smooth, blackened line following around its curve. Another step revealed a tray made impossibly of a single limb of wood, with knotted handles so intricate, I could only think the wood had grown of its own volition.

People had lived here once, Ceena's people, I judged from the way this bowl and tray resembled nothing I'd seen in any town. Nothing Sumedaro. Nothing traded from the south or west. These were older pieces, different, with a grace of workmanship that put our tools and sparse trees to shame.

Leaving the pieces where they lay, I rose quietly and looked about. I meant to walk farther, to explore the clearing at least as far as the woods encircling it. But from far away Dev's voice called . . .

The greenwood dimmed; the sky turned gray, overcast. I felt a rushing through my feet, a trembling as though the earth were too uncertain of its true shape to hold fast.

The light filled out again, yellow and thin this time, enclosed.

"Dizzy." I stumbled. "The haven . . . did you see it?"

"Are you all right, Calyx? The air. It's too close. I didn't think you heard me."

"The field. It was a haven. Here. It's real . . . ."

"That's what I told you just a moment ago. If there's any

power in Aster to give you a dream, it would be here, atop
the earth where the havens once stood."

"You didn't see anything?"

"No, of course not. Only the walls, the light, the carvings.
You shouldn't worry so much. We're safe here. Hershann's
the only one would be a problem, and there isn't a chance in
the north he'd come looking for us."

"No, of course not."

"But please, don't worry if you can't find the lit candle. It
took me weeks the first time—"

"Candle? What candle?" I shivered, stepped back for a
wall to lean against. Whatever it was I had seen, Dev knew
nothing about it.

"Quiet now, and listen," he said. "We should hurry.
Close your eyes. I'm going to touch you here, on the neck
like this, and here on your temple. Syth showed us this the
first week we were here. Be calm a moment. Thus we are
linked. Tonight you will dream of Sharat temple. When you
lay down, tell yourself that you'll go to Sharat and search
for me. That's all you have to do. Think about Sharat
before you fall asleep. Picture me there. When you fall
asleep, I'll be watching for you. I'll carry a candle in my
hand. You need to find the candle. Tomorrow I want you to
tell me which room you found me in. And don't bother
trying to speak to me in the dream. It wouldn't work. As
jarak dreamers, we only watch."

9

That night I went to bed with an image of Dev set firmly
in my mind. He would wait for me in Sharat temple, I
told myself as I huddled beneath the blanket, waiting for
warmth to ease my restlessness and gnawing hunger. Sharat
was a good place to meet. All would be well. Dev was
helping me now, and in my mind Sharat was holy. No
troubling thoughts of Lakotah or Aster's disappointments to

hinder my dream. And it was fitting that the first jarak dream I'd ever shared with a priest would be on temple grounds.

Sleep came quickly, but it began with too many troubled thoughts and wandering efforts. Then sometime later in the night my mind cleared and an image of Dev came to light. Dev, with his smiles and concerns always layered one over the other. Dev with his tall back and slender shoulders. Dev in his orange robes, a priest. Sumedaro.

He was waiting for me, his form pulling across the miles, as though a beacon of light led me on. The land sped by, hills, mountains and valleys all a blur until Sharat appeared, wide and angular, windswept towers and rock-hewn walls. Palpable. Solid.

And I was there, inside its walls. Walking. Searching for Dev.

He was somewhere inside now, watching for me. I could feel his presence, the warmth of his candle. I turned slightly, searching. It only took a moment to find. Even through the walls it seemed I could feel the small blaze of heat and I followed, walking down hallways, passing through walls that never would have yielded to my waking body. The hour was late and no one was about, though I could sense people sleeping behind doors, the shape of an arm against a pillow, the faint path of a priest's jarak dream.

Then I found him. He was standing in Sharat's kitchen, the candlelight drawing a halo of orange on his robes. Behind him, Maura and Serebet's walls were hung with vines of garlic and onions, just as I remembered. The ovens still held some warmth; coals glowed deep within the firebox, and I could feel it, as sure as if I was there again, flesh of my hands raised toward its warmth.

Dev smiled brightly to see me. But, true to his word, he did not speak, and an idea came to me of a game I might play with this priest of mine, a trick to show him he would not regret his decision.

I walked up to his jarak form, intending only to snuff out his candle, to see if I could touch him in the dream. Smiling quickly, before he had a chance to react, I closed my fist around the slight wick.

Nothing happened.

Dev looked surprised; he had no idea what I meant to do. The priests he trained with did as they were told. None of them would think to act without a guide, to risk an error or the dark. And I had forgotten the one lesson I should have remembered: the Sumedaro jarak dreamer cannot change a dream. Dev's real candle burned in Aster, not here. Of course I would never be able to touch it.

I felt like a fool. I'd wanted Dev to know he hadn't made a mistake agreeing to teach me. I wanted him to know that I could keep up with him, make him proud. And so I touched him again, hoping to prove that I would make a strong dreamer. I grabbed a fold of his robes and willed my jarak body away from there, away from Sharat's shimmering walls and courts. Away to the haven room where he had taken me that day.

I had no idea what would happen. My thoughts had leapt so quickly. Sharat was gone—as suddenly as if distance was no more than thought—and we were in Aster again, in the haven room. Dev was standing beside me, a terrible, troubled look on his face.

Then I'd succeeded! Here were the same walls, the same low ceiling and splintered door. The room was dark, ill lit by Dev's small candle. From the shadows Jokjoa's carving seemed to stare down at me, its eyes so rich, I wondered if the wood itself held living roots that still grew down into the heart of the earth. "Jokjoa," my thoughts cried out, "can you hear me?"

I watched a moment longer, wondering. But of course, there was no answer and I forced my gaze away from those eyes. Too real they were, too laden with expectation.

The other murals on the wall seemed to glower down at me, morose now, as if challenging my right to stand there, and I wished suddenly I'd picked any other room but this one. I remembered that other field I'd seen, the sweet grass layered atop Aster's hard stone floor, like two paintings my mother might have done, the one imposed upon the other, covering but not quite erasing it.

Suddenly I wanted to be out of there, safe in my body again, where thoughts and fears of the Silkiyam dead could not haunt me. I let go my hold on Dev's robe and fled as quickly as thoughts could carry, away to my bed, to my own body asleep beneath the rich velvet canopy. Just once I glanced back, barely in time to see Dev's silhouette fading, unable to maintain his hold on that room without me. Back to his own room, to his own dreams.

*   *   *

Early the next morning, I sought Dev out. I meant to apologize, explain. All I knew from the look on his face the past night was that I'd done something wrong. More than anything, I was afraid he'd refuse to help me further, that he'd say he'd thought about it during the night and I was too untutored a dreamer, or he was too busy or too afraid to take the risk.

I broke my fast with the other priests, eating in silence while one of Hershann's elders intoned yet another service. Words. I shook my head. Nothing but words. Habit. Was anyone here truly listening? Some heads were bowed, others snatched at bread, stuffed their mouths, whispered during the repetitions. Did any of them care about their jarak dreams? I wondered. Or was this only one way out of many to spend the days of their lives, as Rija had said. An easy path, with answers too easily given?

The meal finished, we left in a solemn row. But instead of going to the library as I should have done, I turned down a different corridor, following after Dev.

He and Avram were just beginning work together, outside on repairs to a tall hutch that housed a squawking collection of pigeons, chickens, and ill-tempered geese.

I called out a greeting.

Dev stiffened when he heard me, laid down the tool he'd just picked up. "Calyx had a dream last night," he said to Avram, but it was me he was glaring at.

Avram straightened up from his work. "Oh? What was it?"

"We'd been talking about jarak dreams," Dev said.

"Yes?" Avram looked quickly from Dev to me, then back to Dev.

"It was nothing." I shook my head. "Just a game."

"I told her we could see if a dream she had had recently was jarak."

"Still trying to learn to dream? It's a pity you couldn't have studied with us."

Avram held his hands out, overacting, but this time I had no patience for his baiting. "And was it a jarak dream?"

Dev started to answer, to tell him what we'd attempted, but I stopped him: "It was nothing. Dev's teasing," I said quickly. "He was going to watch one of my dreams. That's all."

"Dev's generous with his time. You should bring your dreams to the rathadaro hall," Avram reproached me. "It wouldn't hurt you. Sometimes I wonder . . ." Avram stopped a moment, as if trying to spare my feelings. "You might be Briana's lady, you know. But isn't it time you shared more in Aster's life? To have a dream watched is a blessing. No one else brings their dreams to just one priest. We are children under the same stars, all of us, and our dreams return to the stars."

"She knows that, Av," Dev said drily.

Avram snapped around. "Then why doesn't she bring her dreams to be watched? Why bring them to you, as though there was a secret to them, something she didn't want us to know? Unless they are jarak dreams? In which case Hershann should know. Maybe her own father, Lord Morell, should be told. Was that why he sent you away, Calyx? Because you didn't have dreams. Or because you did?"

"They're not jarak," I said, fighting for calm. "They're just dreams. Same as I've always had. And they're no more the business of everyone in this temple than they were of Lakotah's."

"Then you do have jarak dreams?" Avram was smiling now, baiting me.

"I didn't say that."

"Then you are sensume, as the whispers go?"

"If you already know what everyone's whispering, then there's no need to ask. Dev, would you mind? I wanted to show you something. It's a drawing I did for Kath. That's all. I thought you'd like it."

This time Dev agreed, and as we walked off together I hoped his annoyance with Avram's sharp tongue would shield me. Once out of hearing distance, Dev stopped. "Why did you lie?" he asked.

"I didn't need to listen to that. Avram goes beyond joking. And as for his piety, he'd as soon pay someone to have a jarak dream for him if he thought there'd be any gain to it. Besides, you said yourself we have to keep what we're doing a secret."

"Yes, but Avram isn't Hershann. We don't have to hide from him. And with dreams like that . . ."

"There wasn't anything wrong with my dream."

"No, nothing wrong. Only, Calyx, why didn't you tell me you had jarak dreams?"

I raised my hands as if to argue, then dropped them back to my side. "I know I didn't tell you. And I've paid more than once for that same choice. But I thought you understood. Why else would I have wanted so much to be a Sumedaro? Maybe if you weren't so caught up in your own needs, you'd have seen—" I stopped again. "I'm sorry. That wasn't fair. What matters is that you know I can learn. I only meant to keep up with you."

"Keep up with me?"

"I found you with the candle, just as you told me to."

"Not *only*." Dev shook his head. Then for the briefest moment he raised his hand to my cheek and touched me. His hand was so warm, so surprising. Without a thought I laid my hand over his. Just a touch. But the next moment he looked beyond me, across the courtyard to where someone was walking. One of the elders. A priest, his hood pulled close across his face. Even across the distance it was obvious that we'd been seen, the touch noted. Dev's hand dropped quickly to his side and he turned away from me.

"Your dreams are strong," he said. "Avram would sell his robes to have one dream like yours. Someday you'll be a priest. A teacher. But how did you do that, move us back to Aster?"

"I don't know. We went to that room. The haven room. It was—"

"No, that's my point. We didn't go. You took me."

"We came back to Aster," I said, part of me still afraid I'd done something wrong. "I didn't carry you."

"But you might as well have. You don't understand, do you? *I don't know how you did that.*"

"No. There's no difference between that and what you did yesterday. We were linked when I found you in Sharat. Then, when I wanted to continue the jarak dream somewhere else, we were still linked together."

"All right, maybe that's what it was. I'll ask Syth—"

"No, don't. I'd rather keep it between the two of us. We already agreed. Not Avram or Syth. No one. I was disappointed enough when I first came here, when Hershann wouldn't allow me to be a priest. I'm not ready to risk another, firmer denial. We'll work on my dreams together. When they're stronger and I have something I can show Hershann, proof he can't deny, then we'll go to him. We'll tell him."

"All right, then. As we agreed."

I smiled. "I'll work hard for you. You won't be disappointed."

"It's probably best this way. And it's true Hershann isn't the elder he should be," Dev agreed, his eyes brightening again, as if he'd been relieved of a burden. "At least we aren't leaving your dreams to run wild or risk your getting lost. You won't be abandoned, Calyx."

Two years passed that way. Two years of stealing what I could in the way of Sumedaro lore from the library. Two years at the fire altar living Hershann's ruse of the dutiful daughter, mannered, faithful, and patient. Two years of keeping the Sister's fast with the other priests, though I had never been asked to do so.

And never once did I bring them my dreams. Or grow close, or feel welcomed as anything but a guest, tolerated for my handiwork in copying but no more than that. But slowly, working alone and with Dev, I filled my journals. First one, then another, and another.

When I wasn't working in the library, I watched the other Sumedaro and learned to mark the heart of a dream as they did during services. For weeks I practiced in the privacy of my room, forming the circle again and again until I believed I had in truth enclosed my jarak dreams within. Mouth to ear, ear to heart, heart to navel to eye again, the circle of both the dream and the world, each the other, each united. When I felt ready, I began joining in the ritual. It was simple, really, raising my hand in unison with theirs. Perhaps a head turned here and there, but no one came running to say I hadn't the right. And if Hershann noticed, it couldn't have troubled him or he would have sent Rija with one of her little messages. After a day or two the few pairs of eyes that had watched no longer turned, and I took it as another of my small victories.

Life in Aster went by quietly. We worked the seasons: spring—what little there was of it—the planting, fall the harvest. Before each winter set in the mason priests worked new mortar into old cracks. Carpenters repaired roof tiles and cracked aqueducts. For others it was the carding and weaving and scrubbing, endless scrubbing of walls and floors and bedding and clothes.

Somewhere during that time I took to wearing the long

brown robes of a priest. This time Rija did ask and when I told her—as I had prepared myself to say—that there were more robes to be had than dresses, she nodded, as if it made a kind of sense to her. I worried less about being the outsider then, as if while I understood that the clothes couldn't make me truly belong, at least I was no longer as conspicuous as I had been.

In all that time I had no visitors from home. I should have expected it. After all, who would have cared enough to come? Micah perhaps, but he would never be able to afford such a journey even if he wanted to see me. Nor could Serell have spared him had he found the courage to ask. My mother wouldn't have been able to travel so far, but she could have sent someone in her place . . . Ceena. Ceena would have tolerated the journey, enjoyed it even. The long road, the discomforts, they would have meant nothing to her. Ivane could have paid to outfit her and supplied a horse. I would have given anything I owned to see her, to tell her of my jarak dreams. But no one came.

And gradually life settled into a pattern. No matter the robes I'd put on or the words I mouthed, my special status could not be denied. Aster became more firmly the prison Morell had intended. While I went faithfully to the library tower every day, still I was shut out from the rathadaro couch, where most other priests were required to serve their turn.

At the same time Hershann often remarked, as did Syth and many of the temple elders, that more dreams were being brought to the temple's doors than ever before. And the priests were needed, every one of them, as if the fire of those dreams was too much for any one priest to bear. It was a good sign, Hershann said. A sign that the temples would be better used, more appreciated, and with luck grow a little wealthier again. But if I hadn't realized it before, I saw now that only a few priests were able to speak the people's dreams with any facility, and these were already taking turns in the rathadaro hall, while others doubled up on work loads, covering for them.

Hershann welcomed the townsfolk, saying they were the ones who finally succeeded in chasing off the beggars heckling them, forcing them to disband. But there was another tale making the rounds, claiming that the townsfolk had little to do with it at all. That winter had worsened. And the homeless, no longer able to survive the cold, had waited only till the road opened, then moved on south. And though no one dared speak of it aloud, more than a few of Aster's priests had taken to the road along with them.

With that, and the continuing rage of fevers that plagued the temple through that year, I wondered sometimes that Hershann could afford to keep me out of the rathadaro hall. Of course, most of the priests assumed I was sensume, unable to vault the hurdle that separated the priests from the dream blind. Why else would Lord Morell's daughter be forbidden Syth's lectures, or to spend a turn at the dreamwatch in the rathadaro couch?

One other story was whispered about: that Dev and I were lovers. And though I could not deny having wished for it, still there was no truth to the rumor. The problem was that I didn't know how to deny what so many people thought they'd seen for themselves—without risking the larger truth of our meetings.

Rija was one of the first to give in to the gossip. I was in my chambers one evening, undressing for bed when she said, "It's a pity you haven't the fine clothes you must have had at home, isn't it?"

I looked up, surprised. Hadn't Rija already agreed it was more practical if I wore the same robes as everyone else? "Why is that?" I asked, annoyed. "You said yourself these robes were warmer, less troublesome."

"Oh, that may be," she said. "But priest robes cover you so high, up to your neck, and down to your ankles. I'd think a man like Dev might like to see a little more. Your shoulders are lovely, you know. You shouldn't hide them. And your neck—"

"What are you talking about?" I sighed, annoyed.

"About Dev, of course. Calyx, it's no secret. Not from me, of all people. Not when it's my job to come in here of an evening only to find you gone. And not just once. Mind you, I think there's nothing wrong with it. There's more than one priest here—man or woman—who likes to have their way on the side." She smiled, a little too knowingly. "If things get out of hand, though, well that would be something else, wouldn't it?"

"But things aren't out of hand, are they? And they're not likely to get that way. Tell me, though, who is it you've heard talking about me?"

Rija didn't answer. She glanced around the room, a troubled look coming to her face. If she thought to find some bit of evidence to use against me, she might as well give it up now. Dev had never been in this room, never would be.

"Of course, if he's only a friend, there's nothing wrong with that," she said. "But if you did want him, why shouldn't you do as you wish?" Rija turned to face me, hands on her hips, daring. "If I had half your nerve, I would. You don't even realize it, do you, that you've twice the freedom I'll ever have? Why, if I so much as looked at a man, I'd be booted out of here, no better off than any of those beggars outside the gates. Not you, though. You're perfectly safe. But if you want to know what I think, a little lie now and then is far easier than being a wife outside. And in your position, you don't even have to worry about being forced to marry Dev. Unless . . . you wanted to?"

"We are not lovers," I said more angrily than I'd meant to. "And I have no intention of marrying anyone until I am ready to do the choosing."

"Of course not. Though on the other hand, with you, Dev's prospects aren't altogether bad," Rija kept on, thoughtless and unheeding. "His family has lands. Or Avram—he's always ambitious. Your father could give more, if you wanted—"

"Rija, I've heard enough. You have no idea what you're saying. I'm going out."

"Well, but I don't see the harm. I don't think it would matter to Hershann either. He's too afraid of your father to say a word against you. Oh, other things you'd do might bother him," she said, and suddenly I wondered if there wasn't a hint of a warning in her too sweet voice. "But not that. He'd think it was your own business. And it is. Still, if that's what you want, I won't talk about it. Not unless you bring it up. It's late, though. I'll just pick up the tray in a minute and then I'll be going."

I sighed then, unwilling to carry this argument further. But I thought about it all the next day. Of course they talked about me. If there was one lesson I'd learned sharing a room with Mirjam, it was that people would talk. And in a way, the talk might prove a help. Dev and I did spend time together and the time had to be accounted for. If these people, priests though they were, couldn't conceive of the possibility that it was faith that brought us together, why should I fight to convince them otherwise? Dev was a comfort, just not the sort they imagined.

All through that brief summer we'd met in secret, planning each step forward in my jarak dreams. Whatever Dev learned, he passed on to me. Wherever Syth sent him, so I later went. Corridors, cellars, grounds, none of it was beyond my dreaming eye. Aster town's homes, markets, and guildhalls, I watched them all.

Dev was nearly as pleased with my progress as I was. I kept up with him week after week, matching the reach of his jarak dream, stretching my sight, learning control. For him, devout priest that he'd become, it was the one challenge to Sumedaro authority he allowed himself, his cry of protest that he could not pray harder, dream harder, live harder than our meager lives allowed.

Meetings spent in planning our dreams were the simple ones—a passing word quickly begun and quickly finished. The more difficult times were when Dev needed to watch my dreams. For that, further stealth was required. Silence. More time. Once we'd thought to meet at the rathadaro hall, in the room near the fire altar, but that had proved awkward. There was too much traffic there during the evening hours, and later in the night as well, to pretend our frequent meetings were mere coincidence. Always we were watched, our actions known.

We'd discussed other possibilities. Dev had no room of his own, and meeting in my chambers was far too indiscreet. Dev suggested the haven room, but for reasons I couldn't explain, I was afraid of that place, afraid especially to bare my dreams there. And so it was the library tower we settled on at last, a cubicle in one of the many forgotten corners.

Watching a dream does not require the same lapse of time as the dream itself, which in turn does not require the same amount of time as waking action. Most often I entered the library first while Dev waited in the courtyard. Then when it seemed no one was watching, he'd follow after me.

Watching my dreams, Dev learned what I was capable of doing. And always what I was capable of was exactly what he asked me to see and—since that first time with the candle—never any more than that. When the watch ended, he would be there, smiling and proud, partly of me, but most of all proud of the priesthood he longed to honor.

But as time passed, the seasons began to drag. Midway

into that second winter, when it seemed we'd done nothing but the same exercises over and again, the same dream of Aster town, or Sharat temple, or this or that, a restlessness grew inside me. Even before coming to Aster I'd been able to choose my own dreams, send my sight where my corporeal body could not travel. Was that all the Sumedaro had to teach? What then was the difference between our jarak dreams and pretending that a book I'd read about a distant country was the same as visiting there?

Then one evening, when the routine moved through the same motions it had on every preceding evening, I couldn't slough off the feeling that all this was nothing but childish drudgery.

"Put your hands in mine," Dev was saying. "Close your eyes and listen. Kuoshana's song is the earth's breath. All else is quiet. Silence fills the room. The only sound is in your heart, in your dream. Listen to it. Can you hear me?"

"Yes."

"Do you feel my hands?"

"Yes."

"Our hands are linked, bridging my eyes to your dream. From the gods to the dream, through our hands to the dream, thus I watch, thus we share, thus we free the dream.

"Last night," Dev said, "we shared a dream of a house in Aster. There were two windows beside an arched door. Do you remember?"

Impatient, I nodded. Yes.

"There was a man inside, talking. I want you to show me what he said. Not from memory, but with the sight of the true jarak dream . . ."

As Dev shut his eyes, I pulled my hands suddenly free, and in a rush of words said, "Why not try farther this time? We've already dreamt of Aster. We know we can do that."

"What?" Dev looked up at me, startled.

"I was thinking we might try farther. Briana perhaps. It wouldn't be very different. I have friends there, people who would be markers for me."

Dev sat quietly, considering the thought. "I want to say no because I think Syth would, but I can't think of a reason good enough. Few of Aster's priests ever attempt to see farther. Avram's tried, but he hasn't been able to yet. I can. Syth can certainly. And a few others. It's custom, I think, that holds us back—not Jokjoa's law binding our dreams. I don't doubt you're able . . . all right, then," he said, pulling at his chin. "But not Briana. That isn't different enough, if it's different you want. Your sister's in Gleavon, isn't she? And you've never been there? That would be more difficult, though you'd still have the blood connection to guide you. And I would be there as well, watching."

"Gleavon? But isn't that too far?" I took a sudden breath, thinking of Lethia. "Why not Korinna's court? I've never been there, either."

"Sometimes I don't understand you." Dev looked at me. "If Briana isn't challenge enough, Hillstor's even closer. So what would be the point? Besides, it's your sister who makes it a safe venture. And for a first attempt at any distance, it's safer to have a connection; combine the familiar with the new."

"What if Lethia's there?"

"Lethia? The queen has nothing to do with this. It's your sister you'll dream of."

"But . . ." I hesitated. "Are you certain they won't see me?"

"Your sister isn't the one sharing the jarak dream. I am. I'm the only one who'll know where you are. The power lies with the dreamer; it doesn't pass into the vision. Besides, even if anyone saw you—Mirjam, Lethia, your sister's husband—it wouldn't matter. They couldn't touch you. Only two jarak dreamers can share a dream and even so, they cannot touch. Remember, the Sumedaro is watcher only. And haven't you told me more than once, your sister doesn't dream?"

We spoke for several minutes longer, setting the mechanics into motion—a time, markers along the way. Then we separated, Dev walking lightly while I wondered what I'd begun.

That night as I slipped into a bed so like the one I imagined Mirjam to be sleeping in, my curiosity grew. Mirjam! I tried to remember the surprised look on her face the last time I'd seen her in my father's hall. Mirjam, her hair laced in pearls, her gown cut low for Theron. But what had her life been like these past several years? Had the goddess Seed touched her? Was she with child? What if there'd been enough time for two already! I think I fell asleep smiling, with an image of my slender-waisted sister suckling a baby to lead me toward the tunnel of my jarak dream.

There was darkness, the space of a thousand stars. There was distance. The cold of memory falling away to a new day. Then there was dawn. And Gleavon. Light growing golden on the horizon, pale streaks of amber and gray.

The next moment I was inside Gleavon, the walls rising about my jarak body, tall and strongly built. A warm breeze swept through my hair, surprising me. I had forgotten what it was to feel a land untouched by winter's hand.

And then I felt my sister's touch, familiar but changed also with time. Relieved, I sped forward playfully through the keep's great halls and corridors, marveling as I traveled at Gleavon's grace and brightness. When I found her she was asleep in a canopy bed, her husband, Theron, curled lazily beside her. Mirjam seemed a little older, a little more tractable. She looked drawn, if that were possible. Pale.

I think that even in the jarak dream I sighed then, feeling the melancholy weight of the years that had passed between us. I turned to look for Dev, but he was not there yet, and I knew I should take one more short look, then return.

In one thing, at least, I was right. Mirjam's room was even grander than Briana had ever hoped to be; rich furs and tapestries, cedar chests and soft chairs, filled the wide chamber. But of a child there was no sign, no adjacent nursery, no cradle, and nothing to say that one was expected either.

I relaxed a moment, knowing I was invisible to any who might walk in, imagining her awake, the two of us visiting in this room. I would laugh easily with her, mocking Morell, agreeing that her hall was everything she'd ever wanted— grander than his finest hall or courtyard. If he had one sculpture of Jokjoa and Oreill to be proud of, she had three. If he had two great tables carved and inlaid on which to feed his guests, she had five. We would speak freely, as only the passing of time could allow, sisters now at last.

But it was a game after all, that imagining. And the room, for all its richness, could not hold my interest. Somehow my thoughts betrayed me. Wandered. I found myself wondering about Lethia. Lethia at dinner in Briana, proud and arrogant. Lethia as she must have appeared before the fire altar, her eyes ablaze. And later, speaking her terrible dream to all those people. Lethia, ruling in Gleavon.

And then, as though my thoughts could move this jarak body without need of my will, I felt myself pulled toward her. Walls. Corridors. Rooms. None of it could stop my passing, till my jarak body stood suddenly before her.

Lethia was awake—as I had somehow known she would be—moving about her chamber in a robe woven as light as a cloud. Her dark hair hung loosely to her back. She must have just risen from her bed and stood now at a high, arched window looking out over the towers beyond. She seemed calm, distant, and I was entranced, watching until she turned and looked directly at me.

I reeled back, struck with the power of her gaze. She can't see me, I warned myself. Be still. I am a watcher here, nothing more. The Sumedaro cannot change the jarak dream. Ceena said so. Dev said so. They agreed. She would not be able to see me. She wouldn't.

But she could. She was staring right at me. At me, not through me. Then she smiled, and her beauty was a terrible thing: ageless, white, more a mask than a face. Only her eyebrow moved, rising above her dark eyes; the eyebrow that was the first thing I'd known about her, the way it split, exactly the way a lie would split the truth.

Lethia cocked her chin, nodded, and it was no use pretending she could not see me. She was purposefully twisting a ring that she wore, wanting me to see. I stared at it, at her hands, so pale and long, and the ring, smooth and shining in the dawn light. I knew it then. It was the one my mother had given Mirjam, with Jokjoa's hands carved around its band, one after the other, and on every wrist an image of the bracelet in Aster temple.

The ring. It was one of Jokjoa's tokens.

I looked back at Lethia then. So many questions filled my mind. But she was no longer watching me. Her gaze had turned to something behind me, and I wheeled about, frightened suddenly by the weight of so much I did not understand.

A man was there, tall, young. I don't know how I'd missed him. He must have been there before I arrived, waiting. He stepped forward, crossed silently to Lethia's side, and watched me. Though she was tall in her own right, he towered over her. Handsome and dark, he was richly dressed, as a queen's courtier would have been, his lined eyes caught somewhere between youth and those of a stronger, older man. Foolishly I wondered if he was her lover.

But he grinned at me then, with lips that parted like a

jackal at the kill, and the look on his face was like nothing I ever wanted to see again.

I was trapped. "Edishu," I whispered.

In answer he took Lethia's hand in his and raised it, that I might see the ring. "You surprise me," he said. "Calyx of Aster temple. Calyx of Sharat. Calyx of Lakotah. Coming unarmed, when you knew I had the ring."

"What unarmed?" I answered, forcing my fear to hold still and not betray me. "Is that a question?" I kept my voice firm, trying to think. He spoke in riddles, it seemed to me, and if I turned the questions to him, perhaps I could buy time to think, find a way to escape.

"Three temples you have slept in. And how many tokens touched? Yet you come to fight with no weapons. While this queen was good enough to give Shammal to me—all of her own volition—a present." He laughed loudly. "I am almost disappointed. You were forewarned. More than Lethia. And here I had hoped for a game."

I thought he would take the ring himself and put it on his finger. But he didn't. Instead, holding Lethia's hand fast in his own, he pointed her finger toward me, and she stood there, puppet-like, allowing it, wanting it.

From the ring's center an arrow of light shot out, white and cold. It flew toward me, struck me before I had a chance to realize what was happening. Whiplike, it pulsed through my body, lifting me, throwing me backward till I was slammed to the floor.

For a moment I could not breathe, could not see. Needles pricked my skin. Somehow I found the strength to push up on my hands and take a breath. The pain eased. I sat first. Then stood. Tried to make the world stop spinning, and face him again.

"There. You see," he said, his voice echoing, printing itself on my mind. "You cannot fight me. You will give me what I want."

I bit my lip in, forced myself to answer, not to accept defeat so easily. "And what is that?"

"You will bring me Jokjoa's tokens. One by one. Until I have them all. Shammal. Rath. Gamaliel. Hajthaele. The Fist, the Dagger, and sweetest of all, Oreill's token."

"Is that all?"

"No!" he roared. "Do not trifle with me. That is not all." And he raised Lethia's hand toward me again, pointing.

Again the white light shot out. I tried to hide behind my hands, close my eyes, run away, but it was useless. The light hit me, coiled about me: glowing, constricting, glowing, constricting.

I tried to stand, to fight it. Tried to breathe, to count, to see out of the darkness that closed over me. To see anything. Long moments passed. The world was black. Only pain existed.

But if there was pain, there must be a center. If I can feel pain, I must be alive, I told myself. Searching for a muscle that could move, respond, I found a hand, a fist, dug my fingernails into my hand. Let there be this pain, I begged. Let me feel this hand.

Then somehow I found my legs, willed the muscles to move. Found my eyes, and sight. *Now*, I thought, *if I could reach the ring* . . . But he raised it again and its power coursed through the air, forcing me backward.

What did I know of fighting such power? What were the rules, the methods? Wherever Dev was, I cursed him, cursed the Sumedaros for leaving me as ignorant and helpless as them.

"You will come to me in the end." Edishu's voice tore into my heart. "Naked, weaponless. When I have gained each token. You will come to me and you will ask, will beg for me to take you. To give you life. For without me, you will learn, as this fair queen has already learned, you have no life."

I fought for air, fought against the pain of each breath. At last I raised my face. "Is that what she did?" I asked. Then, before he could answer, I sucked the air into my lungs again, this time allowing the pain to grab me, shock me into motion. I lunged for Lethia's hand, thinking somehow I could gain the ring, turn it against him, hurt him as he had hurt me.

And I caught her, felt the impact of my body slam against hers. I was slow, but it didn't matter. She crumpled, soft. Collapsed without resistance. I felt her arm against mine, blood warm and real. But inside—there was nothing. I gathered my strength, tried for a second leap, this time against Edishu, to strike him.

My fists fell into the space where he had stood.

He was gone, and I lay on the floor, the light enveloping me again, constricting, glowing, constricting. I don't know how long I waited, but eventually the light dimmed and I raised my eyes to look, thinking he would be gone.

But he was there! Standing exactly as he had been! And Lethia was there beside him, the same hungry smile fixed about her silent lips. Edishu came and kneeled beside me, his face so impossibly beautiful it could not be human. Only the eyes inside were as I remembered.

I forced myself to speak. "Where are you?"

"In Kuoshana," he said, his voice a gentle lie. "But only for now. I thought you knew that."

I raised my chin toward the queen. "But she's real."

"Is that a question? We can play at questions if you like."

"Why aren't you the one wearing the ring yourself?"

"Still too easy. If I am in Kuoshana and Lethia has the ring, it is enough that she wears it for me."

"What will you do with the tokens?"

"Again an easy question. You can answer that yourself. Look there, out the window. Tell me what you see."

I forced my arms to work for me, my legs to hold my weight. I hobbled to the window, arms grasped to the sill for support. The view opened out across the walls of Gleavon, out beyond the fields swaying gold and green in the slight breeze and it seemed that there was only one thing that mattered. "Summer," I said.

"There, you see what my forebearance can allow. You did know. You always know more than you think, Calyx flower. And in your own lands, in Aster?"

"Winter."

"And whose touch is it that holds winter there? And who is it granted the queen's request here? Surely not Sister Sunder?"

"You?"

He smiled at me then, his eyes roving over my face and body the way a lover might, deep and searching, as if he meant to know every turn and look about me. "And whose hand will bring the tokens to me, so that I may allow summer to enter her land as well? For you see, I can do whatever I will with this earth. And who is it will touch her lips to mine? Now and whenever I ask?"

"No!" I shouted, backing away. "I will not. Let her bring the tokens to you."

"She already has!" he snapped. "It's not enough. It has to be you. You will bring the tokens. And you will—"

"No! No! No!" I screamed as he reached toward Lethia's hand again. But I couldn't continue standing there, waiting helplessly for him to strike. He was right in one thing. I had no weapons. I couldn't fight. Couldn't even touch him. But then I wondered frantically, How had he touched me? This was a jarak dream. Though I'd felt pain, felt Lethia's body. This was a jarak dream. I'd forgotten. I didn't have to wait till he hit me again.

Struggling to maintain control, I closed my eyes. There was strength enough in my jarak dream to bring me here, I swore. Jarak strength. He cannot take that away.

Away, I whispered to the growing silence. Away.

Inside the dark I found the parameters of my body, found the tunnel that had brought me here, and the path leading me home.

Somewhere far in the distance, Edishu cried in rage. But he couldn't touch me. I was going home to Aster. To my body. To my bed. Away. Away . . .

10

It was weeks before I was able to see Dev again.

A rash of new fevers descended on Aster, striking the elders, the weak. Two of Aster's priests died and were buried in the vaults below ground. Then, just as the temple hoped to be free, to go on with the business of survival, several more priests did not come down to break their fast at the morning table. Syth, always prone to illness, was struck with it, lying abed for days without eating, without speaking. Dev, I heard, lived at his teacher's side doing what little he was able while on the floor above, Hershann ordered us to keep the temple routines moving forward. Still, the loss was heavy. Elders were not easily replaced. There were lifetimes of service in their hearts, knowledge that could not always be passed on through the jarak dream. And there were the living to be concerned with, the glances filled with fear and disbelief.

Whispers echoed in the corridors: that there was a curse on the land, that the deaths were a plague sent by the gods, that Jokjoa had condemned us and never would waken. For my own part, I moved through those weeks as if a pall had surrounded my heart, cutting off the possibility of thought, emotions. Numb with my own unspoken fears, I welcomed the heavier workload, the tension of those days that helped me forget my fear of the night.

But at last a time came when enough dreamless nights had passed that I began to think of Dev again. More than two years had come and gone between that first jarak dream of Edishu and now. Wasn't it true, I tried convincing myself, that I'd been the one trespassing in Gleavon this time? Edishu had not come here, looking for me. This battle I'd brought on myself. But with the control I now maintained, it should be the simplest of exercises to keep my dreams safe, closer to Aster and the northern temples.

In the temple, we'd taken to eating in smaller groups that winter, a habit which seemed to fit the harsher needs of the community. It was a Sister's eve dinner. I'd been seated with Kath and several of the other scribes when I caught sight of Dev passing through the hall. A week earlier, when the close smells of overheated kitchens and boiling unguents had left me feeling flushed and dizzy, I'd taken a knife to the back of my hair and chopped it off short like a man's. Now, when I called, Dev glanced toward the table but kept walking as if he didn't recognize me.

Kath reached out a firm hand, holding me back. "Let him go," she spoke in my ear. "There's more than enough people watching."

I looked around at the table. She was right, of course. Conversations had stopped the moment I'd called Dev's name. There were shifting, uncomfortable glances. I took a swallow from my cup, laid it back deliberately. "Why does it matter?" I whispered back to Kath.

She pulled off some bread from the loaf, held it in front of her mouth as a shield. "You still don't understand, do you—even after all this time—what a curiosity you are to us, Calyx?"

"What I understand," I said, trying to keep my voice down, "is that I don't like being watched."

Kath coughed deliberately, drank some water down, then stood. "Calyx, I was hoping to find a younger hand to help me with some figures," she said aloud. "Would you mind?"

I rose, tall and composed—all mocking propriety now. Kath had always been more diplomatic than I—more than most of the other elders, for that matter. I followed her narrow back, watching the way years of familiarity had taught her to rein in the long, cumbersome elder robes she wore.

"Go to him if you wish, child," she said when we were far enough along a quiet hallway to speak. "But don't expect the rest of us not to watch."

"Why? Why can't I be just another priest?"

"Because you're not. But it's more than that. It's because you fight the world so much that everyone watches you. Our lives are narrow here, circumspect. And a little dull. You see that, don't you?"

"I see what you bring on yourselves. Your fears, your restrictions—"

"Do you never stop arguing? We wear the habits of centuries. And for centuries we've believed that in the temple the affairs of men and women should be discreet. Those of us drawn toward marriage are permitted to leave without dishonor. It's not a written law, because it never had to be. It's the observed custom."

"I've already heard this," I sighed. "More than once. Doesn't anyone understand, I'm not interested in marriage?"

"And I'm not talking about marriage. I'm speaking about the difference between our expectations and yours. Your insistence on choice is something most of us have never seen. In Aster, obedience equals survival. But you? You parade about as though you've the right to mold the world to your own needs. Whether it's fighting Hershann or denying your father or taking a lover. Who else has such expectations?"

Who else has such needs? I wanted to ask her, but in some way I knew she was right. I said, "Then I am different. But you're not the one I mean to argue with, Kath. You've been the only elder here different enough yourself to tolerate me."

Kath's wrinkled face turned up in one of her rare smiles. "What, that I've allowed you to hibernate in my tower, read my books? Didn't you guess you gave an old woman some pleasure, knowing that one other person, at least, appreciates the same dusty tomes she does?"

"Mistress Kath?" I asked suddenly. "May I ask a question?"

"Ask," she said, but her eyes narrowed.

"Have you read, or heard, maybe, anything about the power Jokjoa's tokens could hold?"

"What tokens?"

"Like Rath. Or Gamaliel, the goblet?"

Kath looked at me a long moment and I knew at once, I'd made a mistake. The pleasure had gone out of her eyes. "You'll have to ask Hershann if you want to know anything like that," she said, shaking her head. "But I doubt very much that he knows the answer."

"Do you?"

Kath stared, startled by the question. She opened her mouth to speak, stopped as if surprised herself that she had no answer. "Do you mean to leave us all with no foundation on which to stand?" she said. Then, snapping her robes across her chest, she left with a terse farewell.

I stayed behind a minute longer, waiting for my thoughts to clear, wondering what I'd said wrong. In the end, all I could decide was that I still needed to speak with Dev.

I caught him in one of the passageways just beyond the rathadaro hall. He must have stopped to see how many people were standing in the lines, waiting. I called his name, but when he turned to face me, I didn't know how to begin. Dev had the gaunt look of a man whose face had changed during a long illness; exhausted, consumed.

"Dev, I haven't seen you," I started awkwardly. "Is Syth going to be all right?"

"The elders think so," Dev nodded, but his voice sounded gray and sadly monotone. "The fever took him hard, but it's well passed now. He's eating. Walking again."

"And you? It's been hard for you as well, hasn't it? I knew you were with him. But I thought . . . Rija said you hadn't taken the fever?"

Dev squinted into the uneven light, and the shadows drew lines across his eyes that hadn't been there before. "Calyx, I'm all right. I was ill. But it was nothing. Not the same fever. There was a day there," he tried to laugh, "when Syth and I took turns at each other's sick beds. But I'm all right now." He started walking away and I ran to catch him again.

"Dev, I need to speak with you. It's about that night . . ."

"Yes, I thought you would. Avram told me about it." He looked at the ground as though he wanted to have done with this.

"Avram? What does Avram have to do with my dream?"

"I'm sorry, Calyx. I meant to tell you. I was never there that night. Syth asked me to bring some medicine from the village. I couldn't find you in time to ask, and I thought you would prefer it that way, to have Avram watch for you rather than forgo the jarak dream. I knew he'd do it for me. And it was a good idea, what with the fever that took us after that. But maybe that's why nothing happened. Calyx, it was only one dream. You needn't worry. You'll have other jarak dreams."

"What are you saying? Avram followed my dream? He was there? Not you? I never saw him. But what do you mean, nothing happened? Is that what he said? Did he tell you—"

"That you dreamt of Lethia?" Dev sighed. "Yes, he told me."

"And he also told you it wasn't a jarak dream? That doesn't make sense. How could he say I had a dream of Lethia, but it wasn't a jarak dream? It can't be both."

"Calyx, it was a long time ago. I don't remember every word he said. And really, it can't matter that much. What he did say was that you have a wild imagination, that you were convinced Edishu himself had entered your dream. To tell the truth, he was a little concerned about you, about your imagination. But come, we might as well walk. The hall's too drafty to stand here."

"Imagined?" I repeated. "He said that? Imagined?"

"Calyx, I don't like to say this. I had honestly hoped it wouldn't come to this, but you do go too far. You didn't dream of Edishu. You thought about him in your dream of Lethia. There's a difference."

"Avram said that also, didn't he? And you believe him over what you've seen with your own eyes, inside your own jarak dream?"

"No! Calyx, you're twisting his words around. It's just that—"

"He's the one twisting words. And now you say it wasn't a jarak dream. Then you accuse me of being sensume?"

"Calyx! No, certainly you're not sensume. I've watched

your dreams. It must have been something you thought about during the jarak dream. You could still be a Sumedaro someday. We could go to Hershann together! I've been thinking about it . . . Only don't, please don't tell him any of this nonsense. You'll never have what you want . . . not that way. Your dreams are powerful. More than that even—"

"But not powerful enough to have a jarak dream of Edishu?"

"Those aren't jarak dreams. They're something else. Stories you've read. I don't know."

"Dev, you're the one showed me the haven room. Was that room a story? Was the Elan Sumedaro a story? Why do you stay here and keep the Sister's fast if you believe it's all stories?"

"Of course they're not stories. But whatever we dream, Calyx, you and I, we can't compare ourselves to them. To the gods. It's enough for me to believe. To have faith. I don't require Sister Seed to lay her hand to the earth and bring summer. It's enough for me to believe summer will come. And I've told you, you already have the power to travel farther in your dreams than many priests ever reach. I know that. And you will be a Sumedaro . . . Listen. I had an idea. What if we wrote to Jared? There'll be a messenger going out as soon as the road's passable. Jared could arrange to have you take vows at a different temple. That way, Hershann—"

"It's not enough anymore, Dev." I shook my head. "Not for me."

"Father Jokjoa! What do you mean, *not enough?*"

"Dev, where do you go when you dream?"

"Always with your questions! Calyx, I go wherever I want to. The same as Syth or Avram or any other Sumedaro."

"And I go where I want to. And I dreamt of Edishu. It wasn't the first time."

"Calyx, we all have wild dreams like that. The elders do. Even those who aren't Sumedaro have some dreams—"

"Why don't you believe me? You've seen my dreams."

Dev touched my arm. "Wait," he said, taking a breath. "There's something else we can do. Not an answer for your questions, but a change of walls. How long has it been since you've been anywhere? Or ridden a horse? Or seen the trees? I have some business in the town tomorrow. I want you to ride with me. Meet some people."

"What people?"

"No one important. Just something that might interest you, a look at the world beyond Aster." Dev's eyes grew brighter again, as if he were a boy planning some mischief. "I'll tell you about it later. But for now, don't speak to anyone, especially not to your lady servant, Rija. She runs to Hershann with news of everything you do."

"Rija? No, she doesn't. She's not a servant. She's been a friend to me."

"No she hasn't, Calyx. It's her duty to befriend you. But her loyalty is to Hershann and his loyalty is to the temple. It's a closed circle here. Act as an individual and you'll never be accepted, never be a part of the circle. Rija's never stepped outside. And I step outside too often. Calyx, I wanted to tell you, I think Hershann already knows you dream."

"How could he? I never said anything—"

"He's seen your journal. Rija gave it to him."

"Rija? I don't understand. Why didn't you warn me?"

"Maybe I should have, but by the time I suspected it no longer seemed to matter, not to Hershann at least. In the beginning it would have, of course. But he knows and he hasn't mentioned it. And I don't think he will unless he can use it to his own advantage. Calyx, if you must tell Rija something, just say we're going riding. Let her think what she will. We should be back before the evening call. And please, don't wear those robes down to the village. You'll be safer if no one looks at you as a priest."

The next day, a Sister's fast, broke clear and cold, I woke, recorded my few dreams more briefly than usual, then placed the book back under my pillow. I didn't see Rija that morning and thought that perhaps Dev had been too hard on her. After all, he had no real proof who'd been rummaging in my table, reading my things. And if she had read the journal and passed it along to Hershann, maybe Dev was right, it hadn't been so terrible as I feared. Certainly, nothing had come of it.

I washed, found a suit of brown leggings and a heavy shirt I hadn't worn since the time I'd been traveling with Jared. During the fast there was little else to do but wait to leave. I'd long since sworn to honor the Sisters and keep their fast as the priests did. But I knew well enough I also did it for myself, for the vanity Hershann had wounded when he denied me the priesthood.

True, I'd fought Hershann's edict, taking for myself the outer trappings of priesthood. But there was still one corner of the temple I had not touched: the rathadaro hall with its long couches and lowered floor. At first, when Hershann's bitter warnings still caught in my throat, I had shied away from the pit, determined to follow my old habits and keep my jarak dreams to myself. But ever since Edishu had found me again, I'd begun to wonder how it would feel to follow someone else's dream. What if there was a power in the rathadaro couch that Dev hadn't thought to teach me? If not a weapon, at least a way to defend myself? I'd ask Dev today, I decided, before he approached Jared—or anyone else—with proof of my dreams.

An hour later, with an extra cloak belted over my shirt, a pair of high riding boots over dark leggings, I met Dev at the stable gateway. He helped me onto a horse he'd already saddled, paid a quick but courteous greeting to the few priests who saw us, then led the way out and down the road leading toward the town.

We rode along in silence for a while, picking our way through the half-melted slush and mud. In the open distance, the land looked uncompromising and hard, but I hardly noticed. I'd seldom left the temple since coming to Aster, seldom ridden at all. But if I felt uncomfortable or awkward, I never noticed it for the pleasure I took in the open air, the relief of so many miles traveled without walls or bells or gold-painted letters.

Several times we passed wagons or people riding alone or men and women walking briskly toward the temple. Now and again one of them called out a greeting to Dev, and he hailed them in turn, familiar with their names. The first time I thought it pleasant, the second a coincidence, after that I was genuinely perplexed. I waited for the road to quiet again, then turned to Dev. "Are you going to tell me what this is all about?"

Dev pulled on his mustache. It had grown thicker in the last year and fit his long face more handsomely than when we'd first met. Now, out in the open with the wind brushing his cheeks into color, he looked less tired, stronger than he had the day before.

"There's a house in the town," he said slowly. "It belongs

to a man I know. Lucas. He's a merchant, trades with the temple—with Briana too, so I've heard. He's a good man. I trust him." Dev nodded his head, but it seemed he was trying to convince himself as well as me. "There'll be other people there, ten, maybe even twenty. They meet together . . . to talk. We may see others from the temple. Didn't I tell you that Avram will be there? We usually ride together, but I told him to go on ahead this time. And you need to remember, if you speak to any of our priests, don't use their names. They'll ask me to make certain you've agreed."

"To what? Why the shroud of secrecy?"

Dev stared ahead. "They're hungry, Calyx. And there's been sickness this year, more than what you've seen and heard about at the temple. Much more. Hardly a person in Aster town hasn't lost a child or a cousin in the last year. Sunder's hand is choking the land, they say. Some in the temple say it also. Illness and a barren world. As if the gods had forgotten us as we've forgotten them."

"Hershann doesn't think we've forgotten the gods."

Dev shook his head. "And I don't believe it, either. Calyx, this temple is my life. Everything I've ever wanted; a life of devotion to my jarak dreams, listening to the Sister's footsteps, the stars—there in my dreams—"

"And have you found them?"

"It isn't so simple—"

"But it should be. Ceena always said the truth is there, unchanging. It's only our eyes that have closed out the light. There was a truth here once. I was taught what to believe, to worship, the same as you. But what the priests do—what we do—in the temple, these sanctimonious repetitions. Year in and year out. How would anyone really know if the gods have forsaken us? What we do anymore it doesn't mean anything."

"Enough!" Dev raised his hand in protest. "The only thing I really fear is that you might be right. But we've talked about this endless, endless times. You want answers and I don't have them. You raise a hundred new questions while I'm still grappling with the first. For now let's just agree that these meetings are secret because Hershann has no sense of anything outside Aster's guarded walls. This is more than just 'hungry.' These people are desperate. They need help." Dev stopped, lowered his voice. "There's been some talk of banding together, forming a group to petition Briana—"

"Briana?" I tried to see Dev's eyes. "What does Briana have to do with Aster town? Why not go to Korinna in Hillstor Valley, or Lord Shimoan? They're much closer."

"They've thought of that. But Korinna isn't much better off, and they're unsure of Shimoan's allegiance. Avram seems to think they can reason with Morell. He supports the Sumedaro—"

"He believes wrongly!" I insisted. "My father doesn't support the Sumedaro. He controls them, uses them for his own interests. Lakotah's elders don't move without his word, don't speak a dream he hasn't examined first and approved. Where did Avram hear this? And where do you think my skepticism comes from if not because I've seen what use he makes of your precious Sumedaro truths?"

"Calyx, please! Listen. And remember, these people have no idea who you are. To them you're a guest in the temple, worth more for any jarak tricks you might have than anything. You're safest if you keep it that way. They're not your lost Silkiyam looking for havens in every garden path. They're not raiders. Just people together. We're protected where Hershann's word is still feared enough. But without food and support from the towns, the temples could be starved out also."

"And these meetings. Hershann doesn't know about them?"

"Some of it, yes. Hershann would never allow us complete freedom. He has no use for these people other than the coins they pay for the dreamwatch. He wants only to shut himself away, hide in the past. But Calyx, I didn't choose to become a Sumedaro to ignore the rest of the world. I can't live that way.

"Several of us have been coming here through the winter. In secret. And we talk. Most of these people believe the cold is the gods' doing, Sunder's death magic maybe. They don't claim to know. But they think it's past time for a sign. They talk of the Elan Sumedaro as though they're waiting for him to come again."

This time Dev's words struck hard. The Elan Sumedaro. And Edishu in my dreams. Wherever I turned, those names were linked together. At least these people weren't Sumedaros—maybe they'd have something new to say. In the meantime, my lips were dry, my mouth ill-tasting. I prodded my horse to a faster pace, wishing this day hadn't come on a Sister's fast. Fasting always made me feel anxious and more than a little confused. The hunger I'd tried to forget had grown with its own insistence, and now I tried ignoring it, turning my thoughts to the curving road and the horse's steady gait.

Aster town had been built in what must have once seemed a promising site: a level valley between a series of long, gently sloping hills to the north and a river winding to the south. The town was smaller than Briana, which wasn't surprising since Briana was central to Morell's territories while this was only a single town grown up about the temple. Aster was cleaner, though, with wider streets and more land around each home. But when I looked closer, I saw that the houses were in need of repair, and much of the land lay fallow and hard. Several people passed us as we rode through, but this time no one called a greeting.

"That house belongs to the Orley family." Dev pointed out a large, rambling building. "You won't be meeting them tonight, but they're good people. And back at the end of that street is old Barrow's. In better times he was a merchant. Now he stays mostly to himself. He's a friend of mine, though. You can trust him. We turn here, to the stable master's house. Down this lane."

We dismounted and brought our horses around the back of a wide, steeply roofed building that looked as much stable as house. Dev opened the door on a large entry room, and at once we were assaulted with a wall of noise and people. I watched from behind Dev's shoulder, wondering what I was doing here. The room was crowded with Aster townsfolk. They filled every corner and scrap of space, drinking, eating, talking all at once. I shook my head, trying to clear my sight while the long ride, the arguing, the lack of food, all roiled inside of me.

What did any of these people and their fears have to do with me? I was a librarian, a clerk, a fool in a house of priests, anything but what these people needed. I would have jumped to my horse just then if I'd the chance, but someone turned into the path behind us, blocking a quiet retreat.

A white-haired man, his long beard reaching nearly to his buckle, appeared at the door beside us. "So you've come, priest!" He slapped Dev solidly on his shoulder. "Well and good! We've been waiting on you. And who's this you've brought? A wife?" The man leered at me through his beard, and though in the temple I might have argued, here I turned away.

Dev forced a laugh. "No," he said. "Only a guest."

The man looked at me, his eyes twinkling. "Be welcome then, lady," he said. "We've little to offer except words, but that you'll have in plenty."

"Here," Dev whispered as we made our way farther in. "That's Jains over there against the wall. Watch talking to him. He's council head of the town and has no love for Aster temple. Thinks we're bleeding his land."

Dev started toward a smaller, well-furnished room with the odor of oiled veneers and leather books. The smell was pleasing, familiar, and I would have gone in, but Dev stopped and turned back around. I craned my neck to see into the far corner and found Avram sitting on a makeshift rathadaro couch, a woman's hands tucked securely inside his.

"Shh!" Dev warned. "Be quiet. Let's go."

"Why is he speaking their dreams here?"

Dev hurried me away. "They can't afford Hershann's tithe anymore. And we—the priests—we talked about it, felt it would be wrong to deny them what little help a Sumedaro has to offer. Besides, there's no right or wrong to it. Avram is a priest. These people need to be shriven of their dreams. He'd no more think of refusing them than I."

I wanted to ask more, to try to understand how all this had been going on without my hearing of it. But a tall man walked up and greeted Dev loudly. "Sister's eve, priest," he said.

"Braddock! Greetings! Any news from Shimoan's people? Have your sons returned yet?"

"No, sir. Nothing yet," Braddock shook his head. "It's a slow time of year for travel. But we're waiting. Though I did hear there was news from the Elianor Hills, word of dreams there as well. And you've been kept busy yourself seems like, sir?"

Dev laughed. "Syth tells me he doesn't know when he's seen anything like it before. There's hardly enough of us to hold the rathadaro watch. Twenty people yesterday, and nearly half of them with the same dream. A year ago this time it was half that, two years back it would have taken a week for that many people to come with a dream, any dream at all."

"What's this?" I asked. I'd known that more people than usual were bringing dreams to Aster. But that it was happening across the northlands? Had he said that nearly half their dreams were the same? How could that be? And what dream? "Where do the dreams come from?" I asked.

"No one knows," Dev shrugged.

"I thought she was from the temple," the man—Braddock —glared down at me. "Doesn't she read dreams?" he asked, his smile changing with suspicion. He was an odd looking man with deep jowls under his cheeks and a chin that sat heavily atop his chest. Uneasily, I remembered that in Briana a man of his size would have been searched for weapons before entering my father's halls.

"Her? No, no," Dev laughed as he spoke. "She keeps herself busy. She works in the libraries, does our copying."

"S'at right? Well, I suppose I'm not one to be asking what you priests do year round in your towers. That's your affair, I suppose. Now the dreamwatch. There's something we all share in. What the gods do in Kuoshana lays on all of us here on earth."

"This dream," I asked again. "What is it?"

"Well, that's the thing of it, lady. It's like it wasn't our dream at all. Someone else's jarak dream, more like, that we all wandered into. I've had one myself, Jains there, and Hessy—she's my wife—she's dreamed something of the sort too. There's war in it, battles, fighting usually. Some say they saw Silkiyam people. If that were possible. Gods fighting among themselves. Things like that. Dev here says he's going to stand the watch on my dream soon's we have the chance. But come along. Orley lays a fine table, but all in all, what you don't help yourself to now won't be there later, not with that mutton and bread waiting."

"Thank you," Dev said. "I'll take a drink, if you don't mind. But not dinner. I keep the Sister's fast. Calyx might, though."

"No! You go ahead," I told Braddock, then, glaring at Dev, I added, "I may not be a priest, but I've chosen to dwell among them."

Braddock shrugged his shoulders, then pulled Dev away toward a center table. The aroma of heady wines and the sweet warmth of bread twisted at my stomach. My hands were shaking. Perhaps I should have eaten, I thought. The ride had proved far more taxing than any fast day in the temple. I hadn't been used to the pace, to the wind, to a houseful of new, demanding faces. And wasn't there the return journey still to be made?

I found a corner wall to lean against and closed my eyes, hoping for a moment's quiet.

"A song! A song!" Braddock called, and from somewhere a small, round-bellied lute appeared and was passed from hand to hand until it came to rest in Dev's lap. Someone pushed a chair under him and he took it, shifting the lute to his arm. Dev plucked a note and tightened one of the strings till he was satisfied with its pitch. Then he raised his face to smile at me, and all I could think of was the first time we had met, when he never said a word that didn't leap for joy of its own accord.

Micah had been that way once for me. And he and I had gone on to do more than just smile at each other. Yet touching Micah had been deliberate, with nothing as alive as this one small smile of Dev's or the sudden touch of his hand on mine. Micah had always been more brother to me than anything. What we had done, what I had pushed him to do that day at the cliff tree, wasn't love. There was scarcely any desire in it. I understood that now. It had been a petty act meant more to hurt Morell than anything. It would never be more.

Dev started singing, and his voice was deep and soft, richer than I would have thought possible out of his narrow chest. He chose one of the verses of the Elan Sumedaro I had read recently, a Kareil song—as most of the holiest were. Yet now, hearing the verses aloud in a voice as familiar to me as the rising and falling of my own breath, the words came alive and took on new meaning:

Armed with tokens
Of Jokjoa, thus he rides
Thus he dies.
Elan Sumedaro, through
the skies thus he rides.
He is girdled with
Hajthaele, sacred weapons
of the god.
Bound to fight against

the Night, blind Edishu
seeking life.
Thus he rides.

Through the havens
And the gateways, thus he dreams
Thus he dreams.
You who are Jokjoa's daughters,
Sunder, Eclipse, Sister Seed
Grant him strength
against the darkness
Hear his song of
Jarak need!

Elan Sumedaro, son of skyworld,
son of earth,
With your touch upon our
forehead, thus you rid
the land of grief.
With your tokens from the
Father, Bow of strife
Bracelet. Knife.
With your son
Kareil, the white one,
Send Edishu into
nightmare, raze the
spectre of our fear
Thus he rides.

And there it was, as always. Jokjoa's tokens. The ones
Edishu had demanded that I bring. And these shared dreams
Braddock had just mentioned, they sounded so similar to
mine. Gods and battles, that's what he'd said. And Dev,
knowing of the other dreams must have recognized mine in
theirs. Which could be why he hadn't felt as concerned as I
did.

Except that no matter who else had a dream similar to
mine, as far as I knew, no one else was being attacked. No
one else had to defend themselves against his next attack.
Edishu had said I was a fool to meet him unarmed, and
there was a truth I needed to face. Till now I'd been running
away from him, fleeing back through my jarak dreams to
safety. But what else could I do? It was one thing to sing

about the Elan Sumedaro's weapons, another to find them
and unlock their secrets.

But was there anything else to those shared dreams Braddock had mentioned? What if there was a power to them
that Dev hadn't thought to teach me, something the Sumedaro
took for granted during the dreamwatch? What if there was
something I could gain, another way to protect myself—or
hide?

Dev had finished with his singing. A few of the men
gathered close about him, and I was left standing alone,
watching. Just then Avram caught my eye. He started
toward me, making his way past a close knot centered
around the food trays, but I didn't care to speak with him.
There was a door to my side and I turned toward it, but I
heard Av's voice again, much louder this time, and I stopped
to listen.

He was standing at the apex of a small crowd now, waving
his arms, talking louder and far more eloquently than I'd
ever heard him before.

A woman called out, her voice filled with concern. "If
they strike down our hopes for vengeance, where will we
go?"

"Tell me first what anger will gain you?" Avram turned
to the crowd, whispering just softly enough they had to
quiet their own voices to hear him. "Will it send winter back
to Sunder's blackened skies? I say you move as a whole,
with anger at your back perhaps but with unity in your
heart." Avram stopped for just a moment, glancing around
the room till his gaze found mine, smiled, then moved on.
"Morell's armies could strike you down in one brief morning the way you are now. Unarmed. Without a captain. But
wait. Strengthen your forces. Look to your neighbors. You're
not alone. Then, when you've enough numbers, strike! Morell
will fall and his lands with him, and your claim will be heard
across the land . . ."

Strike Morell? But Dev had said petition him for help,
not move against him. Confused, I pushed toward Dev.
What was Avram talking about? Strike Morell? Arm themselves against Briana? But Aster was so far north of Briana.
Nobody could accept such a plan, surely.

A heavyset man blocked my way. He was talking loudly,
raising a wineskin in the air as he answered Avram's call. I

tried to push past him, but he didn't notice me, wouldn't move.

The room was too hot, the air thick, rancid with odors.

"Dev?" I called, and my voice seemed to grow weak even as I spoke. But he must have heard me because the next thing I knew, he was there, reaching out, just as I thought my legs would no longer hold me upright. "Take me home," I whispered. "I can't stay here."

"No, of course not. It's all right. I'm sorry, I should have known not to bring you. You didn't need to hear that. Avram doesn't mean anything. He's just trying to appease them." Dev murmured a few hasty apologies to Orley and Jains, then with one arm firmly clasped to my shoulders, he steered us toward the door.

Outside in the air, I felt stronger. Dev had the good sense not to bother me with questions, and when he offered me a hand up onto my horse, I took it.

He checked our horses' tack, then jumped to his own mount. We started out at a quiet walk, passing through the same streets we'd come in on. The air brought strength, reviving me. I waited, but I knew what I was going to say. Everywhere I went, I was unarmed and defenseless; against Hershann and his priests, against Avram and these townsfolk, and most of all against Edishu. Except for one final lesson, Dev had taught me everything the Sumedaro had to offer. And it had not been enough. I needed more. Even here, at this unexpected meeting, I had needed more.

We rode on in silence, Dev glancing at me now and again with concern on his face. Not for a good hour, though, till the cool air had cleared my thoughts and the evening light drew a hatchwork of shadows over the road did I turn to him. "I have to find a way into the rathadaro hall," I said. "You've never let me watch a dream, and it's time. I want to speak a jarak dream."

Dev's smile faded. "I shouldn't have brought you here." He shook his head. "But even so, Calyx, there's nothing to entering a dream you haven't already done—and more."

I glared back at him. "No! There's more to it. There has to be. I want to know what these people are dreaming. What it is they're sharing. Where it comes from."

"If this is about Avram, I'm sorry. I didn't realize he'd go that far, inciting them against Morell. It won't work, of course, they're not an army. They don't know how to move as a group, unarmed. No supplies. Briana's far enough away—it's meaningless, if that's what has you worried—"

"No, it's not that. It's the dreamwatch. You do it, the other priests do it. If you tell me that I'm a powerful jarak dreamer, why won't you let me watch someone's dream?"

"You could watch my dream," Dev offered. "It would be the same thing. But Calyx, watching a dream is a simple thing, really. No secrets. No miracles—"

"No, I want to stand the watch for one of these dreams Braddock mentioned, those shared dreams."

"And what if Hershann walks in? Anyone could. Aren't you the one who said you still want to keep your dreams a secret?"

"Not anymore," I said, surprising myself with the surety of it. "Hershann doesn't matter. I've thought about it. I have to learn more, that's all. You heard those people in there. Were their dreams so very different from mine? Perhaps if I witnessed someone else's dream, something else, new, it would come clear."

Dev clicked his reins to a faster pace, and I let the distance between us widen a bit. I didn't have to ask again, he knew what I wanted. It only remained for him to decide what he would do. The road was little more than a rut of wet snow mixed with mud here. Not deep or white and clean, the way the snow lay through less traveled areas, and not the full, dark mud that comes welcomed in spring when the earth is a flood of runoff and new rain, and green shoots vie for a look at the sun.

Spring. Summer. It all seemed so distant, a memory out of childhood. Could it be true what the townsfolk were saying? That the gods had forsaken both the land and the people? That they'd fallen into the web of their own dreams and would not waken? It could explain so many things—the winter, Edishu's return. If only I could sit on the rathadaro couch, compare my dream with someone else's. Maybe then I would understand.

Around and around my thoughts spired, waiting, till at last Dev slowed his horse to a walk and I rode up alongside him again.

"All right." He took a breath. "Hershann isn't always about. And not too many priests pay attention to that hall if they aren't assigned the watch themselves. We'll find a way in."

I smiled my thanks, but didn't feel the need to speak. After that the monotony of the ride lulled me into sleep. Sometime during the ride Dev threw a second cloak gently over my shoulder, and took my horse's reins to lead us forward.

Next thing I knew, Aster temple lay before us, a dark crowd of ravens circling near its towers overhead, gates open wide to the biting morning air. We made a quiet entry, riding in unnoticed past the tattered fragments of the beggars' camps.

"Dev?" I started.

"Your choice," he said without waiting for the question. "Tomorrow morning or now. It's late, but sometimes it happens that people come just the same, then stay till the morning rather than make the return trip out at night. Someone will be there."

"Now," I said, steadying my hands in front of me. "It has to be now."

11

Standing in the rathadaro hall that night with Dev, I found a grace Lakotah had never held for me, a gentle hub of light that anchored itself over the dugout couch, and silence, sweet, sweet silence, to ease away my hunger and fears. Here at last I might find the one room in a Sumedaro temple to equal the haven room, a room filled with the power and force of a jarak dream. Power enough to rival Edishu's dream.

Awed, I bowed my head.

For the first time I saw Aster through different eyes—not the frustrated war she carried on against cold and death, but an ancient hymn to the world. These four walls were not empty. No jarak house could ever be empty. I saw Aster for what she was meant to be, and my heart filled with faith. Here at last I might find a home to make my own, a place the gods might truly dwell. Were I to be allowed to stand here as a priest of the watch, to become that point of light through which the gods channeled their dreams, then never again would I mock the temple's fire altar, never would I doubt the sanctity of this room.

Dev pointed to the farthest of three rooms, each below ground level. I followed behind him, climbing down the few steps to the couch, my eye pleased at the graceful way it wrapped around three walls of the room, leaving an open channel in the center. It may have been the fresh spruce bows scattered on the floor, or a trick of the cooler air in the room, but with each step it seemed as if the winds I'd felt sweeping through the haven below Aster's floors stirred again and filled that room with its power.

Three years had gone by while I waited for this day, for the chance to learn the Sumedaro dreamwatch. Surely here I would find the true heart of the Sumedaro's lore. My heart prayed. Let it be that the Sumedaro had not been forsaken by the gods, had not forgotten the older ways of the clans and the Sisters who ruled us all. Let me become a part of their teaching, a jarak dreamer, a Sumedaro.

Now perhaps I would learn the safest road to follow, a path wherein I might hide from Edishu's hatred. Others came here, brought their dreams, so similar to mine. Others must have known fear and confusion also.

Perhaps I could see Kuoshana in this room as well, find proof that skyworld yet watched over us, a world adjacent to ours as two rooms in a house are connected through a passageway, with doors to enter and leave—here is a door which must be opened, as a hand flexes to open a latch, so we must flex the muscle which permits us to enter Kuoshana. So I would have help against Edishu.

Yet some failed. Sensume they became, unable to bridge the path that separates earth from skyworld, unable to bring the memory of another's dream back to the light of day. No priest could be a full Sumedaro unless they held the dreamwatch. It was not possible.

I must not fail.

A young woman—a girl, she couldn't have been much older than I—was already seated on a mound of rose-colored cushions. She stared at the ground shyly, if that was possible, dressed as she was. I had not seen anyone like her since my sister had sat beside me in Briana. She had circles of black kohl painted around her eyelids and lips as red as the dawn. Still, under it all she was pretty, with a clean skin that made me want to smile in spite of the dress clinging so tightly around her narrow waist. Part of me was jealous—it was true. Mirjam's teasing about my plain face and straight body were never as far away as I would have liked. But I shook the memories away and looked at her instead as though we were dreamers equal before Jokjoa.

"Calyx, this is Sherra, from Aster town. She comes here often," Dev said, his voice steady, as if he'd dealt with his misgivings about coming here and banished them. "Sherra, this is Calyx's first dreamwatch. You understand that she'll enter your dream with me? She'll be present watching your dream. Are you still agreed?"

"Yes, sir. Hello, Calyx," the girl answered with an open smile. She looked at me, but only briefly, and I wondered if she thought it only proper for a priest to be as plain-faced as I.

She sat immediately on my left, her long, colorful skirts floating down over her legs, leaving only the tips of her boots showing. But she didn't bother to fuss and arrange her skirts as Mirjam would have, smoothing the ruffles and making sure I noticed how careful she was. She was an odd mixture, with her face painted red and black, picking at her fingernails like a girl, and under it all an aching tiredness that showed the truth of how hard she must work and how much hunger know. The heavy coat bundled behind her looked too large by far to fit her small frame, more like it belonged to some elder brother or father who'd loaned it to her for the trip from Aster town.

"Sherra, can you tell me"—I leaned forward—"is your dream one of the shared ones?"

She blushed, looked down again at her hands. "No, not that," she said. "It's my own."

For a moment I didn't breathe, but sat there as if I hadn't heard correctly. But then I shook my head, warning myself.

Dev saw my disappointment. "Calyx," he whispered, putting his hand to my shoulder, "it was the dreamwatch you wanted, not the dream. It doesn't matter. Now, listen—" He cleared his throat, started again. "For this dreamwatch, Calyx, you must follow closely. Sherra's dreams are rich and colorful. She's a good one to learn with. And she remembers easily, putting up none of the blocks some people try. Now, take my hands, both of you. Are you comfortable? Good.

"Close your eyes and listen to my voice. The dreamwatch technique is not difficult. Either you are able to achieve the state or you're not. For three years, Calyx, you've been learning to find your own dreams, to choose them and travel wherever you wish, then waken once more in your own bed. There is no other lesson in the Sumedaro apprenticeship than honing this blade. Sherra's hand is the door to her dream. For this first time, I'll help you turn the latch so the door swings more freely. But you must be the key to that door. All you need do this first time is open it far enough to look inside and tell us what you see. You need not cross the threshold. Do you understand? Calyx? Can you hear me?"

"Yes, I hear you," I answered, but already Sherra's touch was working its spell on me, pulling me forward, away from that room. Dev's voice sounded thin and unfamiliar. The disappointment I'd felt hearing that Sherra's dream was not a shared one receded, forgotten as layer after layer of new, rich complexities opened before me.

"Just listen, Calyx, and do exactly as I say. Sherra, think of your dream now. Remember it as best you can and let no other thought cross into your awareness.

"Calyx, you must narrow your vision until you see a long tunnel forming in the darkness before you. If there is no tunnel, imagine it. Create it out of the colors in the dark spaces. Build it long and narrow. Sherra is at the far end of the tunnel and you are linked by touch. Narrow your vision closer and closer. Forget anything else but Sherra's hand in yours and the tunnel you will walk through to her dream. Now, slowly, slowly, picture yourself entering that tunnel. Walking. Closing the gap that separates you from her. The tunnel is god-hallowed, a sacred place, older than the earth itself. It is the bridge Elan Sumedaro walked to Kuoshana, lit by the thousand stars of Oreill's night. Walking it, you are protected by the gods. There is no danger. No fear. Only this long, safe road leading to Sherra's dream. You can reach the end of the tunnel now. Reach out your hand. Can you see the end of the tunnel? Imagine it growing lighter now, brighter and brighter, like the holy band of stars surrounding the night. We are the stars unstrung on heaven's night. We are the black of night that cradles the stars, a pillow to the sleeping god's head. Where the gods rest, there shall we find our dreams. Give of yourself that you may be their pillow. Cushion their heads. Receive the jarak dream.

"Now, open the door. Slowly. Slowly. I'll be with you. Open the door and look inside Sherra's dream."

I remember closing my eyes. And Sherra's touch and Dev's, all tied to me like a line of string. But Dev's voice began changing and the words I couldn't understand, couldn't separate her touch from his voice from my touch.

Dev's voice grew higher, lighter, and as happy as any I'd ever heard. But it was my throat the voice was coming from, my mouth, not his at all.

"Farlin," I called out. "Farlin, is that you?" I had on my prettiest dress, the new one with the bright colors. Farlin would like that, I thought. And I did so want him to be happy. He had spent so much time with that Roshanna girl, what was her name? Oh! It didn't matter. But I wanted him to like me. Not her. I had told him I would meet him out here, in the trees to the north side of my father's pasture. Farlin would know where. After all, wasn't he always the one telling me it would be all right?

And now the wind died down and the sun was warm and sweet on my arms and I felt so happy. "Farlin," I called again, loud as I dared.

"Sherra, over here. I knew you'd come." I heard Farlin's warm laughter.

He was teasing me. At first I couldn't find him and I wandered around the open glade, not daring to go too close into the thicker trees. But then he whistled from behind a huge old aspen and popped out his head and smiled.

I walked right up to him. I knew I looked pretty, just like he wanted me to. I had on honeysuckle scent and my eyes were colored too.

"Sherra, you're beautiful," he said. And he kissed me. Before I could say anything, he kissed me. He had his lips half open and he pressed his mouth over mine, so warm and sweet and close. I felt lost in his kisses. And it went on and on and on. He picked me up, right up off the ground, and carried me over to a bed of moss he'd made up.

*   *   *

"Calyx? Calyx, can you hear me?"

"You're a fool, Dev! You should never have tried this without telling me. And I don't want to know what little trade she offered you for this joke. Or what in Eclipse's name possessed you to bring her to Orley's house. She's not to be trusted. I've told you that and still you act as though it doesn't matter who she is. Morell's daughter! And you go bringing her right into Orley's house."

He was so funny. Farlin laughed and called my name. He held me around my waist and he kissed me again. "Sherra, you're beautiful," he said. And he kissed me. He had his lips half open and he pressed his mouth over mine, so warm and sweet and close. I felt lost in his kisses. And it went on and on and on. He picked me up, right up off the ground and carried me over to a bed of moss he had made up.

"Calyx, you've got to wake up. Avram, bring some wine, will you? Maybe if we sit her up again, we'll get her to drink."

"We haven't time! Didn't you tell me you were watching the dream with her? What happened? Why did you let go? Eclipse alone knows what she's seeing! And send that girl home before she asks too many questions. There'll be trouble for you over this one, Dev. More than the trouble you'll have when Hershann finds out what you've taught her."

"As though you had no part in it? Or was that some other priest there today? Inciting against Morell! As if that would help . . . What were you thinking, Av? You knew she was there. What did you want, to get her attention?"

"If it's me you're worried about, don't be. I wouldn't want her. Wouldn't want eyes like that watching me in the dark. But you now, I keep asking myself why you've taken to her so? Or is that why you don't want me speaking against Morell? You wouldn't mind a small grant of his landholdings, would you?"

"For once, will you just be quiet, Av? I don't want to hear it."

"Farlin, you're so nice to me," I said.

"I want to be more than just nice to you," he said. His eyes were the color of the blue sky at sunset, bright, teasing.

*   *   *

"Calyx? Can you sit up? Can you hear me? Avram, look. I think her eyes moved."

I walked right up to Farlin. I knew I looked pretty, just like he wanted me to. I had on honeysuckle scent and my eyes were colored too.

"Sherra, you're beautiful," he said. And he kissed me. Before I could say anything, he kissed me. He had his lips half open and he pressed his mouth over mine, so warm and sweet and close. I felt lost in his kisses. And it went on and on and on. He picked me up, right up off the ground and carried me over to a bed of moss he had made up.

He was so funny. Farlin laughed and called my name. He held my waist and he kissed me again.

"Calyx? Calyx? You've got to open your eyes. You're here, in Aster. It's Dev. Dev and Avram."

"Shake her, Dev. Hold her shoulders and shake her. Damn it all, what could have gone wrong with an ordinary dreamwatch? Jokjoa's night! We've got to get her to her room."

"You're beautiful," he said. And he kissed me. Before I could say anything, he kissed me.

He had his lips half open . . .

And he pressed . . .

And I felt lost . . .

No. Something was wrong . . . changed . . . different. "Who are you? Where's my friend? You're not Farlin!"

"No more than you are that pretty little child."

"I don't know what you're talking about. You weren't here before. What do you want?"

"Only to live. To be alive. To walk. To talk. To touch you the way you wanted Farlin to touch you—"

"No! That's not the answer! You're lying. But I don't know why. What do you want?"

"You are beautiful now, did you know that? Isn't this what you wanted? To look this way? Your skin so fair, your neck long and sweet. Curving—"

"Don't touch me."

"But you liked it. You wanted him. We can be Sherra and Farlin if you like. You let him kiss you. I could make it feel the same . . . or better. Whatever it is you want. It took me so long to find you. You should not have done that, you know, closed yourself off to me that way. But you can't hide anymore. You don't know how . . . And there's no reason. I can change this face if there's another you like better."

"Better than what? Who are you?"

"Shall I remind you with my other face? Would you like that? But I am disappointed. To have been forgotten! How long ago was it, by your reckoning? A breath, a lifetime, while I searched for you? I want you, you know. Need you . . . My torch. My guide. My vehicle. To carry me to earth. And I will have you, you and all the rest of the world. Willingly. You will beg me to take your body, and not just like this, like two copulating animals, but absolutely, irrevocably. You will be mine. There is nowhere you can hide now. Nowhere you can run."

"Edishu. Yes, I know you. But you're wrong. I've learnt that I can fight you now. You'll never have me. Not like Lethia."

"Never? You know nothing of this word, *never!* Shall I tell you what the Elan Sumedaros thought? There was more than one, of course. Like a line of wooden toys, bending backward through time. Shall I tell you what end they met at my hands? What they learned that this word *never* truly means? Or do you prefer we complete the ritual here, now? Come, take my hand. I give you the same offer I have always made: Power! Riches! The pearls of Oreill's night and the knowledge to use them. And for myself, one touch, only one. A simple joining. Just the one small yes, and it will be done!"

"You can't hurt me this time. You aren't carrying the ring, are you?"

"I have other weapons. I can strike you down to dust—"

"Then why couldn't you raise the ring without Lethia? I think you're lying. You can't strike me. Weapon to weapon, you said, and this time you have none."

"Neither do you."

"That's not true. Look at me. I will not fall down before you as I did in Gleavon Keep. I've grown. Changed."

"You're wrong. You come less than naked here before me."

"No, I am Sumedaro. I have sat the rathadaro watch. I am jarak. I am dreamwatcher."

"Do you want me to show you what you are?"

"I am rathadaro."

"You are nothing."

"It's not true. I have sat the watch—"

"And the watch is nothing. The Sumedaro are nothing. Do you know how many times they have given me what I wanted? Given until now, they've forgotten what they possessed, forgotten there ever was a time when they walked the night as freely as they now walk the day? The Sumedaro gave their strength away. Eons ago. As shall the others. Till there is no clan left on earth who knows how to wield that power save me, the one dreamer."

"No, it's not true. There must be power to the Sumedaro."

"Then strike me. Now. Here. I bare my chest to you. Take up an arrow, a dagger. Strike. What are you waiting for?"

"No, I've another weapon. You just told me yourself. You can't touch me unless I will it. And I won't. Never."

"Never? You use that word so lightly. But listen, I enjoy the game. The hunt. Scenting you out. If I catch you without your consent, do you know what happens?"

"I don't want to know."

"Nonetheless, I shall tell you. Because it's important for you to understand. Have you ever seen insects together, how they mate, then die? One devouring the other. I would do that with you. I can put Sherra's face on one insect. This face that pleases you so much I could put on another. You could die quickly, if you like. Or you could have me willingly. In the end it will all be the same."

"No! Get out! I don't believe you! I don't know what you're talking about. Don't touch me! Don't touch me!"

"What was that? What did she say?"

"I'm not sure. Something from the dream. Calyx! Calyx! Wake up!"

"No . . . Don't touch me . . . Wha's happen' . . . ?" I sprang upright. I was in my bed in Aster. But the pasture, it was gone . . .

Someone must have carried me to my bed, covered me with blankets, but I couldn't see anybody. "Head hurts . . . Wha' happened?" I tried to speak, but my mouth, the words, nothing was right. "Did I fall? Wherth' Sherra?"

Through half-open eyes I found the hearth in the opposite walls. A fire burned against the grate, rising, flickering.

From the heart of the fire two blood-red eyes bore into me, warning, *"You will be mine! There is nowhere you can hide!"*

"Stop it!" I screamed, covered my ears with my hands to drown out the voice. "You're a dream, a dream. You don't want me."

"Calyx! Stop shouting. There's no one here. Who were you talking to? Dev, what did she say? Did you hear her?"

"No. Are you all right, Calyx?"

Dev touched my forehead lightly. I looked up, half afraid the eyes I'd find would not be his. "Calyx, can you tell us what happened?"

"I don't know. I was in the rathadaro hall with you and that girl, Sherra. I was going to watch her dream. But Dev, you were there. Didn't you see what happened? Was that her dream?"

"I don't know what I saw." Dev hesitated, his mouth drawn into a tight line. "Why don't you tell us what happened?"

"You're supposed to tell me! Where did I go? I was with you. Dev, tell me, I have to know, was that her dream I watched?"

"I'm sorry, Calyx." Dev turned away. "I didn't mean to hurt you. I never should have allowed it."

Avram glared down at me. "You watched Sherra's dream. That's all that happened. You just weren't ready for it . . . Dev, I told you not to try anything like this. Not without telling me."

"Avram, please, we don't need to argue anymore. It's over. And I already said I was sorry. But Calyx"—Dev came and sat at the edge of the bed—"it was Sherra's dream," he said. "It must have been. But we sent her home hours ago. Can you tell us please what happened?"

"Make her tell us what she dreamt."

"Avram, she isn't well. She needs time. Just wait. I'll ask. Calyx, you were lost in Sherra's dream. That's not supposed to happen. It's dangerous. You were only supposed to look inside her dream to see if you could find her, then return. But you went further."

"There is something I remember, a friend. She had a husband, a lover. They were together."

"Sherra said you changed the dream, Calyx. Do you know what she meant by that?"

Avram interrupted. "There's no such thing as 'going further.' Sherra's lying! That's all."

"Avram! Enough!" Abruptly, Dev crossed to the hearth, stood there, his arms braced against the mantel. "Sherra's too young to know what happened. And Calyx isn't a Sumedaro. The Sisters know—she can't shape dreams. No one can."

"Dev?" I said, keeping my voice calm. "Please, I need to rest. Everything I know, I've told you. Maybe it's true that Sherra's dream changed. But if what you said was true, that I was lost in the dream, trapped, then don't you see? I couldn't know anything more about it than she does. But I'm tired now. I just want to be left alone to sleep. Avram? I'm asking you to leave."

"We'll go, then," Dev agreed. "But I'm coming back with something to help give you strength. Maybe that's half the trouble. You've fasted too long and I'm to blame."

"Don't say that. None of this is your fault." I spoke urgently, and he turned around, looked at me. There was fear in his eyes. Fear and something else I wasn't sure of. "But some broth would be fine," I said. "Later . . . After I've slept."

They let themselves out of the room and closed the heavy doors as I'd asked, fixing the latch so it would lock from the inside. I didn't want to see anyone else. Not Rija. Not Dev, at least not so soon. The moment the bar slipped into place, I stole back to my desk in the outer room.

I hurried to write the dream down, to record it properly in my journal before I forgot any of the details. No matter what lies I'd told Dev and Avram, I remembered all too well the man who'd taken Farlin's place. Let Edishu wear whatever mask he liked—he could not disguise the darkness of those eyes.

I sat down, started looking for my pen before I realized that anything had happened. My table was completely disheveled. Someone had gone through my papers, books, everything. Not Dev, I thought, shaking my head. He wouldn't be interested in my letters. And my journal he saw often enough. But Avram had been the only other person here, and I couldn't imagine there was anything of value here for him.

I raised the side catch to flip the drawer forward. The journal was gone.

Quickly I ran back to my bed, tore back the thick quilts. Sometimes I fell asleep again after I'd written down a dream. But no, it wasn't there! Under the pillows? That was possible. I picked them up, searching. The journal was gone.

12

After the incident with the dreamwatch, the days passed grudgingly by. Routine set in. Days, I copied long manuscripts for Kath, preferring the company of cold tower walls and silent books than of people. Without two words passing between us, Avram and I seemed to agree it was better we saw little of each other. And Dev, whose friendship mattered most, seemed to be avoiding me.

Nor was my journal found, though I'd moved beyond the shock of having it stolen. Somehow it no longer mattered as much as it would have a year earlier. Dev and I ended our secret meetings and I no longer recorded my jarak dreams. It was almost as if after sitting for the dreamwatch, the time had come to give up pretenses. I had long since learned everything Dev had to teach. My dreams flowed cool and swift and strong, with a touch of power—and danger—we both knew, Dev couldn't hope to match.

And always I lived with one fear: that Edishu would return to fight me. And there was nothing the Sumedaro priests knew that would help me when he came.

I was alone in the library tower one night when Kath found me curled into a knot the way a child sleeps, hands and feet askew, too tired to care or remember about pillows or blankets.

"Asleep again, Calyx?" She stood over my chair, her long face drawn into a frown. "Haven't you left all day?"

Startled, I jumped up, tugged my shirt into place. Kath had caught me asleep in the library before, and while she never ordered me away, neither did she pat me on the back with approval. "I finished my work this afternoon," I said. "The copies are dried on the table. And—oh, yes, we need more of the red ocher. We're down to the bottom and the color's gone too thick."

"That was hours ago, child. And you weren't waiting here to tell me such important news. What is it? Has there been trouble?"

I shook my head, denying it at the same time that I wondered what it would be like to have a friend to confide in—how tempting to simply start talking, no secrets, no lies, no fears of judgment or betrayal. Maybe Kath could be that person for me. Maybe the years spent reading the histories would help her understand . . .

But I didn't answer, and Kath began arranging a sheaf of papers on her table. "And I suppose you've been here half the evening," she said, her back to me. "And never heard all the noise and trouble with the Kareil folk?"

"Kareil folk? Here?" Had I heard right?

"No." She turned around, enjoying her game. "In the riverlands."

"In Aster? But I'd never thought they came through the temples. I thought they kept to their routes, following the Sister's path . . . avoided the Sumedaro. I did see them in Briana once, but—"

"You thought. You thought." Kath shook her bone-thin finger at me. "And did you think they had no more freedom than a herd of elk? Or that we in the temples are of so little use to them?"

"They're inside the gates already? They'll be staying? How many? What do they want?" I asked, my thoughts racing. The temples, the books, the songs. Even Edishu had spoken of the Kareil. Ceena trusted them more than any Sumedaro. Surely they, of all the clans, would know how to ward against Edishu. What if they had news that the Elan Sumedaro had returned and was even now sharpening his blade? What if . . .

"I had a feeling you'd be as hungry as a puppy for their tales. You with your head forever lost in these pages." Kath gathered a load of work into her arms. "So now I've told you. But remember, we are Sumedaro priests here, keepers of Jokjoa's dream. The Kareil path is different than our own. Older perhaps, but different doesn't equal wiser."

"But isn't it also true"—I raised my voice—"that the

nomads followed their path since before there were temples? And every tract you're carrying there is filled with their teachings? And Hershann stands there at the fire altar, holding his bracelet as if he had a right to it when those books, Kath, on your shelves, say the Kareil kept Rath and Gamaliel before there ever was a temple!"

"That's enough, child." Kath's voice was all seriousness again. "If Hershann heard you talking so, he'd have me out of this tower for allowing you such freedom. Yes, the words are there. But what if they are? Those books are too old to trust. I've spent my life trying to make sense of them, and it's no use. And with all your thinking, don't you realize we've enough of our own Sumedaro puzzles without needing to add their pieces to it as well?"

Kath coughed, then took a moment to steady her breath. "Oh, very well. Come along now. Don't look so stricken. We'll walk together. Take your cloak, it's bitter as all night outside. I saw a light burning, thought it would be you. Here, take my arm. My legs are afire, walking all day! Hershann says I should stop, but what does he know about shelves? His work doesn't come to a halt every time he decides to sit down." Kath cleared her throat. "Are you coming, then? Yes? Well, it seems they had some trouble on their journey. Raiders north and east of here chasing them off their routes."

"Raiders? But who would dare?"

"Someone. Anyone, it seems, with times as hard as these. Hershann said something about the towns farther east than Toklat. They've been fighting among themselves, no one landholding strong enough to claim the land, take control. A band was keeping the road shut—so the Kareil must have needed supplies, then, too—but they wouldn't let them pass. Claimed there wasn't enough food. The Kareil knew Aster was here, and I suppose they assumed we wouldn't turn them out. Holy beggars, that's what I'd call them."

"Not beggars," I said as I made my way down the darkened stairs slowly, following Kath's labored steps. "Beggars want land and food. The Kareil claim no home, so doesn't that mean they belong to all the land?"

"Then what are they doing here, tell me that, and not basking in the riches of some southern town?"

Kath left me after that, turning toward one of the elder's offices with her endless stream of papers to be dealt with. I bid her good night, then took a second turn, fastening my jacket closer as I neared the outer courtyard. I'm not certain what I hoped to find, or what I would say if one of the Kareil talked to me. But I felt my blood stir, filled with hope.

They were there, just as Kath had said.

They'd set up a makeshift camp, a small circle of ribbed tents with each door pointing inward toward the center. The tents had high, rounded roofs and irregular sides, nothing like the brilliant cloth-dyed pavilions Lethia had traveled with when she rode into Briana, nor again like the lean-to Jared had taught me to build. These were coarse and black, similar to the Kareil tent I recalled from Briana's market, but larger, made of tanned hides thick and strong enough to fend off the northern air. Later I learned that the Kareil traveled with animals and wagons and didn't carry the weight of those tents around themselves. But that first time, watching from the shadows behind the courtyard pillars, I would have believed they had the power to make those tents float through the very air if they chose.

There were twenty, maybe thirty people in that circle. Many were busy in the open central ground, cooking over a few small fires or sorting through baskets strewn about the courtyard floor. Other voices called from inside the tents, children crying or playing, men's and women's voices. From one tent the thin strands of a song emerged, too muffled by the hide walls for me to catch the words.

As I watched, a young red-haired woman nearly my own age stepped up toward the fire. Certainly there was no magic in the way she moved. She went about her chores as any would have, lifting, bending, walking back and forth. But there was a certainty to every motion, a strength that showed even through her robes, and I was struck by her grace and sense of purpose.

And then the girl stood, pushed her robe from her face, and turned, scanning the courtyard till her gaze rested on mine. She kept her lips pressed tightly together for a moment, then turned, as if to move free of the fire's glare. There was no mistaking her smile or the hand she beckoned with, inviting me closer.

Pulled by my own curiosity, I walked toward her, watching all the time.

In a voice that stirred my memory, she said, "I know you."

She was three years older than she'd been that day in Briana's spring market, and fairer to look at than I remembered. Her hair danced in gentle waves down past the small of her back. Her narrow face was a rich olive color, filled with life.

Self-consciously I ran my hand along the cut-off ends of my hair, hoping it wouldn't matter.

"You're the one who dreamt of Oreill," she said with an open smile. "It was jarak, you know. Though you tried to deny it." The girl, Thekla, spoke as if we were still immersed in our previous conversation, and the three years in between were no more than a passing afternoon.

"It was a long time ago . . . But you're right," I said, remembering again. "It was jarak." I'd forgotten completely. A gentle dream of Kuoshana. But I could make no sense of it. Once I'd had a dream of Oreill. This Kareil girl had watched it and claimed it was real. But that was all.

"And you're here." She spread her arms. "In a temple. So you must have realized it was jarak. And you decided to bring your dreams here?"

I turned away from her deep eyes, ashamed. In spite of all the vows I'd made, what had I ever done with my dreams but hide them—same as I'd always hidden them? How could this girl know what it was like to have jarak strength strong enough to see into any forest city on earth I wished, yet keep it hidden away, a lie sealed in Eclipse's name?

Thekla mistook my silence for agreement. "I was afraid you'd meant to ignore it," she said. "Or worse . . . I spoke your dream to my people, you know."

"You spoke my dream?"

"It was my duty. But even so, I wasn't strong enough to keep that dream to myself."

"What did your elders say?"

"They felt it was a good sign to dream of Oreill. It's not often we find a jarak dreamer in the towns." She laughed as if I understood. "But tell me, you're a sworn priest now? And the life suits you?"

"No." I looked down at the cracked tile floor. "That is no, I'm not a Sumedaro."

"Not one of the orange priests? But you live among them?"

"My father sent me here. To be rid of me, I suppose."

Thekla kicked at an ember that had shot away from the

fire. "Now I don't understand," she apologized. "Your father sent you away from your own people? And you're living here among the priests with your jarak dreams. But you're not one of them. Which is your home, then? Who speaks for you?"

I had no answer. "I should leave," I stammered. "Will you still be here in the morning?"

"Till sundown tomorrow, but no longer than that," she said. "We plan on leaving as quickly as possible. We have some repairs to make on our wagons, a splintered axle, some leather hitches that were torn. Our supply of iron was too low. As soon as we're finished, we'll turn back north toward our late winter route."

"Where is that?" I forced myself to stay, keep talking, not to run from her questions. Since these people already knew of my dream, maybe they'd see I had the right to ask for protection from Edishu: amulets, spells, whatever of the Sister's magic they'd been gifted with.

"We go where we wish. Where we always go," Thekla said. "Our path never changes. Except, of course," she smiled, "that it's never exactly the same, either. Your elder didn't seem to mind us coming."

"Hershann? No, he wouldn't."

"He gave us a glad welcome."

"He would. When it suited him. And when he thought to gain something by allowing you in these walls. He'd want to make certain they hear of it in the town, that a Kareil camp was set up here. Knowing him, he'd send word to the towns and the lakeside inn as well."

"And when they hear of our arrival?" Thekla raised her eyebrows, questioning.

"People need their dreams told. They'll pay Aster the rathadaro fee—if they're able—and Hershann will make up something about how their dreams are blessed by your presence."

"I see. And you find that inappropriate?"

"Inappropriate? Yes, I suppose I do. Hershann's behavior, not the townspeople's. Their dreams need telling."

"But you are glad to see us?"

"Why, yes." I looked up at her. "I needed to see you."

A shadow crossed Thekla's face, and I turned to see a tall broad-chested man, a hint of red running through his silvered hair. "This is my father, Cay LoringHill," Thekla said, taking his arm. "Father, look who I've found. This is Calyx, the one whose dream I heard in Briana."

"Calyx?" Thekla's father shook his head.

"Remember? We never knew her name before. She brought the jarak dream of Mother Oreill."

This time Cay nodded in full greeting. His smile changed, opened wide and joyful with thin, upturned lips that disappeared in the brush of his red beard. His appearance was colorful and bold, with a gray, furred vest over a cloth shirt and wide trousers that, like Thekla's, were gathered at the ankle.

"So my daughter's finally found you?" Cay's laugh lingered in the air, surrounding me in a net of friendship.

"You were looking for me?"

"We asked, wondered, that following spring when we retraced that southern route. We wanted to speak to you. Did you tell her, Thekla, how you dreamt of her?"

"You mean you returned to Briana because of that one dream?"

"Jarak dream," Thekla added, and behind her several other Kareil stopped their work to listen.

"Such jarak dreams as that are worthy of us all," Cay said, smiling but serious. "The dreamer should not be left alone with unspoken visions lingering. We meant only to bring you honor. But now I see you've found your own path. The Sumedaro are not allied with us. And we don't travel the same route. Yet even here you could find a home for your jarak visions. Aster Sumedaro temple should be well met to house a dreamer such as you, Calyx."

"In Aster temple they call me sensume," I answered softly.

For a long time Cay looked at the walls of the inner court. I could see his eyes lingering on the chipped columns and fallen benches that had lain so long unrepaired. At last he said, "I would not have thought it possible to hide a jarak dream. Have these priests fled so far from Kuoshana's path that they can't recognize a dreamer in their own temple?"

"No, sir. It's my doing, not theirs. I don't join them at their fire altar and I've never brought my dreams to their rathadaro hall."

"But to say you are dream-barren before the gods? Is this wise?"

"Wisdom?" I asked, surprised to find myself speaking so

freely. Yet there was no holding back; these people held some secret power compelling me to speak. "How could I know in the beginning what would prove wise and what foolish? I did what I thought I had to, and everything I did was to protect my dreams. Even when I was young, that was the one thing I believed. Hold my dreams inviolable and all else would follow."

Thekla stepped closer. "You should come with us, Calyx. It's not right for you to live this way."

Cay's eyes met mine with a silence so strong, it seemed to hover in the air. Whatever he was thinking, I couldn't read him. His face was a mask, his mouth an unbroken line. Everything about him marked him a stranger. But then, didn't the risk run in both directions? Wasn't I also a stranger to him?

Go with them? Run from Edishu again? Would traveling, hiding with the Kareil be the defense I needed? But if I went . . . My thoughts raced. If I went, there would be time to learn, time to build walls Edishu could never tear asunder . . .

At last Cay nodded. "It's true, Calyx," he said. "We're not a landed clan to offer you wealth. A horse, a tent to shelter you from the weather, there'd be little more than these. But we can teach you the meaning of your jarak dreams and offer friendship against the night."

"You would do this for me?"

"A jarak dreamer should not have to live alone. Your dreams, though a gift, are no small burden. I wouldn't want to think we hadn't offered to shoulder that burden with you."

"I never thought to leave Aster, not yet. And there is Briana, my mother. I'm not sure. I . . . let me think about it, please."

"Of course. It's not a simple decision. There's time to-morrow. Elder Hershann has accepted our offer of enter-tainment. We can speak afterward. But Calyx, understand, we don't make this offer lightly, or often. The mistrust that grows at the heart of our separate paths is deep and firmly ingrained. By accepting our friendship, you sever bonds here that won't easily heal." Cay smiled and reached his arm lightly around Thekla's shoulder.

"I understand. Thank you."

*   *   *

All the next day I did nothing but wait. The priests working alongside me in the library tried my patience; the work was petty and interminable. Kath, in her own fit of irritability—and knowing full well I'd rebel—set me to work on the illegible scratchings of her endless ledgers. Harvest yields, seed varieties, planting dates, storage and receipts, what did they matter? But all I could do was retrace the faded numerals and wait for the shadows to lengthen across the floor.

More than once my hands faltered and I sat with a dry brush resting on the table. Holy nomad Kareil. And one of them had remembered me, not for my position as Morell's youngest daughter, but for the one claim I had to this earth: my jarak dreams. Hadn't Ceena said these people were goddess-hallowed, that they alone of all the clans lived the old ways? And now, if I chose, I could live with them, learn their ways, watch their dreams and if need be, borrow their magic.

If I chose.

But how much more did I know of them than I'd known of the Sumedaro before I'd come to Aster? That they lived in hide tents, that they watched dreams, and maybe or maybe not kept the Sister's fast? That Ceena said her Silkiyam had been allied with the Kareil and perhaps had gone to them again? That they traced their ancestry to the Elan Sumedaro, and some of their folk bore the white-haired mark of Jevniah?

Once I thought the Sumedaro priesthood would answer all my longings, teach me to strengthen and shape my dreams. But the Sumedaro had failed me. If the Kareil failed me next, how would I fight Edishu? I had not allowed myself a jarak dream since the night I'd entered the rathadaro hall. How long could I continue this way? Hiding? Waiting?

At last, just as the first trace of evening light came filtering through the window, Kath appeared behind my shoulder.

"Your work's uneven today," she said.

"Is it?"

"Calyx, there's something I have to say. But—this is none of my argument."

I pushed away from my stool, as if I'd known all day that something would be coming. "What's happened?"

"Hershann spoke with me—"

"It's the Kareil clan, isn't it?"

"I meant no harm. I suppose I understood too well what the attraction was."

"What did he say?"

"Only that you were seen speaking with the Kareil. I thought seeing them would help . . . help distract you from the tediousness here." Kath watched her hands. "But you have to understand: you can't go about saying the Kareil are holiest of the three clans. Calyx, what if you said that somewhere else? In the towns? In your own Briana Keep? In the temples we sometimes forget . . . feel safe. If the townspeople believed that even the priests didn't understand what they were doing . . . Calyx, I blame myself for allowing you so much liberty."

"You told Hershann what I said?"

"It wasn't just that. You were seen talking with them. That's what the trouble was, more than what I said." Kath sat slowly down on a chair.

"And the rest of it? What else did he say?"

"He said you may attend this dinner. But you are not to be seen alone, or speak with any of those people while they're here. There, you see. It's not so bad, not really."

I straightened my back. Sat stiffly. "And does Hershann require an answer?"

"No." Kath rose wearily. "But I do."

I thought for a minute, framing my answer. "I'll be there, at this dinner. And it's late enough in the evening to safely say I won't speak with them alone—today. Tomorrow, I'll make my farewells . . ." to *someone*, I thought. "More than that, I won't promise."

"That sounds calculated. And I ought to know better—but I accept," Kath said, though she would not look me in the face.

I waited out the hour, scrawling my figures with a fury I hardly even noticed. Let Kath think what she would. Let her tell Hershann his message had been delivered. Hershann! Why, he hadn't even the courage to speak for himself!

At last the bell tolled the hour. I threw my brushes into the water, elbowed past the other priests, and raced to my room. Odd that I had once loathed that room, I thought, when now the privacy was so welcome. I leaned against the wall, arms crossed tightly, swallowing hard. "For this night," I said aloud, "let me be Calyx of Briana. Let me stand in clothes of my own choosing unallied with this or any temple."

Carefully, as though the act were holy, I folded the brown robes and laid them across the bed. Then, one by one, I touched the dresses, shirts, vests, and pants layered in the bottom of the clothes chest. I had come to Aster wearing my brother's leftover tunic. Yet that wasn't Calyx either— only Calyx trying to prove she was not Mirjam. For tonight I must choose something else, something with fewer memories, fewer deceits.

Yes, there it was, a white silk shirt, smocked and loose around the shoulders, wide sleeves tapered to a narrow cuff, and black leggings, belted and tucked at the ankles. Black and white. Yes, the colors suited me. Night and day. Separate and united. Calyx of Briana. Calyx the jarak dreamer. And would I add Calyx of the Kareil to my name as well?

There was no time to weigh the questions fairly. The decision would have to come quickly. A word, a feeling. Hershann would say something, or the Kareil would reveal their magic to me. And then I would know.

For the first time in a very long time, I took some care with my brush, smoothing my hair into place until, if it was not as silken as Thekla's shining red hair, at least it wasn't a beehive in a thorn bush. Perhaps it wasn't that I was merely plain, I told my reflection, because that implied an absence of beauty. Wouldn't it be closer to the truth to say my features were unadorned, much as the wildlands were considered unadorned by someone who could not appreciate landscape without a garden?

Below, in the Great Hall, the tables had been rearranged into two concentric circles, the ends of each line open toward the kitchens. Hershann sat at the head of the outer circle with Cay to his immediate right and a red-clad Kareil woman to his left.

Closer to the table ends, I found an empty chair beside Orrin, my fellow librarian. Orrin was a round-chested man, heavily set, with an appetite that could never be satisfied. He had balanced a wide pile of honeyed yams atop a brown-baked trencher, and watching him eat, I wondered at Hershann's largesse.

Not far away, Dev sat beside one of the Kareil men. Dev's face had taken on a healthier color again, and the dark crescents that had lined his eyes were faded now. He seemed to be enjoying the evening, leaning forward to hear the tall Kareil man's words, eating, gesturing. Something about the evening seemed all too reminiscent of Briana and that last dinner where I'd felt so isolated, so watched.

Just then Hershann rose from his place and called loudly for silence. He was cloaked in his Sumedaro finery, with a high, pointed cleric's hat perched nestlike atop his head. He'd pushed the long sleeves of his robe up toward his elbow, not because he felt the closeness of the crowded hall, but to make certain his guests would notice the gentle beauty of Jokjoa's bracelet circling his wrist.

Cay sat patiently beside him, hands folded on the table in sharp contrast to Hershann's graceless bulk. Cay's eyes searched the room, then stopped when he found me. A wide smile crossed his face, and he nodded his head in a greeting I silently returned. A few seats away, Thekla sat with bowed head. Praying, I wondered, or hiding from prying Sumedaro eyes?

Only the sounds of a muffled cough and the grating of a chair against stone broke the hall's silence. Hershann bent toward Gamaliel, then lifted the earthenware goblet to his lips and drank. The eyes of every Sumedaro priest were turned respectfully toward him as he made a great show of returning the goblet to its place. But the Kareils were watching their hands, or the table, or the stone gray walls of the keep that must have seemed so unfamiliar to them. I wondered how they must feel caught in this box of a temple when their world had always been the stars and the earth, and I wondered how I would feel to join them, without those selfsame walls surrounding me.

"Let it be said that in Aster temple two of the great clans met for a time beneath Kuoshana's eyes," Hershann said in that artful, pompous way of his. "And Oreill's starry eyes were content to watch from above. Let it be said that in all the lands, here in the ancient north, the holiest of lands, the first land, the Kareil and the Sumedaro came together and shared their dreams . . ." He paused, then began again. "And now, with Aster's thanks, we accept this gift the Kareil have made for us this evening."

Cay rose from his seat. Slowly smiling, he looked about the hall. "We give you your dreams," he said softly. "Accept them from us as a token of the worlds we walk together. Though you claim no home in the havens of old and we wander the earth in keeping with the Sisters' law, still the jarak dream unites us all. Thekla RiverCross, daughter. Ondine StillWater. Evan GamHill. We listen for your song."

Thekla walked quietly toward the open bowl of the hall. Not until she had taken a stance did the next singer join her. They were dressed much the same: heavy sheepskin vests over long blue shirts and leggings tied close to their ankles. Thekla wore her hair loose to her waist, as did the other girl, Ondine. Last of all, Evan GamHill joined them in the center.

For the first time that day, something like a wind of fear whispered in my ear. Evan's hair was as white as a new-fallen field of snow, pure white, not silver with age, for he was young, nor the white opalescence of a pearl with a hundred colors hidden within, but an empty, colorless white: the white mark of Jevniah. Even his skin was colorless, pale, with veins and arteries visible beneath the surface. He too wore a shaggy vest cut long to his hips, with blue shirt and trousers beneath to match the others. He stood beside the two women, taller and with a sad, distant look to his eyes, laid one pale hand on each of their shoulders and began to sing.

There were no words to the song, at least none that I recognized, only a harmony with a line of melody twining and running free, now drifting easily like a gentle eddy in a river, now rushing, quicker and louder. Then, just as the song slowed to a quiet trill and I thought it would end, Evan closed his eyes. For a moment I feared he might faint, so weak did he seem. He stumbled and searched for Thekla's shoulder. Alarmed, I started up, ready to call out, but before I could speak, he opened his eyes and stared blindly ahead.

The hall grew closer and too warm, with an ill-omened reek of dank wood trapped in a fire. In the center of the floor where Evan stared, a light appeared, its red core glowing without heat. Every face in the hall was captured by that light, watching as it danced and grew. Then, before there was a chance to cry out, a figure emerged from the light, a great-bellied man with three chins where his neck should have been, a spoon in one hand and a pot in the other. Around and around he stirred the pot, working at some concoction he had in there, and singing all the while.

The image held, but only for a minute, then began to fade. But just as quickly another appeared. This one was of a woman, hair spun in long braids about her head, cheeks painted like two roses. From somewhere at my left, one of the priests cried out in surprise, "Essie! It's my Essie! That's her. I dreamt of her just last night. How did they do that?"

The next moment the woman's figure was joined by a young boy, a farmhand from the look of his patched, mud-caked tunic. The boy looked sad. His face was smudged from crying, and a broken panpipe hung loosely from one hand.

Then they too faded, and after that came a soldier in court dress, stepping forward and floating around the center of the hall as if he were looking for someone. Farther down the table, Kath stood, her hand reaching in confusion toward the figure. "Hugh? Hugh? Is that you?" Her voice was no stronger than a whisper. "I'm here! Hugh? Someone call him. Please!"

But already the image faded into the air, and just as suddenly there was an old woman with a cat cradled near her chest, then a merchant crying out his wares, and next a villager high atop his thatched roof.

Faster and faster the dream images stepped from the light, paraded, then disappeared. From every table the priests called out the names of friends or lovers they'd dreamt of. Here and there an embarrassed cry demanded an end to the show, and once I heard Dev let out a deep laugh at the image of a young girl, her pale face tracked in grimy tears. Even Hershann, laughing from his silken chair, laid a sleeve to his cheek to wipe a runaway tear.

Then finally the last of the figures disappeared. Thekla and the other two singers quieted their voices till only a low-pitched hum remained. Slowly, slowly the air filled with the humming; louder it grew, like a storm reaching across the horizon. And just as I thought the light had disappeared, it brightened again, changing from a fiery red to a pure white light. Brighter and brighter it grew, while great bolts of light shot out onto tables and floor.

Suddenly two figures emerged from the core and faced each other.

I looked closer. "No, it's not possible," I whispered as a fearful, cold certainty built along my spine. It was Edishu. They'd conjured my dream, a true jarak dream. How could they know . . . ?

My hands gripped the table, knuckles white. Without daring to breathe, I waited. The Edishu figure stopped moving for a moment, turned his gray face in every direction. He was looking for me. I could feel his fiery eyes peering into each person's heart. One by one he came looking, with his face that was neither hideous nor young. He was hunting out my scent in the cold air, ferreting me out like an animal.

No, I prayed desperately, let it not be true. Don't let them see my dream, not now. Not here in Aster. But he'll remain in the dream, won't he? The others had. They'd only appeared. That was all. They were visions.

But this was no vision. I vaulted from my seat; the chair toppled backward, crashing to the floor. Edishu reeled toward the sound and I stepped backward blindly, until the hard stone wall at my back caught and held me there, like a bird trapped by its own pinion feathers.

Edishu called out in triumph, his voice a mixture of venom and pain. I felt my way along the wall, met the table, started along the inner curve, inching away. But he kept following me, his mouth bared, hungry.

"You will fight this time," he said. "You cannot run away to your little bed. You see, I'm here."

"No!" I cried. "You said we must be matched. Weapon to weapon. You can't fight me here."

"Then bring me what I want." His laughter pummeled across the hall, echoing from wall to ceiling to wall again.

"No." I shook off his words, refusing to allow meaning into the sounds. "Then I'll fight you. However I can." I spun toward the table, grabbed the first thing I found—a silver urn—and hurled it at him, sent it smashing to his chest. And it struck, hard and close. Edishu reeled back under the impact, but only for a moment. Then he picked it up as though he hadn't felt a thing. He held it out, laughing still.

"We can fight with this if you like," he said. "I had almost forgotten how reasonable a weapon silver can be." He took the urn in his hand; it was as long as his arm, curved and slender but thickly cast. He closed his fist around it and began to crush it, to destroy it.

"You like pretty things?" he said. "I can give you pretty things. But in return you must give me something back." He took the wreckage of the urn—a thing no larger than my fist—and pressed it into the pit of his chest and it sank, as if swallowed, whole, into his heart.

And there was nothing. No glint of silver or mark to show where his chest had opened. His eyes were turned inward, silent and still. His face took on a patient, beatific smile, and he waited.

Silence grew again in the hall. Most everyone had fled their seats and stood now beside the walls, watching transfixed. At the table beside me, Cay waited, a grim look where his smile had been. Thekla stood beside him, holding her stance. Hershann was beside her, his eyes stark and bewildered, his fear a sharp contrast to the glowing strength of the bracelet he still cradled about his wrist.

The next moment came a thick, aching sound.

From the flesh of Edishu's chest a dark light tore free, bloodless, cold, and empty. The light grew solid and took on form. Wings appeared first, talon-tipped, then legs, clawed and ugly, a chest with a woman's breasts and a woman's face on the head of a bird: a succubus, clawed and fanged.

The first bird broke free, then another appeared, woman-faced but smaller, maddened, then another and another. In a terrible, raucous line they circled the high ceiling, wings astir, eyes filled with Edishu's hatred. They screeched, spun and dipped, and then, as though they'd never been anything more than a mirrored reflection, the line faded. Only the first, huge succubus remained. Beneath the domed ceiling she whipped around, turned her impossible eyes toward me.

Edishu murmured something to her, and the creature, seeming to understand, spread the lips of her beak-mouth and cried an answer. For one instant more she hovered, and then she sprang toward me, wings flapping, claws outstretched. I dropped to the floor, tried to jump away. But disbelief had made me slow, and one of her claws ripped into my shoulder and the sleeve fell open, dyed with my blood.

Now at last, Cay, Hershann, and the others knew this was no dream vision. The succubus was real, my blood was real. In a panic the priests hurled themselves from the table, toppling chairs and platters. Helpless and frightened, they raced toward the doors, the corridors. Hershann backed away till he stood against the long stone wall, his mouth open with disbelief. But Cay had risen and run to stand as near to me as the creature allowed. When he tried to come closer, the succubus dove at him, spitting its warning cry.

"Thekla," Cay called, his voice low and modulated. "Have you the Wairhisc rock?"

From across the hall, Thekla nodded. With even motions she opened a pouch at her side and tossed something to her father. Cay reached, caught what appeared to be a green-hued rock, small and shining with a crystalline perfection.

From his own pouch he drew its match, a stone so clear, green shadows could be seen dancing inside.

Edishu held out his arm, calling the creature down, and it landed there, flapped its rapier wings once, then was still. Cautiously I found a chair back, pulled myself up to stand. Edishu's eyes shone with contempt. Laughing, he said, "You cannot touch me, Kareil."

Cay looked up but did not speak. Grimly he raised his arms overhead and with a suddenness that shook the hall, brought the two rocks smashing together. "In times of night/ By Sunder's right/ The seed of strife/ . . ."

"You cannot touch me," Edishu cried. "Your weapon is useless. Dead. The time for your Kareil tricks is long since past. Not since the first Elan fought me on the Plains of Duvidan have you been able to raise that stone against me."

"By Sunder's right/ The seed of strife/ Takes life anew/ Be weaponed now/ Wairhisc light."

Again Cay brought the two rocks together and a sound could be heard, rumbling and deep, as though far away an avalanche had begun. But the noise remained distant, powerless, till it faded and the room grew quiet.

Edishu's face lit with triumph. "Now," he said, turning toward me. "You see how little you can do? You cannot run. You are already awake. I was called; there was no need to wait for your jarak dream. Now, give me the bracelet."

Hershann flinched.

Rath? It was Rath he wanted. But of course! Jokjoa's bracelet. "Arm yourself," he'd told me—and I'd thought only of running. When I might have stolen the bracelet myself instead of hiding in Sumedaro halls.

Enraged, I shouted, "You won't have it!"

"Bring it!" Edishu flung the succubus skyward again. "Bring it! Or feel the stinging claws you yourself granted me for a weapon. Or didn't you know that everything you touch shall be as a gift to me? Now let it be your blood that is drawn."

The creature swooped above Edishu's head, then began its dive. Wildly it dropped toward me and struck, its talons snatching at my hair, at my face. With my fists I fought back, blindly beating its wings, body, anything I might reach. At my side, Cay found a dagger and hurled it toward the demon. The blade found its mark, startled the thing away for a moment, but that was all. Useless as the Wairhisc, it ricocheted to the floor.

In the confusion I dropped down, waiting while the succubus soared again, searching the hall. Hershann, his face white with fear, had not thought to flee. He stood against the wall, clutching the bracelet behind him as if he hoped to be forgotten.

I crept toward him, slipping behind tables and uprooted chairs, picking my way through shattered goblets and the bits and pieces of the ruined feast. Whatever happened next, I meant to reach Hershann and pull him somehow from that room and save the bracelet. I came within arms' reach, called out in a whisper, but it was too late. Edishu found me.

"Don't touch it!" His voice echoed against my heart. "Bring him to me. Now. Or your friends will dream no more."

I raised my eyes. Face upward in the center of the floor, Dev sprawled, the bird's claws sunk into his shoulder, its human mouth gaping and hungry at Dev's eyes.

"What do you want?" I shouted.

"Do nothing. Tell the man to walk to me."

"Hershann? Do as he asks."

Shaking, Hershann took a step forward, then stopped.

"Closer!" Edishu cried, his eyes wide in fury. "Closer!"

"Do it," I pleaded, my eyes riveted on Dev. As long as Edishu did not order the succubus further, it held back. Cay had taken up a stave and was goading the creature, pushing into its soft underbelly, prodding its neck. Back! Back!

Ravenlike, it cried out, its mouth showing black inside, wet and unsatisfied. But miraculously the thing jerked, flapped its wings, backing away from Dev. Several others jumped in to help Cay now, trying to ward it off.

Hershann took another step, and this time I moved forward with him, steadily matching his pace, while Edishu's gaze lingered on the bracelet.

I stepped in closer. One thing I prayed: that without my compliance Edishu was powerless. He had needed Lethia to use the ring. He'd needed me to touch the silver urn before he could bring it to life.

And he needed me now.

Hershann took another step. The bracelet was around his wrist, dull as tarnished silver. He was near panic. I could see it in his legs, in the small quaking refusal of his head and shoulders. Edishu was less than ten steps away.

"Closer," Edishu said, this time his voice a whisper through clenched teeth. His gaze was riveted to the bracelet, his lips curled back, hungry, tasting his victory.

One more step I watched, waiting. Watching. Waiting.

Hershann started again.

A shout tore free from my throat and I leapt toward the bracelet. Caught it! Hershann's arm was tense beneath mine, but he didn't matter. Rath was in my grasp, touching me . . . alive. And in that moment the room exploded in light.

Edishu fell back, enraged. The succubus screeched, its wings frenzied as if in its death throes.

Rath's light poured into my veins, traveling as swiftly as blood, as swiftly as thought. Around the hall its stone sent thunderbolts of streaming light, darting, circling, glowing. Like an arrowhead, light struck the succubus. And it shuddered, convulsed, once and again, then another time. Its face twisted, then held, its eyes blind, mouth rigid.

A moment later it fell to the floor. Colors dimmed. Its shape grew hazy, indistinct, then changed for the last time back again to a lifeless silver mass upon the floor.

When I looked away, Edishu had disappeared.

I dropped my hand. Rath too was dull again. Hershann shook himself as though waking from a dream. He looked about, saw the ruin, the disarray. For a long time he stood there, shaking his head in confused disbelief. He composed himself after a while, found his voice, and barked an order to one of the priests.

A few remained behind to deal with the chaos—Idelle and Rija, I noticed. But the elders, Kath, Syth, and Fowler, pulled their robes closely about themselves, and without a glance backward, they began their silent passage out of the hall.

Cay came toward me when they'd left, his face haggard, his eyes dark. But I wasn't ready for his explanations and, wrapping myself in a different kind of silence, I walked away.

13

For two days I shut myself away in the silence of my rooms. I ate if food was brought, slept if my eyes closed. And though I wondered if I'd have the strength to fight, no jarak dreams came to me. Everything seemed empty, hopeless. The Kareil had broken faith with me. They'd stolen my dream unbidden, revealed it to these Sumedaro priests who had no right to it. True, they hadn't meant to open a door for Edishu, but that was no solace. I couldn't find a way either to forgive Cay or forget.

Toward evening of the second day, Rija came knocking on my door with a message—her first visit since the broken feast. She'd been sending others in her place, quiet girls she trusted to follow her orders, drop off their trays of food and get out. Silently.

Now Hershann had sent her to say that the Kareil's stay had gone on longer than expected, but they were ready to leave now. One of their elders, Cay, had asked to offer a farewell.

I stood erect, facing her. "And what does Hershann say?"

She shrugged, looking about the room as if nothing between us had changed, checking to see if it needed straightening, as if I were a child too spoiled to be trusted. "Oh, he's glad they're leaving, I suppose," she said.

But I was too curious to settle for such simple answers. "And about that—that conjuring. What did he say?"

"You mean your dream?"

"My dream? Is that what he called it? Hershann says it was a dream?"

Rija raised her brow as if I were being obtuse. "Of course it was a dream, Calyx. They were all dreams. Yours the same as everyone's. Kath's dream was told. Gregor's. Mine wasn't, but then, I didn't need my private thoughts paraded about."

"And the Kareil? What are the priests saying about them?"

"Just as you'd think. The Kareil stole the dreams. What else should we do? Allow them to go around saying they've the power to conjure a dream without a watch? It's no different than outright thievery! But if you ask me"—she shook her head as if enjoying the sound of her own voice—"what they did wasn't so different from our own dreamwatch. Just that instead of one priest and one dream, the way it ought to be done, they brought the whole thing out so others could see. It's a trick. That's all. But that's what's so annoying. They act as if they've done something terrible, asking to be forgiven and all that. But it was only a trick."

"And the succubus?"

"Wasn't that awful? Such disorder. But what about it?"

"Is that all you thought? That it was a trick? It wasn't real? And this scratch on my shoulder? It never happened? Rath's light—"

"Of course you were scratched. You fell against the table. Everybody saw. But Calyx, why don't you just come with me? Tell Hershann whatever it is you want. Say good-bye to the Kareil, then they'll be gone. Everything will be back the way it was."

"Everything?" I murmured, knowing full well with Rija, there wasn't any use in saying more. She'd brought her news, though it wasn't what I'd expected. Hershann had been quick to use the past few days to quell any talk, discredit my dreams along with the Kareil "tricks." Perhaps he thought I'd go back to my copying. If the rest of Aster believed I was no more than I'd always appeared, not a dreamer, not a threat, and certainly not a priest to stand at the fire altar, then Hershann needn't worry.

Hershann waited for me in the same small hall where the Kareil had conjured my dream. The room had been returned to order; tables, chairs, platters, any sign that a vicious battle had converged there had all been brushed neatly aside. Hershann sat near the fire, the same robes of state gathered about his ankles, the same false smile settled carefully on his too soft face.

Next to him Cay stood, his eyes intent on Hershann, his hands firm at his sides as they spoke.

Hershann looked up as I approached. "Ah, Calyx," he said, changing his tone. "Did you hear? I have glad news for you. You have visitors. Come to take the place of these who would say farewell."

"A visitor?" My heart jumped. "Who? But . . . No one else was here the other night, were they?"

"No, no." Hershann looked at Cay. "If someone was here, you would have been the first to know. But before that, Cay tells me these Kareil have made you an offer of sorts. And it seems they aren't willing to leave unless they have an answer from your own lips. I tried to tell them your . . . retreat was answer enough. That—"

"Calyx." Cay's voice was intent, urging. "We wouldn't leave without speaking with you. We wanted to be certain. This is what you want, staying here?"

"What I want—" I started to say.

"But I haven't told you yet," Hershann interrupted. "Your brother has come for a visit."

"Hayden? He's here?"

"That's what I said, isn't it? Which means, as I was trying to explain to these Kareil, that you would never go against your family at a time such as this. But their ways are different. They seem to think it shouldn't matter what your brother wants. Or that your father is lord in Briana. And of course, they don't understand the implications as we do. Don't value the importance. What would your father say when he sent for you, if you weren't here? No, it wouldn't do. Lord Morell has placed you in our charge here, and that is a trust we will not break lightly." Hershann paused, waiting to see what I'd do.

He was right, and he knew it. I wasn't ready to go with the Kareil, though not for his reasons.

Aster was not my home and I was beginning to doubt that any Sumedaro temple ever would be. The Kareil had deceived me. And if anything had stopped Edishu, it had been Rath. Not the Kareil.

And the truth was, I wanted to see my brother.

I looked up to find Cay smiling at me. Somehow I hadn't expected that; I'd grown so used to Hershann's stubborn remoteness. "So, Calyx," he said. "This farewell comes all too quickly. It is farewell, then?"

"I think so," I said.

"But I think, also, that we will meet again."

I smiled then. "I hope so."

"And you are not angry?"

I thought about that a moment. "I was angry. And confused also." I was going to say more, but Hershann was listening, eyebrows raised, waiting to interfere. "Maybe it doesn't matter what happened."

"But it will matter," Cay said. "And you must be wary. You can find us if you want. You'll always be welcome. And also, we did not fail you, not in the way you think. I had wanted to give you a gift—"

"You don't have to—" I started to say.

"I understand that. But I wanted to. And we talked about it, until I realized that we do not have in our possession the gift you most need. The Wairhisc rock, it should have worked. This is something we'll have to study. But you would be better with weapons of your own. Do you understand?"

I turned to look at the log, cooling to white in the fire. Cay was warning me. He had understood. He'd heard what Edishu had said, and he was warning me.

Hershann coughed as though he wasn't certain whether to allow the conversation to continue. He kept nervously twisting his left wrist with his hand. I watched, then realized that it was Rath he was thinking of, his precious relic. Cay looked at Hershann's wrist also, but intentionally. He caught my eye, glanced back again at Hershann's wrist, then nodded.

I met his gaze, urging his red-silvered hair and bearded face into my memory. *There will come a time for us!* my eyes answered.

Cay bowed his head as if to say he understood my answer and was satisfied. He stooped, gathered up the thick woolen traveling cloak the Kareil wore, and left the hall.

Hershann pushed himself awkwardly out of his chair, then turned, and motioned for me to follow.

"Hayden? Hayden, is it you? But what are you doing here?"

"Coming to see how my sister fares, of course. Why else should I traipse across half the northlands? But come, I was hoping for more of a greeting out of you than that. Not even a handshake or a hello?"

I broke into a wide smile, urging darker memories to the back of my thoughts. Hayden looked wonderful: ruddy-cheeked, tall, different yet achingly familiar at the same time. His face had lost its round contours and grown longer and narrower as he'd come of age, far more like our mother than he had seemed before. His gray, fur-ruffed cape, though richer than any I'd seen in a great while, still showed the dirt of the long road. And though it looked as if there had scarcely been time to open a guest room for him, I felt certain Hershann must have known for days that he was coming.

As Hayden opened his arms, I ran to him, leaping like a young girl, and he lifted me, spun me around and around until finally, laughing, he brought me down again.

"Your mustache is too long! And you smell of horses," I laughed. "Horses and horse blankets. But tell me, did you just arrive? How's Mother? And Ceena? Is she in Briana?"

"I think they've been trying to make a priest of you, sister." Smiling, Hayden held me at arm's length. "You look . . . taller. But thin as a candle. Elder Hershann, you said she'd only taken on the Sister's fast, not taken to keeping it all the week long!"

Hershann stood behind me, arms crossed as if he were a kindly uncle presiding over a family gathering. He was smiling his thick, ingratiating I'll-grant-you-my-blessing-if-you-behave-the-way-I-want-you-to smile that I'd long since lost tolerance for. "Tell your brother how well you're taken care of here, child," Hershann said to me. Then he stepped oddly to one side until certain he had my attention, he patted the outer pocket of his robe. Beneath his hand a small rectangular shape stood out. He patted it again, smiled at me, all the while making certain no one else had seen his hand.

But I knew what that rectangle was, knew its size and thickness. And with Hayden beside me, I remembered all too well what it was to live in my father's court, to know instinctively that beneath every look and comment there was another, deeper meaning.

Hershann had my dream journal, just as Dev had warned. He'd have read every jarak dream I'd made since first coming to Aster. And he was warning me, threatening to reveal my jarak dreams to Hayden if I attempted to say anything untoward concerning his actions.

I almost laughed aloud, the joke was so ill timed. Once, perhaps, Hershann could have frightened me with threats about Morell's intentions. Once it might have mattered who knew of my jarak dreams. But no longer.

"Of course I'm well." I turned back to Hayden. "They

didn't tell you anything was wrong, did they?" I searched my brother's face for the other side of Hershann's threat. How much had Hayden heard? The Kareil's dream conjuring? My watch in the rathadaro hall? Was that why Hayden had come? Because Hershann hoped to relinquish responsibility for me before I caused more trouble?

Suddenly a voice spoke out from one of the dark, curtained walls at my back: "How well can you be when you don't remember the first of Sunder's lessons?"

"Ceena!" I cried as my guardswoman stepped into the light. "Ceena!" I ran to her, my arms open in joy. But she stood straight and unyielding, and I stopped suddenly, catching myself. "And what lesson was that?" I said carefully.

"What it always was: to follow your enemy's eyes. To see the spaces in the dark. Your brother has looked at me no less than three times since you entered the room, but you paid his silences as little attention as you would have paid a sleeping cat."

I glanced back at Hershann, searching for a way to hurry him out of the room. "I'm sorry," I said, offering Ceena a smile. "They drill us on different skills here. And I'd nearly—but not quite—forgotten how demanding a Silkiyam teacher can be. But Hershann, have they eaten already? Ceena? Hayden? The Sister's fast isn't for another day yet, and we should eat together, here or in my rooms."

"Then it is true." Ceena's eyes probed deep. "You do keep the Sumedaro restrictions." She was tense still with a vigilance I'd almost forgotten. If Hayden had matured, then Ceena seemed more ageless than ever. Stronger, more controlled. And after all this time apart, the set of her deep blue eyes and heavy brows, her tall frame, everything about her, sang of her Silkiyam blood, setting her apart.

Hershann stepped between us, listening carefully. "How could I have forgotten?" he said. "Forgive me, but between equals, you'll understand what a difficult day it's been. So many details to be taken care of. No one to depend on. I'll have Rija bring a tray. Wine perhaps?"

"That would be appreciated," Hayden said with a courteousness as calculated as any I'd ever heard. "Calyx, our gracious elder assures us you'll be free to spend the day with us tomorrow. You'll show us the grounds. We'll have time to talk."

Hershann waited at the open door. "You'll have to excuse me, then. There are several appointments I must keep. But don't forget, you promised me news from Jared. And there was a letter, I believe?" Hershann bowed low toward Hayden, then turned and left, the hem of his robes trailing along the floor behind him.

No one spoke until the last of Hershann's footsteps had faded beyond the hall. "So, my little sister," Hayden said, growing serious, "we've a priest in the family, after all? And all along I thought . . . that is, no one thought you'd take any of this seriously enough to choose the Sumedaro vows?"

Hayden's words surprised me, echoing so close to Cay's assumptions. Even Ceena's masked eyes could not hide her interest, her suspicion. Was I Sumedaro now? Was I a jarak dreamer? Had I grown? Had I changed?

Vexed, I turned on Hayden. "Oh? I was under the impression that no one had thought of me at all in three years. Father sent me away, and away I went. No letter! No messenger! Nothing for three years? Was I so much a tiresome younger sister for you too, Hayden? I might as well have turned priest, for all the care you sent after me."

"Calyx." Ceena's voice was low but cutting. "Save your rashness for another time. We've all had lessons in loneliness; yours are neither the least nor the greatest. We've come. Let it stand."

Ceena's words rang true, as they always had, and I caught myself, let out a breath. Then more calmly I asked, "Who told you I was a priest sworn? Not Hershann?"

"But he did, though—" Hayden started.

"No," Ceena said, "he did not. Hershann only said you'd fasted on the Sister's day with the others. Hayden assumes the rest."

"Perhaps," Hayden thought for a moment, then nodded. "But Calyx, from your own mouth, tell me. Is it true? Is this your sworn home?"

"True? That I've become a Sumedaro?" I repeated, the anger gone out of my voice. I walked over toward the narrow window that lit the room and stared out beyond the courtyard, beyond the gray temple walls, as far as I could see across the vast, bitter northland. "A dreamer, yes. But a priest? No. Definitely no. Hershann never allowed it. Though, by Jokjoa's fist, how I wanted it! At first I begged. And when that wasn't enough, I stole. I stole their robes, their prayers, their fasting. All the simple, outer things, I tried to mime. And how did they answer me? They pretended that nothing I did, or wanted, or cared about mattered. However I dressed or acted, I was always Morell's daughter, someone to be indulged, tolerated. And the one true thing, the only real Sumedaro act I might claim, they weren't interested in. It didn't matter. Isn't that strange? My jarak dreams, Hayden. You didn't know about them, did you?" I didn't wait for an answer. "While you at least are a king and a soldier, Hayden. And you, Ceena, a Silkiyam warrior. You know who you are. But what name could I give when I stood before Jokjoa's altar to pray? A wife! That's what Hershann told me I could be. From the first, he said Morell had different plans for my future than to keep me locked away in a temple. But you tell me, Hayden, who exactly would come seeking this alliance, even if I should accept it? Was there a lord anywhere in the northlands who didn't hear Father disown me? Who would believe he'd disclaim a daughter in one breath, and offer a thousand troops for her dowry the next?"

I turned around again, almost expecting to find the room empty, Ceena and Hayden nothing more than rogue images in my imagination. But no. They were real, their eyes followed me; Hayden looked surprised by my words, Ceena looked as if she were searching for the truth. But the way they watched me, gazes lingering, they seemed almost—if I guessed correctly—as hungry for sight of me as I'd been for them.

"A dreamer," I said. "That's what I've become. A jarak dreamer. The one thing I believe I may have been born to be . . . But now, you tell me, Hayden. Why did you come? Certainly it wasn't to see if I was eating my dinner, or what color robes I'd put on?"

"Caly, I'm sorry. I never meant to question you as if you were a child."

"Caly? I never heard that name."

"No? Isn't that what I always called you? It seems I must have. I remember—"

"Sweet brother! You'd have no more ever called me by a child's name than you would have worn a toddler's dress yourself once you were old enough to have the choice of proper clothes. No, only Calyx. But I'll take it as a compliment that you try to find one now."

"Seriously, then. There is a reason. Father sent me to bring you home. He wants to see you."

"Morell? Why? What does he want?"

Ceena stepped closer. "Officially it is Morell. He wouldn't have it out that anyone else gave commands over his. But it's Ivane—"

"Mother? She wants me home? She won out over Morell? I should have known to have faith in her."

"Calyx, wait." Hayden touched my arm. "I have to tell you, she's not well."

"Not well? What do you mean? What's wrong? No, I can see now. You wouldn't have come this far if something weren't wrong."

"Ceena, tell her."

"She's with child, Calyx. Four months, and not carrying well."

I stared, speechless, looking past the walls to a memory of the last time I'd seen my mother. She'd looked tired, far older than her years. I remembered that. And if she'd spoken Morell's name, there was no love in her voice. I turned, set my teeth. "If she's pregnant by Morell, then he raped her!"

"Calyx! No!" Hayden protested.

"She's too old to bear a child." Ceena stepped forward. "Whatever else may have happened, that's what we have to face now."

Just then the door swung open. Hershann entered with Rija close behind, a tray of cheese, bread, and dried fruit in her hands. Rija kept her head down, her yellow hair modestly covered by her hood.

"So, Calyx, they've told you the news." Hershann smiled. "Your father has sent for you! And you'll take him our blessings, of course. And our thanks, Lord Hayden, for his and your generosity while we housed your sister. And I'm sure Morell will continue to think well of us."

"And for your discretion, of course, Hershann. You understand—I'm sure I don't have to explain to a man of your respected position—how much your cooperation means to us. It would not sound well in any court if anything amiss were to happen on our return journey. Or if word had somehow gotten abroad concerning my royal sister's whereabouts."

Hershann shuffled conspicuously from side to side, and I had to stifle a laugh at his discomfort. So I was royal now? I'd never seen this politic side of Hayden before; he must have grown to it while I was away. But I was enjoying it very much.

"Of course not, sir," Hershann answered. "Rija! Set the tray down. Can't you see, Lord Hayden is hungry? Would it be too much trouble, sir, to ask when you'll be leaving?"

Hayden put his arm around Hershann's shoulder, dwarfing the older man, and walked him over beside the hearth as though to confide in him. "What's a little trouble between friends, Hershann? You know we are really very much alike, you and I. You serve the night, I the day; you the gods who grant us all dreams, I the dreams that make us all gods."

"You flatter me, sir."

"No? Really? I only meant to be honest."

"And will Calyx be returning to us? Later? Here in Aster, we're very fond of her, of course."

"That's two questions. You only asked for one. But since we are friends, I'll tell you. Tomorrow and maybe. But tonight, if you don't object, my sister and I do have a good deal to discuss."

"Yes, yes, of course. I'll leave Rija here to help with the rooms. If there's anything we haven't thought of providing, please, consider this your home—"

"Thank you, but no." Hayden shook his head deliberately. "There's nothing. Rija may leave. Now."

Before an hour had passed, we'd made our plans for the journey back to Briana. Hayden had grown in more than stature. He'd grown to manhood and in a way I'd seldom thought possible from the quick, sword-slashing brother he'd been as a boy. He was loving and not afraid to show it. But proud also, and all too aware of the proprieties of face. He teased me, laughed with me, and spoke openly about the past three years and his feelings for Morell, telling stories of their arguments and—most surprising of all—how little they agreed. He spoke less of Ivane; in truth, they'd spent little time together. And I wondered how Morell felt to have him at his side, loyal, as what son would not be loyal to the land that would one day be his, yet principled as well, and defiant when he thought it necessary. Morell had thought to make a puppet of his son, and once I would have believed he might succeed. But not anymore. Perhaps, I dared hope, perhaps it would not be as difficult as I had feared to go home again, with Hayden at my side.

It was Ceena who troubled me more. Whether I moved to the couch beside the fire or the table for a sip of wine, all the while Hayden and I talked, she watched me. Watched and studied. Like the Kanashan warrior she was, she stood outwardly relaxed, but with a center that churned with a volcano's wrath.

Was her dislike for the Sumedaro that strong? Had I changed so much? Was there some sign I was supposed to give her, some password from my younger days, that would put her at ease? Look, Ceena! It's me, quiet, plain-faced, inconsequential Calyx? Why seek more?

But there was more. There were my dreams, and there was Edishu, both of which she knew. What was it Ceena had said when she watched my dream three years ago? That Edishu lies imprisoned in Kuoshana? That he won't easily escape?

But escape or not, he had found a way to reach me.

Let Hayden concern himself with raiders and treachery along the road. I feared Edishu. How could I hope to ride safely to Briana? Anywhere I went, anytime I slipped into a dream, couldn't he find me again? And without help from Dev or Cay or even the temple. Without weapons. How could I hope to escape him when he came closer each time?

Unless I had a weapon . . .

Hershann had a weapon, Rath, and Gamaliel also. But he didn't need them. What were they to him? Ornaments? I was the one who needed weapons. For him they were cold things, beautiful, yes, but dead. The same as it had been for Avram that time in Sharat. But for me, Rath came alive and the goblet would too. What if I took them? He still had the fire altar itself and the carvings. I needed them to fight Edishu. It would just be for the journey. Later I would return them. I was the one who needed them, wasn't I? Edishu had said as much, that without a weapon I could never win. Cay said so also. It wouldn't be stealing . . .

Later that night, when the moon had risen high enough over the temple walls that no lamp was needed to find my way, I slipped out of bed. I'd made up my mind. In the morning Hayden, Ceena, and I would be riding south to Briana with a small company, and this time I would not travel unarmed.

Slowly I opened my door. The way was clear. Rija would have long since retired to her own small room. Back inside, I buckled a pouch to my Sumedaro robes, threw those on over my nightclothes, then stepped into the hall. I needed no tools for this theft, no rope, or knives; only my hands and a quick tongue if I needed a lie. I would go to the fire altar. Prayer would be as good an excuse as any. Who would deny me the right to ask the Sister's blessing for the long ride ahead? And who would think to check, till long after it was too late, whether Rath was safe in its place?

Lightly, as quickly as I could, I made my way through the corridors. The night air burned against my cheeks, and my muscles stiffened. The way was slow. Here and there a priest was still about, carrying a candle, busy with some late-night chore. Each time I heard the sounds of footsteps or a rustling cloak, I slipped into a darkened corridor and waited, blood pounding in my ears, till the sounds faded away again.

The lamps at the fire altar's doorway were not lit, and I slipped inside, making my way forward along the rows of shadowed benches. Ahead, the fire altar candles were ablaze in row upon row of yellow light. Hallowed even in this hypocritical center. The glow burned my eyes, pulled me forward. Overhead, the statues of the gods seemed to beckon, their gilt forms shining. Eclipse smiled down toward me, her eyes knowing. *Guide me*, I prayed, *bless me with your cloak of deceit.*

There below the hem of Eclipse's robe, Rath rested atop its velvet-covered pedestal. Its edges reflected the candle-light back upon the room. Dancing, calling to me. At its side, the goblet rested. Plain, earthenware Gamaliel. What was that line I'd read once, the one that seemed to fit so well: "My father's tokens are never beautiful to the eye"? Yes, that was it. Gamaliel, plain with its own beauty.

Isn't this what my mother would want, for me to carry a weapon, to be armed as Mirjam was? Perhaps these had belonged to Ivane's family once, the way the ring she'd given Mirjam had been in her family line. It wouldn't be theft, not really. Wasn't that why Rath seemed to come alive at my touch? Because it had been in my family? Perhaps Gamaliel had been traded north or moved with a marriage? Mirjam's ring had fallen into Lethia's hands by mistake. Surely, Mother would have meant for me to have something also . . .

The wood railing felt solid under my hand, smooth and warm. I slipped over it, one leg, first then the other. Candles flickered and burned on each side, so close that my face felt as though I were standing in the midst of a hearth fire, flames rearing on all sides. Three small stairs led beyond to the pedestal and I took them, all the while feeling the memory of Rath's first touch in Sharat temple, so strong it lingered on my fingertips. I didn't dare look at the statues on the wall above, didn't dare face Jokjoa's eyes. The only strength was in these two, in keeping my sight ahead. Eyes lowered, mind clear of fear or guilt.

My hand went out, closed around Gamaliel's long stem. For the first time I felt its rough clay surface, warm where the goblet had faced the candles, cold behind. Carefully I slipped it into the pouch I'd brought, then reached for the bracelet. Rath seemed to glow both warm and cold at the same time. The instant I touched it, a light kindled deep within the bracelet's heart. I watched for a moment. When I lay it down, the glowing stopped. When I touched the bracelet again, ever so lightly, it danced, sang, spiraled in a hundred crystalline colors. And then, though it was no easy thing to let go, I slipped the bracelet inside a pocket. My heart stilled. I turned back toward the railing, took the three steps down.

But the candles were glaring in my eyes, and I didn't see the man who'd been watching me from the benches till it was too late.

Eyes forward, the hood of his Sumedaro robes drawn up so close that his face seemed hidden in a cave, he stood waiting for me. "What are you doing?" he asked.

"Dev!" I let out a breath. "It's you."

"What are you doing?" he repeated. "Put them back! You have no right—"

"How did you know I was here?"

"I've been following you since you turned past the last corridor."

"Shh. Keep your voice down. There's priests awake. Out

in the rathadaro hall. Was anyone there? Did they see you?"

"I don't care who's awake. What are you doing with those? Was Avram right, after all? Are you an enemy to this temple? Calyx, if anything I've done or said, led you to this, I didn't mean—maybe you misunderstood . . ."

I walked up beside Dev. "No, you can't blame yourself for what I do. For what would have happened anyway. And witnessing isn't guilt. But I'm going to Briana. My brother's come. You must have heard by now. And I'm taking these with me till I return."

"Hershann will never let you—"

"He isn't going to know. No one's going to tell him, though he'll guess eventually. But that doesn't matter. I'm going to bring them back. Both of them. You of everyone here should understand. I need them, the bracelet most of all. But the goblet also, because without it I don't think I can survive much longer. I have to have something to protect myself."

"Protect yourself from what?"

"You know what I'm talking about!" I started to shout, caught myself, then stopped. Nervously I peered into the shadows. "Hershann can pretend all he wants that that thing, whatever it was, attacking us, was a dream. That my imagination is out of control. But you can't. You felt it. And you know what happened in the rathadaro hall . . ."

"No, I don't. I don't know what that was." Dev shook his head, and there was a look of fear in his eyes. "Sometimes, Calyx, when I'm with you, I don't understand anything."

"But you do understand that I can't risk losing myself in every jarak dream."

"Then you tell me what it was the Kareil summoned. Though I don't think you do know. Not really. Do you, Calyx?"

"Is that what I have to do? Answer your questions and you'll give me permission to take the tokens? All right. But all I know is that my dream was the door, the same as you told me Sherra would be the door to her dream. The Kareil opened the door. Something stepped through. I wasn't sleeping any more than you were. So it wasn't a jarak dream. It was real, the blood on your shoulder as well as everything. The rest of it, I don't understand any more than you do. There's no book, no history to turn to, no one who can explain what it was. No one else even admits it happened. But Dev, I'm frightened. I'm not taking this bracelet because it's pretty. Or because I want to steal the faithful away from Hershann. I don't want to hurt Aster. But I have to have some means of defending myself. Rath has power, and Gamaliel too, though I don't know how to bring that one alive yet. But you saw Rath work. If I can't fight back, I'll never be able to answer your questions. Dev? Please?"

Dev kept his eyes down, and I waited, not daring to speak. It wasn't that I needed his permission, though if he wanted to, he could shout, force me to stop. It was Dev himself that mattered. I needed him to understand.

Finally he looked up. "I know," he said, "you must be frightened, because I'm frightened for you. And you're right, I do know what I've seen, even if I don't know why or how. If you think Jokjoa's tokens will help you, then I have to accept that. Besides," he made an attempt to laugh, "I know it isn't the gold you could sell them for . . . But you will bring them back? Whatever else I am, I'm still a Sumedaro. My loyalty is to this temple. And the tokens, they belong here . . . when you're done."

"I'll come back. Hayden never hinted I might not return."

"But you don't know when, do you? And you've always told me Morell gives you little freedom . . ."

There was more that Dev said, but somehow I wasn't listening. He stood so close, I could feel the warmth of his skin and I wondered if he sensed it as well. Our faces, so close, whispering in the dark. The light flickering behind us. What if he moved to touch me? I closed my eyes for a moment, almost willing it . . . I wouldn't protest . . .

He stopped talking and I opened my eyes. He'd been watching me, but he shied away suddenly, turned as if he hadn't been looking at me at all.

I swallowed, tried to think of something to say. "Morell doesn't want me there. Hayden as much as said so. It's my mother I'm going to see. But the truth is . . . The truth is I'm not certain where my home is anymore."

"You don't love Aster temple. Not fully, not the way I do."

"You've taken your vows here. It's different for you. I've been shut out since the day I arrived."

"Calyx, there will be vows for you someday. And when they come you'll be glad you waited. Maybe Aster isn't for you, even with your jarak dreams. It was probably best all along Hershann never allowed you to enter the priesthood."

"Best! He never stopped for one moment to consider what was best for me. The only thing he cares about is the kitchen. I wanted to be a Sumedaro because I wanted my jarak dreams. I thought the one came only with the other. You showed me that's not true. I have my jarak dreams—"

Suddenly I reached across the empty space that separated us and took Dev's hands in mine, forcing him to look down at me. His brown hair lay curled on his shoulders, loose and free as he'd worn it since we'd first come to Aster. I didn't want to stop looking at him. His face was so light, so quick to sing, as open as a child's. The blood rushed to my cheeks, to my lips. I would have gone to him just then, had he wanted it. I caught my breath at the idea. Who would know? Or care? And there was time. Hayden and Ceena had already retired. I had work to do, packing, but there was time. All I need do was reach up, bring my face toward his. Wasn't this meant to be? Hadn't we only been waiting for the chance all along?

I moved until we were nearly touching, raised my chin upward. For a moment he almost came closer, his mouth ready to answer. And then he turned away. Looked to the door, the fire altar, the floor.

"I thought I heard someone coming," he said shyly. Then, "I suppose you have to go? But it's not fair, how little time there is anymore. And we're always so serious. No time to smile. To joke. It's too bad you couldn't say good-bye to Avram also. He was asking after you."

"What do you mean I can't say good-bye? Where is he?"

"He was called home for a sudden visit. Left two days ago. He didn't want to say much. Something about his parents' landholdings."

"I see. But it's just as well. I never know exactly how to speak to him. But please, be careful while I'm gone. In the village . . . tell them Briana isn't their enemy. Or their answer. Avram should never have said those things. My father's not interested in land this far north. But Dev, if you need anything, send a messenger to Briana. Or come yourself. If nothing else, I could help with the cost."

"You should write to me, Calyx. Send a letter back with Avram if you haven't returned yourself by then."

"Oh, how's that? Where exactly is he?"

"South. In Gleavon. That's where he's from. I thought you knew."

"Gleavon? Avram went to Gleavon? No, I didn't know." My voice was a chill whisper. "I never knew. Lethia's Gleavon? Are you certain?"

"Well, yes, of course. But why should it matter?"

"It doesn't, I suppose. But you should go now. You don't want to be seen here with me. And Dev, thank you."

14

We rode out of Aster temple the next day before sunlight had touched the distant hilltops on the eastern horizon. Those first few days, the wind was against us and the going was slow and the weather rougher than I expected. My first journey north had been difficult, it was true. But memory and the eagerness of those early days had somehow blurred the harsher edges. How different this trip felt in comparison, weighted down by fears for my mother's health, by the tokens hidden inside my clothes, fears that someone from the temple, heedless of Hershann's warnings, might condemn me after all.

Not counting Ceena, six guards had made the trip with Hayden: Jesun, Hayden's boyhood friend from Briana, then Trompson, Solly, Starn, Hannak, and Muley. They were a silent lot for the most part, loyal where it suited them and mindful of their duties.

Jesun was youngest of the six, closer to Hayden's age than the others. The two had been friends in Briana, and through most of our riding they stayed together, two abreast at the front of the line. Jesun's father was Norvin, Morell's closest captain. Along with the rest of their brood, Jesun had always enjoyed a favored position in Briana, secure between his friendship with Hayden and his father's power. Yet somehow the court intrigues had slipped by him, and there was an innocence to him that reminded me more of Dev than Hayden.

After Jesun, there was Trompson, who did our cooking;

Solly, a huge man with arms as solid as a wrought iron door latch; then Starn, the only talker in the lot; Hannak, who pulled thoughtfully on his long beard when I told him I'd known his family in Briana; and old, one-eared Muley, who made certain I knew how well he could fix a blade in a tree from twenty paces.

The five of them made up a motley crew, seasoned and road wary. And while Muley would no doubt make a good ally in a fight, they were older than most guards in Briana's lower halls. And except for Jesun, there wasn't a man among them keep-trained for fighting. Not that I'd ever known all my father's men. That would have been impossible even for Hayden. But I remembered watching the troops Morell sent off as a portion of Mirjam's bride price. Young, well-trained guards they'd been, tall, proud figures who'd gone off with lively steps and eyes all filled with the glory of a soldier's future.

These men cared little about wearing Briana's colors, and they looked as if they were more used to handling a dagger in a street brawl than a long sword, more concerned with the size of the wage they were offered than whose standard they carried.

Yet somehow I felt welcome in their company. And if I could never feel quite as close to them as Hayden and Jesun were, still they were glad company after the years of guarded, cold conversations in Aster temple. Nor did I think we need fear any trouble with them around. No attempt was made to hide the weapons they carried, sideways along their saddles, over their shoulders, strapped to their belts, or waiting in scabbards at their sides. They were as ready for a fight as anyone could be, cautious and alert with their hands near their weapons—listening and watching, always watching.

That entire time I carried Gamaliel and Rath in secret, hiding the bracelet beneath my shirt sleeves, where its steady light would not show. None of the others seemed to notice but for Ceena, who more than once along the way I found watching me so intently I couldn't help but slip a hand down to make sure one of the tokens hadn't come loose somehow.

Whatever Ceena's thoughts, she wasn't ready to share them. She held herself back from me—not aloof, as though I had rubbed myself too closely against the Sumedaro she held in such contempt—but in a colder, calculating manner, as if she were still waiting to render judgment on me.

But how I wished in sweet Eclipse's name that things might be different between us. Hadn't there been a time when I'd counted Ceena as a friend? Hadn't she been first to know of my jarak dreams, to know and not judge me by them? And hadn't she been first to whisper Edishu's name?

I needed her, and she wasn't there for me.

Wait, I told myself as the hills gave way to forests and then to hills again. *Wait. She'll be there yet again*. For now I must content myself with having the tokens near at hand, with remembering the difference they would make if they were needed.

We traveled at a steady rate, not racing—there was no need of that—but stopping when it suited us to stretch our legs, eat, and see to the horses. Hayden thought we could make the trip in two weeks if the weather held. But the truth of it was, we were halfway through what should have been spring now, with not one sign of a pale green shoot to be found above the snow-covered ground. People seemed at pains not to mention how last year had been the same, with winter fading into winter and nothing but a cold white disk of a sun to mark the passing seasons.

As it was, it took more than three days of steady riding to reach Roshanna Lake Inn. We pulled in late of an evening, found the inn less than half tenanted, and quickly fell to eating a dinner of sour apple porridge and flatbread.

Upstairs in the long attic room that served us all for the night, Hayden called me aside. "Here," he said when we were alone, "I want you to change into this clothing. It's Jesun's, but it should fit you."

"But I already took off my Sumedaro robes. What else would I have to hide?"

"You were the only one wearing black out of Aster. You stand out. It's not healthy."

"Healthy?"

"A target, dear sister." Hayden smiled, but he was serious. "There is one prince riding in our company. And in case you hadn't noticed, one princess. Either of them would make an excellent target."

I stood facing my brother, seeing this trip through his eyes. Not since Hayden's first night in Aster—and then it had been for Hershann's benefit more than his own—had he worn the golden circlet Morell had laid on his head. My brother was worried; I hadn't realized it till then. And there were other things that made sense which I hadn't paid attention to before: the plain clothes Muley and the others wore, the lack of a standard or colors, the company itself. We could have been any group of travelers: too large for most raiders to tamper with unprovoked, too bedraggled for thieves to take note.

The fourth day beyond the inn saw us in the wilds again, out in the hill country surrounding the Koryan River. All around us the land was a bleak, crippled waste. There had been trees the last time I came through; thin, tight ones, it was true, fighting for a glimpse of the pale sun, but alive. Now one tree out of every three was dead, and brittle, snapped branches hung like webs, bark-mottled and hollow. Where the farms we once feared visiting had stood, now there was only a wreck of collapsing roofs and abandoned furnishings. Edishu had told me this plague of a winter was his doing, but I wondered: Was such a denial of life possible, that he could turn the season's ebb and flow against itself?

At night, huddled about our fire, Starn took to warning against the hill country. "It's demon haunted," he said, searching each set of eyes as if to take the measure of our faith.

Muley answered him with a grin, "Demon or goddess, take your pick. One's the same as the other to me."

Wordlessly Ceena pushed herself away from the circle and walked to where the horses stood tethered in a line. We watched, but no one moved to join her and she stood riveted, listening into the wind, her face the same unyielding mask she'd worn since Aster.

I looked at Hayden seated beside me. "Let her go," he said as he shook his head.

"This land"—Starn opened his hands, drawing us back—"was once as green as a summer garden. Fields of plenty. A land of power. But the Sisters fought over it, carving it up for spoils. Sunder it was won here. And not a farm left that could salvage its crops from her grasp."

Jesun whitened at the tale. "My mother should have been brought down to Briana," he said. "I tried to make her come, but she can't ever decide anything."

I remembered Jesun's mother, Portia—a quiet, nervous woman who had lived on with her family even after she'd married Norvin, west of here in FelWeather Keep. In Briana we knew her less from anything she said in her own right than from the fuss Norvin and his sons made the few times she did come down.

"Jesun, she'll be all right," Hayden tried to reassure his friend. "She's been there this long and more than managed."

Jesun pulled at his fingers. " 'Should I bring all the children or leave the younger babe?' That's what she used to ask me. Every day the same thing. Then I'd tell her what I thought, and she'd say no, that the baby needed her most of all and the road was too hard for a child to make the journey. Or she wouldn't know how to pack, or who best to leave behind to caretake the large house. Mother would ask me what Norvin wanted, and I'd say, 'Only what's best for you.' But she wanted to be told what to do, then couldn't find the wherewithal to do it anyway. She doesn't know what she fears most, leaving home or being away from Father. So she does nothing, year after year. But Hayden, I can't stand to think of her so far away."

"It's late, Jesun, and you've got to stop worrying," Hayden said. "When you've seen your father, you can talk about plans then."

Jesun nodded. "There's nothing else to be done for now, I suppose. But this time she has to come."

That night we heard wolves in the distance, baying and crying to the stars. I lay on my side, near the fire, eyes open, listening to their calls. Earlier that night Hayden had set Muley to watch beside the fire. It was the first night we'd set a watch, and I felt better for it, though I didn't like admitting the need for one at all. The wolves' cries were distant and lonely. They didn't sound hungry or driven, only a part of the night, of the wind and the dark skies. I stretched a hand, felt for the tokens. Several days back, I'd lashed the pouch behind my saddle, much as Jared had when we'd ridden into Aster. But I hadn't felt comfortable with them out of my reach. A horse could bolt so easily; raiders could steal them, steal our gear . . . The worries had grown overpowering, till I'd given in and fixed the goblet again at my side: awkward but necessary.

The next morning we rode in silence till, blessedly, the road veered eastward, meandering into a series of passes and low valleys. Here the trees grew thicker and taller again, and the tricky underbrush was no longer as dense as it had been. With the riding easier, I thought it time to try talking to Ceena.

She pulled her horse to the right when she saw me, making room for me to ride alongside.

"Does the road keep on like this much longer?" I began. "Was my mother to have any other guard with her—after you left?" I asked again, but this time I saw Ceena wasn't listening.

Her gray horse held his ears flattened back as though there was a scent in the air. He kept flicking his neck away from the upper side of the hill, pulling back on the bit in his mouth. Ceena leaned forward and stroked his long cheek to quiet him, then reached and brought out a silver and ivory dagger and fixed it in her boot top.

"What did you hear?" I asked, thinking of the wolves and wondering that Ceena should be so concerned in the daylight.

"Nothing yet," she said, turning to where Hayden was riding up.

"Get back to where you were," he said, voice low as if he wanted to be certain the words wouldn't carry. "Next to Jesun, and don't look around."

Reluctantly I dropped back, slowed my horse. These were no wolves to have everyone so worried. Nor was it for any pack of wolves that Hayden had told me to change my clothes. Ahead of me now, Ceena and Hayden were talking, heads leaning in toward each other. I couldn't hear what they said, but I saw Ceena nod toward the right and Hayden followed her lead, looking cautiously about.

That night we rode as far into dark as we could while still saving time to set up camp. There was a crescent moon in the sky, with scarcely enough light to see the front of your hand by, but Hayden ordered us to build no fire, not for warmth and not for cooking. Trompson fed us cold cheese and dried meat, which we ate with little ceremony. For drink, he poured wine from the skin without even a sprig of dried spice to sweeten it. Our meal finished, Hayden and Ceena, Solly and Muley, spent the remainder of the evening cleaning and sharpening their weapons.

Later, when those of us who weren't on watch had climbed into our blankets, the wolves started their crying again. Ceena rose, walked a few paces into the dark. I could barely make out the sound of her movements, but even so, the pattern of her steps was etched into my memory. She stood with her feet set squarely apart, her hands resting at her sides as she moved through the paces of the Kanashan breath-of-night stance, her entire being an instrument fined-tuned for listening.

The wolves called each other, answering first from the west, then from the east, their voices rising and falling like wind across a wide lake, hollow and mournful. No one else said a word; we only waited while Ceena listened. At last she returned and seated herself on a log next to Hayden, but all of us could hear. "They are wolves," she said. "But not all of them."

I took a long breath. Human foes, I said to myself, almost relieved. Not Edishu and not his succubus.

Jesun rolled over. "We could ride through the night," he said. "We could make it to Briana in three days. If we start now, racing, we'd reach the lowland road tomorrow. They wouldn't dare chase any farther."

Hayden stared down the shadowed road. "No," he said, "not yet. They've stayed back this far until now. If they don't come any closer, we have a chance of making it to safety once we're beyond the Koryan River and down in the lowlands."

"Why the lowlands?" I asked.

"The closer we get to Briana, the less likely anyone is to risk an attack. There's more traffic on the roads there. And more of our own people."

"They could have made a stand anytime," Jesun said.

"But they haven't," Hayden said. "Which means they're waiting."

Trompson drew a blanket around his shoulders. "Yes, but who are they?"

"Robbers," Solly said. "Who else would be out in this forsaken pit of a forest?"

Muley nodded and I remembered Hayden saying that the two had come to Briana as a team, refusing to be separated when Norvin threw a soldier's cape to the giant Solly and a shovel at Muley's feet. "We don't have to worry," Muley said. "Not if they're robbers. The nine of us are more than enough to hold off a crew that's twice our size. Besides, no band roams this land with more than four men, not that I've ever heard of."

"It's possible," Hayden said. "Yet I'm not convinced. Can you think of anyone else who knew we'd be moving through the valley?"

"There's my mother, and her household," Jesun offered. "They knew."

"No, nobody there who isn't loyal," Hayden said. "Calyx? Who at Aster knew where you were going?"

"Why, most everyone, I imagine. But Hershann wouldn't send a raid against us. Unless it was the Kareil tracking us. They could have found out, I suppose. But it doesn't make sense."

"No." Ceena spoke from out of the dark. "This isn't their way."

"Anyone else?"

"Well, no. Nothing I can think of. Except . . ." I sat back, thinking back to the day I'd spent in Aster town with Dev.

Lightly Hayden prodded. "What is it?"

"Two things, really. I was with Dev . . . No, you wouldn't have met him. He took me into Aster, to a meeting. It was the first I'd heard of it, but apparently Dev had been going for some time. Another priest, Avram, was there. They spoke of organizing a band and going to Briana to confront Morell."

"What's this?" Hayden watched me carefully.

"I should tell you," I said slowly, "Avram is from Gleavon. I think . . . I have reason to believe he's Lethia's man."

"Why? What would she want with another priest?" Hannak asked.

Trompson said, "Or to pick a fight with Morell from Aster? I'd believe it if she set spies to watching us. But this much, it wouldn't make sense."

"Perhaps not," Hayden said, "but it could be her. The farther from Gleavon, the easier she'd think it to be. What more, Calyx?" Hayden leaned closer. "What of this other priest, Dev?"

"Dev had no hand in Avram's doings. He went there as a priest only, to watch their dreams. They were having dreams, the townsfolk. Jarak dreams . . . of a sort . . ." I looked away.

"What sort?" Hayden asked.

"All of them the same dream. Repeating itself."

"You mean people kept having the same dreams?"

"Different people having the same dream."

Ceena's eyes were hidden in the dark. "More dreams of Edishu?" she said.

"There's time to talk of jarak dreams later," Hayden

said. "But what's this about confronting Morell? What else were they saying?"

"Avram was trying to convince the people in Aster that Morell could help them," I said. "Either that, or that Briana would fall to them if they attacked. But I didn't take it seriously. These were townspeople. Unarmed. They were family people, not troops."

"And this Avram, he's from Gleavon. So you think Lethia may have a hand in it?"

"I don't know," I said, and for a while the question lay.

The wolves' calling filled the air again till Hayden said, "All right, let's leave it for now. In some ways, it might be like Lethia to send her men out in secret that way, far enough so we'd never be able to name her—though I can't see her reasons. And even if we could prove it true, there isn't anything to be done out here. For now, Muley, and you, Solly, take next watch. After that I'll sit with Ceena."

I must have dozed off because the next thing I heard were the sounds of wolves again, closer than before, but now the stars seemed to have shifted. Hayden and Jesun were sitting watch: Hayden facing east, across to the other side of the road, and Jesun west, through the black forest. I fell back to sleep thinking of Rath's circle tight around my wrist and wondering whether any of Jokjoa's weapons could be used against living men rather than dreams.

When I woke next there were voices nearby, low and murmuring, and the sound of steel being drawn from a scabbard. Two, four, eight heads I counted, the full number of our company. One of them, Trompson, crawled up beside me, his hand on my shoulder warning me to silence.

"Hayden says we move. Now. There," he pointed, "to the deeper trees for cover. Mind you stay quiet. And low."

Quickly Trompson helped bundle my gear out of the way while I pulled on my boots. Hayden was already leading the others away from the clearing, back toward the promise of shelter. Beneath the trees the snow cover was lighter, with open stretches of ground showing through. Trompson showed me how to choose a path through the snow where the sounds of brittle twigs were less likely to give us away.

At the rear of our line, Starn and Hannak led the horses, two abreast, their heads ducked well below the rise of the horses' backs. It was then, just as I thought we might make it to the cover of the trees, that the attack came.

A shout sounded behind me, and I turned to see a man vault out at us from behind the trees. Before we could move, he dove between the rear set of horses and drew his sword on Starn.

Starn reeled to face him, but his hands twisted in the reins as he turned and he lost his footing, stumbled to the side. There was a desperate quiet for a moment, then a moan and another sound. It was Starn, a sword sliced through his stomach so quickly that none of the others had time to realize it had happened.

I stood there almost without understanding—watching as the dark figure above Starn yanked his blade free and leapt away.

"Get her down," Ceena shouted, and Trompson was suddenly pulling me, dragging me toward cover behind the trunk of a wide tree.

Trompson pushed my shoulders in, but I peered out the other side just in time to see Hannak reach Starn's side. He was trying to grab him around his shoulders, drag him away to quiet. But he never had the chance. Another man ran up on Hannak, knife drawn to his throat. Abruptly Hayden jumped in, smashing his boot into one man's back and hurtling him backward, away from Hannak.

Somehow Hayden and Hannak shook themselves free of the attack, regrouping and joining the others around the trees. Only Starn's motionless body, sprawled across the blood-soaked snow, was left to mark the battle.

"Pull the horses in," Hayden called to Jesun. "Muley, move that log, the split one. Are you ready?"

In answer, Muley's two short daggers disappeared into his boot tops. Hands free, he grabbed the opposite side of the log from Hayden, started shoving it toward a second tree. Warning me to stay under cover, Trompson ran to help, but I had no intention of sitting uselessly about. Quickly I jumped in behind, grabbing an end of the log with the others, heaving it closer till a wall began to form.

"Solly, you there next to Muley? Ceena? The next—" Hayden started, but there was no time. Three shadowed figures jumped from the trees. Trompson grabbed my hand, again urging me back to my place behind the trees.

From the left this time, a handful of new men jumped at Jesun, matching us, outnumbering us. While Jesun fought on his right, Hayden sprang after one of the others, whipping his outstretched sword across the man's stomach. As I watched, the man doubled over, both arms crossed desperately over his middle till his knees buckled forward and he slumped to the ground.

Trompson jumped away from me, pulling his dagger free as he ran to help Hannak.

I started up on one elbow, but Ceena saw my move. "Get down," she shouted, and I did as I was told, though my helplessness frightened me almost more than the battle itself. Ceena was in the middle of the fighting now, her sword raised to mid-height to meet another man's weapon. She tried a feint with a quick lunge, then a side sweep, but the man was already waiting. I watched her parry attack after attack, but she made no headway and seemed tense with the effort, as if she were waiting for something.

At the exact moment I thought she had him, the man jumped backward, away from her reach. All in a moment he reeled about, came up facing a surprised Muley, and before there was time to react, he buried his sword in the old man's back.

Muley cried out, staggering under the blow, then fell forward, his face choking on muck and snow. Caught by the cry, I started after him, thinking only that he wouldn't want them to have his dagger . . .

A gravelly voice away to my left called out, "The girl! Get her! There she is."

For a fraction of a moment, the fighting seemed to stop, the man's words echoing in my ears. I looked up once to see Ceena poised in her fighting, watching me. I thought surely she'd push me back to cover or shout for me to get away, but she said nothing, just watched me as if she'd been waiting for some sign. Still I kept half in a crouch, half in a crawl till I reached Muley's body. His back was turned so I could not see his face. His dagger was on the ground where he'd fallen, slippery and cold as death, but I grabbed it, started crawling backward again.

Somehow I made it back to the safety of my tree, holding Muley's dagger awkwardly in my hand. When I looked out again, the first thing I saw was Ceena standing alone in the center of the fighting, watching me.

Our eyes met and she turned suddenly away. A fury seemed to have come over her, as if whatever she'd been waiting for had come to pass and she was ready now. With a cry Ceena turned her short sword upon herself, drew a line across her forearm till the blood ran red and free to her elbow, spilled onto her shirt, to the fractured white earth. She let her sword fall to the ground, unneeded. But her bloodied arm she raised skyward, and in a voice that shattered the air, she cried, *"Kanashan, Sunder! Thanun, Sunder! Cruor, Sunder!"*

Overhead, she traced a pattern in the air, triangular and intricate. And then she leaped, as sudden and high as a whirlwind. The first man she reached fell over with a single deadly blow. There was the sound of bone meeting bone, a cracking and splitting sound, and then silence. Another of the raiders stood watching, too frightened to move. Ceena spun toward him, her body a riot of motion, Sunder's daughter now more fully than ever before.

She struck his neck first, then brought the side of her hand slicing down toward his temples, and he reeled away, his legs carrying him clumsily toward the tree where I'd been watching. For a moment his eyes cleared and he looked at me . . .

So close . . . Time froze. He could reach me. Kill me still. And I knew it; sensed it inside his desperation; in his hand, still clutching his knife; his eyes, surprised by pain. So close . . .

"Jarak witch," he groaned, and in answer I hefted Muley's dagger, quickly found its point of balance. Then I raised it without a thought; raised it and brought it down into his chest; denying his words; felt his flesh grab and hold, muscles tearing, felt his falling, felt the dagger being pulled from my fist.

His eyes widened, and a choking sound came from high up in his throat. His knees buckled and he slumped to the ground, then lay still.

Ceena was at my side, pulling me back, away toward the trees. Away from the man's too-white face. "He's dead," she said. "Are you all right?"

I forced myself to look at her, but I couldn't answer. I was trembling, surprised by my own audacity, by the death I'd just witnessed. Ceena turned, yanked the bloodied dagger from the man's chest, wiped it on the ground, then again on her leggings before handing it back to me. And I took it, not knowing what else to do.

The fighting kept on for only a little longer. Several of the raiders watching Ceena had already turned to flee. A moment later the first touch of morning light opened across the sky, and the few remaining raiders signaled each other to pull back.

"Calyx!" Hayden called. "Calyx, where are you?"

"She's here," Ceena answered for me. "She's all right. But lower your voice. And no names. We're not free of this yet."

Beside Hayden, Solly kneeled over Muley's body and lifted him up to a half-sitting position. He was talking to him, the words coming faster than I'd ever heard him speak, but whatever it was Solly needed to say, it was too late.

Hayden surveyed our company, then called to Jesun, "Get Starn. Move him and Muley closer to our side. We're riding out of here as soon as we've given the rites to Sunder."

With Jesun's help, Solly lifted his friend up in his arms. Dead, the man looked too frail to have ever walked. Solly held him to his chest, a giant next to the still, white-bearded man. Solly's face was wracked and speechless now. Jesun stood back, allowing the man his last words of farewell.

Hayden, Ceena, and the others worked over the mass of weapons and wasted supplies, but I had no stomach for such things. Heedless and numb, I turned away, watching a bird fly from its tree. I needed to walk. To move. To try not to think about the faces of the dead I'd just met. The dying man's curse. I followed the bird's path, closer to the road where the bushes grew gnarled and tall. Looked up.

Not ten paces away, three archers stood aiming back toward the trees. Their bows were already cocked, arrows fitted to their strings.

I came to suddenly and cried a warning shout as I ran, tripping back toward the others. Behind me Hayden turned, but Trompson had been looking the other way, his back a ready target for the first of the three arrows.

Trompson lurched forward, then fell, his voice stifled by the earth.

"Get down!" Hayden warned, but it wasn't necessary. The warning spray of arrows had already ended. Hannak grabbed the shuddering Trompson by his arms and pulled him back to our circle. By the time Hannak had ripped open Trompson's shirt to find the wound, the third man was dead.

*   *   *

We spent the rest of that day digging three shallow graves. Starn, Muley, and now Trompson, all of them good fighters and all of them gone. After a hasty burial—Sunder had already claimed her due—we quietly assembled what little gear remained in our reach. But the raiders must have been watching us the entire time. From our left a warning arrow sped suddenly past one of our horse's shoulders, nicking the poor thing before it settled to the ground.

Ceena jumped to the fallen arrow.

"Do you know it?" Hayden asked.

Ceena studied the arrow, its shaft and fletching, then passed it to Solly's waiting hands. "It's as common as any could be," she said, and Solly nodded his agreement.

"Could be from anywhere in the northlands," he said.

Hayden's mouth was set in a hard line. "Then unless something happens, we have no way of knowing who we're fighting."

"Avram," I whispered.

"What's that?" my brother asked. Hayden was keeping me close at his side now, and I sat huddled against a log, feeling the cold, the utter loneliness of death so close by I could taste its hollow cry.

"It's Avram. I'm sure of it," I said.

"How?"

"You heard what he called me, didn't you?" I forced myself to look up, meet Hayden's eyes first, then Ceena's. "Jarak witch."

"Why?" Ceena demanded. "Why?"

"There was trouble with a Kareil dream watch. They showed my jarak dreams to the entire hall. Strong dreams, they were. Dangerous. Then later—this was just before you arrived—Hershann put it out that the whole affair had been a farce. Only Avram didn't know, or didn't care. He'd already left the temple, ridden south for Gleavon. But not before he had time to come through here, hire raiders, fire them up on his story."

"It's possible," Jesun said. "He could have heard at the inn that seven men had been traveling toward Aster. Put together several different possible plans and hired raiders to keep a watch along the road."

Hayden was standing beside me, listening, but without giving Jesun his full attention. He was twisting a ring about his little finger, a plain band of gold with small jewels set inside. I had never seen the ring before, and I wondered if it wasn't an amulet of one of the Sisters. He stopped when he saw me watching. "Queen Korinna," he said, his mouth tight. "You remember her?"

I nodded, yes. And Hayden tried to smile, but ended shaking his head instead. "This is my fault," he said, and I was surprised again at the kind of man he'd grown to be. "You shouldn't be here. You should never have been threatened this way."

"It's not like that." I started to reach a hand toward him, but he turned away and began pacing.

"Morell didn't want you to come back. Not now. Not with Ivane ill. If I had listened to him, you'd still be safe in Aster temple. But, no! I had to have my way, pretend I could make peace in the family."

"But I wasn't safe in Aster."

"I thought I could make Ivane happy," Hayden said. "Just once. Seed knows, I'd done little enough for her before. And it was such a small request she made, to see you again. Maybe I'm only the young fool of a soldier Father makes me out to be. Not fit to lead my own troops."

"Hayden, stop." I walked after him. "This is none of your doing. Didn't you hear? It was me they wanted. And they would have found me here or in Roshanna Inn or even in my bed in Aster. You could as easily say that I'm better off at your side than not. Solly? Jesun? Isn't that true?" I turned, looking for agreement, but the two men would not meet my eyes.

I reeled back toward Hayden. "Get the girl. Jarak witch. That's what they called me!"

"You say it like you're trying to convince me it's true," Hayden said.

Ceena came over and stood behind me.

"Jarak witch!" I said again. "Maybe it's true, Ceena. Maybe you should give me up to them."

Ceena put her hands on my shoulder to calm me. "There's no blame to be taken. Not you, Hayden, or you, Calyx. I don't know what happened to you in that temple, but we're caught in the god's dream. You. Me. All of us. Though we try to make our choices freely, the world is not always ours to deliver."

15

We made our beds in a tight circle that night, with no fire to light our faces or watch by. No moon lit the sky, but overhead the stars spiraled in a white band, the only light in the world, opening its arms toward distant Kuoshana.

Beside me, five other people—four men and one woman—slept heavily and, I hoped for their sake, without dreams. Even Hayden, who had taken late watch for himself, had fallen asleep, his forehead heavy on raised knees. I tapped his foot, startling him, and he peered into the darkness. We had talked of the morning, of risking an escape before another dawn lit the sky. Hayden had favored the idea. What other hope was there? he had asked. There had been some talk of sending a scout out later in the night, and a second plan of waiting to see what daylight brought. But the day had been lost to the task of burials, and firm plans somehow had never coalesced. We had eaten what food we could, then silently tried to make ourselves comfortable, till one by one the company had drifted to sleep.

For myself, though, there was no hope of sleep. No matter how I tried to think only of the uneven ground, the biting wind, the sound of a night owl skimming the air, it was impossible. No one had uttered the words or dared meet my eyes with the thought, but how could I miss the bitter set on Jesun's or Solly's mouths? We would never leave this forest alive! As long as Calyx, *the Jarak witch* remained, they would pick us off one by one.

"Hayden," I whispered. "I have to walk."

My brother looked skeptical.

"At least let me stretch my legs. I can't sleep . . . Just once?"

"I suppose it's dark enough, there shouldn't be any more trouble tonight," he whispered. "Go on, then, but hurry right back if you hear the slightest sound. And keep me in sight. See that tree? Go no farther than that. And sister . . . I've missed you. Don't go taking any foolish risks. For my sake, please."

We agreed on an owl hoot for a signal, followed by a clicking sound as of a twig snapping if I wanted to call his attention. Carefully I crawled away from our circle. Stopped. Waited. Then, hearing no other sounds, I stood upright. The snow here was sparse, the branches overhead so dense they formed a roof against the sky. Underfoot, the forest floor was a scattering of old leaves, brown grasses, and pine cones. It felt good to be walking, to move, to feel the open air dancing across my face, and for the moment not to think of the coming morning or the new dead.

The tree Hayden had pointed out was a thick-limbed, stately birch with a tapestry of branches circling upward. I stood beside it a moment, touching it, feeling the strength of its wood against my hand. There was another tree beside the first, equally tall and round, its white bark so clean in that dim light, I thought no pen could ever touch a finer sheet.

But when I looked closer, the tree seemed to take on a reddish hue, a different, stronger sort of light.

I moved a step to the right, trying to look upward to where the red seemed almost to dance against the black sky. But now I was certain: there was a light. I moved, and the light moved. I stopped. Tried again. When I held still, the light rose up, not so much along the line of the tree as between that birch and the next, illuminating a space between them. I moved again.

Then something else caught my eye. A different light.

Somehow Rath had slipped free of my sleeve. It was loose, exposed against my wrist, and it was glowing, shimmering. A beacon of red-hued light emanated from it downward, tracing a path along the ground, then up again to the space between the trees.

This time when I stepped forward, Rath's light held steady. I held out my arm, following. Now a vivid warmth joined the light, blowing out of that space between the trees as though it were a doorway to a house and the warm air was reaching from within, inviting me in. I followed it until I stood between the two trees, their branches locked and towering over my head. I had the feeling that it was somehow very important to look at this opening from the other side, to see the tree from another view. I stepped back and looked to either side. But where the forest had seemed open before, another tree now stood backed up tight as a wall against the first, then another and another stretching endlessly in each direction, a wall of trees set side by side, their branches woven tight.

Nothing in all the world seemed to matter more than to enter that doorway and know for myself the touch of warmth living inside. I raised my arm. Rath led me forward.

With the first step a shaft of warm sunlight poured out to guide my path. With the second step it seemed as if one world ended and another began. With the third step I found myself in a wide clearing inside a ring of trees. It was daylight again, broad, welcoming daylight with the forest green and pleasant around me. It couldn't have taken me all night to follow that entryway. Hayden would have come searching. Yet here was a new day, the sky clear, the bloodied ground swept clean as if the attack had never happened. As if winter had never been born.

"Hayden?" I started to call, then stopped. What if the raiders still lurked about the woods? Surely they could have followed me inside, or seen the light through the trees. But no, I was safe. I could feel it in the warm ground and the sweet scent of ferns and wildflowers in the air. No enemy could ever follow me into this place. Eclipse's hallowed touch was on the land, as real and palpable as the glowing sun beaming down on my face.

With the surety borne of a lifetime of waiting, I knew Rath had brought me to one of the havens. Not a vision such as I'd seen inside Aster's ancient room. A real haven. Found again. One of Ceena's havens . . .

Now I saw the lavender and hollyhocks growing wild in the grass and farther out, at the circle's wide rim, rows of towering weeping willows tight as a palisaded wall separated the haven from the outside world. Off in a branch, two songbirds shared a tune. The earth here was verdant, healthy, and alive like a longed-for memory of childhood before the chill of age and loss.

The only thing missing was a sign of people such as I'd found in that earlier vision. The Silkiyam might have lived here once. Wouldn't they have left something behind, some long-lost tool or cooking implement forgotten all these years?

Holding Rath aloft as if it were a lantern, I started toward the center rise of the haven. It wasn't far to go; the mead was no larger than a pasture. The only thing I did find was a small pond, a mirror of still water nestled in the tall grass. The water held a fragrance all its own, honey rich and heady as the finest wine. I knelt down to drink, making a cup of my hand. Sipped at it, savoring it. Then I thought of Gamaliel still tucked away at my side. How fitting it would be to accept the gift of this water from the god's own goblet.

I untied the lacing, drew out the goblet, and dipped it full down into the water. From the goblet, the taste seemed even richer, ambrosia-like. I lowered the goblet, ran a finger along its rim. Something was happening.

Inside the goblet the water was changing, darkening. An image appeared, a vision reflecting a sky far different than the one overhead.

I saw a granite wall shimmering behind me, a wall of dark gray, striated rock, ancient and so smooth that I thought no human foot could ever dare its ascent. At its base a lake sat, clear and patient.

Slowly, as if by looking, I would be able to hold every curve and fold in the rock, I kept gazing into the goblet. Then, finally I found a darker space, there along the bottom, a tall, angular shape that could not have been formed by any action of the land. It was a door, I felt certain, opening into a land on the other side.

People lived on the other side of that wall; I could almost hear them. Ceena's people. But I didn't know how to reach them.

And then it faded. The water cleared. The haven stood as it was before.

I emptied the water back into the pond. The few drops remaining were clear again. Curious, I refilled the goblet and waited. Nothing happened. I spilled it back, filled it again. This time I dipped one little finger into the center, sent a tiny ripple washing across the surface. The scene returned, exactly as before: towering cliffs, lake, and boulders.

Again I repeated the process: filled the goblet, waited, touched the water, and watched as the scene reappeared. Each time it was the same. There was a method to the magic, elements that must be combined for the result to occur. Gamaliel, always silent till now, required water to release its power. Water plus a human touch, and its fire could be kindled. Rath was similar in some ways—a human touch was also required. But there the similarity ended. Rath was a thing of light, Eclipse's token, with the power to reveal things hidden by magic. Gamaliel must be one of Seed's tokens, needing water, one of the elements of life.

I rose, returned the goblet to my side. There were enough mysteries here to occupy an entire temple full of skeptics, I told myself. But I had others to think of, and the night was too short to spend on musing upon what might be.

Turning around, I cupped my hands to my mouth, shouting, "Hayden!" I called, giving the signal we had agreed on, half expecting to see him come riding through the trees. But no, he couldn't hear me, could he? I called again, then waited. Still no answer. The trees were a barrier, separating the haven from the rest of the world.

But what if I went back now and convinced Hayden to follow me? Wouldn't we be able to hide here, all of us, together? The raiders wouldn't know how to follow. Of that I felt certain. Rath had led me here. Without the token no one else could enter.

I started back again, down toward the far wall of branches that stood like a curtain against a dark window. Already I could hear the sounds of horses nibbling on shoots of dried grass outside. Anxiously I circled around the outer edge of the haven, searching for the opening. The leaves were warm, soft to the touch, and I followed them until finally one set seemed cooler than the rest. I pushed the tangled fall aside, found the doorway, and stepped back into the night.

And then I was through, out in the dry, wintry forest once again. Once more I turned about. The haven had slipped again into a patternless fall of trees and earth. Where the birch doorway had stood, a speckled brown spruce hen perched to defend its brood. The hungry branches of a sparse alder tree reached toward the distant sun.

Within moments I was kneeling at my brother's side. "Hayden!" I shook his shoulder lightly, praying he would be too glad of the haven to fear his sister who'd found it. "Hayden, wake the others. We can hide. We'll be safe!"

"There's no one here." Hayden stepped through into the haven's warm air, his voice hushed and reverent—and surprised also, for I'm certain that until that moment, my brother hadn't really believed my tale.

"Can you feel the air? It's warm . . ." Hannak dropped his pack to the ground and stood with a fresh smile starting out through his silvered beard. "Feels like a spring day when I was a boy," he laughed. "Look there, look at that!" he shouted, and we all turned to catch a glimpse of a yellow-crowned song bird skirting high over the willow's bowled rim.

For a while no one spoke. Ceena stood slightly apart from the rest of us, but we were all strangers on a foreign soil, watching. Overhead the bird soared and glided in wide circles, playing with air currents and waiting, perhaps for its mate.

"Will they see it as well, out on the other side?" Hannak turned to me. "That's what I want to know."

"I don't think so," I said. "When I was just inside, alone, I called for Hayden. Called as loud as I dared. He never heard. And I couldn't see him from inside. Couldn't see or hear anything either, until just the moment I stepped outside."

"It's too dark anyway to have seen so far."

"But he would have heard. And I didn't see the haven until I was standing inside." I looked to see if Ceena was listening, but she was too far away, deep in her own thoughts.

"The truth is, it was here all along. And to find it . . . I suppose . . ." I searched for an explanation. "It was Eclipse's hand that led me. Anyone could have done the same. It was her power that hid it in the first place, wasn't it?"

"No," Solly said, watching me closely. "Eclipse might have led you to it. But it had to be you who was out there in the night. Not any of us. I doubt we would have ever found it on our own. Even if we'd tripped over the same spot, we wouldn't have found it. The goddess might have allowed it. But it was you she led to the haven, Lady Calyx."

"No!" I paled. "I was led. Any one of us could have found it. It was a trick of the light—"

"What is this place, Hayden?" Jesun spoke out suddenly. "We shouldn't be here. We've no right! Can't you feel the air? It's different. Wrong. No mortal should set foot in a haven. We weren't meant to. What do you think they're hidden for? And I don't know how you found your way in, Calyx. But I want none of it. I'm leaving. Solly? Hannak? Are you with me?"

"I don't know," Hannak said. "Maybe you're right, Jesun.

This place, it doesn't feel right. But I can't very well walk out, only three of us, leave the others behind."

"Jesun, wait," Solly said. "Starn woulda known what to say, but I'm not so quick with words as he was. It's not that simple, whatever you think. We're dead if they find us. Haven't a chance. What's the harm if we stay hidden, long as we're here already? We'll leave soon enough. It doesn't look like there's anyone here to trouble us."

"Harm?" Jesun repeated. "Harm? You think one raider's blade will hurt compared with the wound you'll take trespassing on the Sisters' ground? No! I'm for taking our chances with weapons we understand, not this—this jarak magic."

"Well, maybe you're right about that—" Hannak said.

"Enough!" Hayden cried, his voice cutting sharply. "You will not speak so! Not now and not again. Jesun, will you commit treason in my name?"

"Treason? Hayden, what are you saying? I said nothing against you. Nothing! I swear it."

"Then you will say nothing against my sister, either. Not without understanding that to speak against her is to speak against me. You will follow my lead here as elsewhere. And if you must, then say it was I led you through the birch entry into this haven. Hayden, Briana's lord."

Jesun looked at the ground, then back up squarely to Hayden's eyes.

"And we will speak no more of magic. We are soldiers here, not priests that one of us should lay a greater claim to the gods than another, even if it be to deny any claim." Hayden's face was red with anger, but when he turned at length to look at me, it was forgiveness I saw there. "Calyx, sister," he said, choosing his words, "I don't know how you found this . . . haven. But neither does it matter. We are here, and from what I can judge of that forest barrier we passed through, we're safe. For that I thank you. We all thank you. And we should rest. Yesterday's battle was no easy sight to stomach, not for me, and I think not for a sheltered northland cleric either. We'll make our beds there, tucked up against the line of trees. And we'll sleep in a peace we wouldn't have known were it not for you."

We spread our blankets out on the grass, Hannak near Solly, Jesun near Hayden, with Ceena and I drawn off a little farther away. Nearer to the line of willows, Jesun, in his sweet, light voice, began a song I had not heard since I was a child playing in Briana's courtyard:

> In the town
> The dreamers grow.
> Shunned in forest
> Silkiyam know.
> One, two, one, two.
> Stones throw
> Dreamers go.
> Sunder finds what Eclipse knows.
> One, two, one, two.
> Stones throw. Dreamers go.
> Forest hides
> What Seed did sow.

"Calyx?" Hayden whispered my name in the silence after the song had ended. "Calyx?"

"I found it, Hayden," I said. "That's all I know. Or perhaps it found me. Let them call me jarak witch or whatever they will. But for now, let's take it as a gift, and praise the Sisters who set it here. I don't have any answers."

"It's not your fault, Calyx. The fighting—"

"Let the child sleep, Hayden," Ceena offered from my other side. "What we need now is a plan. I say we hold here one day. Longer than that the raiders won't trouble themselves to wait. They'll think we slipped away during the night . . . that we put a sign of Eclipse's magic on the forest, or forced them into an unnatural sleep. Whatever they decide to call it, they'll be far enough away from here."

Hayden lowered his voice, and in the stillness I must have fallen asleep. Nearby, Ceena and Hayden were speaking, their voices hushed so as not to wake the others.

"Through all the ages of the northlands," Ceena was saying, "the havens belonged to my people. And they were my home for as many years as it takes a girl to grow to womanhood. Until one day I came home to find our houses burned, our people disappeared. I was forgotten, by the dead, by the living as well. And if not forgotten, forsaken. I've lived outside the havens now for more years than I lived within. There's so much I've forgotten. But what I've told you is true."

"Then we are truly safe and the raiders won't find us, so long as we remain inside this circle?"

"Look, there. See the willows, how they bend away from the circle? The border on this side seems to follow that line. But outside, where the raiders watch, there is only the one birch tree Calyx first saw. Outside, there is no wall of trees, no path to follow, nothing. That world does not enter the havens. The three Sisters saw to that."

"But tell me again how Calyx found the entrance? And how were your people found?"

I raised my head over the line of Hayden's shoulder to see better. Ceena's dark, prominent features seemed at war with each other, trying, as were the rest of us, to understand. "That is the question, isn't it?" she said. "One answer may do for both, but I'm not sure I have all the pieces yet. The Sisters' magic has been failing. That much we all know for certain, though you people of the towns may not remember when life had ever been different. But none of us are so young we can't remember an earlier time when season did not bleed into season with no healing to mark the separation.

"But it was long before this that the Sumedaro's jarak magic had begun to fail. The Kareil, as keepers of our history, speak of a time when all the townspeople were Sumedaro—not only the priests as it is today—and all had jarak dreams. I don't know which came first, whether the Sumedaro built their temples to regain their dreams, or the construction of the temples and villages themselves brought on the weakening of their dreams. But inside these questions somewhere, are the real beginnings of the tale. Perhaps it's true that the earth is reacting to Edishu's presence. There's a tenacity to the cold that never was there before, as if something was preventing the sun's touch from reaching the earth, remembering.

"So too it may have been with the havens. They were old. Ancient. Perhaps their magic wards were weakened, as summer had been weakened, the earth itself failing as the gods' power failed. I'm not sure how, but the barriers continued eroding, enough so eventually a band of raiders found a way to slip through . . .

"As to what Solly said, that it had to be Calyx who found the entrance, he's right, though she tries to deny it herself. Somehow she's part of the cycle. She's a dreamer, you know. With jarak power stronger than I've seen anywhere before. Anywhere!"

"But she said she was no Sumedaro—"

"Not a priest, no," Ceena corrected. "A dreamer. It's taken me all this time to understand there's a difference, that even after living with them in the temple, she could grow to one and not the other. The one has nothing to do with the other, you see—though I know that's not what they teach you. But Jokjoa would never allow his power to wane if he did not leave a means behind to shield the earth from Edishu's touch."

Ceena's words seemed like a whisper spoken in a different language, sounds that fell without meaning. I felt dizzy suddenly, overwhelmed. I reached across to Ceena, longing for her more solid strength. Gently she put her arm around my shoulder and pulled me close to her. I could smell the tangy sweat on her clothes, the smell of horses and woodsmoke, dried blood and tears, all mingled together in her touch.

I loved her, my sullen Ceena, and I loved Hayden, my gangly older brother who had grown into a king. And the laughing, frightened Jesun and Solly, poor Solly, who had shed a man's tears for his friend. And Hannak too. And somehow, though I didn't know how, I had brought them here, to the sanctuary of this haven. But I didn't know if I had failed them or saved them.

Though the air was warm, I shivered. I was safe here, for the time at least. Safe from Edishu's threats. And if what Ceena said was true, that the gods meant to fight Edishu, then I was not alone. And if my dreams were a portal for Edishu to reach me, so they were also open to these havens and to the Sisters who had shaped the havens. And I might yet be safe.

I stayed awake a little while longer till at last even Hayden and Ceena let the easy sleep of the haven fall over them. Then I too slept. When I woke again, the moon had turned in its course. A gathering of stars danced across the clear, dark sky. Beside me, Hayden's silhouette rose and fell in easy breaths. I sat up, looked about. Jesun, Hannak, and Solly were asleep. Only Ceena's blankets were empty.

There was no path to give away her footsteps, but once I started walking, I couldn't help but find her. She stood tall, facing the northernmost point of trees. Her back was to me, so I could not see her face. But I could hear her and watch.

In her hands she held a small, dead animal—a ground squirrel perhaps, I couldn't be sure. But it was newly dead, its body limp, tiny feet upright. Its neck must have been broken, judging from the way its head hung foolishly awry. Then, as if that broken body were some hallowed libation, Ceena raised it aloft, marking her invocation to the gods. While its blood ran in dark rivulets down her arms, she sang a slow, beseeching song; the words the same as those she had cried out in the midst of the fighting: *Thanan. Kanashan. Cruor. Thanan. Kanashan. Cruor. Thanan. Kanashan. Cruor.*

Over and over she repeated the fragments, her voice trembling, sometimes tired, sometimes angry. She stopped, then started over again, shaking the animal's body as though she were threatening the sky, her need so palpable it was carried to me, a thing on the wind, in the air.

And then she stopped and hung her head. She dropped the animal's body to the ground, then sat, back hunched, arms hugging her knees.

Quietly I joined her. After a while she asked, "Do you remember the day I first talked to you about the havens?"

"Yes. You said the Silkiyam had lived in the havens. But Ceena, I never knew, never imagined . . . How could you have endured Briana after this? It must have been like death."

"Hush!" Ceena shook her head. "I never lived *here*. This haven I never knew. There were so many. Like doors in a great house. Yet you are right also. And this one"—she plucked a blade of grass—"is not so very different from the others."

"What were you doing just now? What were you saying?"

"I asked Sunder to let me go home. In return, I promised her service, my life in service. I dared to hope if I offered a blood sacrifice, she might accept me."

"And . . . ? Did she answer?"

"No." Ceena forced her voice to hold steady. "I fear sometimes that the door was closed to me when I first left the havens. That they can't hear me, or won't let me back."

"Ceena," I said slowly, "it wasn't I who found the havens. That is, not exactly. I know I was the one who found it. But I was led—"

"Led? By Eclipse? But no, I see. There's something else, isn't there?"

In answer I pulled the pouch from my side. Stood Gamaliel up for her to see, then took Rath from my wrist and laid it on the grass beside the goblet. "Rath and Gamaliel. Jokjoa's tokens."

Her eyes flashed. "I can see that," she said, and there was anger in her voice. "What are you doing with them?"

"I took them from Aster. Borrowed them. I needed protection for my dreams. But I wanted you to know it was Rath that led me to the havens. I never would have found the entrance without it."

"I see."

"And Ceena, there was something else too. When I found the haven earlier today, Gamaliel showed me something. Maybe you'll know what it meant. There was a wall of rock towering overhead. Higher than Briana Keep's highest tower. High as a hill. But it wasn't a hill. Though it wasn't a wall, either. Not exactly. It was a barrier, I think. And I had the feeling there were people on the other side. Hiding, maybe."

"Hiding? Yes." Ceena turned, the anger gone out of her again. "I don't know if I dare think of it. It's almost beyond hope that the Silkiyam found a way to go deeper into the havens. And the goblet's magic revealed the place. Still, you see, it's no less hidden than before . . . But that I might dare hope . . ." She shook her head, as if forcing herself back from her own bright vision. "So, you think it was the bracelet and not you that found the haven?"

"Of course it was the bracelet. It led me. It opened the door."

"There's too much here, too much I don't understand. Though it does make sense that the bracelet's power led you. But the door . . ." She shook her head. "The inner door? Where would that be? Not here, surely. That would be too easy. But somewhere, just as this haven had a door from one world to the next."

"Ceena . . . Do you want me to use it again? If you think there's a door . . . ? I'd use them to help you. Or for my mother, if there was anything I could do."

For a long time Ceena stared at the tokens. Then, finally, in answer, she pushed the pouch back toward me. "No," she said. "Put them away. I don't know what you could do for Ivane, but they're not for me. I don't think you understand what you're offering here. Thank you. But it's not time yet. Someday—soon, I dare hope—I'll start searching in earnest again. And if I find them, ask them to take me back, if they would, then perhaps I could finish my learning, be fully Sunder's daughter."

"But what you did today, the way you fought. That was no small thing."

Ceena rose to her feet. "The Silkiyam were given the forest to live in. And I was taught that what lives in the forest, so we also may become. Stone, wood, water, the natural things of the earth. When I touch stone, I too am like stone, hard, unyielding, and strong. With wood I can flex, be light enough to stir in the wind yet strong also, in the way that the trunk of a tree is strong. But knowing that hasn't been enough. I need more."

Ceena's gaze turned far away in thought. "I told you once," she said. "Kanashan incomplete is useless. And so it is. It takes me the greatest power I can summon to do the smallest act. With more knowledge I might have done more and used less power. What I can do anymore, it's only a shadow image of what I might have been . . . But I don't remember. For whatever reason, part of my memory's been locked since that day my home was destroyed. Burned out of me like so much smoke coming from the houses. The fire. I was outcast in every sense of the word, denied even my memories . . . Perhaps that was best, though. Perhaps there were secrets I wasn't meant to bring into your world. But sitting here like this, I can't help but hope that soon, very soon, the time will come to search for my people. If you can show me a haven, Morell's daughter"—Ceena forced a laugh, reached toward me—"then surely I may yet find the Silkiyam."

16

We left the haven near noon the next day, then rode for three days at a hard gallop, through wind and freezing rains that stung our faces and pelted our chests. All had gone as Ceena said. The raiders weren't fool enough to linger in the forest, sulking over lost prey. And though we all feared the chance that they'd raced on ahead, hoping to outrun us, that we'd stumble onto them farther along the road, Hayden said no. They would have awakened to find us fled into the night, he said, the prize they'd hoped to catch stolen away and nothing but a tale of Eclipse's tampering hand to take home to their master—whoever that might be.

How strange it was to meet anew the man my brother had become: as strong-edged as Morell at times and then again, a man you could trust for fairness and true concern. His soldierly side kept us to a hard pace, scarcely allowing time to rest or eat. But the strange thing was, we felt stronger for the effort, as though the few hours' refuge the haven had granted us had done more than merely hide our bodies. It had succored our spirits and offered us renewal. Hayden saw that and acknowledged it, using his concern for people in a way Morell would never have conceived.

We didn't speak of it, this feeling of redemption, not then . . . Could we have discussed a maelstrom when we were yet inside its belly? But I knew what I felt and I could see from the horses' long strides and my friends' heads bowed to the wind, hair and capes flying free behind them, that we had all been touched by the Sister's hand.

And then suddenly, the afternoon of the third day, we reached Briana. Now the sounds of the horses' hoofbeats changed, and the dull remarks of the soft road were replaced with the hard ringing of cobbled roadways clattering in my ears.

Briana had changed. I saw it at once, but not in ways I would have guessed. Everywhere I looked, new wealth showed its garish face. Lethia's gilded touches rimmed the avenues and pathways, and where one inn had stood on a main route there were three now, all full of shouting and drinking, all marked by trailing lines of refuse and mangy dogs rooting about the gutters. Morell had paid, but with a different coin than he'd bargained with. And Lethia's wealth that he had hoped to make his own looked as if it had remade Briana in her image instead.

Then, all in a whirl of guards and gateways, kitchen maids with great baskets of washing slung across their laughing hips, priests and gawking stable boys, we crested the hill and passed through the high walls of Briana Keep. Hayden glanced back as if to make certain he hadn't lost me along the way, and Hannak rode dutifully to my side—though I looked with disdain on the hand he tried to offer. I took a steadying breath and promised myself not to think of my cropped hair and windburned face that had once been the standing joke inside these corridors and kitchens.

Inside the first yard, a stable boy ran up and took the reins from me, his curious eyes aching to figure out who exactly I was. I tried to look straight ahead, but even so, the heavy glances and hushed whispers that followed me about the courtyard were difficult to ignore.

A swarm of men suddenly surrounded Hayden—soldiers, servants, merchants hoping for a quick sale. They plied him with questions, laughing, begging for a word about the road, the travelers, whether there'd been any women, whether the northern lands had worsened or not.

Not until Hayden had arranged for someone to see to the horses and answered a few of their questions was I able to reach him myself.

"Hayden, wait." I pulled him away from the crowd. "Before we go in, I need to know: what do you plan on saying to Morell? I have no love for surprises."

Hayden smiled affectionately. "First, take my hand, Calyx. Walk with me. You do look awful, you know."

"No worse than you."

"Well, that's true. But I'm used to it on my face."

"Be serious. Morell knows what I look like. And it's not the dirt he'll care about. Are you going to tell him about the haven? I won't argue about your decision. I only want to know."

"I've been thinking about the same question. All I feel for certain is that there's no need to tell him any more than I have to."

"But that doesn't mean anything."

"Not exactly," he said. "It means we need to agree on this. Let me do most of the talking. That's what Morell will expect anyway. And if I happen to leave out some details, don't feel called upon to mention the fact."

I shook my head, hoping for a more direct answer. "Then you won't tell him?"

"I'll tell him that we were attacked and that Starn, Trompson, and Muley died in the fighting. Father's always concerned first with the details of a battle. And he'll mourn them, you see. They were good men, loyal to him. To Morell that means a lot. He'll be more interested in finding out who the raiders were who killed them than how we escaped. Unless one of us says something. And I don't really think that'll happen. I've already sworn Jesun to silence. Hannak and Solly wouldn't do more than sell the story in the streets and call it a jarak dream, if they've a need. There's no reason Morell shouldn't believe us. If it comes up at all, just tell him you dreamt that Sister Eclipse showed you a path."

"Yes," I said. "Except that I'm tired of lies . . . But Hayden, I wanted you to know: I meant to thank you for coming to Aster, for your loyalty to me."

"No." Hayden stopped me. "I'm not the one should be thanked. We were completely exposed. Taken by surprise. They had the advantage, had probably picked the site ahead of time. And even with Ceena's strength on our side, they had more than double the men and weapons. If I thought Morell needed to know about the haven, if it made any difference to Briana's future, I would tell him. But the truth is, Calyx, I'm not really sure what happened myself. We hid. We weren't found. That's all any of us know. For now there's no reason to make more of it than that."

Morell was waiting for us, as I knew he would be, seated stiff-backed and righteous in his great carved chair in the inner hall. He looked at me once when we entered—it never took him longer than that to make up his mind. He rose to greet us, kissed me stiffly on one cheek it was more a matter of protocol for the attendants, guards, and clerks surrounding his chair than anything else. For my part, I did as Hayden wished, smiling and full of pleasantries, saying nothing my brother had not said first. And then, the required etiquette met, Morell led us into a smaller, less formal room, one with decidedly fewer ears.

With a punctuated abruptness Morell led Hayden to a long, map-covered table and began shuffling through papers. He was ignoring me already, dismissing me as if I was of no more import than any of his clerics. I was angered at first, but then I saw—wasn't that exactly the face I'd shown him? Why should he act differently when his expectations had been so thoroughly met?

While they spoke, I watched my father. Like Briana itself, he had aged. His hair was whiter and his back not so straight as I remembered. His dark beard was streaked with gray now and clipped short. But what struck me most was his neck, the way the skin was looser now, the muscles faded. All this time I had pictured him at the height of his strength still, domineering and proud. Now he seemed to have shrunk, both in size and demeanor. He was direct, committed to action, but he let Hayden lead the conversation and rather than arguing, followed along the path he was led. The mystery was gone out of him, and I was no longer afraid.

"Tell me again what they wore," Morell said, his hands tight against the table edge.

"Dark leggings, vests, wide leather belts. No different than any of our own soldiers. They could have been anyone."

"But they weren't," I said, and Morell looked up at me, his eyes narrow, always the pragmatist. For a moment I thought he would say something, but no, he lowered his eyes, went back to his maps.

"I don't think so, either." Hayden shook his head as though this had all been gone over a hundred times. "I told you, they followed us. And Calyx says any number of people knew she was traveling south. Aster town and the surrounding territories aren't well known for cautious behavior."

"True enough," Morell said. "But the question is, were they raiders or soldiers? You say they were soldiers, Hayden. Why?"

"Because it fits. Calyx spoke of a priest, a man from Gleavon himself. He rode out of Aster just hours ahead of us."

"That's not enough to go on."

"No, sir," I said. "But also, he was no friend of mine. Nor of yours. I'd heard him speak out against you, against Briana."

Morell pulled on his chin, and I could see him considering my words seriously for the first time that day. "Is this true?" he asked Hayden. "Have you heard of this?"

"Only what Calyx told me."

"Well then," Morell turned back to me and I saw at once that three years apart had changed nothing. "My apologies. This is a poor beginning for a homecoming, isn't it? Here we are speaking of all these matters when you must be impatient to see your mother. It'll be good for her to have a daughter to talk to again. And don't you worry yourself, either. She'll be all right as soon as her time comes. These things happen. And she knows of your return, of course.

But not of these difficulties. We wouldn't want to upset her, would we?"

"No, sir," I said tightly, seeing that he'd say no more of import till I was dismissed. Whatever news he needed, he would have in private from Hayden.

"Of course, of course. She needs cheering up. I'm no good at it, seems I never say or do the right thing. Ah, well. That's an old story. But you now, go on up to her. See what you can do."

A girl I didn't recognize was already waiting for me at the door, clean towels and a smock folded carefully over her arm. I followed her to one of the smaller kitchens, scrubbed my face and arms till my skin burned red, but I wouldn't accept the clothing she offered. Instead I called for a mug of hot wine, drinking down first one, then another before I was ready to leave.

After that I made my own way about the keep, trailing my hand across once familiar walls. Here was the turn to the temple courtyard and there the corridor leading out toward the soldiers' quarters, and this one which I would come back to later, the hall to my own bedchamber. All the same and yet different, as my father had been, as I was.

By now Ivane would be waiting for me. Ceena, who'd been her companion as well as guard since my sister and I had left, would be with her, and perhaps Allard, her manservant . . . And where would Micah be?

Micah! Once again I realized I'd hardly given my old friend a thought. Why? Didn't I still feel any of the childhood ties that bound us together? What had changed? Was it that I had moved into realms he couldn't share, that he had once called himself sensume? But no, that didn't explain it, for in the end, no one had ever truly shared my jarak dreams. Witnessed some perhaps, but shared? No. Even home in Driana again, I felt the loneliness that had shadowed my years, the differences.

At my mother's door I stopped, sloughed off the illwrought mood. Here of all places I need not feel alone. I tapped lightly, then pushed the door open without waiting for reply. The room was dimly lit, the shutters closed against the sun. I blinked; in all the years I had lived here, I had never seen my mother's room darkened.

"Mother?"

Ivane was sitting up in bed, her back supported by several

bolsters. She had been waiting for me. "Calyx, daughter! Come here where I can see you. Sit down. Here, on my bed."

I came around to her bedside and sat down. Thin candle-light shadowed her bed. Her hair hung in loose strands about her face. She had tried to pull her gown together, but I could see she had not risen to change her clothes and she seemed lost inside the faded lace. Her once lively eyes were rimmed in dark circles, and where her body had once been narrow and fit, there was a great rounded belly pushing the covers into a mound she could not hide.

She knew I was looking at her, and she took my hands in hers. "I'll be all right," she said in a soothing voice. "Haven't I been through this three times before, and three times borne fine, healthy children?"

Something in her voice made me stop. Hadn't I heard her say those very words once before? But there wasn't time to ask now. "How . . . ?" My voice cracked with the anger I had tried to push aside. "How could he do this?"

"Hush, child. You're so young. Even gone three years," Ivane smiled. "What do you know of the ways of husbands and wives? You shouldn't be so quick to place blame. We'll be fine, this babe and I."

From the far side of the room I heard a rustling sound, and Ceena was suddenly at my side, her hands on my shoulders, holding me back. "She needs your help, your comfort. Not your condemnation."

"Tell me, what do you hear from Mirjam?" I made my-self ask. "Have you seen her? Has she children yet?"

"Of course we hear, often. These days there are more couriers and soldiers traveling between the lands than mer-chants. But no, Mirjam has borne no live children. We heard once that she had conceived, but the child miscarried and she was ill a long time after. Perhaps I should give her this new one to raise." Ivane's hand moved to her blankets and she tried to laugh, but the effort caused her too much discomfort.

When she'd settled down again, she seemed even more tired than when I'd entered the room, and I thought she had fallen asleep. But shortly she looked up at me again. "Come here. It's you I want to hear about. Have you been happy? Have they treated you well in Aster?"

I glanced toward Ceena. "They took care of me," I gave

a little laugh. "Too well. They treated me as if they'd been sent the other sister, Mirjam. Did you get my letters?"

"There were several, yes. I enjoyed them."

"Remember the one that said they had given me a great chamber all to myself? And I thought I never wanted it until—"

"Until you realized how much you needed your privacy," Ivane finished.

"Did I write and tell you that?"

"You didn't have to. You're enough like me that I could guess as much."

"Except for painting," I laughed. "I found out the hard way. Not that I minded. I enjoyed the work. It was one of the few things I did enjoy. It's not the same as what you do, of course. But I learned to handle a brush well enough to do straight lines—and realize I'd never be as good as you. And you, have you been painting?"

"No, no. I'm sorry. I've been so tired . . ." Her voice trailed away and I wished I'd said something else. Of course she hadn't been painting. I could see the room well enough for myself. Where were her easels? Her paints? When had that too moist, overheated smell chased away the familiar odors of linseed oil and thinners?

"But," she started, one finger drumming on her coverlet, "you haven't told me . . . and Ceena refused to speak for you . . . are you Sumedaro now?"

"No." I looked away. "Though it's odd how everyone asks the same question. Now, when it no longer matters. At first I thought Morell's exile would prove to be my good fortune. I had—I have jarak dreams, Mother. Strong ones. I wanted to learn to use them as the Sumedaro did. To see the world. To stretch them as far as anyone ever could. To wield them however I needed. But Hershann laughed when I mentioned the idea. He said my father sent me to Aster for safety. That I would be a queen someday. Not a priest."

"Is that what Jared told you as well?"

"Jared? Jared said nothing. He never spoke a word that didn't agree with Hershann."

"I see. And so you gave up the idea?"

"Give up?" I laughed. "When did you ever know me to give up? Oh, on the outside maybe. I knew about hiding—"

"As did I," Ivane nodded.

"But I kept on with my jarak dreams."

Ivane raised her hand to my cheek. "My child, my darling girl. You sound so much like I did once, with secrets and longings that couldn't wait for an answer. I also thought it might be best for you to be a priest. Why did you think I let him send you away? And surely it hasn't hurt you to have been away from here. But don't you hear your own words? When Jared was young, or so he's told me, the reason he wanted to be a priest was to dedicate his dreams to the gods.

"But you speak of your jarak dreams out of pride. You glory in them . . . Which well you should. But the Sumedaro are taught to speak of their jarak dreams with humility. Of serving the gods through their dreams. Not of stretching their power to reach across the earth, or treating with Jokjoa."

Ivane grew suddenly quiet, exhaustion falling over her again. Ceena motioned to me that it was time we left her to sleep.

"Wait," Ivane called, her eyes unfocused and dark. "There's so much to talk about still. I was wondering, do you think perhaps it's time for you to consider leaving Aster? If you haven't taken a priest's vows yet, I doubt there's any more they can teach you. If you're willing, no one would dare speak against me . . . now . . . if I said I wanted you home again."

At first I didn't say anything. I had thought of it many times. But I hoped I was no longer such a child as to imagine stealing away in the back of a wagon, with nothing between me and my future save a layer of hay and a basket of chicken eggs. It was difficult to imagine my future, any future. Like a gray cataract covering my eyes, the way was shadowed and indistinct. I owned no wealth to call my own. I knew nothing. I fit nowhere.

"It's inevitable, I suppose," I said. "I doubt I'm little more than a burden there, a nuisance at best. I could go back, clean up my few belongings. But what would I do after? Live here again? I'm not certain . . ."

My mother's gaze shifted to Ceena's stern face and remained there, though her words were directed toward me. "Or you could travel. Perhaps go south and visit my people. You once had two aunts, you know. And an uncle, my older brother. We called him Sail." She turned toward the wall. "I suppose I don't really know if they're still alive. But there would be cousins to meet. Ceena could go with you. She has people of her own to find, though she thinks she can't leave until I'm well."

"South?" I mouthed the word, as though wondering at its flavor, but Ceena stopped me before I could answer. "Come," she said. "Your mother needs to sleep now. She's already talked too long. It's difficult for her."

Ivane tried to smile. "Give me a kiss, then go on. I'd like to sleep. But come again. Soon," she said. "In the evening if they'll set you free. Or the morning."

Outside in the corridor, Ceena laid her hand on my arm. "We should speak together. Your mother's words may have some truth. She's suggested much the same thing to me, that we should travel together."

"And what did you say?"

"Wait," Ceena said, looking first for intruders. "Come with me." Ceena pointed toward a closed door that had led to Hayden's chambers when he was young. The room was small, but I was surprised to see how well lit and airy it was. A long wooden trough hung below the windows, with green herbs and flowering plants growing inside.

Ceena smiled at my appraising eye.

"You do this?" I asked, running a finger along the red-veined leaves on one plant. The leaf felt like velvet, thick and substantial, not at all like the poor crops struggling in the northern towns. "I never knew plants like these could grow indoors."

"With sunlight and warmth and a little of Sunder's touch, it's not difficult."

"Sunder's and not Seed's? I'd never have thought this was in your nature to try."

Ceena pinched a brown leaf from one of the plants. "We've all been pushed through a crucible these last few years, haven't we?"

"But it never ends for you, does it?"

"Never," Ceena said. "Though it's the search for patience that has consumed much of my time of late. Patience and doubt. But we can speak of my gardening exploits another time. Calyx? You saw your mother?"

"She's thin, but I expected as much. Later she'll gain her strength back."

Slowly Ceena said, "There will be no later. This child will kill her."

I stared at my hands, at the plant, the window, the floor,

anywhere but at Ceena. "No. You can't be certain. Women have always gone through this—"

"I've spoken with the midwives. The best in all the surrounding territories. They have more skills in these matters than I, though I could see it for myself. She's bleeding. And she can't eat. She hardly drinks."

"I thought that passes?"

"It should, but with Ivane it has not."

"Haven't you any skill with medicine?" I said, my voice harsh, rising. "Look at what you're growing here, in this godforsaken winter. If you can grow flowers, why can't you grow medicines?"

"No. I've tried, but my hands are useless. Plants like these I can grow. But to use them, to know how one must be blended with another, the soils, herbs, no. Only the Silkiyam dedicated to Seed's Heya magic learn the properties of growth, not those of us who were Kanashan. Whatever we do for Ivane, it will only ease her passing. We cannot alter the end."

"What are you saying?" I shouted, denying her words. "That she's going to die and you aren't going to do a thing to stop it? I can't believe this. You're a Silkiyam. You practice Sunder's rites. You can't just stand there and say there's nothing we can do. I won't believe that. I'll think of something. I can, you know. I will. I'll think of some way . . ."

"Yes, Calyx, but how? Don't you think I've tried? Look at these plants, this room. Does this speak to you of death only? Isn't healing the other side of fighting? Sunder doesn't demand a black ritual of her followers. My people were healers as well as warriors. And I've tried. But there's nothing I can do. Saying you'll do this or do that . . . It doesn't work that way. Bargaining doesn't work."

"But it might," I said, suddenly quiet.

"What?" Ceena looked at me.

"There is one I might bargain with. One who has a stake in listening to my terms."

"Who?"

"Edishu." I looked up, met Ceena's eyes.

"Is it true, then?"

"What? That Edishu walks the earth again? You held my hands. You watched my dreams once. Do you remember his face? I do. He's touched me. Not only in my jarak dreams, but in the light of Jokjoa's day. Don't you believe me?"

"I believe you found a haven, Calyx, where none had been found before."

"Not me. I told you, Rath led me there."

"Rath. All right."

"Then you'll help me? Tonight?"

"Calyx, it's too fast. What terms would someone such as he require in trade? A bargain has to have terms. And if he tries to trick you? How will you fight? How can you be sure . . . ?"

"I'm not. But you just said Ivane doesn't have time for sureties and so I can't wait for them. I have the tokens. He wants them. I know that . . . Ceena, I'd like it if you stood guard over my bed tonight while I dream. Will you?"

It took Ceena several moments to answer. "Not because I approve," she said, "but because you ask."

That night I lay in my old bed, wary as a soldier before dawn. The room was dark, my alcove tight and confining. Outside the door Ceena waited as I'd instructed. She was to waken me in one hour—no matter what she thought she heard. One hour. No more and no less.

Eclipse had passed through this room, I told myself, and run her hand along the walls. Nothing was as I remembered, nothing as I'd expected. There were shadows and memories, to be sure, but they were new ones, not the memories I'd left behind. I shivered under the cold wind of my fear, refusing to turn back from this jarak dream. I didn't know how to raise the tokens against Edishu at my command. But if there was any way for me to help my mother, I would do it. I would give it. It was that simple.

"Edishu!" I called, my voice hollow in the empty room. "Edishu, I have a bargain to offer . . . If you're not afraid of a game. Tonight. In this room. A dare. A chance."

If Eclipse's power were with me, Edishu would not see the desperation behind my bid. If he did . . . If he did, his demands would escalate beyond my reach.

And the prize?

A lie first, for the one thing he wanted most was the thing I was least willing to give. How could I bear it, the thought of his hands touching me, his mouth, his eyes peering into mine . . . But if I could hold him off, or trick him, or lie and swear some lesser boon, perhaps then he would help Ivane.

Rath or Gamaliel in exchange for medicine. These I would consider. Not as Ceena had said, merely to ease Ivane's pain but something to keep her alive. Surely Edishu would know of some way to cure her?

"Edishu!" I called as my eyes grew heavier, and I conjured an image of his face to guide me into sleep.

My shoulders and back grew cold, and for a moment I thought I was awake. But no, there was an acute ether in the air and the precarious sense that but for my outer shell of skin, heart and mind would lose contact with each other.

I was asleep, walking in the midst of a jarak dream. And I knew exactly where I was.

I called again, then waited. "Edishu?"

I was in the small garden behind Micah's house in Briana—a fitting place to bargain with Edishu—neither on my territory nor his. I looked down at my clothes. I was wearing the black trousers and white shirt I'd been wearing when Hayden and I first left Aster. My hair was longer than I'd ever worn it, but even in a jarak dream such details often blur.

For the moment the garden was quiet, and I wondered in what guise Edishu would appear. He'd tested me in battle, wearing the scarred face of a warrior. And he'd borrowed the mask of a young man and spoken his lies in the sweetest voice. He'd sent his succubus and he'd raised his tokens against me . . .

Then I saw him. He stepped out from behind a tree as simply and as eloquently as if he'd never done anything but wait for me. He'd come in the guise of a man Hayden's age, perhaps a little older, with a silvered, trim beard and a sleek-fitting vest over his shirt.

"So this time you've come seeking me?" Edishu said. His hands were on his hips, his feet set firmly apart, waiting. "For what?"

I steeled myself, set my feet as wide and as firmly planted as his. "To bargain," I said. "To play a game."

"I knew," he smiled thinly, "that you'd come to me eventually."

"To talk, Edishu. Only to talk."

"Did I say more?" His eyes gleamed; he was baiting me already, testing, but I had no intention of backing down.

"I have an offer to make," I said.

He cocked his head to one side. "There is little I enjoy more than a true match, a game of wits," he said. "Lethia came to me for the promise of power. She was too easily won."

"It's not power over people I seek."

"Wealth? No, not you. Kingdoms to rule? No . . . But I could offer you power to control your magic. Power to control your dreams."

"And what about you, Edishu? What do you want?"

Edishu threw his head back and laughed, "With you a willing consort at my side, creation would be mine."

"Is that it? Dominion over the earth?"

"I want what I have been denied." Edishu's voice rose to a higher pitch. "Everything Jokjoa dared deny me. Reparation a thousand fold. It was from Jokjoa's dream that I was created. And so I am real. I exist. But Jokjoa keeps me trapped. Kuoshana's gateway keeps me trapped . . . Look at my face." Edishu lowered his voice. "Do I not hold within myself the full extent of all things possible? Look!"

I watched. His eyes widened for a moment, met mine, then closed. When he opened them again, his face had changed. I held my stance, forcing myself to watch. He was hideous, his face a match of the one I'd seen the first time I'd dreamt of him: blistered, leprous, death-like but alive, impossibly alive.

"You are everything I want . . ." he said, and now his voice became the man's voice I remembered from Sherra's dream. A lover's voice, seductive and too, too sweet. ". . . Everything I've been denied: arms, hands, legs. Dreams as strong as the gods. Waking dreams—this too I demand—with power to shape the earth."

He paused a moment, but only a moment. He was changing in front of my eyes. Face, clothes, demeanor. He aged, his hair whitened and a beard grew. Ancient he looked, but his face was a man's again, no longer a demon's. His clothes turned like ribbons in the wind. Orange robes, full to the ground now. When he spoke, it was with the voice of a Sumedaro elder, frail but honed on wisdom.

"Birth, death, and deceit," he said. "On these the world turns. Oh yes, and dreams, the unformed energy which binds us all together, like air, surrounding and sustaining us.

"And when I walk again on earth, all dreams will be

mine. Life, death, change, and dreams. All will be mine. If I say the earth shall be barren, then the desert will conquer. No field will remember Seed's touch but I grant it. If I choose to raise a storm or call a behemoth from the sea, it shall be. If a man cries for death, I will be the slayer.

"I shall be worshiped in fear. And no one will dream. Not a jarak dream. And not a waking dream. I will destroy the havens and hold the earth forfeit against any who seek to defy me. With those tokens"—he raised a finger and pointed to my hand—"I will create for myself a body. Hands that move and crush. Hands to turn my dreams to day."

"No!" I shouted. "Not yet."

"What then?" he asked, and he changed once again, became the man who'd first entered the garden.

I calculated, took a risk. "We've been well matched, have we not?"

Edishu smiled. "Perhaps."

"No. Not just *perhaps*. I say matched. I carry the tokens. But you have found me."

"Round one."

"Then I propose round two."

"A game then? And the stakes?"

"My mother, the Lady Ivane, is in childbed. Ill," I said quickly.

"What does that have to do with me?"

"I want medicine to restore her."

"Entice me."

"In return, I give you Rath. Round two."

"Willingly, is it? And why should I believe you?"

"For my mother's sake, I would—"

"Spare us both your gentle intentions. I much prefer your lies. Your hatred will sweeten my victory when you come to me. Besides, I have already tasted what mortal women deem *willingly*, and it is not enough. No." Edishu threw back his head and laughed. "It isn't enough. But listen, we can play your little game. After all, it's only fitting. Someday—it is true, you know—someday, you will come begging. And in the meantime, you will help me pass the time. I shall give you a riddle, an easy one. Bring me back the answer and I'll tell you where to search for what you need: a single leaf of a twisted elderberry bush ripened in the light of a Sister's eve moon. Will you do it?"

"Have I any choice?"

"Choice? Of course you have a choice. You always will. That's what makes you so enticing. You hate me yet chose to face me, and I enjoy the taste of your hate. I could almost lick it off your lips, like a kiss. And I do enjoy the game.

"Now hear the riddle. *What dwells in Kuoshana in spring-time, in summer journeys the earth, yet come winter sleeps caged and trampled?*"

17

We take vows and we break them, using them for our own gain. With each self-betrayal the hurt dies a little, but what does it matter? Only in the end, looking back over our brief lives, can we judge whether there was any point to the small treacheries committed against ourselves. Only in the end can we know what mattered.

Dinner the next evening fell on a Sister's eve, a night I should have fasted. In Aster temple I had vowed not to partake of flesh or food of any kind on that holy evening. The Sumedaro fast, or so the priests teach, in remembrance of the Elan Sumedaro's quest for Kuoshana's gateway. That vow had not been asked of me. I had given it freely, telling myself that small sacrifices were necessary if I was to find the strength for each new, larger task That and, perhaps more to the point, I made that vow because I was still naive enough to believe that what I saw as the outward face of the Sumedaro was a match to the inner face: the Sumedaros live their life in thus-and-such a manner; Sumedaros walk the path of their god; Sumedaros are filled with the light of their god; Sumedaros dream . . .

It is not so. Somewhere else lies the truth. In some other temple perhaps, but not in there.

That night Morell laid out a small feast on my behalf. And why not? I had vowed to him that whatever else passed in Aster, I had never become a priest-sworn Sumedaro and could do as I pleased. Now I needed to pay for such bragging, forcing myself to swallow down the bits of meat and vegetables the servants heaped high on my platter and pretend to enjoy the meal, wondering through it all if I had done anything more than make one lie work for another, greater one.

We were seated in one of Briana's smaller halls, the feast laid out on two long tables that had been set up across opposite walls. Protected in the center floor, a large fire burned, its smoke and warmth curling around, then out the rafters overhead. The company was smaller, more intimate than the dinner served in the Great Hall three years earlier, and I was glad of the difference.

Morell sat at the head in a wide, throne-like chair—another of Lethia's additions that hadn't been present three years earlier. Ivane, of course, had not come down to dinner, nor Ceena, who would be at her side. Hayden sat on Morell's right, then I, with Morell's captain, Norvin, across from me. Norvin's elder son, Arun, was there, but I had not seen Jesun since we had returned to Briana.

I leaned closer to Hayden's ear. "Where's Jesun?"

"Returned to FelWeather. He feared for his mother's safety and talked Norvin into granting him a good-sized company of men. He hopes to persuade her to return here with the younger children."

"She never wanted to live here, did she?" I asked, trying to remember something about Portia besides her wide cheekbones and the long yellow hair she wore braided around her head.

"No. But times are different. She'll come now, if only to save her sons the danger of making the trip for her sake. She can't be doing well there. Norvin said FelWeather has suffered the same hard frosts as most of the northlands, and they haven't enough hands left to till the fields. Bring in more people to work the fields in these short seasons, and you have to hunt game to feed them while you wait for harvest. Then the game runs scarce and you're worse off than when you started." Hayden shook his head and I started to ask another question, but he wasn't listening.

He was watching the young Queen Korinna, seated directly across from him at the table, though the word *watching* did the scene no justice. He was staring at her every motion, drinking in the sight of her hair, her eyes, her smile. I looked across from Hayden to Korinna to Hayden again. She kept her eyes steadily on those around her, but whenever the talking slowed, she sought him out, returning his gaze. Then Hayden would smile back at her, and I thought I'd never seen his face lighten so.

Hayden twisted a ring on his finger, the small, plain band which he'd shown me only briefly. It was the ring he'd worn in the haven. Now I saw Korinna's ring was a match to his, and I wondered how long ago they had exchanged gifts.

They loved each other. It had to be so, and for a brief, foolish moment I felt twice betrayed. Once because I was left out. Second because I had only just found my brother, spoken with him as two equals—no longer the younger sister trying for her brother's attention—and though Korinna must have been often in his thoughts, he had scarcely mentioned her name to me! Next he would have this woman I didn't know taking up residence in Briana, eating beside him, confiding in him, sharing his bed.

But later, after the dinner, when I saw Hayden take Korinna's arm and stand with her before the cooling fire, the light dancing across their faces, my anger faded. Whereas Hayden was dark and tall like Morell, she was light and fair-cheeked and small of build. His shoulders were wide and solid. She was graceful and small. He laughed loudly, throwing his head back freely while his joy flew about the hall. She was quiet and even-keeled, yet as strong-willed and determined as a queen should be, for all her delicate features.

Korinna was already queen in her own right in Hillstor Valley, west of Briana, at the base of the Westrun Mountains. Korinna's mother had died years earlier and her father had never remarried. As the only child she'd been raised at her father's side, knowing she would be queen one day. It was in the year before I left for Aster that her father died—a head injury, I'd heard, taken when his horse had missed its footing on a jump. What would she do? I wondered. Live as Norvin and Portia did, Hayden taking over rule of Briana when Morell was no longer able, she remaining in her own court, so far away? I never minded Mirjam's marriage into Theron's family at Gleavon Keep. Mirjam had never expected anything different. Though Mirjam had had little to do with the decision or settlement, Theron had seemed a good match. Had Morell set this up between Korinna and Hayden? It hardly seemed likely. Such love as passed between their hands could not be arranged or planned.

It was Seed's doing, her trail left stamped on the earth, and where she bestowed her favor, few ever turned their hearts away.

I took a deep breath and forced myself to look away. What was the use of all my striving in Aster, or the bargain I'd only just made with Edishu, if one look at Hayden and Korinna, so content in each other's arms, left me feeling as hungry as Sherra had been in that meadow beyond her father's house?

No, for me there would be no lover's arms—not when the night was a battlefield and the lonely darkness the one chance for victory I could find.

The dinner over, Morell pushed his chair away from the table and called for musicians. The music was pleasant enough. Hayden returned to his seat, this time with Korinna on his side. Then, halfway through a lively roundelay, Morell raised his goblet and called for a toast. Instantly the musicians faded toward the rear, and everyone in the hall raised their goblets to meet my father's.

"Let us drink to Calyx, Hayden, and Jesun," he called out. "To the good tidings we take in their safe return home!"

"To safe journeys always," Norvin replied, his deep voice more grating than usual.

I drank the sweet wine quickly, letting its flavor warm my throat. Then, before I had time to set my cup down on the table, Morell spoke again. "As for you, daughter," he said, his gaze locking on mine, "we have been thinking of your future, as well a father should. You are a woman grown, older now than your sister was when she married into Gleavon Keep."

I flushed under Morell's demanding stare, somehow knowing what was coming. Morell was at his best at times like this, relishing his power, Briana's true lord though he had never taken back the crown he'd given Hayden. Slowly he looked up and down the table, his gaze stopping briefly on each person's face, always the judge, always including and warning. "We are all family here tonight," he continued. "There is not one of you I do not trust and love as I love my own son and daughters. You know the dangers Briana faces, the dangers we all face in the north. We have news of a great migration of people out of the northlands, east of Toklat across the Yestar River. They move south in hard numbers, forsaking useless farms and empty keeps. You've heard of the attack against Hayden's party. You know we must build alliances if we are to remain strong."

Morell waited a moment, letting the silence work for him. "I have sent couriers east of here, to Istyak Keep, Lord Sawill's land. Calyx, you may remember him. His territories border just east of Gleavon, though admittedly the journey is longer."

"No sir, I can't think that I do," I said.

"He was here five years ago," Norvin offered.

Norvin was a part of this with Morell, then, working against me in ways Hayden never would have agreed to. "But not three years ago?" I said. "Not at Lethia's dinner?"

Morell raised an eyebrow. "No, he was not here then. His first wife, Hava of Ruax, had just died at the time."

"Then he only remembers me as a child?"

"I suppose." Morell started drumming a finger on the table.

"And he knows nothing of your . . . decision . . . to send me away to Aster? Or of my slight indiscretions three years ago?"

"No, of course not. But he's a fair-handed man, older than you, to be sure. But certainly you would have . . . You understood, you could hardly have hoped to find a younger man?"

"But you misunderstand me," I said in a honeyed voice. "I was not troubled for my sake. Only that if you seek political alliances, you had better be careful not to tempt the horse with a rotten apple. You promised Lord Sawill a daughter of your own heart?"

"What's past is past, Calyx." Morell raised a questioning eye, and I wondered if he didn't honestly believe his actions could be so easily dismissed. "What matters now," he went on, "is his opinion of Briana Keep. We've already explained the size of your dowry to him. It's handsome enough—you needn't fear a lack on that account. Besides, an alliance between Istyak and Briana could mean a great deal. Sawill is no fool; he understands the need for our combined strength as much as we do."

"And Lethia? Does she approve? Three years ago I would have thought Lethia was alliance enough for you."

"Lethia? Damn Lethia! Damn her to all Jokjoa's night! She's too strong for her own good. She can't even control her own people. And by whose right does she think to—no! Wait. For once this is none of Lethia's doing!" Morell stole a quick swallow of wine, then roughly lowered his goblet. "Enough of this! How you twist my words! What's the matter with you, girl? I offer you a husband, a lord in his own right. The proposition has already been discussed. And you dare sit here, at my table, questioning my decision!"

Deliberately I flung back my answer: "I have already been upstairs, Father, and seen for myself your opinion of the rights of husbands who rule their own keep."

"What? Upstairs? . . . Why, you . . ." Morell grabbed his goblet from the table and raised it up behind his head, his wine spilling against the wall behind him.

"Father! You swore peace in this household." Hayden was suddenly at his side, catching fast to Morell's shoulder.

Morell froze, glanced from Hayden to me. Hayden took the goblet from his hand, but there was no struggle. Norvin rose, whispered something in Morell's ear, then stopped and fixed his chair aright.

After that, my father did not look at me again.

Hayden and I met outside, in a corner of the courtyard where both the keep and Lakotah's walls joined. He wore a thick cape pulled tightly under his new growth of beard. He looked dark and strong, his features a mixture of Morell's coloring and my mother's sharp lines. Watching him, the way he reminded me first of one, then the other, I couldn't help but wonder where my parents' argument had begun. Or that if his resemblance to either of them had won over the other, we would never have been able to meet each other that night.

"I'm leaving, Hayden," I said. "I've already explained. I've an idea where I can find medicine for Mother. It's not certain, but I mean to risk the journey. No, wait." I put my hand to his. "Hear me out. There's more to it than that, of course. I can't stay. At least not too long. As long as Morell goes on making these demands, there's no shelter here for me."

"But I rule here also, Calyx," Hayden said, as if he had already guessed my plans. "And I swear by Jokjoa's oath, he won't be allowed to make a marriage for you unasked."

"I believe you mean that. But for whatever reasons, our disagreements run deeper than that. And I'm too old now, too much a stranger to live here beneath his roof. Hayden, you know as well as I, I say red, the man says black, I speak of priests and vows and promises, he counts soldiers and horses and land. We're different. Don't deny it. You knew it when you lied about the havens."

"I did not lie."

"Of course not. But you may as well have. Together we deceived him. We knew he wouldn't accept the truth of the havens. But I can't live that way, in Eclipse's harness, scheming and inventing lies to soothe Morell through each new day. Not that I don't lie, I do. All too often. But I'd much prefer to choose the need myself."

"But to leave so soon? This is ridiculous. How can we be standing here even pretending it's safe? And alone, Calyx? At least let's make some preparations. Two days, that should do it. You can wait two days. Mind you, I'm not saying I want you to leave. But if you must, two days should be enough to arm a group of guards, gather provisions."

"No, Hayden. I mean to go alone."

Hayden flung out his arms. "This is impossible. You can't. Calyx, those raiders have to know we're here. And if it were you they were searching for, as you suspect, what assurance is there that they've given up? The word could easily have gone out to others."

"Hayden, would Morell move against Lethia?" I asked.

"On your word?"

"Or on yours."

"No." My brother shook his head.

"Would you?"

"Calyx, don't turn this around against me. You haven't been here. You haven't seen how deeply she's dug her way into Briana's soil, like a taproot. Her people are everywhere. Her soldiers ride freely on our roads. Her coins are traded in every tavern and market. She's the one who sent the gold to pay for our roadwork last season. Two years ago when the frost ruined the winter wheat, she shipped her surplus here to fill our bins. And there's our sister, Mirjam, living in Gleavon Keep. What would it mean to her?"

"What has it meant to me?" I asked sharply. "To be called a jarak witch?"

Hayden winced, but he remained calm. "We don't really know those were her men. Not for certain. Morell already doubts her. You heard him for yourself, shouting her down.

She's meant well, outwardly at least. We've no grounds to fault her on that. But she's meddled heavily in our doings, and with each week it's more and more difficult to shut her men out of our meetings and keep her clerks from our books. But move against her? No. It's far too early for him to think along those lines."

"What of the dream she spoke that night, when she said I meant to kill her? How would Morell take that, along with this new story of raiders?"

I waited while Hayden, his lips pulled to a thin line, considered the question. "Dreams, Calyx. No more than that. He never spoke of her dream again. Nor, for that matter, did she."

"She didn't have to. She'd already accomplished what she set out to do."

"But why set herself against you?"

I didn't answer at first. I wasn't certain Hayden either needed or wanted to hear the entire answer. But three times now Hayden had stood by me—before Hershann, to Jesun in the haven, and now to Morell. I owed him at least the partial truth. "Because it's true that I'm a jarak dreamer," I said, "and Lethia knew it. And hated me for it."

"But after all this time? I could understand if she was jealous of you because you'd found entry into a haven. But Lethia couldn't have known you would do that. Not three years ago. What else was there?"

"I can tell you she's a jarak dreamer also. We met in a dream before she ever reached Briana. She wants me out of her way, perhaps so she can be the stronger dreamer."

"How can it matter so much?"

"You'll have to take my word for it, Hayden. It does."

Hayden turned away to stare at the rising walls of Lakotah temple. "Father sent you away, but none of us ever thought he wanted you to be sworn to the Sumedaro. I think more than anything he just wanted you out of his sight, as if he didn't want to be reminded of you."

"He hates me, Hayden."

Hayden looked back at me and smiled. "I must not have been watching when you still lived at home, Calyx. You were just a child, and I was little more myself. I never saw those things. Did the two of you plan it this way somehow? Did one of you do something I missed from the start, to turn against each other?"

"If only it were that simple. But how could I have done something on purpose? I was supposed to be the child, not him. Unless the fault was mine by doing nothing. Being nothing he could understand. And that may have been the heart of the problem. We both know Father never could stand to see a daughter of his looking like some innkeeper's bastard child—"

"Calyx!"

"Hayden, no." I shook my head, but I smiled to show him I took no offense in what I was saying. "We're both too old for pretending games. Our father never knew what to make of me."

"All right," Hayden said reluctantly. "But what of Ceena? At least you could take her with you."

"She won't come."

"Why not? Did you ask?"

"I did. And she said she wasn't ready to leave Ivane."

"But if Ceena said that, surely you can see the wisdom yourself . . . ?"

"Ceena is talking about staying to help. I'm leaving to do the same thing . . . to help. To fight if necessary—I'm not afraid of that. Sitting here watching her pain, waiting to see if she makes it or not—that I cannot do."

"But don't you understand what a chance you're taking? What if something happened while you were gone?"

"I've thought about it in every way I can, Hayden. You have to try to see, I can't sit here and do nothing. Ceena's reluctance comes from a different place than what you're saying. She'd come, I think, if she weren't fighting herself still. It's as if she's been waiting so long for word of her own people, she's forgotten what it means to act. She isn't ready to commit herself to anything yet except waiting and caring for Ivane.

"There's one other thing. I know how to find a safe route now. There won't be any danger."

"The havens, of course. I was wondering . . . But Calyx, are you certain enough of what you did to guarantee you'll be able to find them again?"

"There's no guarantee, Hayden. If I needed one, I wouldn't be leaving. But Ceena believes there are others. There were in the past, when the Silkiyam lived in them. And even if there's no trace of people, I have to believe that the havens are hidden only, not lost."

"How do we go back, Calyx?" Hayden asked softly. "What is it that's so different now from the past? The havens gone. The gods asleep. The priests powerless without the lords. What is it that's changed? Us, or the earth?"

I looked across the courtyard with Hayden to where a young priest in dark robes had stepped out to lock Lakotah's heavy door. "Both, I think," I said. "The one feeding off the other as surely as day turns into night."

"But how to stop it? We're only people. We haven't the power to change the wind, the seasons."

"No, but some things might still be in our power, though we don't recognize them. And we haven't lost all our weapons. We still have our jarak dreams. And the havens may be opened again. The Kareil clan. Each portion of our history, waiting to be retold." I started walking toward the stables, Hayden at my side. "I've been afraid sometimes," I said. "Afraid of what's happening to me. I don't know why I found a haven, but I did. Or why I have the jarak dreams I do. But while I fear them, they're also the only thing I trust for sure."

There was a pale gathering of color just beginning to light the horizon when I left Briana. The more I protested, the more adamant Hayden grew, insisting he be allowed to help outfit me in all the hardiest gear he could gather. While I was trundled off to the kitchens to gather whatever prizes the larder had to offer, Hayden wandered through the soldiers' quarters, helping himself to anything he thought I could carry. Before I rode out, he had loaded me down with two daggers, a broadsword, shield, leather riding boots, and a heavy mail shirt I swore by Sunder's arm I'd throw away the moment I rode beyond the first hill.

At last I climbed on my horse's back. "I'll never be able to sleep, let alone dream with all this weighing me down." I laughed.

"You don't sleep in them," Hayden said, adjusting the stirrups with a hard tug. "You use them. Besides, you've promised me you wouldn't need them. You're the one who said you'll find the havens and be safe. Now don't go worrying me again, or I promise, you'll never get beyond Briana without two score soldiers following behind you."

I leaned down and grasped my brother one last time. "Thank you, Hayden. I don't think I would have had the courage to do this if you hadn't understood . . . Or believed in me."

"Just ride," he said. "And don't worry about Morell. I'll tell him something."

"Thank you. And tell Mother I'll be back quickly as I'm able. She thinks you don't love her, that you're more Morell's son than hers. But I think she doesn't know just how much like her you really are."

Below us on the road, Briana town was just beginning to stir. Here and there a door slammed, an ax came down heavily against a log. The clanging of milk pots and wagons creaking under the weight of the morning's load all mingled together in the brisk morning air. Hayden started to say something— a warning, I imagine—but he stopped himself, gave the horse a slap on the rump, and sent us riding away beyond Briana.

18

Three days into the northlands and the snows began again. The land was nearly as harsh as when Hayden and our small company had ridden down, the ground stretching white and hard in every direction. On each side of the road, the forest and underlying brush were covered in waves of frost, and the mud-speckled forests we had fought through earlier were gone. During the days the wind bit constantly through my hat and burnt my ears with its high-pitched whistle. With each mile I felt certain the wolves we'd been hearing would have dug up the shallow graves we'd left and were now waiting at my heels for more.

For the first few nights, while Briana seemed close by, I'd built a hurried camp in the trees just off the roadside and, thankful that I'd carried enough supplies and needn't hunt for my food, I slept heavily and long. By the next night I was camping near the Koryan River, just outside the hill country where the raiders had attacked us. Shadowed in the bright moonlight, an owl hunted nearby, and with each new sound I imagined the raiders stalking closer in toward my camp.

Hayden had given me weapons, but what help would they prove in real combat? I'd never been trained as a warrior, nor did I look forward to relearning the feel of a blade ripping into flesh. And what good would it do me to use my jarak power if I couldn't first protect the hollow shell of my body asleep on the forest floor?

Anxiously I tossed about under my blankets. I meant to ride in secret back to Aster, to find Dev and ask him to help me find an answer to Edishu's riddle, then back to Briana. But the way was long. What if Hayden had been right and the raiders were still out there, waiting? Anyone could have followed my trail; there was so little traffic along this route—an occasional horse and rider and little more. True, my horse was still and calm, but that alone meant little. Hadn't the raiders already proven they could sneak up on us unaware? I'd been brave to tell Hayden I would camp in the havens. Truth was, I wasn't certain I could find one again—if there was more than the one to be found.

What had I done that first time, other than stand in mortal need? And need in and of itself couldn't bring miracles. I thought hard, trying to reenact the scene. There had been the road and then a slight clearing veering north and south.

I rose, counted off the steps in the dark. There had been one birch and then another and then an arching wall of trees.

But no, there was no haven—only the night surrounding me, empty and cold. Of course I couldn't do it by myself. I hadn't that first time, either. Not really. Rath had led me. How could it be otherwise?

So be it, then. But I was too nervous, anxious. Every noise seemed louder and closer than it really was. If I was to have any rest, I'd have to try finding another haven.

I slipped the bracelet from my wrist. Such a small thing. Certainly it didn't look as if it could hold such power, or once have belonged to the gods. I touched it, ran my finger along its crisp edges, then held it aloft. At once the bracelet began to glow—a small, steady light that shone out in every direction. I stood there, doubting and hoping at the same time.

What if Eclipse had tricked me? What if the first haven had been only a well-hidden clearing after all, a trick of the forest that had somehow held winter back? Hadn't that first haven been farther north than here anyway, in a thicker part of the forest?

And then suddenly away in the distance I saw it, the unmistakable light of a haven—not the one I had brought Hayden to, but another—wide and golden and waiting in the distance. I sprang up the shallow hill where I'd built camp, peered into the dark. This time, where I'd thought to find one haven, I saw three, two lying east of a distant ridge line and the third faint in the distance. The second one could have been as much as a full day's ride away, as were the two that lay in the opposite direction. But they were there, lit up like a village at night, golden and warm against the evening snow.

Within minutes I had packed and saddled my horse and was urging her forward into the snow, away from the hard track of road. She complained at first, pulling her head sideways against the reins as if to say she would not work until she'd gotten her sleep. But she sensed my need and picked her feet up higher, stepping over the layered snow, then walking head on into the wind until Rath's light led us into the first of the havens.

After that I slept in a haven nearly every night of the journey, pacing my riding so that come evening, there'd be one in reach. And if there was one, I told myself joyfully, then couldn't there be more? Ten havens? One hundred? One thousand? All crisscrossing the northlands, all a tribute to the Sister's ancient promise?

Once I knew how to look, it wasn't difficult to find them. By the second night I had taught myself to use Rath's glow as if it were a candle, lighting my way into a darkened room. On the third night, as I grew more confident, I learned to find them in my jarak dreams, to feel out the lay of the land, the way its hills and gulleys wound their way into a pattern, Eclipse's pattern, so that what appeared true by day was not the truth of the land at all. The dream was the truth and I needed only learn to trust it.

And perhaps because with each breath drawn in the havens I felt stronger, more certain of myself, it never occurred to me to wonder how it was I could find the havens at all—that whether I was awake or dreaming made little difference. If a haven lay hidden on the land, I would find it. Rath was with me, I told myself. Stolen or not, the bracelet didn't care who its owner was. The relic's light burned straight and true, rising in answer to my need. It would have revealed the haven no matter whose hand held it aloft.

It was midweek on a bright afternoon when I finally caught sight of Aster valley, the temple's brown-gray stones serene and patient below me. I camped on a hilltop through the night, waiting for the quiet of the morning to slip inside. I didn't want to be seen if it could be avoided. Hershann would not be expecting me, but if he found I had returned without a guard, without a letter, he'd be more than suspicious. And he'd be missing Rath and Gamaliel.

I slipped off the bracelet, hung it on a chain around my neck, where it wouldn't be seen. Gamaliel was more difficult. It was larger and the pouch seemed too obvious. Instead I slipped it into my food bag, hoping it wouldn't look like anything more than another turnip or onion. After that there was nothing left but to wait for morning and Eclipse's trickery to ease my path.

Garret, one of the priest-masons, was posted at the gatehouse. I never would have noticed him at all but that he stood a full head taller than any other man in Aster. He was chinking a hole in the stone when he heard my horse's stamping and hailed me from afar.

Garret opened the gate and let me in to the temple's wide courtyard, then held my horse's lead rope while I dismounted. "You picked a fine day to return," he said kindly. When I didn't answer, he said, "We hadn't been looking for you so soon, Calyx. But I'm glad to see you. You're alone?" He looked backward over my shoulder as if expecting to find a train of quarrelsome horses racing behind me toward the gate.

"Alone? Yes," I said, my voice sounding odd after so many days alone.

"Well, I expect you'll want a meal. And someone to take your horse. I can take you to the kitchen." He looked at his hands, picked at a dark smudge across one palm, then brushed them off against his brown vest. "And Hershann will want to know you're here. I'll run and tell him."

"No!" I said too loudly. Then, lowering my voice, I went on, "No, thank you." Garret was a simple man, goodhearted and well intentioned. I had done well to meet him first at the gates. Eclipse would indeed be with me if I met no one more threatening than he. "That won't be necessary," I said. "That is, I'm not planning on staying long."

"Not staying?" Garret looked down at me, a flat, curious look on his face. "Why, you only just returned. Kath's been talking about how she can't find anyone to copy so straight as you. Why, I'd do it, if she let me. What's the difference between running a straight line out here or up there, where it's warm . . . ?"

"Can you tell me where Dev is?"

"Dev? He'll be in the western tower, in the armory hall. But he won't talk to you. Too busy. It's all like that these days. Elder Hershann's put us to work, two jobs now to every man and woman of us. And wouldn't you think we already had enough to do? But listen to me telling you what you know for yourself! And me nothing but a northern priest, too old to sit the watch anymore. Too old." He shook his head. "Now, you're sure I can't get someone for you? Nothing's the matter, is it?"

"No, nothing's the matter, though you're kind to ask," I said, smiling. "But if you don't mind, I'd rather you don't tell Hershann I'm here. Not yet at least. My father—Lord Morell—he wished my whereabouts to remain secret. Only to tell those I most trust." I touched Garret's arm. "But tell me, why isn't Dev in the rathadaro hall? Shouldn't he be sitting the watch?"

"Hershann says it's not needed."

"Why? Have the shared dreams ended?"

"Oh, no, the people still come. They come. And with a hand out at the kitchen more than anything. But Hershann says there's hardly a dream among them that's worth the time, or any different, one from the other."

"And that is . . . ?"

"Oh, it's as good as any song. There's Kuoshana's gateway all green as spring. Lit up like a palace. And a man—no, two men. They're fighting. One's trying to get in the palace, the other out. Or something like that. I'm not too sure, exactly. I haven't been called to speak a dream in . . . must be five years now. Maybe longer?"

"Yes, of course," I stopped him. There was no need to hear more. I sighed heavily. Ivane had been right: Aster temple didn't feel like my home, not anymore. I had come to find Dev and, if I could, persuade him to come with me. Afterward there would be no looking back.

"Thank you," I said.

"Oh yes. I haven't seen you. Not at all."

*   *   *

It didn't take long to reach the western tower. Once out of Garret's good-natured reach, I slipped into a corner, waited till I was sure there was no one about, then changed my riding clothes back to the Sumedaro robes. With a little luck no one would think to notice another orange-robed priest walking the halls.

As Garret said, Dev was in the lower level of the western tower, his head bent over the edge of a crossbow he was oiling. But he was not alone. Avram sat quietly beside him, chiseling out the broken remains of an ax handle.

They saw me at once, raising their heads almost in the same motion.

"Dev?" I said, my voice too shrill.

"Calyx! When did you return?" Dev stood, a broad smile dancing unmistakably across his face.

Behind him, Avram laid his work on the bench and nodded once. He'd cut his dark hair shorter than most priests wore theirs—far more in keeping with the harsher needs of a traveler or a soldier.

I held his gaze. How could he show his face after . . . after what? No one in Aster temple should know of the attack against us, I reminded myself, unless they'd been told directly. And if Avram had been the one who'd stolen my jarak journal, no one would know of that either besides Hershann. Nor would anyone care that Avram had been born in Gleavon territory; that once Lethia and I had met in a jarak dream. What accusation could I bring against him for speaking out against Morell? At a meeting in Aster town that was never supposed to have happened?

"I've only just now arrived," I answered. "But I was hoping to see to some of my things in the library, Dev . . . Will you walk with me?"

"Well, yes, of course." Dev looked down at the half-finished bow. "That is, if you can wait just a while longer. I have to finish this work. Gregor, he's the new arms master now. He put us to it, and we promised to finish the lot."

"I see. But I had hoped—"

Avram's smile was a dare. "You needn't go all the way to the library tower just to talk, Calyx. I promise not to say anything you won't like."

"What will you say, Avram? Will you ask after the safety of my journey?"

Dev looked from one to the other of us. "How did things go?" he asked. "Is your mother well?"

"Not so well as I'd hoped," I started, then abruptly I decided to say more. "The truth is, I've returned for medicine for her."

"Here?" Avram didn't try to hide his interest.

"Not here. But maybe you can help after all, Av. How well versed are you in riddles? Unless you already know the answer to this one?"

"Try me," he said. "I'm as good as any. Better than some. We play at riddles in Gleavon sometimes. It helps the nights to pass. Sometimes it helps keep you alive longer."

"What kind of medicine needs a riddle to work its healing?" Dev asked.

"This one does," I said. "I already know what I need: the leaf of an elderberry bush. But it has to be picked from a certain place and at a certain time."

"Rules," Avram laughed. "And here I thought you were the one person in Aster temple who wasn't afraid of breaking rules."

"But I'd have said the same of you."

"No, I believe in rules," Av said, watching me closely. "Some there are for keeping and some for breaking. That's the difference between Dev and I."

Dev scowled, trying to find the source of tension.

"He believes in keeping rules while I'm far too much the realist for that. I believe only in using them. Why don't you break your rule, Calyx, and ask the riddle?"

"I think I will, then," I said. *"What journeys the earth in springtime, dwells in Kuoshana in summer, yet come winter sleeps caged and trampled?"*

"I don't know," Dev shrugged. "What do you think it could be? A dog of some kind, an animal?"

"No," Av said. "But no one could have thought to trick you with that for long, Calyx. It's water. The streams break up and go crashing past their banks in the spring. In summer the lakes are full. Then winter comes and the river is frozen— caged in ice and walked on. Is that all? Is there anything else?"

"Which water?" I asked.

"Roshanna Lake?" Dev suggested. "It's the largest body of water near here."

"That's it," I said. "I'm sure it is. When is Sister's fast?"

"In two nights," Dev said. Then more slowly he asked, "Why, Calyx? What are you planning? What have you two been talking about?"

"Come with me, Dev. To Roshanna." I took his hands. "I mean to go alone, but I'd prefer your help if you'll give it."

Dev kept his hands in mine for a moment, his brows knit, then he stepped back. "You can't go so soon, Calyx. You've only just returned. And how could I go with you? You mean, leave the temple?"

"Let her go, Dev. She's old enough to do what she wants. Ask her father, he'll tell you so."

"Of course leave the temple, Dev. It's just to Roshanna Lake. Help me find the elderberry, then you can return to Aster."

"Go with her, and Hershann will have your vows stripped away. He'll do it. After that hoax with the Kareil, he wants nothing to do with her, not again. Unless it's to ask her about the tokens she's stolen. You didn't know that, did you, Dev? She's the one who stole them. But you, you're jarak sworn. You belong here!"

"Calyx"—there was pleading in Dev's voice—"I can't just leave. Whatever else Avram says, he's right about that. You're free in a way I won't allow myself to be. Your vows are to yourself. Mine belong to Aster. Of course, Hershann isn't perfect, he's only human. But that doesn't change anything. When I needed to offer my dreams to the gods, it was Hershann who took my vows. The elders are symbols, it's true. But they're symbols that I need. Forging a path between my faith and the gods . . . I can't turn away from that."

"Such pretty words." Avram crossed his arms. "What are you going to do now, Calyx?"

"The same," I said. Av knew now I would turn south again toward Roshanna Lake and Briana. And more likely than not, there would be raiders again. But he could not know of the havens, and I would see to it that all the rest of his knowledge availed him nothing. "Unless you'd like to come with me? Or do your vows prevent you?"

"My vows?" Av laughed. "What vows?"

Dev's face clouded over. "Avram . . . ?"

"Your vows to Lethia. Those are the only ones that matter to you, aren't they?"

"I've already told you, I'm far too realistic to chain myself down with vows. Even those."

"Even to her?"

"In Gleavon we have a saying, it has to do with staying alive, maintaining a hold on your property."

"But . . ." Dev's voice was almost too low to hear. "What of your vows to the priesthood?"

"The priesthood? Yes, I took vows to the priesthood. But there are other loyalties that come first." Avram's voice was loud, but I thought he meant what he said. "I'm here because we knew from the first that one of our family would serve Lethia in the north. My elder brother Alain wears her judicial insignia. My second brother carries her keys. Stacia, my sister, wears the robes of council in her own right. In another year, two at the most, Gleavon's Sumedaro elder will need an arm to lean on, someone who both the queen and the temples can trust. My father taught us which vows matter . . . vows of the blood."

"You know, Avram," Dev said, sounding more certain of himself, "that's the first time I've ever heard you speak clearly. Thank you for the lesson."

Av smiled.

"But it seems to me, now that we're talking of vows, that if I want the ones I've taken to mean anything, it seems I'd be wiser to give them in service where they're needed." Dev turned to me. "Calyx, I pray you know what you're doing. But if this is what you need, I'll help you."

By late evening Dev had packed all the clothing and possessions he cared to take: a small, gold-hilted dagger, a brooch, two bound volumes he'd taken as a present from Sharat temple, and little else.

When the corridors were least crowded and I was certain the gossiping Rija would not be about, I stole away to my old chambers. What was there that I needed? Two gowns, a pair of light gloves—all of it too fine for riding. So little of Aster had ever been mine really. Hershann's trinkets, the bed, desk, chair, all lent to the room to fill its lifeless walls.

Dev seemed quieter when we met back together, as if he'd spent a good deal of time thinking, but he offered me a smile and pointed out a stolen ham and a wedge of cheese he'd hidden under his shirt. All seemed to have gone well. Hershann, as far as we could tell, had not heard of our plans. Garret had somehow managed to keep his own mouth shut—at least for the time. Though I knew if he was questioned, he'd tell. The stable master, a lazy, oafish priest I had never known well, was easily paid off for a second horse and his promise of secrecy.

Dev and I had no time to speak of plans—whether we would return, where I would go after I'd taken the elderberry to Briana, how we would buy our food. But I think Dev understood that I had no mind to return to Aster. More than anything, Avram's words seemed to have hurt him, unbalanced the sense of mission Dev had always carried as a shield. The rest of it—the temple, his possessions, his fellow priests—all were easily put aside. Only his faith that had sheltered him had been wounded, and I was afraid the wound may have cut deep.

All through that first night, we rode at a hard pace. When we made camp, Dev spoke little, avoiding me, and for the most part I left him to his private musings. Later I would speak of Avram, of my thoughts concerning the priesthood and his loyalties. For now, I reasoned, Dev had given up enough. It was time that he needed most.

The next day we picked up the route again, following south toward Roshanna Lake. From there the road eventually joined back in with the other routes: FelWeather Keep and the Hills of Elianor to the west, Toklat toward the east. Near dusk we found a sheltered copse and made camp on a level patch of ground so securely protected, I felt no need to search for a haven. I had hoped to talk, to explain something more about our need for haste, but within minutes Dev was wound up in a nest of woolen blankets and had fallen asleep. Tomorrow was Sister's eve and I had decided to fast again, to use hunger to strengthen my senses, my resolve.

Tomorrow night the moon would be at a quarter's face over Roshanna Lake and I would be there, watching for its rays to dance across the shining spine of an elderberry leaf.

I sat with my back to Dev, unable to sleep. With Dev asleep at my side and no voice save the wind's to answer me, I felt more alone than during the entire journey back to Aster. Too much could still go wrong. What would happen to Ivane if I failed to find the elderberry? What if Edishu changed his mind and refused to help my mother?

Sometime close to dawn, I must have fallen asleep. The

next thing I knew, Dev was shaking my shoulder. The early light was moving in across the trees, outlining each snow-covered branch with a pallet of dancing colors. Dev had already kindled a fire in a circle of gray stones, and a pan filled with stripped meat sizzled over the banked coals.

I sat up, hoping Dev would be too polite to notice my half-opened eyes and tousled hair. "What day is this?" I asked, squinting against the white sun.

"Sister's morn." Dev smiled, then purposefully pointed out the first meal he'd ever cooked during a fast. "A good day for hungry travelers. We'll make Roshanna Lake Inn by evening, but we'll need our strength."

"Thank you but no," I said. "I'll eat later. But you go ahead. I need to rinse my face, wake up."

Dev laid his knife down. "Calyx, if I can, you should. They never were your vows."

I sighed, forced myself to come awake. "No, Dev, this business of making choices may seem new to you, but for me, it's the same as it's always been. I fast or not—but it's my choice. You eat to show yours. We mean the same thing in our different ways."

"Sometimes I wonder." Dev turned away, his voice sullen again. Whether he ate or not, he couldn't have enjoyed the meal very much. When I walked back from the bushes, the fire had already been trampled, the pans stowed back in their places.

All during that cold day we rode south, shoulders huddled into bulky coats, eyes fixed on the distant Hills of Elianor. Around midafternoon the first unmistakable signs of Roshanna Lake cropped up, and we rode past miles of wind-bent trees and the frozen husks of splintered cattails. Later, with an hour or more until dusk still ahead of us, we reached the inn. From this vantage and for as far as we could see, Roshanna Lake was one vast, unbroken field of snow, marred only by the shadowed berms created wherever the wind had blown up against a captive log.

On the outside, Roshanna Lake Inn was no different from any inn in Briana: dark, milled wood, moss chinking against the wind, a sloped roof which in recent years had been shored up against heavier snows. Several outbuildings huddled beneath snowdrifts: shed, stable, a small barn. As soon as we dismounted, a churlish, ragged boy ducked out of the low stable door, took our horses, and left without a word of greeting.

I felt weary and shaken from the long ride and eager for a warm fire. But still I had enough sense about me to be cautious. The inn was more crowded than when I'd come through with Hayden. Avram had sent Lethia's raiders after me once already—couldn't he as easily do it again? Dev and I stopped in the doorway, waiting for our eyes to adjust to the dim light. The inn had a dark, high-ceilinged common room. Off to the left were a series of long tables with the best lying closest to the fireplace. Along the far wall, a double staircase snaked away upstairs while from below, the smells of long simmering meats filled the room.

Lightly, as though I were long used to such confidences, I laid my hand on Dev's arm and whispered, "You must decline when they ask if you want a room. And order supper for the two of us, and spiced wine. I won't eat, but we don't want anyone thinking we're Sumedaros observing the fast. Can you do that?"

In answer, Dev gave a laugh as subtle as if we were two young lovers seeking nothing more than a warm meal before the waiting night. He was smiling broadly, as though he had not a care in the world, and once he bent low and pretended to whisper something in my ear. I'd forgotten what an actor Dev could be, how he'd spent more time in the towns than I had and had seen more of this sort of thing. But though it was a sham, I couldn't stop myself from imagining what it would feel like if his touch was real, if his kisses were meant for me and not a show put on for a room full of broad-faced strangers.

Dev led us toward one of the corner tables and sat down close beside me. Anyone who looked would have taken us for lovers. The room was loud and thick with smoke. Odors from the kitchen mixed with the stifling air and left me feeling shaky and ill at ease. When a lanky, sweat-streaked serving girl finally stopped to ask what we'd be having, I stared down at the table, wanting nothing more than to be left alone.

In a few minutes, the girl returned with two large mugs filled with a sweet, steamy wine. She pushed them loudly in front of Dev, then waited, her skirts pressing rudely into his back until he found her a coin from his pocket. When she left, Dev spoke in a low voice. "There are four men watching us," he said. "No, wait! Don't turn around. Let them go back to their game first."

"Do you know who they are?"

"I'm sure I don't. Could be from anywhere."

"What are they wearing?"

"Wait, I'll tell you." Dev turned, pretended to be looking for the serving girl. "Three of them are dressed in heavy furs and over jackets. Nothing rich, just thick, warm clothing, more for riding than town or a farm. The fourth man—he's the one in the middle with the reddish hair—he's a soldier. He's wearing a uniform."

"A uniform? Here?" It was all I could do not to turn and stare. "What color?"

"Gray and purple. Do you know it?"

"Know it? Yes." I laughed loudly, looking up at Dev and pulling a stray hair from his shoulder as I imagined a lover might. At the same time I stole a look toward the table closest to the fire. "Lethia's colors," I whispered. "The gray and purple of her private guard. Yet it makes sense."

"What makes sense?"

Before I could answer, the girl returned with two platters heaped high with meat and stewed vegetables. While Dev ate, I pushed the food around my plate, my stomach turning at the thick odors. I felt weak, tired. But the thought of swallowing any of that food seemed more than I could bear. I would hold this fast, I promised myself. I would be clean when I picked my mother's elderberry from the earth.

"I haven't told you yet what happened on the trip down to Aster," I said, with a smile that I hoped appeared outwardly bright. "We were attacked. Three of our men were killed. Good men. But it was me the raiders wanted. And only someone from Aster could have known where I was heading. Same as now, except that they wore no markings on their clothing. The only difference seems to be that Avram no longer feels the need to keep up pretenses."

"What do you mean, they wanted you, Calyx?"

"We heard them say it. *Get the girl. There she is.*"

"But that could have meant anything. Why should her raiders be looking for you?"

"She wants me dead. Out of her way."

Dev made a show of putting his arm around my shoulder, pulling me closer up against him. "What do we do? We can't stay here."

"We hide. Dev, listen to me. That night, after the raiders first attacked us, I went walking in the woods. Not far. I could still see Hayden. I found a path into one of the old havens. We spent the night there, all of us. Safely hidden. It was as if we had slipped through Kuoshana's gate. By morning the raiders had given up."

Dev was silent for a long time, then finally he asked, "How . . . ?"

"You remember when I took the tokens? It was the bracelet that led me to the haven. I knew I was doing the right thing, taking it. It saved my life. We have to find a haven again, before they catch us. It's our only choice. If we're followed, and I don't doubt but it will happen, we'll be safe."

"How do you find it?"

"Them. There's more than one. I found the first when I wasn't looking for it. There was a tree, nothing more. But it made an odd pattern. Rath was on my wrist. It started glowing, like a beacon. I can also find them through a jarak dream. You could too, I think, if you tried. But in another way I've learned to see them. Not see with my eyes, because there's nothing of our world that marks them. No stone or tree or different-colored bush, nothing like that. But a way of looking at the land, understanding the patterns of hills and ravines, valleys, trees. The havens were here first, and they still stand, Dev. They've faded, or maybe been blocked, I'm not sure which, but they're still out there."

Dev was staring down at the table, his fingers absently tracing the worn grain. "They're watching us."

"We'll talk more later," I said. "It's time. We have to find the elderberry." I pushed my chair back and stood.

Too fast!

I hadn't realized how weak I was, how much I'd drunk without food to slow the wine.

The floor reeled up toward my face. Blackness! Everything was spinning, black and spinning.

Desperately I dug my hand into Dev's shoulder. Just in time he caught me, put his arm around me, pretended to laugh, all the while propelling me closer to the door. "Try to laugh," he whispered. "They're watching us. One's up by the table, the dark-haired one."

Somehow he kept me upright, half carrying, half dragging me across the floor, our cheeks close together so that anyone who looked would see only two young lovers eager with too much drink.

I held on, fighting back the nausea until we were outside and the cold slapped my face. "Get the horses," I stammered. "I'll be all right. I'll meet you up ahead."

"No, I'm not leaving you. They'll be after us in a minute."

"Then get the horses. I just have to catch my breath. I'll be all right." I sank to the ground, let my head fall forward, waiting for the cold to revive my senses.

Night had closed Roshanna Lake in her dark arms. Soon the moon would appear and I would have my chance: *A single leaf of a twisted elderberry bush, ripened in the light of a Sister's eve moon.*

I sucked in a deep breath of air. Burning, sharp, it woke me up, sent the blood pounding to my head again.

Now! It had to be now!

Dev pulled me along behind him in the dark, the icy wind forcing my muscles to work against their will. The stable wasn't far. And for whatever reason, Lethia's raiders appeared to be taking their time. If only we could make it to the horses, I would be all right. We were so close now. My mother's life waited on Edishu's promise. Soon enough, the raiders wouldn't matter.

19

We raced out over the eastern road, following Roshanna's southern shore. Dev took the lead, sprinting past the lake's frozen banks as if he were a boy again, loose upon his father's wildest horse. I galloped hard behind him, following the shadowed tracks his horse left in the snow, edging away from a fallen tree where he did, cutting closer to the shore when the path grew too uneven. This was Dev's country, the wildlands surrounding Sharat temple. If anyone could keep the raiders from our back, he would be able to.

We'd been riding for a while like that, solitary figures along a seldom used road, when Dev looped back around and rode up beside me, slowing his horse to a cautious gait. "Do you hear anything?" he asked.

"No. Have you?"

"I thought I might have, but the wind's too strong in my ears. Stop your horse so we can listen." We came to a halt on a slight rise and stood there, turning our faces first toward the inn, then out toward the center of the lake.

Dev's face was a calm study, his attention focused outward. "What is it?" I asked. "Horses?"

"Five, six, maybe more. There must have been more of them upstairs. They're riding hard."

Damn Avram! I couldn't have made it easier for him, could I? "Then we'll have to ride harder!" I said.

"It's not going to help. Listen, can you hear? Over in that direction?" Dev pointed a gloved finger. "They're not coming along the road. If they were, we could easily outrun them. They're coming straight toward us across the frozen lake. They'll outmaneuver us unless we ride into the trees and hope to lose them there."

"We have to find the elderberry while it's still Sister's eve. I can't give up."

"Yes, but where?"

I shook my head, then turning, wondering . . . "There!" I pointed toward a nearby clearing, where, surprisingly, a cluster of half-buried shrubs with the dry, brown-paired leaves of the elderberry peeked out above the snow.

I kicked my heels into my horse's sides and turned his head toward the clearing.

Overhead, the gibbous moon rose higher in the sky. Edishu had said nothing about the time of night I must pick the elderberry, only that it must be ripened in the light of a Sister's eve moon.

Ripened in the light of a Sister's eve moon.

Ripened? . . . Ripened? But how—in winter?

I started, reared my horse in, then kicked him on again, plundering through the snows.

I'd been tricked, hadn't I? All this time I had thought I need only wait for a Sister's eve. But that wasn't it at all. Not at all.

Edishu had said it must be ripened under the moon. Not before, not after. But in midwinter in the northlands, that was impossible! I would find nothing but last year's black windfall berries, a dried bush, the leaves brown and withered. He had said *twisted* also, but that was no help. And if I waited until I could bring him the proof of his riddle . . . ?

Why then, it would be midsummer, nearly half a year hence, and my mother might lay sleeping in a box built wide enough to house both her and that stillborn child waiting to claim her life!

I slackened my grip on my horse's sides, no longer caring when the animal slowed its gait, first to a canter, then a walk.

Edishu had said his riddle was a clue to finding the elderberry, not an assurance of success in helping my mother. And yet, wasn't there one place a flower could blossom, though the rest of the world were shrouded in winter? If the elderberry I sought was anywhere, it would be inside one of the havens. Edishu, I was near certain, was still unaware that I had found the havens. And if that were true, then it was probably also true that he hadn't meant for me to find the elderberry at all!

"Calyx, we've got to ride!"

"Dev, just wait. Please—"

"There's no place in there we'll be able to hide—"

"Hold back. I think it's here."

I closed my eyes and turned toward the leeward side of the lake. One moment. A second. I worked to push the sights of this world away. And then it began, a new calm opening around me. The wind slackened. Winter's stillness fled. There was a sudden drift of ripening leaves and bracken in the air, a fresh, verdant smell redolent with summer and vitality. I knew that taste as clearly as if it had been the face of someone I'd loved since childhood, their arms and smile welcoming me after a journey.

But I hadn't found the haven yet, only its scent. The entryway could be miles away, across the snow-covered terrain.

I looked up. Dev was staring at me, his eyes wide with expectancy, and I wondered at the trust he'd laid on me. He was here at my wish, believing in my ravings about gods and havens and jarak dreams.

The lines of panic had fled from his face. Everything about him spoke of waiting, of expectation and hope.

I closed my eyes again, took a deep breath, then slowly let the air escape. These woods were as ancient as I, in my own flesh-bound way, was also ancient. By dint of my breath, my thoughts, my dreams, my body bled into soil, my feet erupted into the roots of wide mountain ranges, my thoughts fled toward the light of Kuoshana's stars. Thus it was Jokjoa had dreamt the earth. Thus were all dreams united: through the heart, through time, each of us greater, each more ancient than we could know . . .

Then I felt it again; felt first, then saw the lighted knoll where the entry to the haven began. All around, the trees seemed to beckon us forward. The undergrowth appeared thinner, the snow cover lighter, as if there indeed was a place touched by the warmth of a younger sun.

"Look, Dev!" I started to say, but behind us the heavy sounds of hooves grew louder and closer.

Dev pulled his horse ahead and it bellowed, reared up. "Where?" he shouted. "Calyx? Where?"

"There, the shadowed path. Just atop that rise."

"You lead," he shouted. "Hurry!"

We kicked the horses forward, but it was no use. The trail was new, the snow deep. The horses couldn't find their balance.

If the raiders found us now, we'd never reach the havens. Already I heard voices one hundred paces behind us, maybe closer. I didn't dare turn around.

Then suddenly the path changed. Dark patches of bare ground edged up against the snow. What we had taken for ridges, we now saw were the half-buried remains of gray, weathered stones, the tallest rising up three and four layers high.

"Dev, what is it?"

"Ruins . . ." he started to answer, but suddenly behind us, a horse's brisk complaint broke through the air. One of the raiders shouted an order to his men. Another voice called across, muffled but close.

"Get down," I shouted to Dev. "Get off. Now!"

We ran on side by side a few paces, bringing the horses up behind us. I veered away from a towering spruce, then stopped suddenly. We were standing before two huge birch trees, their branches woven to form a trellis. "It's all right!" I called to Dev. "We're here. Hurry . . ."

Ahead, a thick web of branches intertwined. I closed my eyes and started through, one hand outstretched as a guide. The trees were warm, their bark resilient, but they opened up a doorway where before there had been none and we ducked through into the kinder air of the haven.

All at once a rushing wind of moonlight and warmth enveloped us. We were in a wide clearing, our boundaries guarded by a circle of intertwined trees. I dropped my horse's reins, leaving it to graze where it pleased, and stood with my face lifted toward the sky, waiting while the warmth chased the tight ache from my body.

When I turned back, Dev lay huddled on the ground. "Dev!" I called, suddenly afraid the raiders had struck him and I'd never known. "Dev! Are you all right?" I grabbed his shoulders, tried to pull him up, but he was sobbing, resistant.

"I never knew." His voice was cracked, broken. "All those years I never knew." With an effort he sat up, but he kept his hands to the earth, stroking the ground as if he were reluctant to give up its touch.

"Of course you didn't. No one did."

"But you don't understand. I should have known. I was—am—a Sumedaro priest. If even the elders didn't know, then what good was any of it? What else were they wrong about? What else didn't they know?"

"Dev, I'm sorry. I know it was hard for you to leave Aster— "

"No! That is, yes, it was hard. But if I hadn't . . . if I'd never known you—or worse, if I hadn't trusted you—then don't you see, Calyx? I never would have come here. And this"—he dug his hands into the ground, brought up a clump of grass and black earth, clutching it in his fist—"this one handful of dirt is more real, more important than anything the elders ever taught me, ever knew. I'm glad, Calyx. Glad!"

Softly I touched my hand to his face. His cheeks were rough and in need of shaving. His hair was littered with leaves, but just then I thought I had never known a finer man. Thoughts mingled with a hundred half-forgotten memories: Dev taking my hands on the rathadaro couch; Dev helping me back to Aster temple, hungry and frightened from that ill-fated trip to town; Dev in Sharat temple, warning Avram away from me; Dev, my friend, my confidant. My lover?

Tentatively I let my hand wander down to his shoulder, his arm. I did not think any of the Sisters would object if Dev and I made love in their haven. Surely, I would be committing no trespass . . .

But Dev seemed not to notice my invitation. He took a

deep breath and smiled, a wide, brotherly smile, then stood up to look about.

I let my hand fall back to my side. Later, perhaps later would be a better time for such thoughts.

After that there was little time for such concerns. I sent Dev out, exploring the limits of the haven with instructions to come right back as soon as he found an elder tree. Then I turned away, needing the few short moments of solitude to think . . .

I had come to this haven with a mission. Now only a few short hours of moonlight remained. I had to know for a certainty whether to trust Edishu. He'd tricked me already, sent me raging about the northlands for something he imagined I'd never be able to produce—the ripened elderberry.

And I had found the elderberry, but the question now was whether it mattered. If he'd tricked me once, wasn't it possible the entire story was a fabrication—that there would be no medicine regardless of whether I produced the elderberry or not? Would he truly have risked anything of import? Or was I the only one foolish enough to have done that? I was the one who had promised him the tokens. I was the one who stood to lose. Not him. For him it was only a game—exactly as he'd said.

And where was the gain for me? I'd left my mother's side for him. Left Briana. Left Aster. But perhaps there lay the catch. The one thing I'd turned to my advantage was the havens. If I'd been allowed to find them, then perhaps I'd be permitted to use them as well. Perhaps dreams woven in a haven would be the strongest of all? Jarak dreams powerful enough to pry the secrets I needed out from the unwilling earth . . .

A slight breeze blew up against my neck, chilling me. There was power here, I knew it. I could feel it in the earth, the heat rising up from the ground into my feet, whispering; the air touching my neck, playing with my hair.

I could wrest a dream from this ground, I told myself. A dream powerful enough to see Edishu without being seen, to find him undetected.

Suddenly I felt very tired. Dev will find the elderberry, I thought, taking one last look at the moonlight-shrouded sky. He will not fail. Edishu doesn't know where to look for us.

I lay down, and it seemed as if the ground reached up an

arm and pulled me to her soft bed, changing and reshaping itself so I would be comfortable. I fell asleep with the hope that from inside the haven's safety, I might have a farsight dream: find Lethia, find Edishu at Gleavon, find why she sent her raiders and whether Edishu's riddle held any promise at all.

I remember the familiar whirring sound, as of a strong wind in my ears heralding a jarak flight, then a myopic distortion of valleys, sky, and mountains until at last that too settled out and all that remained was a deep, unspoken calm.

I was inside Gleavon Keep, in what must be an antechamber in one of the main halls. There were two doors. One, I supposed, led to the corridor, another, if the jarak dream was strong enough, directly into Lethia's private quarters. I started toward the second door, then waited. There were voices coming through the other, east-facing door.

I shrank back and pressed my shadow body against the bare wall. Please, I prayed, let her not see me. Let the haven protect me. Let Sister Eclipse hide me. I peered through the wall out into a spacious, extravagantly furnished bedchamber fitted out with reclining couches, ornate screens, and wide mirrors. No one was there. The floor was a minute black-and-white mosaic, a pattern of a single flower unfurling its leaves toward the edges of the room. The bed and draperies were opulent and lush, more fitted out for entertaining a king than to house a lonely widow.

I turned my attention back toward the antechamber and the second door.

She was in there. I could sense her presence through the wall. But there was someone else as well, a powerful, threatening voice. Slowly, cautiously, I sent my jarak body through the thick door and watched, all too aware that I had seen this before.

Lethia was locked in a deep embrace with a young man. One of her arms hung low around the curve of his back, pressing him toward her; the other was behind his shoulder, comfortable, familiar. After a moment Lethia pulled away from the man and sat down on a bed near the corner.

They seemed to have done with each other. Lethia's loose white gown hung open over her shoulders. Her hair was loose and tangled, and the odor of scented oils, sweat, and lovemaking hung on her skin.

I looked away, feeling somehow ashamed for them. How little of what I would call love appeared in her eyes, and how much desperation. Then for the first time I noticed my surroundings. Except for the narrow, unadorned bed, the room was completely cold and unfurnished. No carpets, no silken canopies, no chests or tables: the entire chamber stood in sharp contrast to Lethia's luxurious private quarters. Even the bed seemed to have been brought in as an afterthought, as though if they weren't to romp on the cold floor, anything would do. I felt confused. Why wouldn't Lethia invite her lover to her own bed? If it was gossip that troubled her, I didn't understand. Morell, I knew, had brought women up from Briana. Surely a queen with armies of her own could command a servant's wagging tongue?

I looked briefly at the man. He seemed ordinary enough, tall, wide-shouldered, clean-shaven, and young. He wore nothing but a pair of tight leggings that outlined his muscular lower build. Light hair, almost white it was so blond, and beardless. And his eyes, blue . . . But never again would I be deceived. His eyes were too familiar, haughty and soulless. I willed my jarak body closer, closer, meaning to win a better look, but instead I fell back.

The man's body emanated a white heat, an impenetrable wall that would broach no scheming intrusion, not even from the body of a dream. He had set up guards around himself. Eclipse's magic, Sunder's, or his own, I didn't know which. But then I saw his eyes again, and it didn't matter where he gained his power, only that it was a part of him and I must be wary.

Quickly I backed away, wildly afraid my simple defenses would never suffice against a nightmare-god. I backed toward the door, already preparing myself for the cold wind which would carry me home.

But then Lethia spoke, and I waited to hear.

"You aren't satisfied with the ring, are you?" she asked.

Edishu turned his young man's mouth up in a vulgar laugh. "It will do. For now."

"But you've used it. It's the one you wanted. You told me it was enough."

"It was."

"Then you'll come again, as you promised?"

"I already told you. I want more."

Lethia's face whitened. "But you need me. You said so. I

promise, I'll bring you another token . . . Gamaliel. No one
else can do that for you. I know where it is."

"You're too late. She's taken it. Did you think she would
sit quietly forever, waiting for your useless attempts—"

"You said we would make a bargain between us."

Edishu's voice was an empty mask. "I gave you what you
wanted."

"But you promised more!"

"Did I? A bargain is not a promise. And your smile is not
so fetching as you think. Or shall I be plainer? Bring me
another relic or I will not come again."

"All right, I can do that. Anything she can . . . But tell
me how. If she's taken the goblet, I can steal it back. I could
even bring her to you."

"No, I won't have her that way, dead at your idiot soldiers' hands."

"What else do you want, then? I'll find the other tokens.
But this time I'll name my reward first."

"No!" Edishu thundered. "You do not set the terms of
our agreement! I do." He raised his arm, his hand gathered
in a fist. But I had seen enough. The haven had brought me
safety that I dared not abuse. I shut my eyes. Quickly, like
a trailing wind over a winter lake, I fled, turning my inner
sight back toward my sleeping body, back toward the goddess-
wrought haven.

Back . . . Back . . .

I sat upright. I was in the haven again, awake and safe.
Not more than a few paces away, the two horses stood
quietly grazing. Dev was asleep beside me, his blankets
pulled up as far as his shoulders. On the ground between us
lay a sprig of elderberry leaves, ripe and fresh as if they'd
been picked at a Springsnight festival and laid as an offering
at my side.

Except that now I was no longer certain I wanted it.

I forced myself to think clearly. I was in the goddesses'
sanctuary. Edishu could not enter this realm. He had no
power here, nor did he know where I was. And I had the
elderberry we'd bargained for . . .

Bargained.

The word sounded bitter in my mouth, and I shivered
with a cold far harsher than the haven's sweet air. Lethia
had said she'd made a bargain with Edishu. Is that what I
had done?

I hung my head in despair. No, please, Jokjoa! Please, Oreill! Let me consecrate my jarak dreams to you, to the havens, to everything that is real and holy on this earth. Let my dreams be a light against the winter. But please, help me! Grant me a way to ward against Edishu, to hold him at bay, tight in Kuoshana's prison.

The hours passed over me like a cold blanket, stiff with my fears. Sleep seemed to lie forever beyond my grasp. At last, searching for solace, I rose, took Jokjoa's Rath from my wrist and the goblet from its pouch. Once before Gamaliel had shown me a vision. Since then I hadn't thought to look inside again. But I should. There was so little I understood of Jokjoa's magic. Rath revealed things near at hand. Gamaliel's power seemed to work beyond time and place.

Hadn't I seen a narrow brook over by the stand of trees?

Deep inside the goblet, the clear water began changing. The goblet was glowing again, its clear water changing, turning murky, heat rising like a corona about my hands.

I stopped, waited.

Soon a warm light began to glow, stronger and stronger. I could feel its power welling up around me, including me, holding me. A light different from any I'd felt, neither jarak nor vision . . .

And then suddenly I was lifted up into its center, carried—a bird on the wind! Away!

I was flying over the blue fields of a mountain range. Far below, a formation that could only be the great ice sheets of the north spilled out across the earth, deep and blue and ancient.

For certain, this was no jarak dream I'd spun. I was neither awake nor asleep. And this path, this northward pulling—it was none of my doing but was propelled instead by Gamaliel's invisible hands. Yet I was safe, secure knowing that the goblet had heard my voice and brought me this newest dream.

Above, the stars turned: the bear, the dog, the tree. Distance slipped by with time and it seemed I neither thought nor slept—only watched. Then at last, as though I had been held safe inside the hands of some invisible giant, I was let down in a frozen field.

The winds stilled. I caught my breath, felt for the two tokens at my side, then looked about. Hard, cracked blue ice covered the unending countryside. Though I was in the highest glacial passes, far above any possibility of a tree line, the frozen air did not touch me. Before me, a small farmstead had been built into the rear of a hillside. It looked almost comical, it was so out of place in this isolated world. All the details of a farmhouse were there: slate-roofed dairy, barn and a house, planked and trimmed, all so comfortably laid out. I think there was even a light glowing within.

It was impossible, of course. No farm could have been built here, so far from roads and mills. Where would the timbers have come from? The bolts and hinges? There wasn't a tree growing anywhere in this vast, frozen land, only miles of stone and ice, chiseled into shape by eons of upheavals and thaws.

I hesitated, trying to decide whether to venture inside the house. For all the comfortable outer touches, I was certain no one lived inside. But as I looked, the house seemed almost familiar. There was something about it, too perfect, too simple, almost like a dollhouse, as though if I walked around back, the entire facade would be open so a child's hand could reach in and rearrange the furnishings.

But I had seen the house before! I was certain of it. Could it have been in Aster's library? Perhaps the illustrations in one of the manuscripts I worked on? But no, those had none of the realism of this farm. Only my mother painted pictures like this.

Ivane! Of course. It was a perfect likeness to the cover on Ivane's book, the present she had given me the same day she had given the ring to Mirjam. What had I done with it? I hadn't taken it to Aster? No, I remembered. I'd wrapped the journal in a scarf and laid it in my old chest in Diiana. I'd forgotten all about it, pushed so far down toward the bottom where I'd hoped it would be safe. And it had been. Safe from my hasty departures. Safe from Avram, who'd have brought it to Lethia. Safe from Edishu, who'd have found it in my heart.

Jared had said the journal was his idea, and that may have been true, but the cover, the cover came from my mother.

I faltered, trying to remember that day. Hadn't there also been a dream of hers I'd watched? It hadn't been jarak perhaps, but a dream of something she'd remembered. Not

the book. That came later. There was a man in the dream.
Not Jared. Maybe someone who was Sumedaro? A lover? If
only I'd had the skill then to follow a dream as well as I
could now. There was so much more than I could hope to
understand . . .

But it was Gamaliel that had brought me here. The god's
own token wanted me to see this. Knowing that, I found
courage again, rose up tall and defiant, arms thrown wide
toward Kuoshana's unending sky.

The white sun bounced off the wavering ice, nearly blind-
ing as it distorted the pattern of ridges and moraine.

Ivane had known about this place. Whatever else might
be true, she had known something.

"Mother . . ." I screamed, and the thin, cold air carried
my voice toward the distant mountains.

"Mother . . . Mother . . . Mother . . . What does it mean?"

The echo returned, *What does it mean? . . . mean? . . .
mean?*

"Mother?"

Mother? . . . Mother? . . . Mother?

"Why didn't you warn me?"

Warn me . . . warn me . . . warn me . . .

But there was no answer, only the wind-born pattern of
my own voice, laughing as if in jest.

One thing I believed: there would be no reward in returning to Edishu just now. I must first come back to this
place—not in a jarak dream or vision such as this, but in my
own body, strong and ready to act. Were I to try to enter
the house through a jarak dream, the door would never
open. That would be to change the dream. And I knew I
didn't have that power. Ceena's people perhaps or the Elan
Sumedaro could shape their dreams, but not I. If I intended
to find out what was hidden inside that house, I would have
to twist its handle with my own hand and claim whatever
awaited inside.

Only after that could I return to my mother and ask her
what truths had been hiding in the remainder of that dream
and how she had known about this house.

20

Late the next day, when we were reasonably sure Lethia's soldiers had given up their search, we left the haven. The lake winds had calmed and the air was still. Overhead, the chalky gray sky spoke of snow and incoming weather. But our plans had changed with my vision of that house, and we were sworn for the northlands now, not Briana as I'd originally planned. If Lethia's soldiers had orders to follow us, they would look toward my father's lands, not north into the wastelands beyond Aster.

There was no road north of Aster temple, but Dev knew the trails that wound through the dark woods there and which led into the forests and which wound back to the town itself. We would go there first, to Lucas, the merchant Dev trusted, to sell us warmer clothes, food, and supplies without fear of Lethia's spies hearing the tale. After that it would be my turn to lead, across the last of the foothills, then north and east following the path toward my mother's book house.

All through that first day back toward Aster we rode in an uncomfortable silence. Dev had shut himself away with an unyielding demeanor, and no matter what I said, he offered little more than a word or two in answer. I was glad then that I hadn't told him about Edishu, that it was his riddle which had sent us on this brash journey. It seemed better that Dev find his own answers because surely, from the way he acted, it didn't seem he'd be content with mine.

I wasn't certain what had happened or if anything had happened at all. There'd been no fear on his face when we first entered the haven. Hadn't he said he was glad to see the truth of those holy places? Yet some inner battle raged. I could see it in the tension in his shoulders, the grim set of his jaw, and his cold, unanswering eyes. Twice I tried to ask, to offer him what comfort I could, but both times he looked away with veiled eyes and finally I gave it up. When he was ready he would speak. That, or find a corner in his heart to bury the trouble.

We made our brief stop in Aster town, always keeping out of the open streets and shops, then turned our horses north again. Now, with each day's journey, the trees grew more stunted and bare, until within two days, only the willow bramble and black spruce were strong enough to survive the wind. During the days that followed, we added layer upon layer of warmer clothing. Then late on the fifth day, those trees also faded and we crossed the tree line into the heights of the ridges. From that vantage I had my first view of the jagged western mountains towering higher than I could have imagined possible. And eastward beyond us, the great ice fields I'd crossed in my dream, vast as all Kuoshana's stars.

Each day brought new, unforseen hazards, from the sledge we hauled together over the glazed ice to the wind-carved ridges that sometimes forced us to a crawl. Mornings we'd look out across a valley where narrow lines as fine as pen strokes crisscrossed the blue earth. Crevasses, great cracks in the ice, opened like the mouth of a behemoth in the distance. Progress was painfully slow and where I'd hoped to cross half a field or ridge line in one day, it took two. Where I'd hope to wake to a still, clear morning, we'd find blizzards of pelting snow driving us, long hours when the sun's glare narrowed our vision to a confused blur.

Yet for all the toil and exhaustion, the journey's toll could have been far more serious. Near dusk each day, we halted our progress. Then, as though enacting a sacred ritual, while Dev stood silent at my back, I stretched out my jarak vision in search of hidden lights and found the havens.

They were more plentiful this far north than they had been in the forests, and most nights we needed walk no more than a quick span to reach the flickering circles of light. There was no pattern to the havens, no tricks to make them appear. But wherever I closed my eyes and turned my inner sight to search, they were there—a doorway of light against shadow, waiting to be found.

Stepping into a haven was like entering a portal to another land. Always it was summer, with a warm sun overhead and soft grass underfoot. Inside, famished from the day's ordeal, we'd eat voraciously: meat first, then anything with fat or sugar, with a drink of the haven's sweet waters to quench our thirst. Then, almost before we'd swallowed our last mouthful, we'd fall asleep, more needful of rest than talk.

Mornings we worked. We woke with that sense of renewal peculiar to the havens, as if the very air were enough to nourish us, restore our strength. Breakfast was our one cooked meal of the day. After eating, we'd pick extra grain for the horses and fruit for ourselves, eating our fill, then repacking our overburdened sledge with as much food, firewood, and gear as we could safely pull—until the next evening, when my search began again.

Though they began the trek with us, it became evident early on that the horses' smooth hooves would never follow on the ice. By tacit agreement we rifled our packs and saddlebags, taking only the lightest, most absolutely necessary food and gear. Then, with a slap on their rumps, we sent the horses back into the safety of the haven to fend for themselves on the sweet grass and windfall apples that grew there, reassuring each other that after the book house, we'd return to the haven and find them again.

This also I knew: without the havens to rest in at night, Dev and I would not have survived. No one could conquer that country, no matter what provisions they carried, the gear, the clothing—it could not have been enough. Always we were aware that we had only to keep moving, to keep from freezing, to keep alive until I found another haven. Though we traversed but a mere five miles a day, it didn't matter. Eventually, we believed, we would reach the book house.

As long as I continued to find the havens, I felt safe. Something in their nature blocked Edishu's entrance, denied him clear sight into my jurak dreams. Yet during the days I felt a shadow overhead, a dark premonition that told me, yes, he was there, waiting. The months of intermittent visits were over. Edishu was growing impatient. Lethia's attempts, no matter how desperate and wild, were failing him. He meant to win the tokens by any means available. And though I prayed he hadn't yet realized I'd broken with my side of our bargain, I knew it would not be long until he came searching.

Then one evening, when we'd long since lost track of the number of days and nights, I found no haven.

Dev stood behind me, his heavy pack thrown against the sledge. "Shall we go farther?" he asked quietly.

I looked back over the trail we'd taken. The last haven was a full day's journey back across the ice. Retracing the route seemed insanity. Yet if there were no haven now, wasn't it possible the next would not appear either, or the next—that we'd gone beyond the limit of the Sister's country and wouldn't know until it was too late?

We were both suffering from exhaustion, Dev no less than I. My legs ached where I'd pulled a calf muscle slipping on the ice earlier that day, and my hands were half numb and cramped from the cold. And I'd long since grown irritable with Dev. Most mornings he watched me closely, a strange look in his eye, then if I approached him, he grew distant and morose, speaking only when there was a need, only about the most immediate tasks in front of us.

Was the fault mine that I could no longer find a haven? Had I ignored some propriety, or crossed some invisible barrier that I should have lost favor in the Sister's sight? Did Dev see something I could not?

No! I told myself, insistent. There was no special magic to finding the havens—unless it was Rath's—nothing anyone could not have done as well. Only a way of looking at the earth and listening to the changes in wind, sky, and ground. This was not a skill the Sister confered, like the Sumedaro with their talk of lessons and dream watchers, rewards, and vows.

If the haven was there, I would have found it. And if it was not, I must not sleep, no matter how tired my body. Edishu must not find me, not now, so close to the book house.

"We'll build a camp here," I told Dev. "It's too dangerous to travel in the dark. And without a haven, I don't dare sleep."

In answer Dev only nodded, his dark eyes turned uncomfortably away from mine.

We untied our packs and set up the wedge-shaped tent we carried, cutting blocks of snow and ice with a trowel to help weigh down the corners. Inside was dark and narrow, but the walls held out the wind and the air warmed quickly. There was space enough to set up a sleeping area—Dev toward one wall and my place to another, with our packs forming a proper wall in between. There would be no spruce boughs waiting to serve us as bedding, but we did the best we could, carefully protecting anything we put below us from too much moisture. We battened down the tent door, hoping the snow would not drift too high against it during the night. Perhaps, we decided, it would be best to stay there only until the first light of dawn, then pack our gear again and begin walking. There was always the hope that we would find another haven sometime during the next day and take a longer rest then.

In the shadowed gray light we shared a few berries and bread spread with a thick butter, and agreed to finish off the last of the wine. Dev seemed sullen again and I thought I knew what he was thinking. That I was leading him into the wild northlands, far beyond warm hearths and barking dogs. That I had no idea where or how far this book house was. That I didn't know what I would do when we found it, or how we would return. That I was ice blind and sick with the cold, the wind, the loneliness. That though the havens had saved our lives, there was something wrong with me for finding them at all.

Yet I needed Dev's help, even beyond the obvious dangers of the ice fields. I had to stay awake. Sleeping outside the havens was too great a risk. Edishu was waiting for me. By now he must have learned that I'd found the havens. He'd have grown more wrathful, his anger and wariness raging in turn. Within the light of my next jarak dream, I feared he would come for me. I could feel him searching, waiting to snare me as soon as I began a dream. It had been too long, too many easy nights in the safety of the havens. But if we reached Kuoshana's gate before he found me, surely there was a chance something would happen. It must be so! Why else would my mother have shown me that picture if I wasn't meant to go there?

"Dev?" I asked cautiously. "Dev? Will you talk to me? I don't want to fall asleep, not here, without a haven to guard us."

At first he didn't answer. He sat huddled as far away from me as that tiny cave permitted, absently tracing lines on the wall. Finally he looked up, scratched the stubble of dark beard growing on his cheeks, and nodded. "We should talk," he said.

"I suppose I owe you an explanation."

"No, that's not true. I trust you." I looked into Dev's

face, not sure I understood. "But if you need to, I'm more than willing to listen."

"You don't hate me for what's happened?"

"Hate you, Calyx?" Dev looked surprised. "How can you talk of hate? How could I presume to judge you? I'm only glad to be allowed to follow you, to serve you. I thought you understood that. I'm grateful for how much you've already done for me. I was afraid you were angry with me."

"Angry? What for?"

Dev looked away. "For deceiving you, for pretending I didn't know all along. But Calyx, I'm sorry. I only meant to help you by it. But I let you down instead, when you needed my help. I was frightened at first—I'm sorry, I didn't understand. I left you alone, to deal with it by yourself. Because I was too afraid—I didn't know what I could do. But now, ever since you've brought me to the havens, I have understood. I never doubted you, Calyx. Never!" Dev stretched his hand out to me, reaching, as though to ask my forgiveness.

"But for what, Dev? How did you deceive me?" I crawled across our packs and sat beside him. He was hunched over like a small boy, head and neck bent low, shoulders lost beneath the layers of heavy clothes. He gave no resistance when I took his hand, pulled off his glove. His fingers were finely shaped and long. I closed my hand over them, glad for the warmth, the closeness.

Awareness of his touch, his smell, burned through me. I longed to be near him, to feel the surety of his arms around me, the brush of his beard against my cheek. It was far from the best place to lie down together, but after everything, surely some things no longer mattered?

I took off my hat, shook free my hair, then leaned over, closer toward him. I meant to kiss him, to tell him that being with him was what I'd always wanted. But he gave an awkward cough, tensed his shoulders. Pulling away, he said, "I knew it was Edishu who entered your dream, Calyx."

I sat back. "What did you say?" I shook my head. Then: "How—?"

"You remember when we sat your first jarak watch together, in the rathadaro hall with Sherra. Avram was there?"

"I remember."

"You were lost in her dream. I said you'd joined too deeply, that you lacked the training. And Sherra claimed you'd somehow changed her dream."

"Yes, but why does it matter now?"

"There was more. I didn't tell you because Avram was there, and somehow I knew you wouldn't want him to find out. Then later, when I hadn't told you, when I was ill for a long time, I was afraid to tell you. I didn't know how to say it. I had waited too long. That part at least was the right thing to do, wasn't it, not telling Avram?"

"It wouldn't have mattered. But Dev, how did you know about Edishu?"

"We were holding hands, Calyx. You, the girl, and me. No one ever realized. It hadn't ever happened before. But then, no one else's jarak dreams have ever been as strong as yours. I witnessed that dream with you. When her friend, Farlin—that was his name, wasn't it?—Farlin disappeared and Edishu was there. I saw him, Calyx. I shouldn't have, but I did. And I knew who he was. I remember what he said; I've thought about it over and over again, a hundred times. He said that he would have you. You and all the rest of the earth. That you would give it to him willingly . . . and there is nowhere you can hide."

"That's what you meant when you said you deceived me? That you knew Edishu had entered my dreams and you wouldn't tell me?"

Dev kept his gaze directed toward the snowy floor, unable to look at me. "Can you forgive me? I don't have your strength, Calyx."

"Of course you're strong! Dev, how can you say that? Don't you know how much you've meant to me? You've been my friend, my only friend, ever since we came to Aster. And you trusted me. You believed in me. You don't have to apologize. Not telling me about that dream, there's nothing wrong in that. Come, Dev, won't you look at me?" I took his hand again, brought his chilled fingers to my cheek.

"How can I show you how much you've meant to me, Dev?" I asked, feeling that at last the time was right, knowing he wouldn't be able to misunderstand again. Slowly, tenderly—his hands were so beautifully wrought, strong and delicate both at the same time—I kissed his fingertips, then purposefully moved his hand down toward the open collar of my shirt.

I watched his face the entire time. I thought he was shy,

unsure of himself. At first he wouldn't look directly at me, then he seemed confused, almost hurt.

Should I have waited for him to speak first? Or what if I'd blundered and he'd never made love with a woman before? Perhaps as a Sumedaro priest he'd had no time.

He tore his hand free from my grasp. He stammered, tight-jawed, unable to spit out the words. Then finally, with a breath that seemed to wrack his body, he said, "I can't. Can't!"

I backed away, aching and confused. Was I so terrible to look at that the thought of touching me galled him so? "Can't?" I shouted at his cowering eyes. "Why can't you? What's the matter with me?"

"I could . . . could never touch you . . . that way. You—you're . . ."

Dev fought against himself, trying to speak. Then, abruptly, I could wait no longer. I grabbed him by his arms and shook him, trying to wrestle the words out of him. "Am I so ugly, then? Am I not good enough for your pretty eyes and hair? Is that it? Go on, say it, already. Say it!"

Dev looked as though I had struck him full force. When he answered, his voice was so low I nearly missed it: "Ugly? You, Calyx? Can you make so light of my feelings? To think my loyalty, my love, goes no deeper than the shape of your eyes or face? No! It's more . . ." He shook his head. "You're . . . you're the Elan Sumedaro! How could I think . . . dare . . . to touch you?"

I let my arms drop to my side. "What are you saying?"

From somewhere Dev took courage, and for the first time in days he looked directly at me. "Only the Elan Sumedaro could have the strength to withstand Edishu's touch."

"What are you talking about? Elan Sumedaro? He was a man!"

"I know. I thought about that. But in the end, I couldn't see why it should matter. In one legend the Elan Sumedaro is young, another time, he's older. Another time . . . a woman."

"I'm not a legend! I'm a woman. Here! Now!"

Dev looked away for a moment, toward the blue-white walls of our strange cave, but he was no longer cowering under the burden of his guilt. He looked back at me, his eyes offering up devotion and hope. Dev's face was radiant with his belief and love, not for me but for what he beheld as the Elan Sumedaro.

"Calyx?" he said. "It's all I've been thinking about. The Sisters know, I've tried to understand. But I didn't know what to think except that I didn't have the right to think at all. Calyx, I saw your dreams! So many of them. Though why you ever wanted to share them with me, I don't know. Who am I to tell you . . . ? But how could you not know, not even suspect? No one has ever had jarak dreams like yours before. No one. I would have believed you were the Elan Sumedaro even before I watched the dream of Edishu. Though that alone would have been sufficient. Then the townspeople started coming with their dreams. And all of them the same. Your dream, Calyx! Yours and Edishu's! The same dream as the Kareil sent, no matter how much Hershann tried to deny it. And then you found the havens. And that would have sufficed. But I never spoke of it! I didn't know how."

"No, of course you didn't," I said, laying my hand on his with a touch that had grown cold.

Dev talked for a while more, but I had lost the will to argue or even listen. Everywhere I turned, the thin northern air seemed waiting to fling Dev's words back at me. *Only the Elan Sumedaro! The Elan Sumedaro!*

Finally I urged Dev to rest for a while, less for his comfort than because I needed desperately to wrap the uneasy quiet around me and wait for Seed to bring a new day.

Dev slept four, maybe five hours, his head fallen aslant his shoulder, his back leaning into the curved wall. And all that time I sat awake in the strange half-light of our shelter, thinking.

Couldn't Dev have found the haven's hidden entrance as easily as I? He had jarak dreams. Perhaps if his need had been as great, he could have been the one to find them. Yet it had not been him, any more than it had been Hayden or Ceena—not with Rath, not with the havens, not though a score of raiders chased after them.

Nor had it been Lethia. Much as I loathed the thought of allying her name with mine, her dreams were more a match to mine than anyone else's. But Edishu had scorned her, laughed at her, while it was my defeat he craved, not hers or Ceena's or the Kareil's, or any of the others'.

Then why me? I was a woman, born of woman and man,

born of flesh, wearing flesh. What did I know of Kuoshana and gods and dreams and power? My own father had looked at me as though I were less than the dirtiest scrub maid in Briana Keep. My sister scorned me. The priests called me sensume and laughed behind my back. The sensume called me a fool and told me to go back to my father's land and find a husband.

Yet by the same light, couldn't I be the Elan Sumedaro? Couldn't the gods grant power wherever they chose? Oh, Elan Sumedaro! What was it like for you? You at least knew who you were: World Walker, Waking Dreamer. Was it so lonely for you also? Had Edishu hunted you as he hunted me now, with his venomous eyes and hungry mouth?

And what of my mother? How did she fit into these doings? How had she known enough about Kuoshana's gate to paint it, enough to wrap the waiting pages of a dreamer's journal in that one cover?

At last morning came, with a sky so clear and endless it seemed I had never known anything else. I prodded Dev. I had to walk, could no longer keep my thoughts coherent or my head erect.

Quickly he came to, the lack of sleep scarcely touching him. He looked once at my face, at my red-rimmed eyes, and didn't need to ask whether I'd kept my vigil. From then on he took charge of our trek and he seemed relieved of a burden, happier even, as if the offer of his devotion had been accepted and his gods were content. First he retied our packs and gear. Then he cut one of his lighter shirts into strips, knotting them into bands to shield our eyes from the sun's glare. For the first time he uncoiled the ropes we'd been carrying on the sledge. With a quick hand he rearranged the loops, tying one end around his chest and between his legs, then with the same series of knots, ran the loops again for me, until we were yoked together on a line, our lives depending on the safety of our footing.

Dev showed me how to walk forward, testing the ice for hidden fissures and deceptive frost, probing and poking with his axes before daring a step forward. Now we wore the strange boots Dev had brought with us, with rows of nails dug in the heels to help us grip the ice.

Only by starting west, then skirting wide around a mottled rock outcropping, could we see a path. We tested our gear, then started out, crossing in one long day a span of miles that should have taken only hours. I walked without thinking, trusting wherever Dev led, whichever path he chose. It was all I could do to help with my share of the pulling, make my legs keep on with their methodical rhythm.

Dev's back was always in front of me, leading us around a series of low, sloping hills where the ground was covered more in snow than ice, then due west again, the earth so deceiving that each aching step had to be perfectly placed for fear there would be no other.

That evening when again no haven appeared, we camped, this time stopping as soon as we found a boulder large enough to serve as a windbreak. With Dev's prodding, we had the tent up even more quickly than the previous night. Inside, Dev slept first, eating only enough to still the gnawing in his stomach, so that later when I could no longer fight my dreams, he would not be lulled into sleep.

Two nights now I had gone without sleep. I was shivering, delirious with exhaustion and fear. Without the havens Edishu would find me. I didn't dare sleep, didn't dare dream.

My mother's book house. It was somewhere up ahead. Not too far. I was sure of it. The vision I'd had in the haven was true as a map etched in my memory, as firm as if I'd grown up in its shadow.

But I had to keep moving. Couldn't stop, dared not sleep . . .

"Dev?" I shook his huddled shoulders. "Dev, can you wake up? Please?" But he lay in a heavy sleep, too tired himself to respond. I tried walking outside for a while, then stood about, stamping from foot to foot. I chewed on a bit of dried meat, tried anything that would keep me awake and moving, but no matter what I tried, every action began to take on a soothing rhythm, lulling me ever so easily.

At last, nothing seemed to make a difference. I could have fallen asleep standing as easily as lying down. I moved back in and sat down beside Dev—just for a moment—near the crook of his knees, just to steal whatever warmth I could.

What could I do? I was dizzy, weak with fatigue, while in my heart a second weariness cut even deeper. Always the questions were there, gnawing, searing their way into my thoughts until finally, even sitting brought no peace.

I tugged at my clothes, searching for warmth. Then I

weakly forced myself back to my knees again. To my feet. I needed to walk outside to stay awake. I'd managed it all day, hadn't I? Just a few steps. I wouldn't go far, I promised myself. I only needed to move. I would be careful. Just a short walk. Nothing would happen.

Like a drunkard, I took one step, then another, swaying uncertainly. I wasn't going to go far. Stay within range of our tent. But there, just to the east and not far away, I saw a group of rounded boulders standing in a near perfect circle.

Strange, I thought, that we hadn't noticed them before. I started forward. Twice I almost gave in and sat down on the frozen ground to rest, but I caught myself, *Don't stop*. I shook my head. *Don't rest*. I scooped a ball of snow into my gloved hands, thoughtlessly rubbed it on my forehead and face. The cold stung, but only for a little while.

At last I reached the stones. They were nearly as tall as I, twelve in a circle, like sentinels guarding the entrance to the far north. I had no idea how they came to be there; surely no one had come this way in a hundred lifetimes? There were no human markings on their gray and white faces to show how they'd been dragged or carted into place. Yet no natural movement of ice could have arranged them in such a pattern. In an odd way, they reminded me of the entries to the havens, deceptively plain on the outside, god-hallowed within. Then, because there was nothing else I could think of, I reached a hand out and touched the first, a white, granite-etched rock.

Nothing happened. I waited, touched it again, but still nothing changed. On a whim I tugged off my glove and touched the rock with my bare hand, a stray thought warning me away from the blistering cold.

But this time, instead of the empty wind, a song began rising up as if from the very heart of the stone.

I listened eagerly, hungry for the gentle rhythm. There was a high phrase, then a trilling, then low, lower, reaching out toward me from a dim memory, and I recognized the song. It was a Kareil ballad of the Elan Sumedaro. A Kareil song waiting for me in the stone as surely as if Cay LoringHill had left it for me, knowing I would find it: a greeting and a map:

*   *   *

There is that within the northland
Aching fist of flaming night.
There is that which stills the tempest
The Waking Dreamer's name and right.
In all times Edishu's waking
Longs for earth with death and hate.

Great the strength of deft Hajthaelc
Jokjoa's bow of ebony might.
In your hand the arrow is courage
In your heart the truth of light.
Let it lock Edishu's prison
Let it sever all his might.
As the summer buries winter
So the bow begins the fight.

Fist to fist and armed in combat
Thus the two must ever fight.
Brave Hajthaele
Of Sunder's bounty
Dark Edishu craving life.
At the gateway to Kuoshana
There the sacred bow does rest
Life to life, the dreaming father
Lays his tokens on your breast.

I sank to the icy ground, no longer caring that I was colder and more tired than I'd ever thought possible. What was I to do? What could I say? The Kareil had met me twice. Only twice. Were they too, like Dev, ready to proclaim me Elan Sumedaro?

Me, Calyx of Briana, who had spent half her life hiding her dreams from one person or another. Now, with no birthright on earth to call my own, they were ready to hand me the crown of Kuoshana! If Dev had been the only one to lay this onus on my head, I might have shrugged it away. But now the Kareil, whom I had once trusted—and Ceena, who was Silkiyam born, waiting in Briana. And what of Micah, shouldn't I count him? He'd shared my dream. It wouldn't be much longer before he asked the same questions. All the people I'd loved. All of them!

Elan Sumedaro. Elan Sumedaro.

I didn't feel like a hero. No, or a god or a legend. I was afraid. The real Elan Sumedaro fought with Jokjoa's weapons at his side. Hajthaele, the bow, Shammal his ring, Rath, Gamaliel, Oreill's pearl, plus his own magic to guide him. And when those failed, his son, the white-haired Jevniah, added his sword to the battle, so that in every generation someone had been there, ready to meet Edishu.

Unlike the Sumedaros, who could only watch dreams, the first Elan had been a dream shaper. His was the power to shape dreams, touch them, change the fiber of the very world through them, so that what he dreamed, the world became.

True, I held Rath and Gamaliel, but I knew almost nothing of their power. What had really happened that first time I'd touched Rath? Avram had grabbed it from my reach—but only after the bracelet had brushed my hand. It had glowed at my touch, hadn't it? While his—and Hershann's—had not the power to ignite its center. And the ring, when Ivane first gave it to Mirjam—it had glowed that time too, though I hadn't understood. Was it possible it had been meant for me all along?

Abruptly I raised my gaze from the darkness of my hands. Looked out.

The book house, it was there. Rising from the blue mist ahead of me, just out across the frozen flats. I turned around. Where was Dev? Sleeping? But there was the book house, and for the first time in days, I felt my courage return, felt the strength flow back into my legs, let them move, stand strong.

I took a step, tottered, but I was too excited to wait. The book house was there, just a short distance away. I was going to reach it. Dev would find me when he woke. He would see it, know where to follow. I had to reach it before I fell asleep. Had to see my mother's book house, Kuoshana's gateway: one and the same. I stumbled away from the towering cairn, forgetting Dev, forgetting everything but my need to reach the house. Just another step. One more step.

I never saw the crevasse. I was far too blinded by giddiness and exhaustion to understand what I did. The soft upper layer of snow hid the edge, the shadows touching at exactly the wrong angle to see the lines marking the fault.

Suddenly I was slipping, my legs scraping ice as sharp as blades. I went down hard, grabbing the ledge at my elbows. But it was useless. I was too weak. There was no hold to find. I screamed, then slipped again, scratched with my fingertips for a hold, then that too failed and I plunged down and down, tumbling, smashing over and over against the knife-edged sides.

Falling . . .

I remember the brittle, stinging cold and my aching chest crying out for breath. I remember the milky darkness and the light of a sun stealing through a narrow crack of ice a hundred feet above the ledge where I had landed. And I remember the pain in my skull, echoing with a silent cry. Then nothing . . .

I passed into a sleep deeper than anything I had ever known before: deeper than night, deeper than winter, deeper still than sorrow. And for a long time I waited there.

Dreaming . . .

21

World Walker.
   Waking Dreamer.

Those were the first words that came to me. In the song, Elan Sumedaro had been called the World Walker, Bridger of Worlds, Waking Dreamer.

I struggled to sit upright, straightened first one leg, then the other, and pulled myself up to a standing position, waiting for the ache of twisted ligaments to cry out.

Far overhead, the sky exploded in a rainbow of night. Stars reeled and danced. Thin clouds hovered, then flew on. Black-shadowed birds screeched their songs to a distant moon. I took a deep breath and wondered why I could breathe at all when my ribs ought to have been fractured with that fall. But they weren't. I was whole. Unhurt.

The farmhouse stood not three paces in front of me. Close up, it looked even more inviting than I remembered: wide-grained wood trim outlined the door and windows, floral carvings delicately framed the eaves. At that moment there was nothing in all the world I could have wished for

more than to spend an easy day sitting upon that door-
step, watching the sun and moon exchange places in the
sky.

For a brief moment I decided I was awake and had
somehow, with the strength of desperation, struggled out of
the crevasse and up to the doorway of my book house. But
no. That was impossible. Even as I stood so near my goal,
my real body lay crumpled somewhere in a dark crevasse,
limbs locked in impossible angles, face bloodied by daggers
of cracked ice. And all the days of fighting to stay awake,
hiding from Edishu, were wasted by one mistake.

This was my own jarak dream. But this time instead of
lying safely asleep in a bed, I lay injured at the bottom of a
crevasse, helpless, and with little chance of rescue.

A golden light peered out from the eastern window, warm
and inviting. I took a breath, refusing to consider thoughts
of failure. Later I would think about my real self. For now,
here was everything I'd been waiting for. I stepped closer,
reached for the latch.

"Wait!" a man's voice called behind me.

I kept my hand on the door, but I didn't move to open it
further. When I turned around, I knew I would see a man I
had never met, with eyes as unyielding as winter.

"Won't you let me talk to you?"

"Edishu," I whispered, and turned as if all along I'd been
waiting, knowing he would come.

He wore the body of an older man, fatherly and understanding. "You wrong me," he said, his voice aged but
gentle. His hand was stretched out to mine, offering
forgiveness.

We stood in the small border of grass that surrounded the
house, facing each other. I could take his hand, let his
strength engulf mine, erase my burdens . . . cessation. It
was the one true gift he had to offer. Respite from the
battle, from my doubts, the hopeless yearnings. How like
my mother's bane these years had become, always longing,
waiting for something that neither of us could name . . .

Ivane. Wouldn't she understand if I gave up the battle?
She never had, of course, but then hadn't I always been
the one who ran to her for shelter, not the other way
around?

But no, she would never have wanted me to give up.
Otherwise, why would she have given me that journal?

What was it she'd said? That she'd seen the painting whole, in a vision? Which might mean she'd been shown this house for a reason . . . Not in a dream, she'd said—because she never remembered her dreams. But a daydream. Or an idea. A sending.

And what if Dev was right and I was the Elan Sumedaro? Would the Elan Sumedaro yield so willingly to Edishu, without even raising the dust on one battlefield?

"No!" I shouted suddenly, breaking the spell almost before I realized it had come over me. "I won't listen to you."

"When have I ever sought to trick you, Calyx? Come over here, won't you? Walk with me. You don't want to go inside that house. It's there that your fears wait. Not here."

I stepped back, away from both the house and Edishu. He looked so kind, so gentle. He was smiling, waiting. But wasn't this his magic again, working against me? Fight him, I warned myself. Concentrate on his eyes.

"You should not have lied to me," he said.

"Does it matter?"

Softer, he tried to hide the venom in his voice. "You hid from me! That was lying. When did I ever do anything but ask your help? You of all people should know what it means to be alone, lost within a dream, with no one to share . . . no one to understand—"

"You're lying."

"I never meant to hurt you. Let me show you what I will give you. Gifts of knowledge, wisdom. Our strength could merge together, growing, dwarfing all earth. And I—we—would be free . . ."

Edishu swept his hand before me, and where grass and a low hedge had bordered the house, I found myself standing within a marble courtyard. Two rows of fountains sprayed silver waterfalls. Beyond them a mosaic pathway led toward an inner chamber. Servants stood along the walls, male and female both and all naked to the waist, all holding flaming torches to light my path. Ahead lay a wide, carpeted chamber with a silken bed spread with rich coverlets and brocades.

"Was it so much to ask?" Edishu said. He looked younger now, stronger, capable. "To want to love you? Who else could share such nights as we have? Who else could speak through their dreams? Think of it! Won't you come with me now? Let me share my secrets with you . . . And I ask so little, only to let me know you, only for a moment. But you must desire it of your own will, as I do."

I listened, thinking of Dev's refusal. But it was Lethia's face I recalled most, her arms around the back of a different, younger man—one who Edishu thought Lethia would find appealing. As he had assumed this face would appeal to me. And what had Edishu given Lethia in thanks for her service but a filthy pallet, scorn, and his flaring demand: *"You must give more!"*

Edishu looked more closely at me, then stepped back, his face contorted in sudden rage. "So you saw that, did you? How . . . ?"

"Saw what?" I shook my head.

"You won't tell me? But it doesn't matter, you see. Nothing you do can change the course of events. Not this time. In the end I shall have what I want, and like her you shall beg me to come for you. To call you mine! Do you hear? You shall come begging."

I turned my face away, hoping to hide my thoughts lest he read them against my will. Why was it this always seemed to matter to him, that I make the choice *of my own will?* And I wondered, did Edishu know I had already taken a lover, my friend Micah, that day on the hilltop outside Briana? Why? Why would it matter? Unless it was simply that I had made a choice of my own defiant will? Acted . . .

Did my will, my choosing, mean so much that Edishu could not touch me unless I came willingly to him?

"Look at me!" he screamed, and he raised a fist high over his head. "Claim power over me, will you? You're nothing! Nothing! Useless as your priests! As your guards and your weapons and your songs! Useless as the . . ."

Edishu raged on, but I had already closed my ears against his maddening threats.

Slowly, hoping he would not notice, I took a step back toward the door. If I could open the catch in time and slip inside, perhaps the elderly body he wore would slow him down, slow his reflexes.

But no! Edishu had no need of fists or speed. He'd seen me, guessed what I was doing. Out of the hurricane of his words a wind gathered and turned against me, raging and inescapable. My face was pressed helplessly against the wooden door. My legs were pinioned beneath me. I tried to push away, but my arms were no match against the wind.

Through the crack in the door a dim light showed out, golden, welcoming. If only I could stretch my hand out to that light, I could open the door, steal inside . . .

Against Edishu's storm I forced my hand upward toward the latch. One more length and I would have it. I watched, pushing, pushing. The wind roared against my ears, and I set my legs, anchoring one foot against the door.

But then the wind changed and I was cut loose, caught up in a whirling gray shadow, blinded and dumb. And all I could hear was the ringing echo of Edishu's grotesque laughter as he hurtled me away from the door.

Once again the house and the glaciers and the stars were upended, torn from my grasp. I was flung head over heels through a swirling, layered sky, spinning and spinning until I no longer knew the difference between night and day and up and down. I felt sick, almost as if the night would never end, and there was only the endless blackness drawing me forward.

And then silence.

I opened my eyes on a blue-gray world of ice. I tried to turn, but my sides screamed out in protest. I was awake, back in my own body . . . trapped within the glacier's narrow fissure.

Awake.

I peered toward the distant sky. There was no sign of Dev, no way of knowing if he'd come searching, or how much time had elapsed while I lay unconscious.

My head felt as if it had been split open. Slowly, carefully, I sat up. There seemed to be no heavy blood loss. No broken bones, no fractured ribs. I'd scraped the sides as I fell, but my heavy clothes had taken the brunt of it, catching and tearing against the walls as I fell. Below the ruined layers my legs showed several minor scrapes and cuts. Oh, but my head ached, and I shivered with a deep, unyielding cold. My arms shook of their own volition, like muscle spasms, tense against the confining air.

I closed my eyes, wishing I could escape into a deep, untroubled sleep, just to forget, to waken later on a new day. When was the last time sleep had been merely restful? When would it ever be that way again, a child's sleep, innocent and deep?

I took a breath, tried to ignore the stabbing pain. Then, cupping my hands, I shouted, "Dev! Hello! I'm in here! Hello! Help!" I held absolutely still, waiting to catch a distant voice. When there was no answer, I shouted again, somehow knowing all along he would never hear me.

I leaned back against the frozen wall. Eventually I had to do something—either face Edishu's power or curl up in a knot and fall asleep, my heartbeat the only blanket against the long night.

Sleep. It would be so easy, so sweet . . . I shook my head. No, to sleep now would mean failure. It would all be over. There had to be another way. On hands and knees, I crawled toward the edge of my narrow ledge and peered over the precipice toward a black, unending drop. As far as I could see there was nothing but an endless night-blue world. The only hope in that direction was death itself.

I crawled back to the wall, forced myself to stand. The crevasse's walls rose sheer overhead. I ran my hands over the layered ice, then—however foolish—pulled off a glove to better feel the surface. There was a handhold, small but perhaps . . . I searched for a foothold, slipped, and listened below me while shards of ice scattered over the ledge. What a fool I'd been to walk from our camp empty-handed, with no tools or weapons. I tried again, climbing with my face pressed to the ice. Left foot, right hand. Right foot, left . . . But no, the next step revealed only a mirror-fine surface. No holds, no pitted depressions. Nothing. I tried a step sideways, searching with one blind foot till I found the smallest of shelves, tested it for strength, then edged sideways, slipped, and fell again to the ledge.

Again I sat there, knees drawn up, arms huddled in close for warmth. Waiting was useless. Dev would never find me, never know which direction I'd walked in. And while it might be possible to find my way out through a jarak dream, in the end it would not help. Left alone, my body would only grow weaker, more disoriented. Whenever the jarak dream ended, the reality of day would return.

There had to be another way. Defeat couldn't come so easily. It was not enough to reach Kuoshana's gate through a dream. My mother would not have meant for me to come so close only to fail.

Elan Sumedaro? Waking Dreamer? What would you have done?

World Walker? Was that what I had become? Waking Dreamer?

And if it was true? If I had indeed become the Elan Sumedaro born again, would there be another kind of dream, a magic that either I'd always possessed but never understood, or a new magic that I'd grown into? Jarak magic, power born of my dreams!

But how could I mold myself closer to the image of an Elan Sumedaro? What could it mean to be a Waking Dreamer? Uneasily I shook my head. What good had any of this power ever done except to lead me here, to the borders of Kuoshana, to grapple with a need for power as great as the world had ever known, power enough to bind Edishu back in Jokjoa's dream and lock the gates behind him.

Power? What did it mean to possess such power?

In vain I stared at the distant line of sky overhead. It was nearly dark now, evening. Possibly Rath or Gamaliel could help. I still had them with me. But I'd never been able to actually command them. And from what I'd learned, their power worked with magic and jarak visions, not the needs of a corporeal body. For a while I spun the bracelet around my wrist.

Nothing happened. All I could see was the outline of my own hands.

My hands. The hands of an Elan Sumedaro? Was it possible? The skin was red and blotchy, the fingernails underlined in crescents of black dirt.

Familiar hands. Strong, capable. But something else as well.

Faintly outlining each finger, a haze of clear blue light glowed. Not Rath's light this time but my own, a light so pure the color was nearly a match to the winter sky, the light of my jarak power, so unmistakable even I could not pretend it wasn't true.

The light of my jarak power. Glowing, waiting, undeniable. As much my own as each callus and wrinkle was my own. Mine to use, to direct, to build. My birthright somehow, bequeathed to me by my mother's ceaseless longing and this, my own—and the world's desperate need.

The light rippled and glowed brighter, as though answering me in a language all its own, saying, *Where you walk, so go I, each with the other. I am all that you are all that I am.*

Slowly I laid my hands down in my lap, holding them

together. Yes, it was true. I could enter a person's dreams simply by touching their hand, by willing it to happen. I could send my dreams where I would, and the eyes of my jarak body would follow. I had found the havens, both in my sleep and in the full light of day.

And now? Now I must become Dream Shaper, use my jarak dreams to change both the dream and earth's waking moment. I must make for myself a waking dream so that the empty shell of my Calyx-body would not be left behind.

World Walker, Waking Dreamer, Elan Sumedaro!

Was that what it meant to be the Waking Dreamer? Was that what you had done, Elan Sumedaro, when you had first fought against Edishu?

And if I failed?

If I failed, I died here, the warmth sucked from my blood as surely as Edishu had stolen spring from the northlands.

That was the answer, then. I had to dream my way out of this tomb, and I had to do it while I was awake. *World Walker, Waking Dreamer.* Then I had to dream my way inside the book house, not just my jarak body but this half-broken, frozen body as well. And it must be inside the book house that I landed, not at its entry, not on the great ice fields. If I waited much longer, I would die. Either Edishu would take me, or the cold. Only in the book house would I be safe. Edishu's power would be weaker there. The house was too close to Kuoshana, too filled with Jokjoa's own dreams. And once inside?

Inside, Hajthaele waited for me. The song had promised it. Hajthaele waiting to be claimed. Jokjoa's bow, which I could wield against Edishu.

I stood, raised my hands before me, watching the blue light of my jarak magic grow. Then higher over my head, I brought my hands together. Everywhere light blazed and flared around me, growing, dancing, enfolding my entire body within its warmth.

I closed my eyes and the light exploded.

This I knew!

Here was the trembling dance of my waiting jarak dreams, and here the pulsing warmth of the haven's doorway. Here was the light of the Kareil's fire, the song of Elan Sumedaro . . .

My song! My dream!

The light shattered and grew, splintered and darted in a

thousand directions as if wild with freedom. Then somehow, with the strength of my vision, I healed it, called it home toward me from the thousand stars of Oreill's pearls, called it home, and fused it into the soft, glowing light of the book house.

I felt one brief, untamed shuddering, a black, spinning vertigo, then I opened my eyes.

I was awake and whole and it was over—body and jarak self melded into one. I was inside the book house, standing inside a wide, open room. In the center high overhead, a large candelabrum shed its light in a circle about the floor. There were few furnishings, a table and chair, nothing more, and these only simply decorated: a plain room well fit somehow for a god who commanded creation.

Of Hajthaele, the bow, I saw nothing.

Then for the first time I noticed three doors on the far wall. They were small doors, closer to my own size than to a man's full-shouldered figure, and I walked carefully toward them. Each door looked exactly the same as the two others: fine-grained wood, glistening finish, golden spun latches. But there was a riddle here. There had to be. Kuoshana's gatehouse meant to test me, to have me make a choice before it yielded up Hajthaele.

I stepped up closer to the center door, ran my hand along its sleek grain. I wasn't ready to open it, not yet. I only meant to touch it, to see if there was anything more than the surface allowed. Then, almost as if they were pulled forward, my fingertips grazed the golden latch, and with that touch a song filled my ears.

It was Kuoshana's song, a rainbow of impossible notes trilling through my blood. Now high, now low, they cascaded over scales I never knew existed. Each note a star, a god, a life, each blending, splitting, changing, and all of them filling me with more music than I could contain. Open this door, the song whispered, and all of Kuoshana's hopes would be mine. Open this door and I would be as the song I heard, greater than any mortal, richer than the pearls of skyworld. All this and more, forever at home in Kuoshana.

The song ended. I dropped my hand to my side, numb. Without that song I would never again be complete. Kuoshana had been offered to me, and I had met her beauty with a longing deeper than anything I'd conceived. How could any other song possibly matter next to that?

But a choice must be made, and freely. Those were the terms I had defied Edishu with, the terms I would use to claim Jokjoa's bow.

Quickly, lest I choose the notes of Kuoshana's song without knowing the others, I moved to the right-hand door. This time, without waiting to be invited, I touched the golden latch. Again a song took my hand. This time the tune was one of pure joy, laughing notes, rippling with the resonance of earth's promise: a bird's call, a river's laughter, the loneliness of a mountain echo, the hope of crashing waters, of cities, people, the songs of birth and rebirth, and all of it, every note and pulse and meter, calling me to claim my part in the world's extravagant rhapsody.

Kuoshana or earth? How could I ever choose, how live without one once I had chosen the other? And what more could a third song promise? Yet here was the next door, and I had no more will to resist this third golden latch than a fish could resist the call to migrate back toward the headwaters whence it had been spawned.

The instant I swept my hand toward the latch, it was too late. The song struck full against my chest as if I'd been assaulted, sent me reeling toward the corner in despair. Dreams! A song of dreams filled with all the painful longings of a million jarak dreamers striving to remember the promise of Kuoshana's song, their own godhood, the hope of earth's living melody. A song of pain and death and separation; of lost children, floundering parents, of friends and lovers dead in battle, of disease, of hunger. A dream song of waiting, of promise, of mortal longing. A song that demanded an answer.

Then silence.

I sat huddled in the corner where I'd fallen, head in hands, crying.

I felt empty. Lost.

I tried desperately not to move, not to take the step that would sever me from the two songs I could not choose.

For already I knew what choice I must make. Had there ever been any question? *World Walker? Waking Dreamer? Had you stood here and listened to the same songs? Had there been any choice for you?*

The only regret I had was that I must always carry those two other songs in my mind's ear, struggling to remember them, always chasing some forgotten rhythm, always wondering if they truly might have been mine.

When I caught my breath, I stood and walked grimly back toward the third door. My sides still ached from the fall, but the pain was forgotten in the face of this newer, more desperate loss. The songs of Kuoshana and earth would never be mine.

The Door of Dreams! The only door I would ever know. I reached out toward it.

The door swung open into blackness.

It was a closet, but deep enough for a person to walk in. I took a breath, then quickly, half afraid that there would be no floor and I would fall into the endless well of despair that marked the dreamer's song, I stepped over the threshold.

At once I found myself in a second room, the exact duplicate of the first. But here on the table, under a dimmer light, lay an unstrung wooden bow and a worn leather quiver full of arrows.

Hajthaele! Jokjoa's bow!

I grabbed the curved bow, surprised at its weight, far heavier than it appeared. The arrows I gathered in my arm, then sprang back through the door into the light of the golden room.

Hajthaele was simple but in another sense as beautiful as anything I'd ever held. The bow curved in graceful arcs inward, then out again, perfectly balanced, perfectly worked, yet like the room, the table, all of Jokjoa's tokens, it was plain and unadorned. A spun silver cord was wrapped around one end, waiting to be strung.

I found the loop, stretched it toward the other end, but it wouldn't reach. I walked with it to the table, leaned my weight down, pushing toward the tip, cord ready, but it hardly bent. I found a different angle, tried again, pushing, the bow's sides cutting into my skin, but it was impossible. I lacked the strength. The cord hung loose.

After that I took out the arrows and laid them down on the table. Gently, reverently, I touched the narrow shaft and feathers that lined its end, the pointed blade at its tip, clean and deadly. Five arrows all together. Five.

I wondered how many chances I would need to wound Edishu deeply enough to send him careening back into Jokjoa's dream. And I wondered how I could use the bow at all if I couldn't string it.

Five arrows. When the time came, would that be enough?

Then suddenly out of the silence, I heard a shuffling at the door. I ran around behind the table, thinking to hide the bow, to protect it. Who dared enter Kuoshana's gateway? Surely not Edishu . . .

The latch opened, the hinges moaned.

Dev! He stood in the open doorway, his silhouette obscured by the light.

I let out a deep breath. "Dev, it's you. Thank the Sisters. How did you get here? Oh, no, never mind. Tell me later. But are you all right?"

"Yes, Calyx."

"Look! This is the bow, Hajthaele, Jokjoa's bow. I've won it. It's mine to use now."

"Put the bow down, Calyx," Dev said, his voice raspy and uneven as if he hadn't spoken in a long time.

"What? Put it down? No! Come here and look at it. It's beautiful. And the arrows. Look at the quiver, the leather work. Do you know the story of this bow?"

"I don't want to know it, Calyx. And neither should you. It's poison, a thing of evil. Put it away. Come outside with me."

"Dev, what are you talking about? It's not evil. It's mine. And I'm not evil—"

"Come outside, out into the moonlight, where we can talk."

"I . . . I don't understand. What do you want to talk about that can't be said here, in the safety of Jokjoa's house?" I stepped backward, closer to the table.

"I love you, Calyx," Dev spoke stiffly, as though the words had been rehearsed. "Didn't you want me? I've come for you. I need you. And when we're done, Briana will be ours. Just as you wanted . . ."

"Briana?" I looked at him, confused. "I never wanted Briana. What are you talking about?" I lifted one end of the great bow, sliding it along the floor.

"Calyx, I need you. Don't forsake me now." Dev's voice rose, angry, insistent. "Put the bow down! Put it down—" Dev stopped short, blinked his eyes hard several times. "I love you, Calyx." His voice changed to a falsetto softness. "I need you . . . outside! Throw the bow down!"

He reached out as though he meant to grab me and steal the bow. He took one erratic step closer, then another.

And suddenly I understood he wasn't Dev at all. It was his body only, with Edishu using Dev's arms and legs to do his work for him, a ploy to trick the gods and gain entry where he was forbidden.

Dev's eyes glared like two hollow graves leading toward blackness. Here! Even here, inside Jokjoa's house, Edishu dared challenge me . . . And I'd been wrong again, foolish to think he could not enter.

I had to stop him! Wasn't that the very reason I'd been granted the bow: to seal Edishu's exile once again, to render his dreams powerless?

The bow! It was meant to be used here.

But what if it was Dev I killed? What if his body died?

"No!" I shook my head. Sunder couldn't be so uncaring, could she? I slid the bow closer, balancing it on the floor, then grabbed the first arrow.

Dev watched, his mouth turned up in a half smile, daring me to raise Hajthaele, almost as if he didn't believe I would use it against him.

But the cord hung loose—the bow too large for me to bend. Useless!

Dev laughed, his voice strange with a gloating triumph. Edishu had known all along I'd lack the strength!

Incensed, I let the bow drop . . .

Dev rushed forward, his hands like claws . . .

I raised the arrow higher overhead. *Don't let it be Dev,* I prayed and I brought the arrow down, drove it down, straight toward Dev's shoulder.

It struck.

I felt it, felt the jarring of metal against bone. Felt the shaft pulse through my hand, quake. And then nothing. The arrow was gone.

"No," he protested, his voice harsh, fading. "I will not permit . . ."

Dev's body crumpled to the floor.

I dropped to his side, lifted his head to my lap, and cradled it there. Please, I whispered, please, Dev, don't give in to him. Don't leave me alone. I pulled the collar of his jacket open, searching for a sign of life.

There!

He was alive. My fingertips lapped up the rhythm of rushing blood. Alive! I held my cheek to his, too tired to move, and for a long time sat there, waiting.

Edishu was gone, fled beyond my reach to Kuoshana as the legends repeatedly tell. For how long, I didn't know. I had wounded him, I was sure of it. But when I bent to look at Dev's shoulder, the mark that should have been there was already healed, the skin as smooth and whole as if nothing had ever happened.

Jokjoa be thanked!

I sat with him awhile longer, stroking his hair, waiting. After a while, when Dev still hadn't moved, I tugged him over to a more comfortable position on the floor, used my torn vest to pillow his head. While he slept, I curled up against him, matched myself to the curve of his warm back and let a much needed sleep come take me.

When I woke, Dev was still lying beside me. I talked to him, tried to rouse him, but this sleep was far deeper than anything I'd ever seen. We would have to leave, of course. Kuoshana's gateway was not a place where I meant to convalesce. Yet even rested, I could never hope to survive a second trip across the ice fields.

Elan Sumedaro, what would you have done? Dream Shaper?

I chanted the litany of his names, hoping that an answer would come. If the true Elan Sumedaro could shape his dreams, change the fabric of the world through his dreams, maybe I could also, in a very small way. Hadn't I done just that already when I entered the book house? Used the magic of a waking dream to free myself from the crevasse? Briana was farther to go, but perhaps it was possible. Distance had never been a barrier in my jarak dreams before. This needn't be different.

I closed my eyes and let my thoughts wander about the darkness, searching lightly, not yet ready to make the attempt, but watching. Gradually a picture of the ice fields took shape, white and barren and endless. And like a word with two meanings, I saw the havens hidden within the ice, warm and confident, marking the miles, just as once, eons ago, three Sisters had played their games here and wakened the earth to their touch. I saw the roads beyond the ice fields also, Aster and Roshanna, Korinna's distant keep, Istyak and FelWeather, mile after mile, remembered but whole.

Then again, I felt the leg of the upturned table at my back. Slowly I opened my eyes. Hajthaele lay on the floor, Rath on my wrist, and Gamaliel at my side. Dev slept, but his breath was even and natural again. At last I felt ready. I hefted the bow to one shoulder, arranged the remaining arrows in my belt, then as best I could, gathered Dev into my arms so we would travel together.

"To Briana this time," I said, closing my eyes. "To my mother's chambers, with a gift and a question."

22

For a long time the waking dream pulled us forward through a world of utter blackness. I saw nothing, knew nothing, only the deep, cold yearning after light that marked the way beyond the ice fields, away above Aster, Roshanna, Elianor, and Koryan. They were sightless miles yet tangible, led by the cry that issued from my breath like a mandate: down, down, down toward Ivane and Briana.

Then suddenly it was over, and I felt the hard earth beneath my feet and the sting of wind on my cheek. I opened my eyes, felt at once for Hajthaele. The bow and quiver were intact, tucked safely into the hollow of my shoulder. Rath and Gamaliel were at my side.

Dev lay on the ground beside me atop a small, frost-hardened knoll. He was sleeping still, his eyelids flickering with the last tremors of Edishu's touch. In the valley below us, Briana sprawled in ever widening circles. Gray columns of smoke leaned sideways from their chimneys. When I narrowed my eyes, I could just make out the shapes of wagons, animals, and people moving about the roads and markets below us.

I had done it, then. I, who was no less or more than any other woman, had somehow spun a waking dream. And it was not so different after all from other jarak dreams. A matter of shifting vision while awake rather than sleeping. I smiled, half surprised at the cunning simplicity of it all. Why had I never thought to try it before? Yet at the same time I understood that it was not simple at all. The dream had been born of absolute necessity, and I had paid greatly to cross the barriers Eclipse set me, barriers through which there was no going back.

But there was little time for musing. Dev moaned quietly and I dropped to his side, taking his hand in mine. He shuddered once, as though waking from a fever, and slowly opened his eyes.

"How do you feel?" I asked. "Are you hurt?"

"Hurt? No, not hurt. I don't think so." He pushed himself up to a half-sitting position, his eyes narrowed against the bright day. For a moment neither of us spoke, and I could see him struggling to piece together half-remembered events.

"We're in Briana."

"Briana?" He started up, then as if there were a pain somewhere—in his shoulder? I wondered—he sucked in his breath and wrapped both of his arms around his chest. "How? What happened? I remember waking up and going to look for you . . ." He shook his head. "And then nothing."

"You don't remember anything else?"

"Some. But it's difficult. Hazy. It was Edishu, wasn't it?"

I nodded slowly. "He tried to use you to reach me. We were at the glacier, at Kuoshana's gateway."

"Yes, I remember. But stop, don't tell me anymore. I don't want to think about that part. I can't. It was like having your speech and your sight torn from your body, and you're still alive. Howling. Hoping for Sunder to close your bloodied eyes and let you die. Tell me something else. Anything. How did we come here?"

"I brought us here in a waking dream. You, the elderberry you found for my mother, this bow. It's Hajthaele, Jokjoa's token." I answered carefully, remembering the look of worship he'd shown me in the haven. I had to take my time, watch my words. Dev's friendship was too precious to exchange for worship, not when it was love I'd asked for and only just learned to accept the friendship at all.

Dev stared at the giant bow. He looked tired and much older. His eyes were dull, with none of the dancing mischief they used to carry. His voice low, he asked, "What was it like, this waking dream?"

"More like a jarak dream than anything. After all, my

sister, Mirjam, would give away a chest of pearls for one of the dreams you command every night."

"No." Dev shook his head. "Mine are not waking dreams, Calyx. Any Sumedaro can learn to choose their dreams. What you do is different. It's the mark of the Elan Sumedaro on you, that you can shape your dreams and the world through them. You can't deny them. Not with me. Make light of it if you must, but whatever you say, it was given you to fight Edishu."

"You're braver than I am," I said. "And you have more faith. I've never had anything but my dreams."

"Dreams of power, Calyx. You would have known it years ago if you hadn't spent so much time hiding them."

That made me laugh. "Hiding? Is that what I did? Hide like a coward?"

"Maybe. But maybe not. There's a wisdom to silence, for both of us. What would have happened if your father had known of your dreams? Or Hershann? Do you think they'd have let you stumble onto your power yourself, or with me, an unknown Sumedaro priest for a tutor? Or would they have tried to use your dreams for their own gain? Holding you back, keeping you locked away in a guarded keep or temple?"

I pulled Hajthaele across my lap. "Look how plain it seems. Like the name my mother gave me—not a flower but the strong, plain calyx that protects the flower. Odd that Jokjoa would fashion his greatest bow and not adorn it with jewels and carvings."

"He didn't need adornments to prove his strength."

"Or Kuoshana's gate. It's his house. He could have made it a royal temple."

"But he wasn't interested in furnishings."

"Perhaps. But you know, I keep wondering how my mother knew what it looked like, knew how to paint it so clearly. So real." I stood, pulled the bow up—all the time trying not to show how worried I was for my mother. "We could both use a warm fire," I said.

"And a decent meal," Dev agreed.

With Dev walking laboriously at my side, I led the way down through the trees toward the outskirts of Briana town. We walked at a slow pace, the slope of the hill easing the way down while our boots pushed through the new-fallen snow as lightly if it were meadow grass. Hajthaele was heavy and awkward, but after a bit I found a way to carry it strung sideways across my shoulder, its tip riding just off the ground. But it made my efforts to help Dev too awkward to be of real use, and after offering him my arm several times, I gave it up and we continued side by side.

In a little while, we were down in the center of the town walking through familiar, crowded streets. For a minute I worried that I might be recognized, but then I laughed to think of how I looked: hair cropped as short as a stable boy's, layers of torn, filthy clothes, and traveling with a young man who looked, if it were possible, even worse than I.

I stopped outside Micah's house and asked Dev if he would mind remaining silent while I spoke with my friend. I must have expected trouble. Certainly, I'd been less than polite with Micah when I passed through Briana that last time, never taking the time to pay him even a courtesy call. I had told myself I didn't want to see him, that he would make me uncomfortable, not understand about Aster temple or my jarak dreams, that I had grown, changed. But no matter how many reasons I'd given myself, they meant only one thing: I was afraid to see him. I was afraid he would look at me with his deep-set blue eyes asking of me what I had once asked of Dev, and I would have to tell him that I felt nothing.

I took a breath, quickly noted the unchanged walls and cluttered yard, then walked to the rear workshop door, and called out Micah's name.

One of the younger brothers peeked his scampish head out the half-open door, yelped, then ducked back inside. In a moment Micah appeared, his arms gray to the elbows with a dusting of clay. Dark circles lay under his eyes and he looked paler than I remembered.

"Hello, Micah."

"You're back again."

"Yes, to see my mother. Have you news? Is there word?"

"She's the same. Is that what you came here to ask?"

"That—and a favor. Some clean clothing if you can spare it. Something I could wear into the keep. I—we only just got here. It doesn't have to be anything good," I said, speaking too quickly but not knowing how to do anything else. "Only better than this. And something to eat. For Dev also."

Micah looked behind me to where Dev stood. "Of course, I'm sorry, I should have offered." He stared at Dev with open curiosity and without a smile to be found anywhere on his face.

"I'll need a small cooking fire, a pot, and a glass vial if you have one."

"What? Oh, of course. Yes," Micah said, then ordered the boy to run back to the house and fetch clothes from his mother's chest.

Inside the warm shop, while Micah brought what I'd requested, I washed my hands and face in a basinful of warm water, then started to work on the elderberry. The stalk leaves I chopped into small pieces, then ground that to a pulp with a mortar and pestle. I talked only a little with Micah, though I could see the disappointment darkening his face with each question I shushed aside. He kept on watching Dev, waiting, I think, to see if he could catch him staring familiarly at me. I meant to say something, to explain, but I felt rushed. My mother was waiting. I could explain to Micah later.

At last, using boiled water, I mixed what remained of the green vine into a liquid and, pushing aside containers of glazes and potter's tools, laid it on the counter to settle out. In a back corner, I changed into the clothing Micah's brother had brought: a blue shirt too large by several sizes and a pair of pants that wrapped around the waist and tied.

Then, worrying over the vial, I held it out toward the window and peered through its brownish, darkening water. For now I'd done as much as possible. Nothing remained but to trust to the elderberry. True, there was no reason to trust Edishu. But perhaps, having been picked inside the havens, Sister Seed might lay a healing breath to the plant and Ivane would recover. Carefully I slipped the vial into a pocket, then hoisted Hajthaele heavily over one shoulder, and turned toward the door.

Dev had already crawled to a small cot and was stretched out, nearly asleep. Edishu's touch lay heavy on him still, and I hoped that rest would help. In the opposite corner, Micah had gone back to the steady rhythm of his potter's wheel, his back turned resolutely away from where I stood.

For a minute I watched Micah's quick hands working the clay into a cylinder, soaking up his patience as if we were five years younger again and there were nothing more to trouble us than being home in time for dinner. And I remembered how I had loved those hands, the veins etched like rivers around his muscular arms and the long, narrow fingers suited, yet at the same time too delicate, for the work his mother put him to.

"Thank you, Micah," I said, walking up beside him. "I'll return as soon as I can. There shouldn't be trouble. But if anything should happen, Dev will know what to do. Take care of him for me, please. He's tired and needs rest more than anything. I have to see my mother first. You understand that, don't you?"

Micah nodded, then without meeting my eyes, asked, "Then what?"

"Afterward? I'm not sure yet. Not until I've seen my mother healed. But Micah, I promise, we'll have time to talk later. After I've seen Ivane."

I turned to leave, but abruptly he called out. "Calyx . . . ? Dev, your friend . . ." He looked quickly toward the mound of blankets on the cot. "Is he your lover?"

"No, Micah, I have no lover," I answered. "I'll be back as soon as I can. We'll talk then, all right?"

I didn't wait for an answer. The cold glass in my pocket seemed so much more important than Micah's sad eyes. He was such a child sometimes. Later I would talk to him.

The road running uphill to Briana Keep was crowded with the familiar traffic of carts, horses, guards, and temple goers. Caught up in the midst of the rush, eyes down and dressed as inconspicuously as I was, I slipped easily past the gates and entered the large main courtyard. From there it was a simple task to duck down a seldom used corridor behind my father's dog kennels and make my way up one of the numerous stairwells. When I was younger, few strangers would have been permitted to visit the family quarters without leave. But this was not the Briana of fifteen years ago—or even ten—and though several people did see me, I kept my eyes respectfully lowered and approached my mother's rooms unchallenged.

No one answered my light knock. I opened the door and slipped inside. The windows were shuttered against the light. The room was dim and too quiet. Ivane lay in her bed, her head propped high on pillows. She was sleeping soundly. Her hair hung in loose braids over her shoulders, and she almost looked younger than the last time I'd seen her. But there were the covers taut over her rounded stomach, and her skin, as I looked closer, seemed a pale, unyielding color. She had not fared well this past month, and for a moment I was afraid I'd come too late.

"Mother? Mother?" I called, but she slept too deeply to answer.

I looked once toward the door, laid my bow on the floor beside her, then, with a shaking hand, took the small vial of ichor from my pocket. Carefully, so as not to lose one precious drop, I pressed the rim to her lips.

"Please, Sister Seed," I whispered. "Let your kiss finish what the havens began. Please, let her live."

I waited and watched, but still she did not move.

Again I pressed the vial to her lips, this time pouring nearly half the contents into the side of her mouth so she could not help but swallow the elderberry down. When I was certain she'd taken some of the liquid, I mopped up the single drop that had fallen to her chin, took her hand in mine, and sat back to wait.

Nothing changed.

I waited what seemed a long time, then looked up to notice the room. Her tapestries, all her brocade coverlets and thick carpets had been torn down and stripped away. There was a bed, one stark table, a small chair. Nothing more.

And the walls . . . The walls were bare, her work all gone! Not a single canvas remained. Nothing. Her paintings had all been ripped from the walls, stolen or destroyed as she lay there, too weak to protest or care.

Who would have ordered such a thing? Whose word could have wrought such punishment?

Stricken, I circled the room, running my hand over the smoothly carved sill, feeling the distant warmth of the sun as it tried to pry its way through the shuttered window. Nothing of the woman who had confided her life to these walls remained. They'd already left her for dead, stealing what they wanted even before Sunder had sealed her lips.

And did she even know I was there? Did she care about the babe stealing the life in her womb, or was she as close to death as her naked walls proclaimed?

I took a breath, shook my head. Edishu had never meant to help. He'd lied from the start, never believing I'd find an elderberry ripened in winter. I was a fool to have thought it could ever matter.

I stopped pacing at one of the adjacent alcoves, a servant's room built much like my own sleeping quarters that had been built off Mirjam's larger suite. The small room was bare, stripped down like everything else. But inside, where I had seldom looked before, stood another door.

I glanced once toward Ivane's bed, then, satisfied that she was still sleeping, opened the door and peered inside. It took a moment for my eyes to adjust to the dark, but when they did, I began to laugh.

Laid up in carefully stacked rows was a handful of my mother's canvases. They were an unfinished batch, tacked to plain wooden stretchers and waiting for their frames. Morell's handiwork—for who else wielded such authority?—had been so slovenly, so ill planned that whichever servant he'd sent to gut the outer room had not even taken the time to search thoroughly beyond the first layer. Gently, oh so gently, I drew out one of the canvases and carried it over to the light.

It was a painting of Jokjoa, the father god, arrayed in Kuoshana's splendors and peering down from his bed of stars to look earthward. He had a mischievous gleam in his eyes, like a young boy. Ivane had painted him beautifully dressed, with rings and bracelet, dagger, and even the great bow was there, angled back over one shoulder—easily, I couldn't help but note, as if it fit. And the bracelet, it was Rath, cut for cut an exact image of the bracelet around my wrist. The ring also, it was Mirjam's, each minute detail as exact as I remembered it.

But she could have seen the bracelet and the ring, I told myself. The ring had belonged to her once, hadn't it? And the bracelet she could have seen in a temple. She could have been to Roshanna at some time. After all, I didn't know everything about her doings. Or she might have seen them in another painting somewhere, in a manuscript perhaps, a library where eons ago another priest had copied letters out, just as I had done in Aster's library. But Hajthaele, how many years had it been since Hajthaele had been seen on earth? And even if she'd seen them, how had she known they belonged to Jokjoa?

I propped the canvas against a wall, peered closer. It was the same exact image. Huge, graceful, dark-grained. And the arrows: the same fletching, with the case mounted just so between the string and curved limbs.

How had she known? Where had she seen the tokens? And the painting she'd done on my journal, why did she paint the book house?

I flipped through the stack. There were others: Elan Sumedaros with Hajthaele; Edishu escaping Sunder's death grip; jarak dreamers mounting toward Kuoshana. One after another the canvases illustrated tales from Kuoshana, each done in fine detail, and always the ring on Jokjoa's finger resembled Mirjam's and the bracelet looked as much like Rath as anything could; Hajthaele, Jokjoa's bow, always an exact double for the one I'd carried out of Kuoshana's gate.

I pushed the stack back in place, then carefully closed the door. Whatever Morell might have ordered, I had no intention of allowing these to be destroyed. They were my mother's legacy and, if she died now, my inheritance. I meant to claim them, to fight for them if I had to. Anything rather than see them lost!

Then I remembered—there was one more painting I had not seen. The one she'd given me, my small journal. Quickly, surprised that I'd forgotten it again, I ran back to my mother's bedside, kissed her chill forehead. "Wait for me, Mother," I said. "Rest. Then we'll talk."

Quietly I closed the door, backing out to find Micah's father, Allard, carrying a tray with a small bowl of broth and warm drink.

"She's sleeping?" he asked as though he weren't surprised to find me there.

"Yes. But how long has she been this way? And who sent her women away? Why wasn't anyone with her?"

"Calyx, she's not well—"

"I can see that myself!" I shouted, anger and fear suddenly rising together.

Allard stared at the floor. "Two days now, she hasn't woken."

"Who said she was to be left alone? Was it Morell?"

"Calyx, the midwives said the child died weeks ago."

He was right, of course. I must have seen it the whole time I'd been with her, something in the way the covers fell across her middle that was different from the last time I'd seen her, filled with waiting for the child. Was that why Morell had ordered the midwives away, leaving Allard to watch her? Because the child—his child—was dead and the mother was nothing but a broken vessel waiting to be discarded?

"And what has that to do with Ivane? She's not dead yet!" I cried. "She's not!" I grabbed Allard by his shirtsleeve, and without meaning to, I pushed him back into the door. He was lighter than I'd imagined, frail and tired. I didn't mean to hurt him, but I couldn't hold back my anger. He was like a hollow pile of clothes, the strength gone out of his bones. The bowl toppled to the ground, spilling the broth and all the drink about the stone floor. Allard bent down to gather the load.

"I'm sorry," I said, ashamed, as I helped him gather up the tray.

"No, no, I understand," he said in a voice inseparable from my memories of Ivane. "It's hard is all. It's hard to watch her so. There's nothing to be done, Calyx. Nothing but wait. And that's what I'm doing. No one's to blame, though. You ought to know that."

"Will you be staying with her now?"

"Later, I'll be back. I have only a few more errands to run. Seems I'm always busy around here. Can you stay with her?"

"I'm going down to my rooms, then I'll be back. I'll wait with her, of course. And Allard, thank you. I'm sorry. You loved her too, I know you did." I hugged him closely a moment, and all I could think was that if anything happened to Ivane, he would be like the husband who could not live alone very long.

Outside my old room I stood a moment, my hand on the door. So much depended on these next few hours, so much waiting, so many decisions. I already knew what I would find inside: an old wooden chest and buried within the dark of a young girl's scarf, a small, blank book. I'd envisioned these moments so many times in the last few days. Book in hand, I'd confront my mother. "How," I would ask her, "how did you know?" And she would wake up from her fever, look at me with her tired eyes, and tell me everything was going to be fine.

Inside, the room seemed as abandoned as Ivane's. I pushed past a misplaced table and made my way into the smaller alcove that had once been the limits of my world. Here I had confronted my first jarak dreams, thinking them imaginary adventures such as any small girl would know. And here I had huddled in terror, defenseless against Edishu's claim to my life. The last time I'd slept here, I'd lain awake through half the night, wondering at Lethia's hatred.

I reached down into the chest and there, at the lower corner, found the bundle. It was smaller than I remembered, inconsequential. Exactly the way a secret ought to be hidden . . .

Slowly I unwrapped the scarf.

The book house. It was the same! Now I recognized the golden light that had hung over the table, and here the corner where the three doors had called me to choose a song. Edishu had stood at that very same threshold. The house had been waiting for me, as Edishu had.

How had she known, my mother? How had she known?

At that moment the door swung open behind me. It was Micah. Even in the dark shadow I knew at once the breadth of his shoulders, his posture and height. "Calyx?" he called out in a low voice.

"I'm here," I answered. "How did you find me?"

"My father told me where to look. I wanted to talk to you. Alone. Your friend, Dev, I left him sleeping in my bed. He'll be all right. It's just that I wanted to see you alone before you rode off again, the way you did last time, without giving me a chance to talk."

He came over and stood next to me, his face drawn inward. "First tell me that you're all right, Calyx. That all this secrecy of showing up at my house in those clothes, with that man, that no one is chasing you and you're not in trouble. Because if anyone's hurt you, I'll stop them. I'll do anything for you! You know that, don't you?" Micah sat down beside me on the bed and stared into my face. I watched as he struggled with himself, reached for my hands, lost confidence, and let his hands fall back to his lap instead.

"How could you help me?" I almost laughed. Then all at once I saw the pain he had gone through for me: the waiting, the loneliness, and the waiting again. Now though he couldn't know it, Edishu could be watching him. Whether I'd wanted to admit it or not, we were tied together, perhaps because of our friendship, or because of our lovemaking. Or for no other reason than that he was sitting near me, just as Dev had been the nearest person at hand when Edishu needed a way to enter the book house. And if Micah was found, what defenses would a shared birthdate grant him against such venom?

Micah turned and the brown curls at the back of his neck danced suddenly, reminding me how I'd once clung to them and buried my face in them. I had told Micah I loved him, that I would never love another man. But I'd been a child and I'd only meant it as a child means such things. Hadn't I wanted to love Dev also and been denied? And if I were the Elan Sumedaro? Did that mean no man would ever love me again? Worship me perhaps, as Dev already did, but love me, touch me? Then my child's oath to Micah would prove more binding than I'd meant . . . that I'd never love another man . . .

"Micah," I said, shaking the vision away. "You came here to talk."

"It's about my dreams, Calyx. I've been having dreams. Some the same, some different. But always you're in it."

I listened, somehow not at all surprised. Edishu had thrown his net wide, not caring which fish were dragged up along with me. "And?"

"I thought you had died, Calyx. I saw you trapped somewhere. You were bruised, bloody, and cold. I tried to call, but I didn't know how. All I could do was watch. And there were other dreams. You were fighting with someone, hand to hand. You had a bow . . . like that one." He pointed to the table where I had lain Hajthaele. "But it was too heavy for you to draw. Another time you're with the same man; his face is different, but it's him. He's stroking your arm tenderly, like a lover. Or there's another dream and you're wrestling, and it's the same man again, I know it is, even if his face is different."

"Micah, did you know the man in the dream? Have you ever dreamt of him without me? Or seen him? Has he spoken with you?"

"No. In the dreams, he never sees me. But Calyx, I know who he is. Don't try to deny it, I won't let you. And I can't live with this. Not alone. It's Edishu. I've known for a long time, though at first I couldn't understand what he would want with me."

I waited while Micah paused.

"And then I understood. It wasn't me at all. It's you, Calyx. You and not you. Not you, my friend, Calyx, Morell's daughter, but you . . . an Elan Sumedaro. No, don't try to tell me it isn't true. Ceena already spoke with me about the havens. I came to her when I didn't know what else to do with the dreams. It was so new and unexpected. Me, having jarak dreams. I had to have someone to talk to. Between the two of us, we pieced together what we knew of your dreams. And I agreed with Ceena. Edishu doesn't fight out of battle lust, though he's plenty of that. He fights for his freedom. And there's only one person the gods ever granted the strength to resist him. The Elan Sumedaro. You, Calyx."

While Micah spoke, I looked at my hands. The blue light that had circled them so clearly in the ice fields was gone now, waiting. I was Calyx once again, but more and more now, Calyx and not Calyx.

"I've wondered the same thing," I whispered. "A hundred times and more. And the answer always seems the same, though I don't understand the how or the why of it."

"It's true, then?"

I looked down at the small, painted journal, wondering again. Then I turned it over. "Do you know how I came here, Micah?" I said. "I spun myself a waking dream. We were in the northlands, Dev and I. Edishu had followed me, and we fought. I won, I think. At least for the time being. If the arrow wound he took means anything, he'll be held in Kuoshana for a time. But I couldn't have made the return journey, it would have taken too long—if we had survived at all. *I brought us home in a waking dream.* My will became fact—so that where we'd been at Kuoshana's gateway one moment, the next we were on a hill looking down at your house. But a waking dream, Micah? I keep thinking that if a jarak dream is a means to witness the world without affecting it, then a waking dream is an extension of this, a means to command the world. Not so different from a jarak dream, only more concentrated, heightened. If that's what it means to be the Elan Sumedaro, to be able to do this thing, then I suppose I have done it."

"Then you can do anything, make anything happen by having a waking dream?"

"No," I stopped him. "It can't be that simple. The waking dream was limited by need, immediacy, and, I think, the potential to do things for the good . . . To fight Edishu."

"Calyx, I'm coming with you. I've thought about it. I'll follow you. Don't try to say I can't. Whatever happens next—"

"Of course you are, Micah. You have to. Though I hadn't understood till now. But listen. I'm afraid for you. You're sharing my dreams somehow, following the paths that are meant for me. It shouldn't be happening, but it is. I'm afraid that Edishu could try to use you to find me. He's done it with Dev. I want you to ride with us. You're not safe alone."

Micah met my eyes straight on. "Where will we go? Can we hide?"

"Not easily. My dreams are like a beacon to him, leading him closer and closer. I can't hide. Yet I have to. I have to buy time to gather stronger weapons, and learn to use Hajthaele against him. But . . . will they let you go, your mother and father?"

Micah laughed. "It's what she always feared, that she would lose me the same way she lost my father. To Briana."

"It's small help, but will she accept coins to hire an apprentice in your stead?"

"Out of anger, maybe. But she'll let me go. There's any one of my brothers could do what I do. But I'll talk to her myself."

Lightly, I put my hand on his, as a sister might. "All right. But for now, I need you to stay with Dev. Please. Here, take this money. Tell Dev to buy what we'll need for clothing, horses, supplies. He'll know what to choose, but he'll need you to show him where to go. And make certain it's only to someone you trust. Tell him we'll be riding out together, the three of us and Ceena. I'll come as soon as I can."

In the corridor Micah tried to look grim and determined, but he could hardly contain the smile that opened across his face. For myself, I felt easier once he was gone and I was able to turn my thoughts back toward my own questions.

The hall was quiet again outside my mother's door, though even the air had the smell of a sickroom, a false cleanliness, scrubbed with lye and boiling waters incapable of disguising the underlying scent.

Inside, Ivane lay as I'd left her, though she breathed more heavily than before. There was no color to her cheeks, and the skin lay slack and mishaped, as though there weren't enough underlying muscle left to buoy her up.

"So, Mother?" I whispered, laying the journal on the bed between us. "How did you know what Kuoshana's gateway

looks like? Was it that man I saw in your dream who told
you about the tokens . . . ? Mother? We could have had so
much together. We could have helped each other, just a
little, to be less lonely."

I meant to say more, to tell her—though I wasn't certain
she would hear—something of what it was to find Kuoshana's
gateway like a memory lost out of childhood. To tell her
how it felt to spin a waking dream. And not just the idea of
it, but to share the awareness of that ability, to have her feel
it with me. And to thank her for that, as well as her other
gift to me—that she had never told me there were things I
could not do. But when I moved to brush a grayed hair from
her cheek, she cried out and drew a startled breath.

"Mother! No!" I screamed, and threw my arms behind
her shoulders, thinking to lift her so she might breathe
easier. But her head hung sideways when I tried, then fell
backward, too heavy, too weak.

"Not yet, please. Not yet! It isn't fair! Edishu?" I shouted
at the walls, "You tricked me! But you'll never win! Do you
hear? Not though you chase us through a thousand dreams . . ."

My throat twisted in a knot and I sank down beside her,
searching for calm. I was not ready to cry, to give in. There
was breath in her still, however faint. And as long as Ivane
lived, her secrets lived.

And if she slept, didn't she dream?

And as long as she dreamt, didn't a path remain open for
me to follow? Couldn't the Elan Sumedaro follow one more
dream? Granted, it was without her permission and I had no
way of knowing whether she would deny me this boon. But
everything had come back around to this one dream. And I
had to follow it deeper, retrace the tangled paths to their
end this time. If I wanted any hope of learning what she'd
known, it had to be now. There would be no other chance.

Now! I swore. *It must be now.*

Allard had left a flask of wine upon the bedside table, and
I helped myself to a long drink, feeling the heat burn through
the knot in my throat. I wiped my mouth with the back of
my hand, took a second drink, then looked at her again.

Ivane's narrow features seemed more at rest now, almost
as if she understood what I meant to do and had acquiesced,
falling from her feverish state into a deeper dream. What
troubled me was the possibility that there might be a difference between the memory I needed to trace and an un-

schooled dream. Dreams I could follow, touch, change even. But memory? I wasn't certain. Unless the path that mapped her thoughts welded the two together in a line so strong that memory became dream just as dream became memory.

"Mother, forgive me," I whispered, and reaching across the pillow, I brushed my lips against hers in the lightest kiss. Her mouth was dry, her cheeks cool. No matter what, I warned myself, this last vigil must be kept—and quickly.

I sat down close beside her on the bed, took one of her hands in mine. She seemed so small, almost childlike. There was no resistance, no response to my touch. I slipped her fingers into the dark cave between my hands and held them there.

Then, eyes closed, I began my jarak search for Ivane's dream. Slowly, slowly, winding through the web of days and nights, the longings borne of all her lonely days, I searched.

Through it I never heard the door opening behind me, the two sets of footsteps entering so lightly into the room, or the hand that lit on my shoulder and rested there, joining the search.

Ivane's dreams drew me in and led me back, one through the other, the strands knotting and furling, and through them all, a single leitmotif running straighter, backward, through the heart of all others, the one that was as much memory as dream. Until I found it, recognized it from so long ago, and the relentlessness of its strength pulled me in . . .

I am inside my mother's dream. The red embers in the fireplace have kept the room warm. There's a noise, slight but enough to rouse her.

My mother opens her eyes and searches the dark room. "Who's there?" she calls out. "Allard, is that you? Morell?"

Someone is in the room with her. A man, but not my father. He leans closer and his hand brushes her forehead, traces the outline of her face. *Does she already know him?* I wonder. *There's acceptance I feel in her heart, not fear.* She turns toward the warmth of his shadowed face.

"Who are you?" she asks.

"That I will not answer," he says, and my breath catches. I remember the voice now. I had heard it before. But this clarity hadn't been there that first time, beating inside. "For if I speak too loudly, my name will be heard and known. And my name is a thing that you especially, little queen on earth, must never repeat."

"But how can you expect me to—"

"Quiet! There is danger in knowing, lest my name be used against you and against the child we shall make together this night."

"Why me, then?" she whispers. "I'm not one of your Sumedaro priests. I paint pictures, that's all. What do I know of your ways?"

The man laughs. "That is your own assumption, little queen. But I will tell you something else. Not all the people in all their little houses remember how to reach Kuoshana, whatever your priests may tell you. And this we must change. Then again"—he smiled—"neither do they know what it is to be locked in sleep, wishing for the beauty of one mortal woman and waiting for a morning that doesn't come."

Ivane raises her hand to the man's cheek, brushes his face. The motion is tentative and light. She feels his smooth, beardless face, and my own hand savors that touch, almost against my will. Is this then the real face of my father, his eyes my eyes, his hair my hair? With one slender finger my mother traces the outline of his lips, asks the question I've come so far to have answered: "What are you, then?"

"Do you not know already?" the man answers. "Open your eyes. Look this once. For never again will I allow you to see the face of Kuoshana save perhaps in the few simple dreams you may invent in the morning light."

For a long time my mother doesn't answer. I can only tremble with her, awed. Together we stare into the clear, shining face that dares us both to come to him.

He says, "You are beautiful also. And it is as I have always wondered, that the ways of mortals are not so very different than the ways of the gods. And what is beautiful and desirable in Kuoshana is also thus on earth."

And then I feel his hands—my father's hands—warm and searching, and my mother closes her eyes.

Time passes. A dull light is shining through her window. The man is no longer at my mother's side. She feels a cool breeze spring up and realizes suddenly that she is afraid of being left alone.

"Wait!" she calls. Near the open window she can just find the silhouette of his broad shoulders outlined against the brightening sky. For one long, worried moment she is afraid he will not speak. Then she hears his voice again, kind and soft with the memory of their lovemaking, and I too am listening, urging the words into my memory.

"What would you have?" he asks.

"For myself, I accept the charge you lay on me, but for the child who will be born . . ."

"Ask, little queen. Ask and it is yours."

Ivane's thoughts race against the growing cold, but the stranger's body is shimmering now, growing insubstantial. "A token," she calls out quickly. "A token that the child may someday use to call upon its father."

The reply comes couched in wild laughter that echoes against the walls, bounding and rebounding until Ivane cannot find its center. "Well asked, sweet woman. And it is done. The child is conceived in a dream, so she shall find the tokens that lead to me through her dreams. But it will be in the full light of day that she uses them."

"She?" Ivane's words are little more than a whisper, but I hear them and I understand. "Then we shall be alone together, this child and I."

When next I opened my eyes, the sun had moved farther down the wall. I felt weak, tired from the prolonged contact. Ivane had given me what I asked, and so much more besides.

"Thank you," I said softly, "for waiting for me to come back to you."

"Calyx?"

Morell's voice startled me. I jumped, turned about. He stood but a short arm's length from my side. At the door, Norvin stood sentry, his eyes oddly downcast.

With Ivane's dream a calmness had settled over me, an acceptance, and I no longer feared for myself. But Hajthaele . . . What if Norvin mistook the bow and tried to seize it? I lunged suddenly, grabbed for the bow, half expecting Norvin to draw his sword and challenge me. But no one moved. "That bow is Hajthaele," I cried, "and I swear, if you move to touch it—"

"Hajthaele also?" Morell's whisper stopped me, so unexpected it was. Without challenge, without malice.

Norvin's gaze roved across the bow's strong curve, staring at its shape and size. But he did not move.

Morell sank to his knees on the floor beside Ivane.

"Is she gone?" I asked.

"Yes." Morell studied her face, then looked back up at me. "You don't know, do you?"

"Know what?"

"I was in the room just now."

"And . . . ?"

"You were sitting there at her bed. I didn't know you'd come back, you see. Didn't know what you were doing. And there was that blue light shining all around you. I thought maybe . . ." He shook his head as if uncertain what he meant to say. "I don't know what I thought. That you were doing something to her. And then I put my hand on your shoulder. That's all I did. Just touched you. And I saw . . . It was her room . . ."

I stiffened, realizing what had happened. "You were pulled along into her dream, weren't you? Whatever I saw, you saw. And now . . . What are you thinking?"

"Hayden was right." Morell looked about the room, taking in the bed. "I loved her," he said, gently running his hand along her cheek. "But we were too different in the end. And I never understood her. I wanted to. I tried. Or I thought I tried. But the things she wanted, they had no real importance. None that I saw. For her it was the gods. The gods and her painting. How could I, with the damn fighting and the famines that never ended, how could I have time for painting? Or all the praying she wanted me to do? The hours wasted with some dream priest? You tell me, Calyx, would it have brought a better harvest to our farmers? Fed the people? Or kept our men from dying in the border wars?"

I don't think Morell expected an answer but the question mattered. "I don't know," I said. "But, maybe yes. Maybe that's exactly what it would have done."

The room was terribly quiet, then finally Morell said "We—we weren't there for each other, your mother and I. Though I suppose she felt the loneliness more harshly, shut away up here the way she was. While I was too busy to see how the years had a way of sliding by, without ever the time to sort through the arguments. Always the same arguments."

He walked to the narrow window and stared outside till his breath condensed on the frigid glass, obscuring his view. "All I ever wanted was to hold this land of mine together," he said. "And then five years ago, Lethia sends an ambassador. What was I to do? An alliance seemed so reasonable

for us all. You remember, don't you, Norvin? Her wealth in
trade for our soldiers. You thought it was a good idea too.
Mirjam married to Theron. Lethia came herself, several
times. And oh, by Oreill's sweet breast, she was beautiful.
A goddess. Funny," he said, shrugging, "in some ways, she
reminded me of Ivane. Ivane the way I had wanted her to
be. Proud, beautiful, and oh so full of fine ideas. Real
ideas, not paintings of some unattainable Kuoshana. And I
believed her."

"Were you lovers?" I asked, my voice no louder than a
whisper.

"Lovers?" My father—I still would call him that—shook
his head. "The word doesn't fit with her. She seduced me,
her body, her honeyed words. But what we did together,
that wasn't love . . . And you tried to warn me, didn't you?
Though of course, by then it was too late.

"Norvin." Morell drew a sharp breath. "We have work
that cannot keep. Accompany Calyx . . . and her bow to the
hall. Hayden will want to know about his mother. Call
Jared. He'll help here. And there's a little matter I'll need
to discuss—even if it must be tonight—with the lady, Queen
Lethia, concerning the garrison of my soldiers who'll be
returning to Briana."

"What? Lethia's here?"

"Yes. These last three days. Didn't you know?"

"No. I . . . I came straight here."

"Well then, if nothing else, this should prove interesting."

I turned once more to the bed. "I'll come back, Mama. I'll
come back and say good-bye. Wait for me? One more time?"

23

Morell hurried on ahead of us, anxious to find Hayden
as quickly as possible. I should have turned my thoughts
more quickly in the same direction, prepared myself for this
meeting with Lethia. But I'd seen and heard things from

Morell I'd have never understood before, and both his words and my mother's passing weighed heavily, distracting me.

The stairway was ill lit and in less than a moment Morell stepped into a wall of shadows that carried him down and out of my line of sight. I walked slowly, paying scant attention to Norvin as he came up close behind me, his step so light I nearly forgot he was there. Another step and we were in the shadows as well, hidden by any who'd look for us.

I felt Norvin's breath near my neck, started to fix the bow so I could turn, but he grabbed me suddenly, taking hold of my arm and forcing me back against the wall.

"What . . . ?" I tried to shout, but he slapped his hand over my mouth so quickly, I gagged and scratched uselessly for his arm.

"Don't bother calling." His voice was low in my ear. "There's no one who is going to hear. And I'll move my hand as soon as you understand that I only mean to take the bow for now. I'm not going to keep it. But call it whatever name you like, I can't have you carrying it down there. I don't want a war on my hands. Certainly not with Morell the way he is just now. And if you're going to turn him as useless as your brother, then you'd better remember that I'm here as well. I don't know what it was you did to Morell just now, but I'm not going to wait around like a milkmaid while Lethia hangs her banner from every tower in this keep. Now I'll just take the bow . . ."

Slowly Norvin let go his hand, but he'd left me more time to think than he realized. I screamed, more as a ploy than anything else, then dropped my weight suddenly to the left, hoping to trick him and pull away from his grip. I don't know what I thought to do—run, I suppose, make for the kitchens or the Great Hall, anything so long as I remained free. But just as he lunged toward me again, Norvin's hand brushed across the bow's tip. A shock went coursing through his arm and his face contorted with pain as sharp as if he'd been stabbed with a knife. Surprised, he sucked his hand in close to his chest, cradled it, while his dark eyes roved across the bow.

"Hajthaele?" he said warily. "Well, I don't know about that. Never did claim to understand what it was they did inside those temple walls. Now why don't you just give it to me nicely? We'll all be better off if Lethia doesn't take it into her mind that you're going to shoot her."

"Don't touch it, Norvin," I warned, testing the fear I saw in his eyes. "Hajthaele belongs in my hands, not yours. And the truth is, I hardly know any more than you what it's capable of. Or how to control it. I'm not your prisoner. Not here, in this house."

Morell's captain seemed to consider my words. "All right then, keep the damned thing. But I warn you, Lethia wants you out of the way. And bow or not, if you move against Lord Morell or trick him into doing anything that'll jeopardize these lands, I won't move to stop her."

"Norvin," I said as calmly as I was able, "I have no quarrel with Morell."

Norvin considered that, then started down the stairs without answering, careful this time that Hajthaele not brush against him. "If Lethia's as taken in by your words as every other fool around here," he said, "it stands to reason she'll only want the bow all the more."

"What is it Lethia says about me?"

"The worst of it is that you tried to steal some jewelry from her—"

"What jewelry?"

"Something about a bracelet, another of your temple relics, though I never did get the whole story. Whatever it was you did this time, it made her mad enough to send her riders all through the northlands looking for you. Toklat, Aster, Roshanna. But Hershann had already sent Jared a letter saying Aster had washed its hands of you, that if you hadn't the sense to marry into Istyak Keep, then they didn't have the means to shelter you any longer—without proper recompense from Briana, that is."

"Did Morell believe her, about the bracelet?"

Norvin shrugged. "I'm not certain just what Morell believes these days. No matter what else you think, it hasn't sat easy with him, the way Ivane's been so ill. And then my own son Jesun comes home with that wild story of you leading them into a haven. And Solly and Hannak, those two who rode back with you, they've been talking like the north wind about it. I tried to convince Morell to stop them, to see we've trouble enough without people believing some god-sent dream's going to save us all. But Morell hasn't wanted to do anything much lately. Then Lethia showed up, angry as a she-cat by day, and at night she's rubbing herself all up and down his side." Norvin stopped, looked over to see how I was reacting, then went on: "And he doesn't like it. I can see he doesn't. But he can't stop her—can't or won't, I don't know which. Though if it were me, I'd tell you what I'd do with that woman and her promises . . ."

Norvin stopped talking then. The stairway we'd come down opened onto the full length of the Great Hall. We looked out to see Morell already standing apart with Hayden, the two of them speaking intently while a fire crackled loudly beside them, masking their words.

The last time I'd stood in this hall, it had been festooned with banners and golden flasks of wine. The dinner that night had been one of the most lavish Morell had ever given. Not far from where Hayden stood now, I'd shamed the man who had been my father beyond the limits of his tolerance. While one seat farther beyond that, Edishu had used Lethia to set his plans in motion.

Now people stood about in small clusters, their low-pitched conversations nervously filling the hall. Some of the men and women I recognized, most I did not. What I did see was that the tight line of guards positioned about the walls were not wearing Briana's colors, but the gray- and purple-hemmed leathers of Lethia's men.

With a move that I hoped would be inconspicuous, I slipped Rath from its pouch back to my wrist and repositioned the heavy bow on my shoulder. At the same time I found Lethia standing among her own people, away on the opposite side of the hall. Closest beside her stood Avram. Somehow I wasn't surprised to see him there. In an odd way, it left me more confidence than concern. Lethia had sent him north from the very start. I was certain of it now. And he must have found it convenient to have his queen's purposes mesh with his own. His stance beside Lethia seemed as haughty as a courtier's, as if he supposed the clothes he wore—Sumedaro orange hemmed boldly in Gleavon's manner—were already a mark of victory.

And then Lethia saw me, and whatever it was she'd been considering, her face became a cold mask. She smiled, dipped her perfect forehead in the slightest acknowledgment. Then, as if I were nothing but a servant bound to carry some precious jewel to her master, she turned to gaze at Jokjoa's bow.

Slowly at first, then like a wave, a hush closed over the hall. Surely now there was not a person present but knew who I was, not one who had not heard the stories in the towns and farmsteads. From somewhere in the crowd I heard my name mentioned, a whisper. "Elan Sumedaro," I heard. And: "The bow, Hajthaele. The Princess Calyx returns . . ."

I looked around, searching the faces to number those whose loyalty would be certain. Ceena I found first, alone of course, but not so far from Hayden and Morell she couldn't reach them when she had to. She saw the bow and started forward, but I sent her a sign to keep posted near Lethia, and she stepped back to wait.

Others were there as well, men I'd once known from Morell's court but whom I'd thought little of in the past few years. On the opposite side of the hall an older Jared than I remembered talked with several of his hooded priests. I tried to see if any stood among them that I knew, but with the way they kept their hoods so close and their eyes obediently downcast, I had no idea which temple claimed their allegiance—or, for that matter, where Jared himself would stand this night.

And then with Lethia and everyone in that hall watching, Hayden made his way toward me. From his look I knew at once Morell had told him of Ivane's death, but what else Morell might have said, I couldn't be certain.

Loudly I said, "Our mother, the Lady Ivane is gone," and the words echoed through the hall.

Hayden reached out, took my hands in his, then pulled me in close against his chest. His arms were strong, his breathing controlled, and he looked for all the world as though he were not a king but only a boy. Yet he would take this well, I thought. Knowing Ivane had been ill, he'd at least be spared the anguish of shock. Even I, though I had fooled myself into hoping I fought against inevitability, had known her death was possible. A time for mourning would come, I knew—but not before I'd faced Lethia and Shammal.

Holding me, his mouth beside my ear, Hayden whispered, "Watch out for Avram. he's carrying a dagger. And Jared's priests—they're Korinna's soldiers."

Then he let me go, backing away with a look that revealed nothing but a brother's shared grief. Lethia made her way toward us, and Morell, from his side of the hall, also approached. Norvin, keeping close to Morell's side, made certain his weapons were in plain sight. "Sir," Lethia faced Hayden, "your sister was found alone in Lady Ivane's room. I have it from one of your own people that there was some confusion as to when exactly—"

"Confusion, Lethia?" Morell cut in, his voice strained. "There was no confusion. We were there together: Norvin, the Lady Calyx, and I."

"The point was made," Lethia said, "in good faith that your daughter—"

"Would that she were my daughter," Morell whispered tightly.

"What did you say?" Hayden asked.

"Calyx is your sister, Hayden. But that is all," Morell said. Then, looking me full in the face, he added, "She is a daughter of my heart. And she is so much more. Your mother, before she died, she told . . . she showed us—"

Carefully, Lethia interrupted, "Lord Morell, these affairs are private and taxing. I too have lost a spouse. A husband. And I understand that in your grief you may want to speak with your family alone. Perhaps if we waited till after the preparations have been made for your wife's concerns—"

"No." Morell turned toward Lethia. "There are matters here that cannot wait."

"Which are best discussed in private . . ." Lethia reached out to stroke Morell's arm lightly for a moment, then took his hand as if to lead him away, but he shook her off and would not follow. A glance passed between them, and while it was not pretty to watch, I loved Morell a little more for the pain it cost him.

"Watch carefully what you do here," Lethia warned. "We have treaties in place. Alliances. Not for you and I, for we will pass. But for Briana and Gleavon, which are far more important than either of us—"

"Treaties whose terms bear looking into."

"I see." Lethia nodded, and she might have said more except that Avram chose that moment to approach from behind us, his voice loud and too sure of himself.

"Have you asked her where she's hidden the bracelet and goblet she stole from Aster? What lies did she tell this time? And that bow, she's no more right to it than I have."

"Be quiet!" Lethia ordered, but Avram's words, and most of what Morell had said also, had been heard by enough people in the hall so that the silence broke again into a confusion of voices.

"The bow is Hajthaele." I smiled, and tried to look as if its weight were not so much more than I could handle. "And it is mine by full rights, as your queen will surely tell you."

"So, Calyx," Lethia said, and her hand went to a golden purse belted around her waist. "It seems Briana has brought us together again."

"The bow and the other two? Is that all?" Avram continued to taunt. "And you not even the first rank of Sumedaro?"

"And it seems," Lethia said tightly, "I should not have trusted your promise, Lord Morell. I thought I remembered you gave your word never to harbor a known thief in this house. But now I think it may be better this way. You save me the trouble of having to find Rath and Gamaliel myself."

Morell looked confused. "Then Calyx did steal the bracelet from you?"

With a show of calm, Lethia opened her purse and slipped Shammal onto her finger.

"In my own name I carry these tokens," I said. "And the only theft we need consider is to ask Lethia how *she* came by that ring Ivane gave my sister for a wedding present."

"Shammal is more mine than those were ever yours." Lethia raised her hand to show the ring, twisting it solidly into place. "For I learned how to fight for it, while you have done nothing but wait till the tokens came to you. Now watch." She stepped back suddenly. "Watch whose ownership proves the greater truth." She raised her hand high overhead to let the ring shine free.

"Edishu!" she cried out so suddenly there was no chance to stop her. "Shammal!" And a wind rose up at her command, swirling and clouded overhead. "Edishu! Shammal!" she cried again, and the wind whipped louder, fiercer, a whirlwind born from the ring's very heart, circling and deadly. Hayden saw it coming and others in the hall jumped from its path. But those who were closest—Morell and Avram, transfixed—were caught up in its force and thrown against the walls.

I stood my ground, leaning into Hajthaele for support, unable to raise my hand against her while the wind struck at me, lashing and virulent. But through it Hajthaele held me like an anchor in a storm, and I waited out the first attack.

The howling kept up, as dark and boundless as a storm tossed between mountain peaks. And then slowly, slowly, it began to weaken. At last, when I was able to look about, I saw how the wind's center had spun no farther than the circle where Lethia and I faced each other, had not reached even to the tables or the fire burning steady in the hearth. Nor was Lethia smiling as I had supposed, but looked thoughtful, strained by the effort of what she'd done.

My thoughts raced back to Kuoshana's gateway and Edishu's last moments—how the wound had disappeared from Dev's shoulder just as Edishu had disappeared . . .

Banished . . . By Hajthaele's arrow, please let the walls that enclose him hold!

I could read the confusion in the hall, the fear, the curiosity. Even Lethia's men had broken their ranks, pressed closer to each other, watching from the walls, wondering.

"If you are waiting for Edishu"—I leaped for the one chance I prayed might be true—"he will not come."

"He will come." Lethia held her ringed hand close. "Shammal brings him."

"What? Shammal and not you, his lover?"

"That's right, I am his lover. And you have never been, fool that you are for that mistake. You thought you could gain his power, didn't you? Thought that if you didn't go to his bed, you'd be all the stronger on your own, that you wouldn't have to share those gifts that came so easily to you? Did you really hope to have any power next to his, when he was born of Kuoshana, and you . . . you're as mortal as I. You breathe. You feel pain. And you'll die. While Edishu will live forever. You're nothing next to him, nothing without him. While it's me he needs, not you. Because I've given him what he wants. And I'll give him more."

"He can't come to you now," I said again.

"I'll call again, only to show you what I am to him, how he will not move in this world without me."

"I didn't say won't. I said can't."

"Can't?" Lethia shook her head. "You don't know what you're saying."

"Edishu is banished. Sleeping as deeply as a dream in Kuoshana. I fought him. And I won. Won Hajthaele. Earned the bracelet. And more, Lethia. While your little whirlwind just now lacked the power to crawl more than a few yards."

"You haven't won anything." Lethia's eyes blazed. "Or if you have, it won't matter. Lord Edishu did not leave me so powerless as that. What he gave me, what I've learned, you cannot touch and you cannot know. There is knowledge in the world you'll never learn. Power you'll never touch. Your fear will be your downfall. I'll fight you, and I'll win. With Shammal first, then Rath and Gamaliel, Hajthaele— and all the others. Oreill's pearls—I'll find them before you even know what they are. And I'll reach Edishu myself. He won't spurn me. Nor will he pretend to want you over me again when you are dead and I am the one who carries the tokens."

"You may wear that ring, but not the power to enable them."

"Morell!" Lethia shouted. "Jared! She's admitted to steal-ing the bracelet. Will you allow your temples to be violated? Your relics stolen? Call your men . . . Or must I take it from her myself?"

Morell had recovered from his fall, but he held his side as though he'd been hit harder than he liked to admit. "I . . . no . . ." He shook his head. "I will not call my guards."

"Make your own choice, then, Morell. Avram!" Lethia snapped.

Lethia's men made an attempt to shift back to attention, raising their staffs and weapons as they waited for the next word, but there was a hesitancy in the way they moved, and though Lethia's back was to me, I could see that she too had noticed the change in their stance. And one thing more she hadn't counted on: the extent of Avram's jealousy for me.

Caught up in our arguing, Avram never heard Jared give the alert or saw our old friend, Beklar, as his narrow smile came to life suddenly from beneath his fallen hood.

All up and down that line, hoods were thrown back and loose-fitting orange robes fell to the floor, revealing a full array of swords, daggers, and lances all unsheathed and ready. Lethia's men drew their weapons and jumped to defend themselves against the attack. For the briefest mo-ment I saw Hayden match his sword against Lethia's cap-tain, while Beklar faced another, drawing first blood. But then I had no time to watch.

In the hall's cleared center Lethia smiled down at me.

"Edshammal! Kuoshammal! Shammkanash! Sunkanash!"

she cried, and as her voice cut loudly through the air, Shammal flared anew.

This time her strength held more certain.

Shammal's power seemed born of skyworld, absolute and irrevocable. World Walker, the ring was called. Dream Dancer. Its power reached me through a haze of blue, almost as if I were back within the silent world of that icy crevasse and staring into its light. I grew as tired and numb as lake water under heavy snows.

Hadn't I tried to fight Lethia once before, the first time I saw her with that ring? And hadn't I lost that battle, run away to my jarak dreams to hide to be safe. Safe where she couldn't hurt me. Safe within the numbing blue cold.

My thoughts slowed. Blue: all the world was as blue and still as Kuoshana's gateway had been. Quiet, irrevocable, a world wrapped in sleep.

A jarak dreamer cannot change the world, I recalled from some long-ago lesson, not change the world, only watch. And I was a jarak dreamer, wasn't I?

And I was watching . . . watching . . .

I thought I saw people moving around me, but their arms and legs were all a blur. Odd, how little they seemed to matter, all their rushing, their noise. Better to sleep, to sleep and watch. Lethia was beautiful after all, wasn't she? And if the three Sisters had given her the ring, what did it matter to me? I had Hajthaele. Though it wasn't so worthwhile at all if it couldn't be used. Couldn't be strung. Too long by an arm's length. Too heavy by ten stones. Maybe I should put it down now. Just hold it: that would be enough.

And watch.

From somewhere there was a crashing sound: Morell with a sword raised against Avram. But they were far away, and too much was moving, with people everywhere. The floor was cold, like me; cold to cold. Lethia could watch for me. She was somewhere too. And wasn't Hajthaele's wood smooth under my hand? Better to put it down, just lie beside it. Later I could try to remember that other thing I used to know about jarak dreamers.

Just to watch. Jarak dreamers watch. That's all they do, isn't it?

Ah, but everything was slow. Cold, yes, but easy. Comfortable. Like blue waves. Lapping. Lapping. If I didn't move, maybe I could stay like this. I felt waves of cold, almost couldn't feel them now.

Almost.

But something was pulling my bow. Hajthaele was going away. That wasn't right. It was nice to touch. Smooth. I wanted to keep it. Even if I wasn't strong enough to use it. Something, no, someone was taking it away from me. Give it back, I wanted to tell them. I like it. I want to touch it. Let me sleep. I don't want . . .

To see . . .

Avram?

What was he doing?

Avram was trying to take Hajthaele.

But my fingers could not, would not uncurl from around the bow's dark wood.

He pulled harder, tried to pry my fingers loose. I could see him, but the bow—I couldn't feel it, fingers so stiff, frozen. Avram grabbed the opposite end, trying for leverage, then pulled again.

Why was he waking me? I wanted to sleep, feel the cold tuck up around me.

Except I couldn't now. There was something on the floor in my line of sight. A goblet. Empty. Clear to its bottom. Clear as a mirror. From where I lay, cheek pressed to the floor, it was the only thing I could see in the entire world. And in it, my own face reflecting back at me. My face talking to me. Calling me jarak dreamer. Waking Dreamer. World Walker. Bridge Builder . . .

That's what I'd been trying to remember. Not a jarak watcher only but a waking dreamer, with the power to touch the world through my dreams.

On my wrist Rath suddenly began to glow. Warmer. Warmth moving up through my arm, rushing through my limbs. Warmth that hurt, like a shallow pool of ice shattering under a footstep. Pain that was life rushing, blood rushing, thoughts . . . rushing.

Rath! The bracelet exploded with its own strength: Eclipse's power to see to the core of truth, power to rekindle memory from my frozen thoughts.

I blinked, found my eyes clear again, as if I'd woken from a long, fever-ridden sleep.

And what I saw was Lethia trembling under the weight of Shammal's power as I had trembled under the burden of

Hajthaele. Lethia had sought to drown me in sleep. And she'd almost won. Almost. Except for what Gamaliel had reminded me, the lesson I'd learned in Kuoshana's gateway: that I was a jarak dreamer but so much more as well.

Elan Sumedaro. Waking Dreamer. And I need not watch.

Then, as if with that one clear thought, the fetters holding down my will broke loose. I rose to my knees, heard Ceena's sudden cry pierce the hall: the Kanashan Breath of Night, the killer breath. At her feet two of Lethia's soldiers lay twisted and still while a third man fought hopelessly to escape her grasp.

Lethia, her eyes darkened with the realization that Edishu would not come, cried out in fury as I rose. She redirected the attack, leveling her arm toward Hajthaele, and Shammal's light gathered again.

But this time I knew what must be done. "Strengthen my arm, Rath," I cried as I found a solid, balanced stance and held it. Hajthaele was long, far taller than I. With my hand on its grip, a new calm took hold, chasing away the years of uncertainty and waiting. And I knew that Ceena had spoken the truth, from her first hushed prophesy until this day.

And I would watch no more . . .

I took Hajthaele's silver cord in hand, this time bending the bow till the cord fit, tight and sleek. I drew an arrow from the quiver, finding it by the soft line of its fletching, then took a breath. A waking dream was not so different from a jarak dream, I whispered, and I turned my gripping hand down, brought the bow parallel to the ground. Thumb and forefinger grasping the nock, I slipped the arrow to the bowstring.

Somewhere lay a pattern to my dreams, a thread that stitched its way from day to jarak night to waking dream . . . a waking dream that would fashion Hajthaele into something I could understand and control, a bow that knew me as well as I knew the span of my own hand's reach, the heft of a stone solid in my grasp.

Closing my eyes to the hall, I narrowed my vision in more and more tightly, until all I could see was the window formed between arrow shaft, string, and bow grip. I aimed the bow skyward. Wordlessly I envisioned the string powered by my shoulder muscles. Pushing . . . pulling . . . drawing back . . . back . . . My chest tightened, my throat stuck with the effort, but I would not let the image go.

Then I opened my eyes, and dream became truth.

The arrow was sweetly nocked, the string pulled firm and true. Pressure welled up inside my arm like a catapult, and I let go . . .

Higher and higher the arrow leaped toward the arched ceiling, its shaft aglow in light. For one precious moment it hung overhead as if it were some fiery constellation in Oreill's hair. Then suddenly it broke into a blaze of fire, fire lit by the power of Hajthaele's magic.

Mine to use, to shape each waking dream.

The arrow began a wide circle, a wake of fire sweeping behind it, red and blue, white and blue, faster and faster. The flames lashed about the room, fire born of greatest need, fire to work Hajthaele's magic.

On the ground my father reeled about, saw the arrow just as it began its descent toward me. He must have thought it was Lethia's doing, her magic that was aimed for my heart. He shouted my name in warning, then leaped, flinging his entire body free of the earth, up and forward, a javelin hurtling through the air.

He never saw Lethia raise her hand, but I shouted as she pointed Shammal toward me.

Arm extended, fist clenched, she stared through Morell as if he wasn't there, stared and refused to stop. There was a quick jerk of her arm, and then a bolt of pure light shot forth.

He took it in his chest, his body rising again even as he fell, writhing as though struck by lightning, but he made no sound. Hajthaele's arrow fell also, but too late to help him; it flew protectively in a wide circle around my feet, and where it sped, a ring of flames rose up. Morell lay just outside the circle, still now, his face to the floor, where I could not see his eyes.

For a moment the fighting stopped. Morell's people wavered uncertainly, but so did the soldiers who'd come with Lethia from Gleavon.

Somehow I remembered to pick up the arrow and return it to its case. If only there'd been another moment, I told myself, one more moment and Morell might have stood inside the fire's protective arms with me. He would have been safe. And his face . . . It was me he had thought he was saving from Shammal's light. But the ring lacked the power to pierce Hajthaele's fire. And Lethia hadn't cared. And Ivane, lying upstairs, wouldn't know. And . . .

Away to my left someone cried out in terror and I listened, half expecting the cries to send the hall into bedlam. But a second, louder chant rose to drown the cry, and there was no fear in the words. "Elan Sumedaro! Elan Sumedaro!" the voices pulsed through the ring of fire.

With it Avram stormed among his guards. "Lies!" he shouted to those of his men who stood, too confused to fight. "There's no more magic in her veins than mine." Then, as if to prove it, he leaped forward, hoping, I think, to reach me over the flame's height.

Hayden lunged after him, but my brother's eyes were too much on Morell and thankfully, he never reached him.

The flame that took Avram burned like no ordinary fire. Scorching white heat came first, then a cry as deep as rock on stone. And though I stood not two arm's lengths distant, the circle protected me and I felt none of its heat or fury. Everything else in that room stopped, all motion, all sound. No one dared move. And then the man who had been Avram was gone: face, sword, clothing, all eaten away to a blackened mass.

Norvin was the first to move again, springing to Morell's side. He'd been fighting when Morell went down, and anger had sent his sword raging to finish what he'd been unable to do himself. Without pausing to clean the blood from his sword, Norvin fell to the floor beside Morell while Hayden, keeping well away of Avram's charred body, moved around to guard Norvin's exposed back.

Lethia stood with her arm lowered again, and I wondered if either Avram's or Morell's death had moved her or if she only meant to save the ring for the next attack. Outside the circle of flames the fighting picked up again, though it seemed the two camps were more interested in watching what happened between Lethia and I than in their own half-forgotten swords. Ceena, at least, fought on, her gyrations causing nearly as much fear as the sight of Hajthaele's flames. Wherever she moved, Jared followed behind, dragging Briana's wounded to a far corner. Beklar also fought not far from Ceena's side, his strong arm sweeping left to right, forcing Gleavon's remaining guards to a tighter and tighter line. At the far end of the hall, Norvin and Hayden carried Morell's body to safety. Hayden limped with a wound he'd taken in one thigh, but he kept on, and I wagered the man who had given it to him lay silent on the floor.

"We are at a draw, then," Lethia called, "if you do not come out from behind that wall."

I shook my head. "This was no draw, Lethia. The fighting's done, and I've not raised a weapon against you. Not once."

"Much to your own regret?" Lethia raised her split eyebrow in attempted mockery, and I remembered how that look had once haunted me. "You won't have me, you know," she said. "Unless you kill me. And I don't think you mean to do that."

"I'll let the fire down if you think it will make a difference. Because, you see, I know you can't touch me," I said, and I twisted Rath around my wrist till the flames multiplied in a hundred reflections, blazed for one last moment, then, as if caught inside a lidded box, snapped out.

"Give me the ring, Lethia. Without Edishu it's useless to you. You'll never reach me."

"You seem very sure of yourself. Why don't you come over here and take it from me?"

Hayden cried out to warn me away, but I ignored him. "Very well," I said. "I accept your challenge."

The distance between the two of us was not very great. One step. Another. Not even a line remained to show where the fire had been. "Give me the ring," I said.

"Take it."

Without shifting my gaze from Lethia, I measured Hajthaele's weight on my shoulder. There'd be no time to nock an arrow to the string, that much I was certain. But if I moved just so . . . I leaned forward as if hesitating.

Lethia was smiling.

With my left hand I slowly reached toward the glowing ring. She was smiling still, waiting.

Farther. My hand grazed hers.

And I snatched blindly at the bow quiver, felt an arrow break loose from the others. Then, just as I meant to grab her by the wrist and pull her off balance, she stepped back. For the first time I realized that her right hand had been busy near my side. Too late I realized what it was.

Gamaliel! The goblet, she'd stolen it, raised it for another attack.

There was a shout. Then a laugh. She raised Gamaliel to her face, pressed its rim to her lips as if to drink.

I swung the arrow as if it were a club, aiming high for her hand. My aim held true. The goblet tore loose from her hand, flew toward the floor, and I dove for it, every muscle in my body tensing as I waited for the crash that would tell me Jokjoa's goblet was broken.

But somehow, impossibly, my hands slid underneath, cushioning the impact. Gamaliel, my goblet, it was safe.

Only then did I look for Lethia.

Where she'd stood there was only cold, empty air. Nothing. She'd used Gamaliel's magic to escape. And she was safe.

Shaken, I hesitated. Lethia was gone. Shammal was gone.

Before I could move, Ceena was at my side, grabbing my hand. "The bracelet!" she shouted. "Look through it."

For a moment I didn't understand, but then I quickly yanked the bracelet from my wrist, held it up at eye level, and stared through its crystal walls, half expecting to find Lethia in front of me again.

Lights shimmered. The floor seemed far distant, insubstantial, as if Rath were a link between two worlds, the one but a reflection of the other with no way to know the difference between the two. But of Lethia nothing remained.

"Is she gone, then?"

"Yes." I lowered the bracelet.

"The coward," Ceena said.

Hayden came and laid a hand on my shoulder. Behind him, Norvin kept on, busying himself with Lethia's men, removing their weapons, binding their arms. Through it they kept staring at me, hesitating, fearful, but with a look of curiosity behind their eyes that made me doubt there'd be any fighting so long as I stood in that hall.

"Lethia a coward?" I said, running my fingers around the goblet's rim. "I don't know about that. A coward would have run from Edishu, been too frightened by the sight and thought of his touch . . . the way I once was. But she embraced him and tried to cross him too. She was willing to do anything, *anything* to be near that much power. I'm not sure a coward could do that."

I turned away from where Lethia had stood and faced the cold wreckage of that room. "How many dead?" I asked.

"Ten of ours. More wounded." Hayden's voice betrayed

the ache of exhaustion. "But less than theirs, I think. Thanks mostly to Ceena."

"And Morell, is he . . . ?"

"Gone."

"He tried to save me."

"I know." Hayden looked at me, then said, "It wasn't your arrow that killed him, you know. And not the fire, either. It was the ring. Lethia knew exactly what she was doing. She didn't need him anymore. And he was in her way. But I love him for what he did."

I nodded, agreeing. "And so would Ivane have."

The next three days I spent mourning my parents. I wished for more solitude, for time alone with Hayden, but little of that was permitted. The priests in Lakotah were in a turmoil of preparations and hardly knew what to do with me. Some went so far as to ask for a show of the tokens' magic, for a sign, for a waking dream that I could not have given them even if I'd had the will. And the people from Briana, they flocked to the rathadaro hall, whispering, staring, a few of them going so far as to reach out and touch my sleeve as I walked by. And with each touch it seemed that more was being taken from me than the childhood I could not bring back or the voices of my mother and father in my ear guiding and shielding, warning and challenging.

On the third day following their deaths, the funeral bier that held the white-shrouded bodies of Ivane and Morell stood in a circle of stones in the open courtyard. Behind it temple walls and stone towers were draped in sheets of black. The flames that had caught and spired were dying now, and little was left to say that Jared and the Sumedaro priests had not already said.

No miracle had come to transport Ivane skyward. No sign that once Jokjoa had touched my mother's face with love. Only the gold thread that joined Morell and Ivane—black and mottled now with a drifting snow—said anything of the ache that had passed for love between those two.

Hayden and I had been allowed to stand a little apart from the priests, and I couldn't help but steal a look at his face, trying to see just how much of Ivane's blood we shared, how much the lack of Morell's marked our differences. Around his forehead Hayden wore the circlet of gold Morell had given him for a crown. He kept pushing it to place it more comfortably atop his head. The kingship it was meant to acknowledge rested fully on his shoulders for the first time now, and I wondered if he was gladdened by it or made lonely as I was under my burden.

"Do you feel that?" Hayden lifted his face to the wind.

"What is it?"

"A breeze. A warm breeze."

"I think not," I said. "Hell's winter doesn't turn so quickly to thaw."

"But I wonder, isn't it possible? That the earth could feel the shift in skyworld and respond. Or skyworld to the earth? You said yourself Edishu was wounded, imprisoned in Kuoshana."

"Stalled perhaps. Certainly not destroyed," I said. "It's what I'm afraid of most: that Edishu will find a way to return before I'm ready. He could win, Hayden. Whatever you think I've gained, there's no assurance . . ."

Off to one side behind us, a restless stamping of horse hooves and cold, rising breaths filled the air. A small company awaited me: Ceena, Micah, Dev, and Beklar as well, the four of them sworn to follow me into the cold eastern forest I meant to travel.

Hayden and I turned together to look at them, the silence drawn tight between us. "You don't have to leave, you know," he said, his voice wistful but guarded. "Lethia won't dare raise a hand against you in Briana. And you could do whatever it is you need to here as well as anywhere. It isn't as if you'd be opposed or questioned. You don't even realize, do you, how many of my men would join you? Or the townspeople. The last few days I've felt more like I'm regent to your rule—"

"Then that's only more reason to go. Briana doesn't need to be troubled with a second crown."

"It doesn't have to be like that."

"No, you're right. It's not you. Not Briana. It's for me, this journey. I need to find the Silkiyam, to ask their help. Ceena's coming with me, of course, and the others—they'd have posted a guard at my door if they thought I'd try leaving without them. But they needn't have worried. I have no desire to travel alone, not this time. We'll start eastward—I won't go north, I've done that already, and certainly not south into Lethia's hands. The mountains block the way west or I'd consider it, though Beklar says he knows a pass."

"But how far will you go, and if you never find them—what then?"

"If you want the truth, Hayden, I'll tell you: I don't know. The gods keep a damnable silence for all the gifts you may think I bear. What I do know is that there's hope in it this time, more than before. Ceena believes the Silkiyam found a way deeper into the havens, that I'll find a door or a way to call them. Something. For myself, I only hope that when I find them, they'll share what they've learned with me before I get hurt." I found a smile, looked up to meet my brother's eyes. "I could lose a finger, a leg . . ."

Hayden's mouth turned up in a crooked smile, then he laughed. "As long as it's not your hair," he said. "It's not like anyone else's I know. I never did tell you, did I, that I used to be jealous of your hair?"

"Jealous? Of what?"

"Just whatever it is brothers and sisters are always jealous of. You had something I didn't. I wanted it." He smiled again, but I suppose we both knew the gaiety couldn't last. He looked away, kicked at a blackened ember lying in the snow. "Calyx," he asked, "do you believe he's your father?"

I took a breath, searched for the words that would help him understand. "I have to," I said. "I've seen his face, the way she saw him. Heard his words. She didn't invent him. And there's Hajthaele. Maybe I took the other tokens, but the bow he gave me. All he was asked was that I take one jarak dream and reshape it into a waking dream. It's what he told Mother. *The child is conceived in a dream, so she shall find the tokens that lead to me through a dream. But it will be in the full light of day that she uses them.*

"There's power, Hayden, and I can unleash it, but not control it—not yet. And I feel unprotected, even dangerous. But Hayden, I believe this: we were three clans on earth, all of us endowed with Jokjoa's dreams. Cleave any one of the limbs from the others and the tree dies. That's where we stand now, and it's as if the earth were bleeding from the wound. Whatever I do next, it isn't for myself alone and I won't attempt it on my own. I need to find the Silkiyam."

I looked away, down the hill and beyond Briana's houses and shops to a road Hayden could not see. Sieges lay out there, and battles and possibilities. Hayden would marry his Korinna. The borders between Briana and Hillstor would fade. Harvests would be stored against the waste. There would be children. There would be dreams.

And none of them would be mine.

Oh, I would have dreams, jarak dreams in plenty. But they would not be the same as my brother's. And yet there was a certain peace I'd come to, knowing that though I could not shed the title my true father had bequeathed me, this quest I now began was mine, and it was freely chosen.

Hayden touched my shoulder, drawing me back from my thoughts. He pulled me close and hugged me, the tears running unashamedly down his face. When we were done, I looked up in his eyes, so dark, so like yet unlike my own. Then I turned and took the first step away.

ABOUT THE AUTHOR

Elyse Guttenberg grew up in New York and moved to Alaska in 1972. She attended the University of Alaska, Fairbanks, where she received her master's degree. She has been a member of the literature review panel for the Alaska State Council on the Arts, and is the editor of *INROADS*, an anthology of fellowship writers. She and her husband and two children live in Fairbanks in their owner-built home, looking north toward the rolling tundra. SUNDER, ECLIPSE & SEED is the first volume in her new fantasy trilogy.